WARMACHINES OF ALEXANDRIA

Book Four of The Alexandrian Saga

Thomas K. Carpenter

Warmachines of Alexandria
Book Four of The Alexandrian Saga

Hardcover Version

by Thomas K. Carpenter

Published by Black Moon Books

Cover design by
G&S Cover Designs

Chapter Headings design by Aleks49011

Discover other titles by this author on:
www.thomaskcarpenter.com

ISBN-13: 978-1-958498-14-9

ALEXANDRIAN SAGA

Fires of Alexandria
Heirs of Alexandria
Legacy of Alexandria
Warmachines of Alexandria
Empire of Alexandria
Voyage of Alexandria
Goddess of Alexandria

Other Books by Thomas K. Carpenter

<u>The Dashkova Memoirs</u>
Revolutionary Magic
A Cauldron of Secrets
Birds of Prophecy
The Franklin Deception
Nightfell Games
The Queen of Dreams
Dragons of Siberia
Shadows of an Empire

<u>The Kingmaker Saga</u>
The Stone Tree
The Crystal Bard
The Ghost Tower
The Champion's Prophecy
The Shadow Labyrinth
The Autumn Empire

The Hundred Halls Universe
SEASON ONE

<u>THE HUNDRED HALLS</u>
Trials of Magic
Web of Lies
Alchemy of Souls
Gathering of Shadows
City of Sorcery

<u>THE RELUCTANT ASSASSIN</u>
The Reluctant Assassin
The Sorcerous Spy
The Veiled Diplomat
Agent Unraveled
The Webs That Bind

<u>GAMEMAKERS ONLINE</u>
The Warped Forest
Gladiators of Warsong
Citadel of Broken Dreams
Enter the Daemonpits
Plane of Twilight

<u>ANIMALIANS HALL</u>
Wild Magic
Bane of the Hunter
Mark of the Phoenix
Arcane Mutations
Untamed Destiny

<u>STONE SINGERS HALL</u>
Song of Siren and Blood
House of Snake and Tome
Storm of Dragon and Stone
Sonata of Shadow and Thorn
Well of Demon and Bone

<u>THE ORDER OF MERLIN</u>
The Order of Merlin
Infernal Alliances
Tower of Horn and Blood

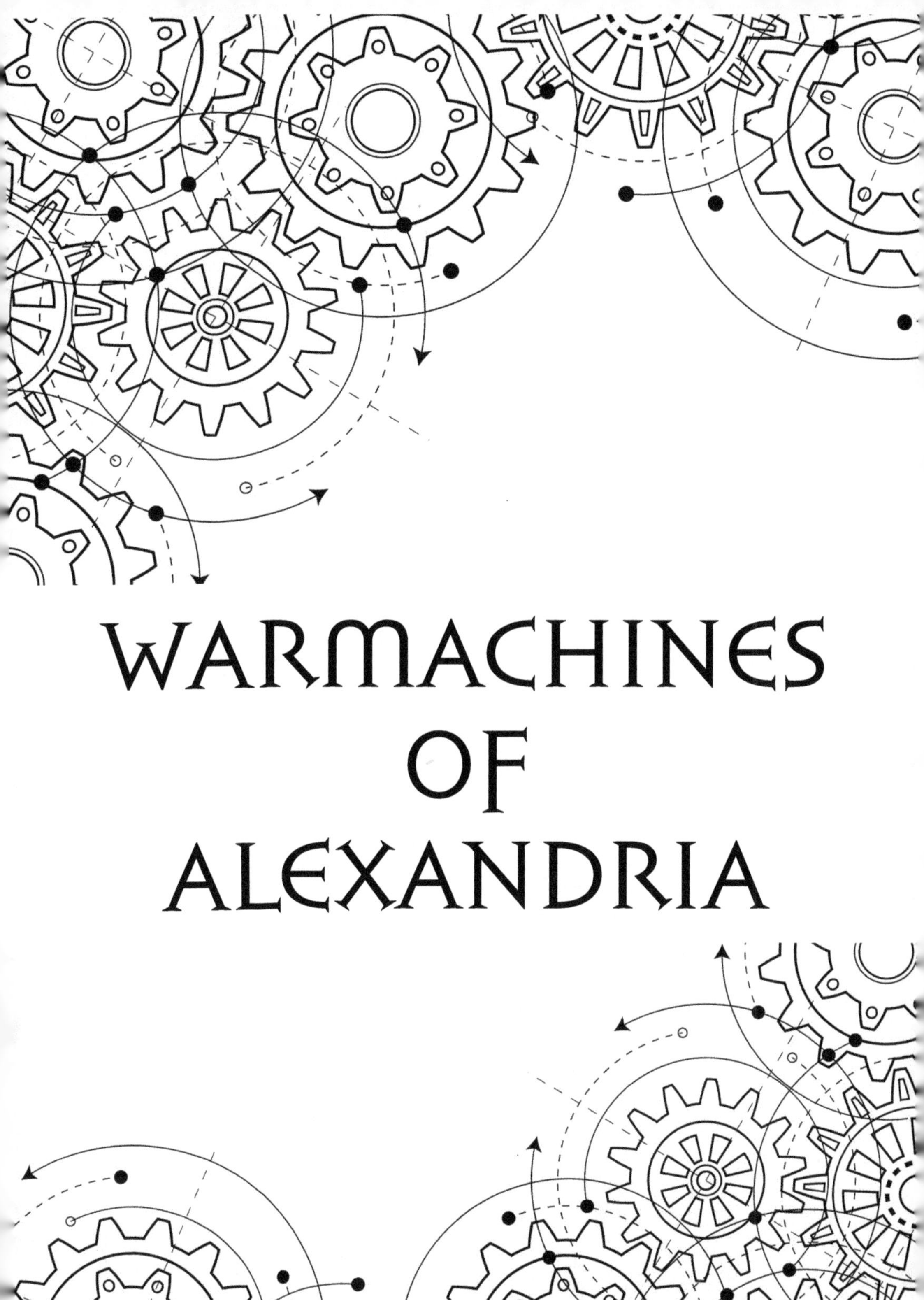

WARMACHINES OF ALEXANDRIA

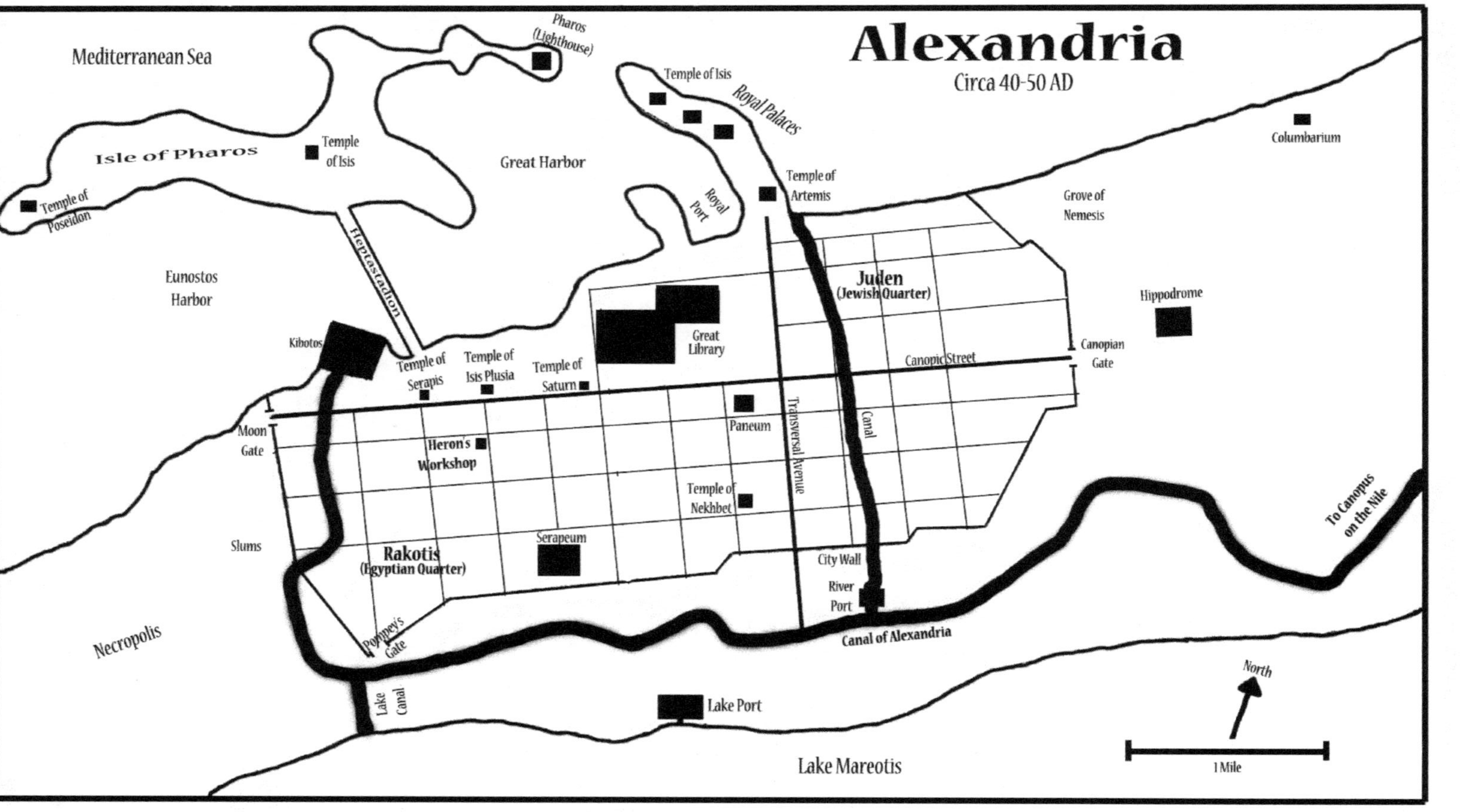

Alexandria
Circa 40-50 AD
Mediterranean Sea
Pharos (Lighthouse)
Isle of Pharos
Temple of Isis
Royal Palaces
Columbarium
Temple of Isis
Great Harbor
Temple of Artemis
Grove of Nemesis
Temple of Poseidon
Royal Port
Juden (Jewish Quarter)
Eunostos Harbor
Hippodrome
Heptastadion
Kibotos
Great Library
Canopian Gate
Temple of Serapis
Temple of Isis Plusia
Temple of Saturn
Canopic Street
Moon Gate
Paneum
Canal
Heron's Workshop
Transversal Avenue
Temple of Nekhbet
To Canopus on the Nile
Slums
Rakotis (Egyptian Quarter)
Serapeum
City Wall
River Port
Pompey's Gate
Necropolis
Canal of Alexandria
North
Lake Canal
Lake Port
Lake Mareotis
1 Mile

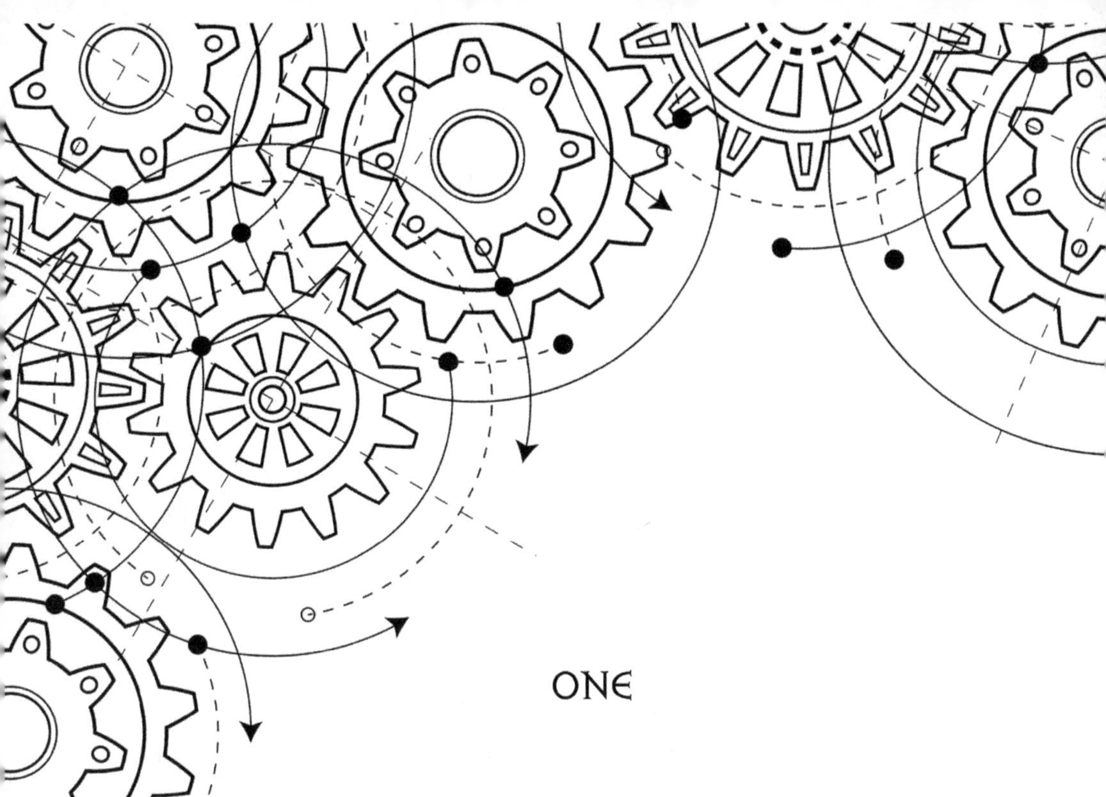

ONE

The domes were the color of bright blood, a wound on the city of Rome, the seat of the Roman Empire. The marble buildings woke to shadow, oil lamps flickering like weary eyes, as sunrise sprayed its color across the city.

Sunrise. To its citizens, the faded pinks of the cloudscape like blood mixed with spit were the markers of a new day. For Magnus Julius Severus, the Consul of the Roman Army, he feared they were the colors of sunset, the ending of the Empire.

Standing on the high balcony, his calloused hands gripping the smooth railing, Magnus felt the throbbing heartbeat of the Legion. With his eyes closed, the beat came - one, and two, and three, and - matching the cadence in his chest.

Two new legions practiced their tactics on the wide fields of Circus Maximus. Their lock-step marching reverberated through the earth, a steady beat that musicians could play to. A thousand-throated war cry carried over Palatine Hill and set the carrion birds to flight from the square below.

The Senate had been furious at his appropriation of Circus Maximus. They had games planned, celebrations to attend. Only the seal of Emperor Claudius kept them from overrunning his office with demands.

Magnus turned his ear toward the distance, but all he could hear was the squeaking of cages, set to rocking by the flight of birds, and the delirious mumbling of dying men. He tried his best to ignore them, as he had more important things to consider, like the training of the new legions. The men in the cages were a sentence he did not care to pass yet.

One, and two, and three, and—the relentless beat was a salve to his frustration. The thudding resounded keenly in his right knee where the warhammer had smashed it when he received his Battlement Crown. He'd been first over the wall in Antioch when he was a young, vain man. That was the last time he ever envisioned himself as the second coming of Alexander. Studying his strategy and tactics was enough.

"Quad!"

The voice of five-thousand soldiers sent chills into his spine. The tempo increased as troops shifted into square formations. Ten-thousand boots ripping at the soil with hobnail soles. It sounded like distant, steady thunder.

When five-thousand shields slammed together, a bolt of steel lightning that ended the thunder, Magnus allowed himself a faint grin. He let the breath out that he hadn't realized he'd been holding.

Turning, he opened his eyes just in time to see Praetor Scipio approaching.

"I think the new legions are ready," said Magnus.

Scipio saluted and handed over the scroll tucked neatly under his arm. The Praetor was a dour, overly-serious man, but Magnus had never met a better military organizer. The Legion was only as good as the supporting auxiliaries and supply trains, and his Roman soldiers were never left wanting.

"Ave, Consul," said Scipio, standing at attention. "How can you know when you have not seen them?"

Magnus frowned at the stiff pose of his second. Discipline was the backbone of the Legion, but rigidity also led to brittleness, which in his eyes, had led to the loss of Alexandria. It seemed no accident that the Praetor's name meant 'rod'.

"Stand down," said Magnus. "A muscle must first relax before it can clench with power. Real strength comes with flexibility." He looked to the cages filled with prisoners in the square. The carrion birds had returned and he caught the scent of rotting flesh on the wind. "And I know the legions are ready because they are like blood through my veins. When I close my eyes, I feel their heartbeats, not mine. I breathe their breath, taste their sweat, bleed with them."

Scipio shifted uncomfortably and Magnus had to turn away to smile. To his second, the army was ledgers and numbers, marks on a papyrus. He received his orders and performed them, regardless of the consequences.

"The scroll, Consul," said Scipio. "The barbarian prisoners, the ones alive anyway, need decisions."

"Not yet," said Magnus. "What about the other legions in training?"

Again, Scipio shifted uncomfortably. "The Senate won't agree to the doubling of signup bonuses. We're still three cohorts away from a full legion."

Magnus slapped the scroll against his palm. "Not even one? The army needs forty legions if we're going to fight two wars and keep the borders safe from marauding barbarians."

"But you broke the Britons in months when the Legates said it would take years," said Scipio with a fair amount of adulation.

"My victory paid a heavy, but necessary, price and Caratacus still lives.

You can be sure he'll rally the resistance and attempt to take back the island as soon as I move even one legion from Briton," said Magnus. "Until we can get our soldiers south to the field, our advantages are the alliance with Parthia, and Archimedes' gifts."

The upper lip of the Praetor twitched and Magnus glanced away from the balcony where the colors of sunrise had faded and the domes of the capitol had turned bone white. In the distance, the shouts of soldiers in training punctuated the morning air.

"Out with it, Scipio, I've told you before not to censor your opinions," said Magnus.

Scipio blinked and tightened his chest. "I'm not even a tenth of the strategist you are, Consul. It's the opinion of the Legates that you are the finest Roman military mind since Caesar."

"Everyone always wants to claim Caesar's mantle, just like they do with Alexander. I'm neither of those men," said Magnus simply. "Therefore, I need the advice of seasoned soldiers like yourself. So if you have an opinion, give it now, or learn to lie better."

"Yes, Consul," said Scipio nodding. "I was thinking the alliance with the Parthians improved with the deaths of the old king and the older prince. The younger brother is neither too cautious like his father, nor too bold like his brother."

"Good, good, you're not too lost in your ledgers for real analysis," said Magnus. "The assessment is correct, but what would you do with their army?"

The compliment seemed to knock Scipio back a bit, but he recovered and continued, "I would...ahem, the proper course would be to wait for the legions and march down *en masse* to siege the city together. We outnumber them ten to one and the Legion is the finest fighting force in the world. This is what the Legates expect us to do. It's the safest way to victory."

Magnus shook his head and wandered back to the balcony, tapping the scroll against his palm. The opinion of the Legates worried him most. Praetor Scipio had no designs on a Consul position, but the Legates, they were the future Consuls and they thought of war as only a way to gain glory and power in Rome. Victory was assumed.

A couple of the big, black birds began scraping and cawing, distracting him from his thoughts. Their wings spread like angels of death as they fought over a dead body in a cage. Magnus ground his teeth. The men in the cages vexed him, both the living and the dead. Especially their leader, the one captured from the iron boat. A boat made of iron. Magnus sorely wished they could have towed it back so he could see it with his own eyes.

"Have I said something wrong, Consul?" asked Scipio, who had nervously returned to his attention pose.

"Hmm? Yes and no. Based on the Empire's teachings on the arts of war, your assessment is correct. That is the safest way to victory."

Magnus paused, even with his political stature, he wasn't sure he should be saying what he was going to say, especially when the Praetor was beholden to the Senate.

"But I've found the safest way is often the wrong way," said Magnus.

Scipio furrowed his brow. "What do you mean, Consul?"

"The safest way is the easiest for our enemies to figure out and find a counter," said Magnus. "By taking the easy route, we signal our strategy."

"But how can they counter our superior numbers and soldiers?" asked Scipio.

"I don't know," said Magnus, "but ask Consul Aulus if he'd like to rethink his strategy now."

"But Consul Aulus is...well, the Senate passed a measure absolving him of the loss of the navy. Consul Aulus was a great admiral, his strategies and discipline were widely admired."

Magnus poured himself a goblet of water and took a long drink. He would drink no wine until the war with Alexandria was over.

"If that's what the Senate thinks passes for real legislation, they are sorely tempting the gods," said Magnus. "But despite his failure, Aulus was a good man. He had an exceptional naval mind and that's what worries me. He outnumbered the Alexandrians ten to one, just like we do. But they were able to counter that advantage through clever use of superior technology," said Magnus. "And that was *before* they started using the iron boats. I shudder to meet a navy full of them on the high seas. Only Archimedes' secret war technology allowed us to take these prisoners."

He gestured to the square with the scroll. The flapping of wings was unsettling. Magnus could tell the living prisoners by the absence of the big carrion birds.

"Consul, that gift, you call it, from Archimedes. It worries me and the Legates do not speak highly of it. Too unpredictable," said Scipio. "Some call it sorcery."

"I don't care what you call it, as long as it works." Magnus felt his voice rise and took another drink. The traditions and superstitions of the Empire would be its downfall. "And I don't understand them. They want this—" Magnus slapped the scroll against his hand, "—but hesitate when they are presented with something new. Don't they know Archimedes' ingenuity held the Roman army in check for three years during the siege of Syracuse?"

Scipio cleared his throat. "Maybe the other secret warmachines of Archimedes will be more amiable to the Legates."

"You have to find them first," said Magnus.

"Our man in Alexandria says he can find them, once he gets his hands on the right documents," said Scipio.

Magnus sighed. Relying on spies and assassins to win the war was the Senate's game. It'd done nothing so far.

"Consul, may I ask how you plan to attack Alexandria if waiting for the additional legions is the wrong strategy?" asked Scipio.

Magnus leaned on the railing. Stringy, white clouds stretched across the sky. Sunlight fell upon his face. It was a pleasant spring day in Rome, too pleasant for his taste.

"Never allow your enemies to know where you'll attack next, Praetor Scipio. Always keep them guessing, keep them off guard. Turn their strengths to weaknesses, their weaknesses to devastating failures. Let them believe they have every advantage, and then demoralize them."

His heartbeat thundered in his ears. He could almost taste the blood, hear the crying of the wounded on the battlefield. There would be no second chance. The fate of the Roman Empire depended on him destroying the Alexandrian upstart. Even its defiance could bring other challengers. He had to wipe out the barbarian and his allies, once and for all.

"We only have one legion in the field near Damascus, rallying with the Parthians, and the Alexandrians know the rest of our legions cannot get south until the fall. While they prepare for siege, they believe we will not attack with the full might of our army for many months," explained Magnus as he gripped the railing until his knuckles cracked.

"But while they prepare for a long siege, we will learn from their tactics, and rush down a force of our cavalry, the Parthian cataphracts, and our few steam chariots, and attack them before they are ready. Using the chariots and Archimedes' gift, we will take the city with one quick strike."

"A risky maneuver," said Scipio. "What happens if the sneak attack fails?"

"The best strategies reward failure," said Magnus, turning toward his Praetor. He knew every word he said would get back to the Senate and the Legates, but they would have to find out eventually. "With our cavalry and chariots spent, the barbarian will believe us desperate, and wish to counterattack. They know we're still fighting a war in Briton."

"How can you know this?" asked Scipio.

"I don't," said Magnus, "but it's what I would do. And this barbarian they call Agog, or Wodanaz, is no stranger to war. He waged an impressive campaign against the Germanic tribes some years ago. We let him do our job for us until the tribes offered fealty and we put an end to his little war. But he got his revenge in the end by taking Claudius' prized jewel, so I think he's willing to take risks. Like Alexander against Darius, a major victory on the battlefield brings rewards of more allies."

Scipio seemed to be deep in thought until he asked, "Where will he attack?"

"The better question is where do we want him to attack," said Magnus, "and I have a place in mind that will nullify the advantages of his steam chariots."

"And you can steer him there?" asked Scipio.

Magnus rubbed his chin. "Only if I'm good."

Scipio saluted. "Shall I assemble the Legates then to lay out the strategy?"

"The Legates? No need, the orders for the sneak attack went out weeks ago. I'm expecting them to reach Alexandria any day. Who knows, maybe in a few weeks, the war will be over," said Magnus as he slipped his finger beneath the wax seal on the papyrus.

"Sent weeks ago?" Scipio's normally stoic face broke with concern. "But the Senate hasn't approved this strategy, nor the Legates. We haven't even finished torturing the prisoners for information."

"Yes," said Magnus, looking at the scroll in his hand. "We haven't. And I'd like to keep it that way."

"But they could have important information," said Scipio.

"If they talk, which I doubt they will, since they haven't so far, the only thing they'll tell us is what we already know," said Magnus, with his thumb under the seal. The waxy button flexed and cracked.

"No." He shook his head. "Send this back. I will not dishonor them."

Praetor Scipio took the scroll, saluted, and stiffly marched from the room, leaving Magnus to his thoughts. There would be consequences for his defiance, and the employ of his strategy without approval, but he didn't care. Magnus leaned against the rail, letting his leg hang slack, so the knee didn't ache.

No. He would not torture them. Kill them because they were his enemy on the field of battle, or as their executioner, that was the unspoken agreement of war, but he wanted no part of what the Senate wanted.

Magnus closed his eyes and inhaled deeply. He did not smell the rotting of dead men below. Nor did he hear the coarse shouts of soldiers in training. Or feel the slight breeze on his face. His body was in Rome, but his mind wandered south to the fighting force streaking towards Alexandria.

The thunder of horse-hooves filled his ears, the smell of sweat from long days in the saddle, his nose. He could feel the wind and sun on his face, the cadence of a full gallop in his gut.

While he hoped the forward force would strike hard and true and the war would be over, vindicating his defiance of the Senate, part of him wanted them to fail, so the barbarian would sense weakness and strike back at Rome. Then he could take his reforged army, and the gifts of Archimedes, and lure the Alexandrians to the land of the three rivers and batter him against the anvil of the mountains, crushing the resistance forever.

Magnus opened his eyes. A carrion bird lifted into the air, rising past the balcony. A hunk of bloody flesh hung from its beak. The birds would feast from here to Alexandria before the war was finished.

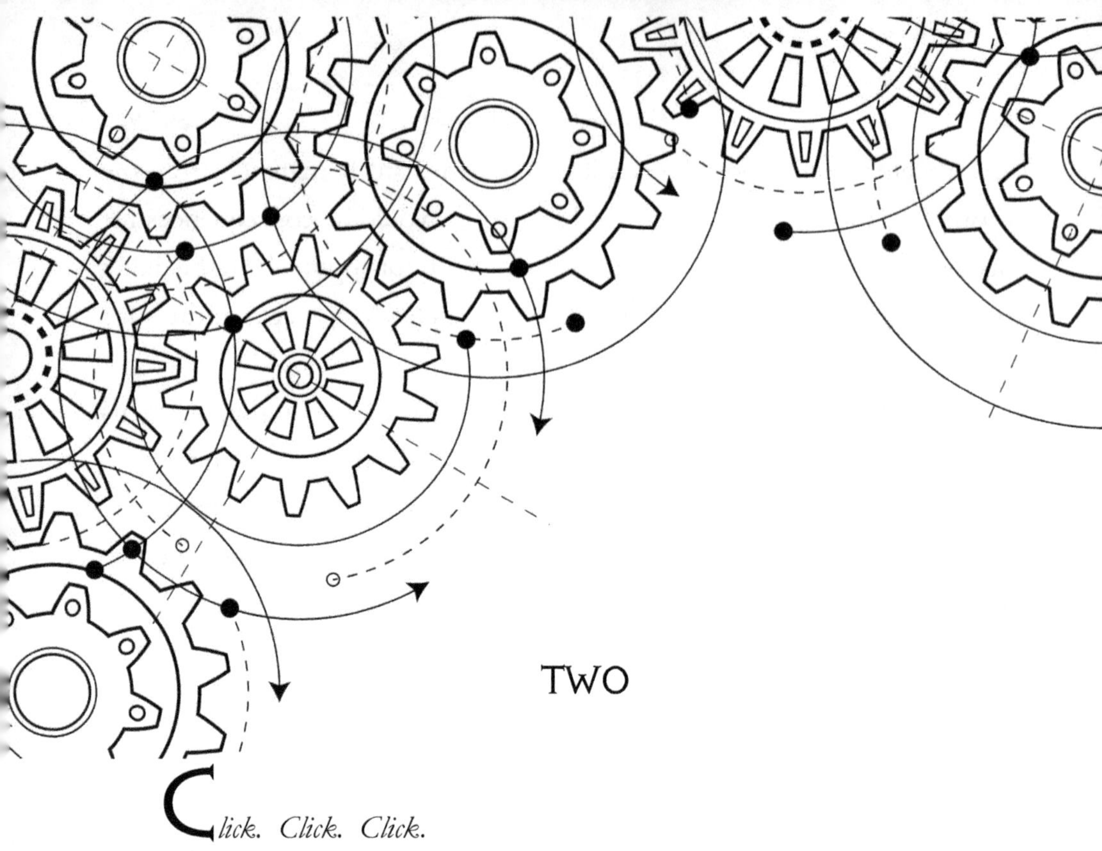

TWO

lick. Click. Click.

Eyes closed, Heron leaned against the wall in the side hall of the Curiosity Rooms. The mermaid scrollwork bit into her back, but it'd taken some maneuvering to get into this position, so she ignored it. Or at least tried to.

Click. Click. Click.

Sunlight warmed her legs, even the mechanical part of her. The velvet cushion inside the brass leg that connected to her knee was sweaty and stunk from days of effort. The buckle on the straps grew hot. Heron adjusted the ivory cane resting across her thighs. Its smooth scabbard soothed her fingertips as it slid back and forth across its length.

Click. Click. Click.

Tiny brass levers smacked against the gears. She counted them despite her exhaustion. The brass Sisyphus would reach the summit soon and release his bronze boulder to slide along the tracks to the bottom with a heavy - *thunk* - before doing it all over again.

Heron opened her eyes the moment before Sisyphus tipped over. The ball sped away from the little brass figure, spinning across the suspended tracks, whirling through the air, the slick kiss of metal on metal, until it came back down to rest at Sisyphus' feet.

Click. Click. Click.

There was a hesitation in the gears. Heron sighed and began the laborious process of climbing to her feet. First, she got on her hands and knees and then set her mechanical foot flat, before using the cane to push herself up. Reaching out to steady herself, she chipped a shard of stone from the scrollwork with her metal hand.

Heron stared at the notch in the stone mermaid. The tail had been knocked clean off. She searched for the piece of stone briefly before moving to the Sisyphus machine. With her real hand, she wound the spring, giving it energy for its labors.

She'd just finished giving a lecture on the steam mechanical and had come to the Curiosity Rooms for a moment of quiet thought. The lecture, the fourth one she'd given this week, had been a failure. The scholars had been attentive enough, even more so due to her new bodily additions. But their questions had only been about the knowledge of how steam mechanicals worked rather than the application.

With the Sisyphus machine wound, Heron left for the Demetarium. She wanted to visit it one last time before she returned to her workshop. There were new weapons to test before King Wodanaz came for a visit.

"*Michanikos!* What an honor!"

A scholar wearing a toga more appropriate for a festive occasion appeared, blocking her way. Heron tried to step around him.

"It's me! Gnaeus Genucius Gurges, a friend of the king and a servant of Alexandria."

Her mind whirled with duty. She blinked him into remembrance. "Ave, Gnaeus."

"What a superb lecture," said Gnaeus. "I feel I am now an expert on the steam mechanical. Maybe next week I will begin my papers on the subject."

"But, I...well," said Heron, eventually deciding not to bother, for what was thought without action.

Gnaeus touched her on the arm, her good arm, his eyes flickering to the other. His smile was somewhat awkward, as if he were asking a prostitute to bake bread.

"This evening," he began, "those of us with an excellent background in the ways of the barbarians are planning a round table discussion on what we have learned since they invaded our city. Many of our notions have been overturned by the up-close observation. Did you know many of them could read and write? Some even Latin? It's a wonder that makes me dizzy with excitement."

The urge to strike him over the head with her heavy brass arm was overwhelming, but she prevailed in restraint.

"I must go," she said and attempted to step around, but he blocked her again.

"Apologies, *Michanikos*," he said. "But would you join us? It would be a great honor for me to bring the Machine Man, himself, to our humble discussion. You've lived and worked with the barbarians. Who better than you to educate us?"

She bit back her rage and pushed past him using the cane as a lever, ignoring the improper clutching at her tunic. When he took a step to follow, she turned, which took an embarrassing number of steps to perform the maneuver.

"Don't you see we're preparing for war here?" she seethed. "Your scholarship into the *barbarian* ways of my friends does not interest me and smacks of ignorance. I would prefer you funnel this idiocy into something useful like the defense of the city, but it seems I am alone in this."

Gnaeus placed a hand against his chest. He seemed ready to offer a retort, until he took a second look and closed his lips.

Heron was about to resume her ambling walk, when Gnaeus dug into his toga and pulled something small and shiny out. He stepped forward and placed the smooth object in her palm.

"A gift, *Michanikos*," said Gnaeus before leaving her.

Peeling back her fingers revealed a brass gear. She sighed heavily and tucked it in the pouch at her side. "I'll put it with the others," she mumbled before resuming her journey.

The way to Demetarium was not made for mechanical legs. The rough hewed hallway was slick with moisture. Summer made the stone weep and the Great Library's eternal war with moisture went unheeded here.

Atop a winding section of stairs without handholds, she paused and cursed the crocodile that had taken her leg. Faint, green slime covered the stone steps. She would not make the bottom of these steps without incident.

Crawling backwards on her hands and knees, she could make the bottom, but what if someone saw her? The alternative was to slip and smack her head against the stone. The passages to the Demetarium were mostly unknown to all but the most highly regarded scholars. She'd never seen another soul in these places. It was more likely that she'd hit her head and die, bleeding out without another person to help her. Only the wrinkled doorman at the end of the hall would ever know, and she wondered if he ever left them.

It would be prudent to crawl. Her metal limbs provided a reason for her new eccentricities, not that she didn't know her reputation from before. But she couldn't make herself get down to the ground, no matter what the danger.

Heron placed her hand against the wet wall. Greenish slime smeared across her forearm. Wedging her cane into the corner of the stair, she lifted her leg, using her upper thigh, and set it on the next step, ignoring the blister that had formed from the rubbing of the buckle. She'd fixed the cane inside her metal hand, a notch Sepharia had added so she might have more mobility, but it didn't give her a sense of control.

The next few steps were treacherous and Heron was certain she would fall, but she went slowly and deliberately, adjusting her weight before making the next step. That had been one of the surprising challenges of the mechanical limbs. They were heavier than her flesh-and-blood limbs and created an imbalance. She was thankful it hadn't been an arm and leg on the same side. She'd be forever leaning one way.

With her ponderous journey complete, Heron glanced up the stairs and tried to forget that she would have to return this way. At the end of the hallway, she found the door warden of the Demetarium asleep at his desk, which she thought odd, since the door was slightly open.

"Ave?" she asked, her voice falling to a whisper.

Upon closer inspection, she realized the old door warden was dead. A pool of dark liquid collected on the floor beneath the desk. In the flickering light, he seemed peaceful, but the frantic blood smears on the parchment book said otherwise.

She hesitated, looking back the way she'd come. It was doubtful that the killer was still here, but the blood looked fresh. Heron thought about climbing the steps again so soon and decided she would rather investigate the Demetarium first before attempting them.

As quietly as she could, she unsheathed the blade and rested the cane on the table. Her metal foot against the stone sounded like a hammer strike and she cringed. Heron moved to the door and prepared to open it. If the killer was still in the room, she would be standing between him and the exit. But better to make a stand here than for the killer to find her teetering on the slick steps.

The sound of a book slapping shut startled her. Heron froze and started to bring her dagger around when the door swung open, catching her metal arm. A man barreled into her and their legs tangled.

They fell together, him on top. The impact knocked the air from her lungs. Something sharp was wedged into her hip. Grimacing away the pain, Heron looked into the killer's face and saw someone she knew.

The unexpected recognition was so strong, she gasped out a 'No'. He was supposed to be dead.

The killer seemed to recognize her, his eyes widening. He scrambled for his blade as Heron tried to bring hers around, but her arm was pinned. She lifted the other arm as a shield as he thrust downward, the blade aimed for her chest.

The knife skipped off her metal arm and slammed into the stone near her head, sending a chip into her neck. Heron heaved upwards, knocking the killer away. Scrambling to his feet, the killer stared at his knife as if blaming it for the failure to kill her before he tucked the book under his arm and sprinted away.

Heron stood, momentarily considering chasing him before realizing the foolishness of that endeavor, even if she climbed the steps on her hands and knees. She checked her arm to find a scar in the metal.

Then she paused, her mind reeling with the identity of who had just tried to kill her.

Philo.

Philo just tried to kill me, she thought. But she knew it couldn't be true. She'd put the knife in his belly beneath the temple of Nekhbet. Watched him die beneath her hand.

Philo. It couldn't be.

But Lysimachus had come back to haunt her. Why not Philo? Could it really be Philo? But Lysimachus had never died.

Philo.

She reviewed the details of his face in her mind. The man who just tried to kill her looked almost the same, but then she remembered the eyes. They were different, closer together, and a different color. The lips too, thicker, less slug like.

A family member, probably. Maybe a brother. Yes. Philo's brother. It had to be. Philo was dead. But he had family in Rome and strong ties to the Roman Empire.

What was Philo's brother doing in Alexandria?

Heron limped into the Demetarium to determine what he'd stolen. It didn't take her long to figure it out. She'd seen the book briefly in his hands and her memory was flawless.

The book was one of the oldest in the hallowed library and to Heron, the most valuable. Philo's brother had stolen the journal of Archimedes, a book she'd read countless times, despite her knowing it word for word.

Heron checked around to make sure nothing else had been taken. It'd only been Archimedes' journal, her mentor, and who she believed to be the greatest inventor of any age. But what she didn't know was why he'd taken that book. Heron searched her memory and could find no reason.

Satisfied with her examination, Heron left the Demetarium. She would contact the Library scholars about the theft and the murder. They would have to find a new door warden. But the stolen book, that bothered her.

Lost in her thoughts, she almost missed the folded parchment on the ground near the location of their struggle. It must have fallen out of his tunic. After the unfolding, a careful process involving both hands and the actuating of metal fingers to pinch a spare corner, she examined the contents, but was immediately stymied by a message hidden in code.

"Plato have pity," she muttered.

The coded message made the theft even more remarkable and practically anointed Philo's brother a spy for the Roman Empire. It seemed this book was no ordinary theft, but why?

Heron sighed. She had a hundred other more important things to do, but the coded message would have to be her first priority. Thankfully, the Great Library was the best place to solve such a quandary. The scholars she had given the counting machine to loved codes. She would give them the parchment before returning to the workshop to collect her things, including her box of violet dust, and set upon the task of the code. Though she hated to give credence to such feelings, Heron knew deep in her gut that whatever was on this parchment, and in Archimedes' journal, would have a significant effect on the war for Alexandria's freedom.

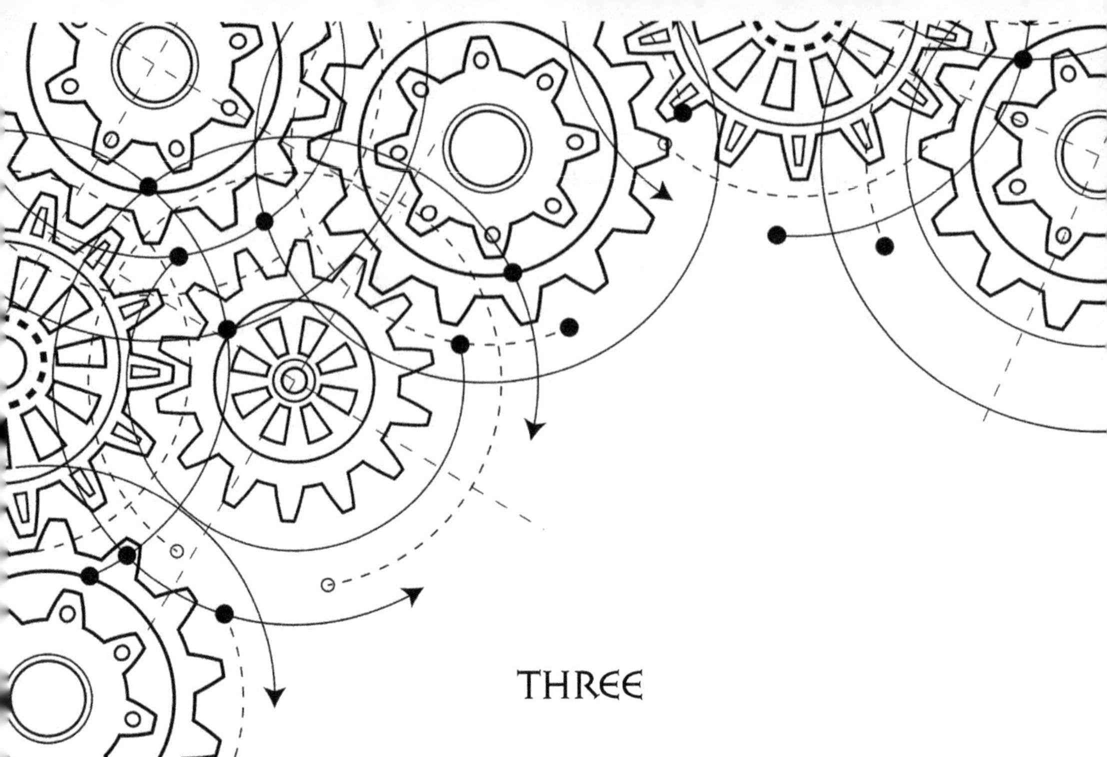

THREE

Black smoke rose on the horizon. The wind blew in Hoth's face and he could taste the burnt wood on his tongue, the pinched-nose scent of cotton tunics set to flame catching in the back of his throat, even the hint of human flesh, sickeningly charred.

Every sailor feared fire. If the ship burned far from land, there was little hope for survival. For the ships large enough to house a kitchen, or an officer's quarters with room for candles and lamps, there were strict regimens regarding their use.

Hoth stood on the quarter deck of the *Mars Valliant*. The shouts of his sailors in the lines seemed muted. He caught their glances forward, toward the smoke. Everyone knew what it meant.

An accidental fire never spread across boats and no one ever died. There was always time to jump into the water. Sharks and other dangers could still claim a water-bound sailor, but fire should be easy to escape.

The *Mars Valliant* and the six ships that sailed with it were meant to rendezvous with the *Iron Spear*, one of the newest iron boats, and two others. The *Iron Spear* carried his friend Agnar and a dozen other soldiers. They had planned to land in Greece to meet with members of the League of Corinth. Polyxena's allies were secretly raising armies in the shadow of the Roman Empire. Hoth knew they were meant to cause havoc for Rome, keeping its legions from the field.

A pair of cross-trees bobbed awkwardly in the water, tilted to one side, smoke swirling from the burnt sheets. As they neared, Hoth checked with the lookout for the all clear. The horizon was empty of ships, but it felt like a trap.

He checked the breeze by the snapping of the flags. The eye of the wind was coming out of the north-east. Not a favorable direction if they had to flee back to Alexandria. Not that he expected Rome to bring enough ships to chase him back, but Hoth never liked to get too comfortable. Keeping a lane open for escape was his first consideration in any battle.

When Nektam made him an iron boat large enough to project power like the *Mars Valliant*, he wouldn't have to worry about wind. The steam mechanicals would let him cut across the wind, and out-maneuver his enemies. But the massive iron boat, the one Hoth planned to name, *Jörmungandr*, would not be finished for another year, if it would be done at all. Increasing the size of the iron boats increased the scale of the problems, and Nektam hadn't been that optimistic last time Hoth had visited him.

Hoth moved to the foredeck to get a better view as they neared. He could see the fallen cross-trees of the wooden triremes that had traveled with the *Iron Spear*, but not the iron boat itself. Hoth hoped that meant the *Iron Spear* had escaped the Roman attack. Otherwise, it was a cause for worry. The iron boats with their tactical maneuverability and steam-based arrow launchers should be nearly impossible to take down by the Roman navy unless they had been trapped by overwhelming numbers.

Hoth climbed on a foredeck railing, holding onto a mast line. The

Mars Valliant slowed as sailors reefed the main sail. Hoth ignored the slapping sheets and focused on the black-green waters ahead. He would instruct them on the proper sail trimming later.

He saw the first body covered in sea gulls long before they reached the ships. With a series of hand signals, Hoth instructed the *Jarl Hammer* to collect the body. He would examine it later.

Something dark and low lurked in the waters ahead, right between the burning remnants of the wooden ships. As soon as Hoth spied it, a stone formed in his gut.

Hoth was momentarily blinded by the shifting winds throwing his hair into his face. He gathered the billowing strands and tied them in a knot behind his head. The eye of the wind had turned, heading out of the south-east. If they were attacked now, they would have to flee further away from Alexandria. Hoth checked the horizon again before turning his focus to the burning ships and the dark shape in the water.

It was too deep to drop anchor and the wreckage ahead was too treacherous to navigate, so Hoth gathered a team to investigate in a row boat while the *Mars Valliant* circled. Dropping into the sea from a moving boat was not ideal, but Hoth had the suspicion they were being baited, and didn't want to spend more time investigating the burning ships than he had to.

Hoth took three men with him, two to work the oars and one the sea hook. They were soldiers more than sailors, full of scars and foul tempers, and wouldn't be missed by the crew if the hexareme had to blow to full sail in a hurry. Hoth could always hide in the wreckage if it came to that.

"Don't move," Hoth cautioned his rowers as they were dropped into the sea by pulley.

A bald soldier with the sea hook in his meaty fists stared white-eyed at the frothing waves below. The lower they dropped, the more he leaned, tipping the boat precariously.

"You, with the hook, straight and tall, now," said Hoth.

The man hesitated, his wild stare bouncing from the hook to the waves and back. Hoth wasn't afraid of getting dumped into the water, but he didn't want to hear about it from his crew if it happened.

"If you don't sit tall, I'm going to come back there and cut your throat and dump you over the side," said Hoth.

The bald soldier's brow knotted. "I can't swim."

"All the more reason to sit tall."

The ropes loosened and the boat dropped into the water, careening immediately into the hull of the *Mars Valliant*. When his oarsmen sat stunned, Hoth jumped into the middle, grabbed an oar, and used it to push off the towering bulk of his ship.

Hoth thought he might have to dive into the water as the *Mars Valliant* smashed the row boat into pieces, but the bald soldier finally woke to the danger and jammed his hook out. Together, they diverted the row boat away.

Safely in the water, Hoth directed his oarsmen toward the dark shape, silently cursing himself for choosing soldiers over sailors for this expedition. As he neared, Hoth wondered why the ships had burned so near each other. If they'd fought a battle, it was unlikely they would meet their demise so close together. As he approached, the flat oar blades slapping the water, Hoth suspected the two boats had been lured in and if the dark shape was the *Iron Spear*, he feared the springing of a trap was almost certain, though Hoth had no knowledge of how even one ship could take down three without warning.

Hoth scooped his hand in the water, bringing up a handful to dump on his head. Clouds had abandoned the sky and the summer sun was growing warmer by the breath. Nearing the ships, the cawing of seagulls filled the air, drowning out even the ungainly slaps of oars in the water.

He directed them toward the black shape. It didn't take long for Hoth to realize it was the *Iron Spear* by the outline of a boat shape sticking up from the sea. Hoth held them in place next to the boat. It appeared the hull was intact, but the wooden structure that formed the interior of the boat had been burned out. A sooty mix of seawater and ash filled the center. Black scars littered the metal ridge above the pitch line that protected the iron from the corrosive sea water.

A great fire had broken out on the *Iron Spear*. There were signs of warping, where the fire had grown impossibly hot. Hoth had never heard of a fire on a ship so hot that it warped iron. Usually, the boat listed into the waters, dousing the flame before it became an inferno.

It appeared the attack had occurred a few days ago. Hoth expected to see more bodies in the water. It was possible that sharks or other scavengers had eaten the bodies, but he didn't think it likely. Not when they'd found a mostly preserved corpse floating not far away.

Hoth smacked the iron hull with the oar, sending a muted gong through the water. Another possibility crept into his bones. What if it hadn't been the Roman navy at all? Though Hoth was not familiar with all the rumored creatures of the southern seas, he knew a few that could cause this kind of destruction. There were even a few from his home waters he feared. The Jormungand serpent had the mouth of a volcano. Or it could be a water dragon of some kind. They were known, even feared, in these parts.

His oarsmen seemed to have these thoughts as well, he could tell, as they stared at the wreckage and the burnt scars on the metal. It would do his crew little good to be spooked by such rumors, even if it might be true.

Hoth put on his most confidant face, smiling as if he was marching to the Underworld, and said, "It seems Rome has a few tricks. I guess they're going to put up a fight on the seas, after all. A welcome sight, for chasing the fleeing white sails of their remaining fleet was getting quite boring."

The soldiers responded with nervous laughter. He hoped it was enough to put them at ease. He'd invite them to dine with him this evening and put enough thoughts of the Roman navy in their heads to crowd out any rumors that floated behind their wide eyes.

Hoth stared at the wreckage, trying to figure out how the Romans had ambushed his ships. It must have been a distressed vessel, but it didn't explain everything. One ship can easily be overtaken by clever foes. He knew, he'd done it himself on more than one occasion. But three? Including an iron boat protected by a brutal steam-based arrow launcher? It didn't seem possible.

He was preparing to investigate the other boats when there were cries of alarm from the *Mars Valliant*. His second was pointing to the horizon and gesturing. Five ships, his hand gestures said. Five ships on the horizon probably meant more behind.

"By the jarl's balls, back to the ship."

They pushed off from the half-sunken iron boat and the oarsman beat good time. Hoth stayed in the center, trying to see the incoming ships, but they were too low.

A second set of shouts and hand gestures told him 'more sails'. Hoth cursed again and encouraged his oarsmen. The ships were coming from the south, sailing with the wind, and cutting off their escape.

When they reached the *Mars Valliant*, lines were thrown down. They abandoned the rowboat and ascended, hand over hand, back onto the deck. Hoth was met by his second as he slipped over the rail.

"Who are they and how many?" asked Hoth.

His second, Ardre, a man who'd sailed with Hoth since he'd piloted his first skiff, saluted.

"Double sheets, triremes maybe. Too far to tell. Eight ships, at least."

Men shouted and sheets and lines were tightened. Hoth moved to the quarter deck to see for himself. Ardre signaled the other vessels to fall into formation.

Seven ships against eight. If the enemy only brought triremes, then they held the advantage, especially with the *Mars Valliant*, but the mysterious burn marks on the *Iron Spear* worried Hoth.

He took a deep breath, filling his lungs with salty sea air, and prepared himself for the battle ahead, when the lookout called down. Hoth couldn't hear him above the snapping sheets and signaled for him to repeat.

After reading the hand gestures, Hoth found he was almost disappointed. He saw it in Ardre's steady gaze as well. It'd been too long since they'd fought any Roman ships.

"Phoenician traders," sighed Hoth.

"I'm sure we'll find some Romans soon," said Ardre. "They can't have all fled back to Rome."

Hoth nodded. "I don't believe they've ceded the Mediterranean to us. Fallen back and regrouped, yes, but not given up."

"It was the *Iron Spear*, wasn't it?" asked Ardre.

Hoth let his frustration pass from his lips with an out breath. "Yes. How the Romans accomplished such an ambush worries me. And the lack of bodies in the water. I fear they took many prisoners and Agog's plans to utilize the League is compromised."

Ardre agreed. "Where shall we go?"

Hoth glanced back toward the smoldering ships. "I want to speak to those Phoenicians. They might be coming from Alexandria and I want the latest news. After that, it's time to return. If Agnar and the others were taken, Agog needs to know."

Ardre began shouting orders to the crew. Booms rotated and lines sung through the air, as the massive hexareme turned south. Hoth tapped on the railing and thought on the mystery of the burnt *Iron Spear*. He couldn't fathom a way that it could have happened, but he knew someone that could. Thankfully, Heron was in Alexandria along with Agog. Together, they might unravel the mystery, and if they couldn't, Hoth worried what it might portend for the coming battles with Rome.

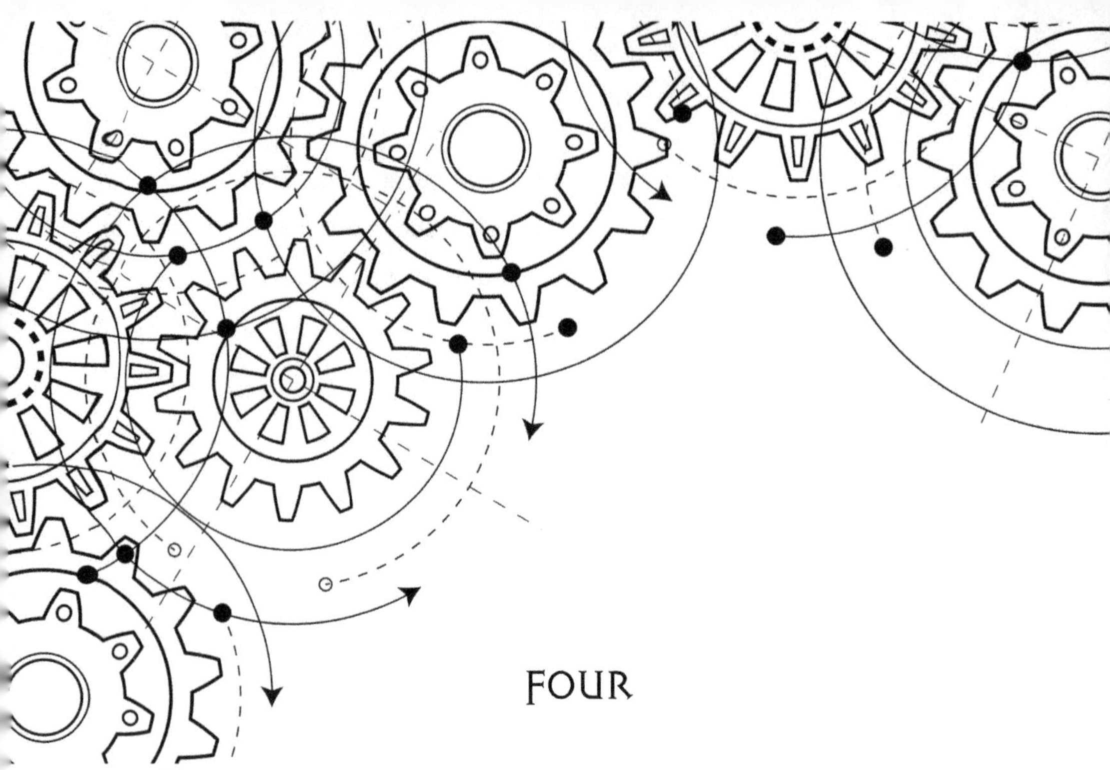

FOUR

Jarngard climbed the inner ladder on the wall, squinting away the summer sun. Agog wasn't far away, giving orders to a crew manning the latest weapon from Heron's workshop.

The men scurried around, looking like mice trying not to get stomped on by a mountain-sized bear. Every time Agog barked a new order, the men hopped a little, and looked more confused, hesitating between the new order and the last. Jarngard stayed back and watched, trying not to smirk, lest the King turn and catch him.

It appeared Agog was trying to get them to set the steam catapult closer to the front of the wall so the lever action wouldn't catch on the stone crenellations. But every time the men moved to follow his command, Agog barked out a new order and the men froze.

"Your Grace," called Jarngard, "may I have a word?"

Agog, or King Wodanaz to most of the population of Alexandria, turned on him looking like a black bear that just got stung by a thousand bees.

"By the jarl's balls, what do you want? Can't you see I'm busy?"

Jarngard stifled his laughter before Agog noticed. He didn't want a repeat of the day he'd been choked by him.

"Vestalis needs those men near the Canopic gate," said Jarngard.

"Are you his messenger now?" Agog grumbled.

"With your permission, can I send them?" asked Jarngard.

Agog sighed and nodded and the men practically jumped down the ladder to get away from the King. Their enthusiasm for escape was not lost on him. Agog narrowed his gaze and tangled his fingers into his scraggly un-King-like beard.

"Was I being that difficult?" he asked.

"You're the King, you can be as difficult as you want," said Jarngard. "But by the many gods of these lands, why are you directing the placement of Heron's new toys rather than doing what you should be doing in the Palace?"

Agog smacked a fist into his palm. "I'm sick of politics and governing. I'm *itching* for a fight. The sooner the Romans get here, the better."

"But we're not ready."

A gust of wind stirred up the ever-present dust and Jarngard found himself spitting.

"We're ready enough."

Jarngard nodded, holding his arm up to block the glaring sunlight. "You should still let Vestalis organize the defense. He's got a mind for anti-siege warfare. You and I are much better at taking cities than defending them."

Agog leaned on the chalky-white stone of the battlements. He smacked it with an open palm. "I have half a mind to attack rather than defend. I hate waiting. I hate *wondering*."

"That's because you know all the ways to take a city rather than to keep it," said Jarngard. "Though we never took a city this big."

"Walls do not make a defense," said Agog. "Nor does this toy of Heron's. We don't even know if the cursed thing works! Heron was supposed to supervise the test, but he's in the Great Library, holed up with those scholars that turn knobs and levers and babble on using words I think are made up half the time."

Jarngard perked up. "I could speak to him. Remind him that we need his expertise on the wall."

Agog frowned. "First a messenger for Vestalis, now to run and fetch Heron. What am I paying you for?"

"Pay?" laughed Jarngard. "I didn't realize there was pay involved."

Agog gave him a sideways smirk. "I guess I forgot I'm supposed to be sharing in the spoils."

Jarngard thought back to the day on the boat with Heron. It pained him not to be by her side. "When the time comes, Your Grace, I may ask for a favor."

"If it's within my power."

"It is. Just promise me you'll do it."

The King's stare turned into a tilted head. "This makes me curious to your price. Care to let an old, fat barbarian in on your demands?"

Jarngard wondered what Agog would make of his relationship with Heron, or even that Heron was female. For some reason, he thought the former would cause more head scratching than the latter. Heron was the exact opposite of his typical conquests. Though *conquest* was too strong a word when it came to Heron. She'd probably stick that knife of hers in his neck for even thinking it.

"When the time comes," said Jarngard.

The King was still staring at him, so he wandered to the steam catapult and tapped on the thick, square base. The whole contraption looked like a hollow steel log on a rotating platform. Unlike the other steam mechanicals he'd seen, this one had no pistons. The steam tank, a huge copper sealed cauldron the size of a fatted pig, sat beneath the launcher and on top of the base; and strange, snake-like copper pipes threaded between them.

"What does it do?"

Agog shrugged. "If we can't get the *Michanikos* out here, we'll have to drag Plutarch away from the workshop to show us."

The wind turned, bringing cool sea air and the sounds of sailors. The gravel on the wall ground under his sandal. Jarngard turned his foot sideways, examining the thin slab of leather on the bottom of his foot, held in place with bindings.

"I miss my boots and deep snow to trudge through," said Jarngard, who had more to say but it was all he could manage.

Agog grunted, an agreement. They stared at the sea and the white sails dotting the horizon for a while longer before Jarngard finally had the courage to ask a question that'd been bothering him.

"Was it worth it?"

A year ago, the question might have brought a fist to the head. Even six or three months ago, Agog would have raged, cursing his name and threatening to send him from Alexandria. But ruling the fractured city, or the summer sun, or the constant threat of the Roman Legion had changed his friend.

The silence went on for a while and Jarngard thought the King had declined to answer until he cleared his throat and glanced over, his eyes absent of the expected disappointment. Jarngard kept his gaze on the sea and waited.

"You really want the answer?"

Jarngard spit over the wall, clearing the dust from his mouth. "I wouldn't have asked if I didn't."

The King seemed to accept that answer with a subtle nod, while Jarngard calmly waited to see if he would answer his first question. They watched a pair of carrion birds sail over, wings crested. The faint thud of workers hammering reflected through the wall.

"Aurinia's dead and nothing can change that," he said finally. "But I think I've realized I didn't take it for her. I took it for me." Agog looked back to him. "Does that change how you feel about coming to my aid?"

"By the cold winds of the north, did you think I was just going to sit in a hut and grow old?"

Agog grunted his approval. "Don't tell the others, but some days I think about taking a steam chariot and setting off to the east or south. See what adventure brings. Leave the city to the Romans or whoever wants to battle them for it."

Jarngard gave his King an appraising stare. "Then why don't you? I'll be the first one at your side." *And Heron with me and a whole, fresh world before us*, he thought.

The King's grin was grim. "Because when I take something, I mean to hold it. And for all the adventure we might have heading south, there's a pile more right here when the Romans attack."

"I was afraid you'd say that," said Jarngard.

Agog squinted into the distance. He cupped a hand over his eyes. Jarngard followed his stare to a dust storm in the distance to the east where the trade roads ran. The rising dust was leagues away.

"Horse trail?" asked Agog.

Jarngard studied the signs. "Could be a caravan, or a wind devil. Maybe even a dust storm brewing."

Agog frowned. "Might be horse trail."

"Wishful thinking?"

Agog chuckled. "Maybe, but fetch the *Michanikos* just the same, or Plutarch if he won't come. We've got five of these steam catapults and not one soldier who can use them."

"Of course, Your Grace." Jarngard bowed, embellishing his movement with flourishes.

"Stop calling me Your Grace," growled the King.

"Yes, Your Grace," laughed Jarngard before heading down the ladder.

By the time his feet hit the sandy street, his heartbeat had doubled, thinking about seeing Heron for the first time in weeks. His cheeks hurt from grinning as he climbed on the roan charger and kicked his mount in motion. He was glad the King couldn't see the look on his face, he might have thought he'd fallen off the wall and hit his head. Jarngard pointed his horse in the direction of Heron's workshop. He would send Plutarch to the walls first, giving him more time to see her.

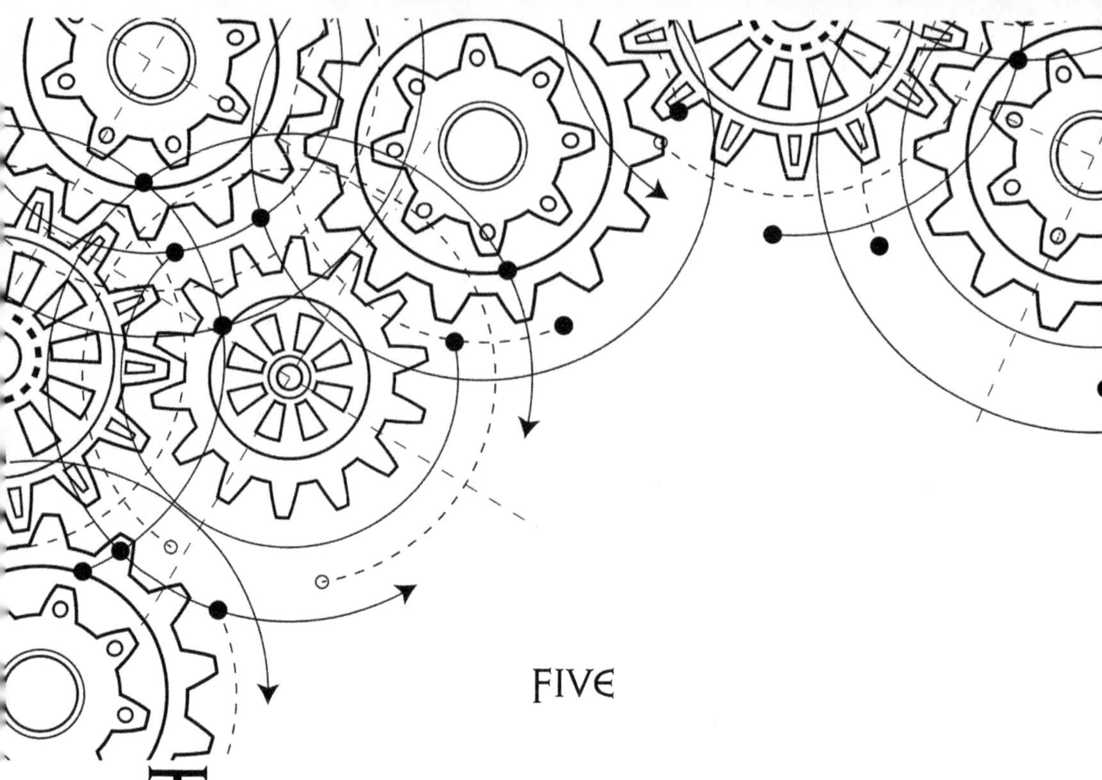

FIVE

The shrine outside the ragged entrance to Heron's workshop spilled into the street. Jarngard gaped at the artifacts piled against the stone-gray wall.

A broken steam mechanical sat at the center of the offerings which lay scattered around it like the city around the Great Library. Surrounding it were pieces of bronze tubing, small gears, gears as big as his hand, dented iron levers, hunks of broken steel, old swords with chipped edges, and even a working miniature automata that had probably been made for one of the city's nobles.

And that said nothing of the hand-carved wooden likenesses of Heron. Some with the arm and leg missing, others had attached bronze tubing to the missing limbs to signify the mechanical nature of the inventor.

Jarngard crouched and examined a wooden Heron doll, carved in exquisite detail. He could tell the Heron doll was female by the soft lips and slender wrists. The carving captured Heron mid-stride, planting the ivory-handled cane forcefully, a look of earth-shattering purpose on her face.

"Come to leave an offering?" asked a shaky, old voice.

Jarngard rose and found an old man in a wine-stained tunic, with breath that could warp glass, grinning a toothless grin.

"In a way," said Jarngard, smiling at his private joke.

"Some say the *Michanikos* is the avatar of Ptah," began the old man as if Jarngard had asked, "others say the inventor is an immortal, born of Hephaestus and forged with Zeus' thunderbolt."

"And what do you say?" asked Jarngard.

The old man teetered on lanky legs, knobby knees sticking out beneath his over-sized tunic. His gaze drifted off and Jarngard wondered if the old man had heard him. Jarngard was about to go inside when the old man started speaking again.

"...the *Michanikos* is a god of the new world, come to throw the old gods back into the waters of creation."

With a foot raised, Jarngard paused and asked a question: "Do others think this?"

The old man belched, spit forming on his lips. The drunken stare was followed by another belch. Jarngard was halfway inside when the old man spoke again.

"Some do, some do."

Looking back, the old man seemed strangely lucid. He even clasped his hand in front as Jarngard had seen Heron do a time or two. Maybe the old guy had once been a scholar in the Great Library.

"Anyone of importance?" asked Jarngard.

"Not yet," said the old man, the earlier shaking in his voice absent. "But when the *Michanikos* saves us from the Romans, more will turn to his cause. He will be the one god to rule the others."

Jarngard went inside shaking his head. He'd spent too much time conversing with the beggar already. Though, if there was any truth to the old man's words, there might be cause for concern. The Temples were jealous folk, and if Heron drained away any of their attention, she might find herself at odds with them again. He might have to take action on her behalf, though she wouldn't like that.

But they need not worry about that now. The Romans at the door were trouble enough for everyone, and while the Temples didn't care who won, they hated the disruption in their profits and would cheer anyone who could end the war quickly.

He was only a few steps inside when Plutarch appeared in the hallway.

"Jarngard!" said Plutarch musically, his eyes sparkling with thought. "It has been too long. I assume you're looking for Master Heron. He's at the Library in the Hall of Numbers."

"I'm afraid it'll be rather short. The King sends for you on the wall. His soldiers need help with the steam catapults," said Jarngard.

Plutarch appeared conflicted, but the King's name was enough to sway him and he bowed and promised to get right to the wall after giving new orders to the workers. Jarngard found his horse in the street again and as he rode away, he looked for the old man, who was nowhere in sight.

Striding up the stairs of the Mausoleum, Jarngard ignored the strange, sideways looks from the scholars. He was an interloper to their great learned ways. These looks were not given head on, but only when he was nearly past.

Jarngard felt like he traveled in a bubble of silence. Pairs of scholars in disheveled togas, signs of old food on the cloth, would approach deep in conversation. When their gaze rose, first a flicker, then a full recognition, the eyes would widen slightly and their conversation would fall to a lull. Upon passing, the two would begin again, but this time at a low murmur. He chuckled as the pattern repeated itself with each new pair.

Three rooms and two hallways past the main entrance, Jarngard looked around, hoping to get an idea of which direction lay the Hall of Numbers. Even though he'd ridden by the Mausoleum numerous times, he hadn't realized how large and confusing it was. Bigger than the Palace, by far.

A scholar stood by, mumbling as he read an unrolled papyrus. His face was hawkish and his hair looked like it'd been cut with a dull knife.

"Apologies," said Jarngard in his best Latin, "can you point the way to the Hall of Numbers?"

The hawk-faced scholar glanced up and his jaw slowly unhinged. Jarngard fought the urge to lunge suddenly at the man, just to see if he might fall over himself to escape, but he decided that was much too cruel and he wanted to see Heron.

As the man's eyes cast about looking for support, Jarngard imagined what he was seeing: an invader barbarian, hair bound by a strip of leather into a Suebian knot, the scars and markings of battle on the nose, ears, and jaw, a pair of blades at his side. Only the tunic would be familiar. The reason Agog had gone about wearing the local styles became clear to him.

The scholar seemed locked in a blank slate, so Jarngard patted him on the shoulder. "I'll find someone else."

"N...n—numbers?" asked the hawk-faced scholar.

Jarngard turned back.

"Aye, the Hall of Numbers. Do you know where it is?"

"Th—they call it, the Pit of All-Thought," said the scholar.

"I don't care what they call it. Can you tell me where it is?" asked Jarngard.

The scholar blinked twice before nodding. "Two halls over. Then down the stairs, three levels, then through the hall to the Pit."

"That way?" asked Jarngard, pointing.

The scholar nodded.

Jarngard glanced back as he left the man to find him still staring.

"It's not like he's never seen a Northman before," said Jarngard to himself.

But had he? As Jarngard followed the directions, he realized the halls and rooms were filled with men chattering on like a thousand deep-throated birds. A war was coming to Alexandria and these scholars appeared unaffected by it.

Maybe the hawk-faced scholar had never seen one of his countrymen, at least from up close. The apartments around the Great Library were filled with scholars. Jarngard rarely saw scholars on the docks or the Emporium or anywhere else for that matter. It seemed by the constant stares that most stayed in the Great Library year round.

The scent of unwashed bodies was thick in the hallway outside the

Hall of Numbers. A short, stocky scholar stood near the entrance tracing his finger on the wall. Jarngard paused, unsure of what the man was accomplishing, before barging forward ready to fetch Heron from her task.

When the stocky scholar caught sight of Jarngard, he stepped into the path, blocking him from entering the room.

"You cannot enter," he whispered. "They're near a breakthrough."

"For what?"

The scholar shushed and pushed Jarngard backward, away from the entrance. When they stood a few strides away, the scholar crouched in a conspiratorial manner.

"They've been at it for three days. The *Michanikos* keeps them going even when they want to sleep," he said.

"At what for three days?"

"Heron wouldn't tell us."

Jarngard pushed his fingers into his hair. These scholars either said nothing or spoke madness. "Then how can they work without knowing what they do?"

The scholar reacted as if slapped, an incredulousness that bordered on insanity. "Why would that matter? We work with the very roots of creation here, the soup of the gods, the language of the universe."

"Well, then," said Jarngard. "Can you go inside and fetch Heron for me? I'm on the King's business and need to speak with him."

"Oh, no," said the scholar. "I'm afraid I cannot. If I disturb them, it might disrupt what they're doing."

A tiny headache formed in the middle of Jarngard's forehead. "But if you don't know what they are doing, then how—? By the jarls..."

The scholar nodded as if he understood. Jarngard put his hand on the man's shoulder and squeezed, hard, hard enough to make the veins in his hand pop out.

"I said, I'm on the King's business. The King of Alexandria. He needs

Heron. Now. Fetch him. Before I throw you into the Pit of All-Numbers, or whatever you call it, and ruin what ever it is that you don't know what they're working on," said Jarngard with gritted teeth.

The blunt talk seemed to get through, because the man finally seemed to notice that Jarngard was not a fellow scholar. Jarngard worried the scholar would grow dumb like the one he'd encountered upstairs when he heard Heron shout.

SIX

"Wrong," she called out, halting progress. The three scholars froze in position, eyes bloodshot and ringed with sleepless dark.

Heron stood apart, watching them work through the sequence she'd given them. They'd been at it for three days without sleep.

And it was utter chaos. Two scholars in untidy togas worked the counting machine, dingy brass levers, worn from use, clacking at each turn. Gears clicked and men called out numbers, while the third scholar scribbled on the round walls of the room they call the Pit of All-Thought.

Normally, this room was reserved for scholars who played with the numbers that made up the fabric of the universe. Work was mostly theoretical - the expansion of numbers, the finding of primes - calculations that had little bearing on the other works in the Library. These were men who enjoyed numbers for the sake of numbers.

"Casto," she said to the scholar at the wall, poised with a piece of chalk in his fingertips. "Aristokles gave you a three digit counter and you wrote four numbers."

Casto looked upon the wall, blinking away his exhaustion. "Apologies, Master Heron, I thought I'd written three, I'm not sure where the fourth came from."

The heat in her chest rose like the swelling of lava. She opened her mouth and only at the last moment as she realized the other two were watching closely, turned the curse into a heavy sigh.

"Your apology is unnecessary, the mistake is understandable given the lack of sleep," she said. "But I would not push if the need was not so great."

Aristokles spoke up, though he appeared conflicted by what he was about to say, wringing his hands and glancing repeatedly to the floor.

"Master Heron. *Michanikos*. We understand there is a danger to the city, otherwise we wouldn't be here." He paused and glanced to his fellow scholars for support. "But we're not a machine like you. We can't keep going without sleep. I'm not even sure what I'm doing anymore."

The heat in her chest fled until it was replaced by an icy calm. A machine. It was the first time anyone had said what she saw in their eyes, what she felt each time she passed the growing shrine outside the workshop.

She looked up. They appeared ready to fall over.

"I understand. We can stop." It wasn't pity that brought the words to her lips.

The men sighed relief.

"First, we must finish this section. We're almost done. After that, we can rest for a while."

She hated giving up. They were so close to breaking the second part of the code, the one dropped by Philo's brother Apion. The first part had unraveled easily on the afternoon of the first day.

Retrieve the warmaster's prize in the temple of thought. The eagle comes so take the flightless bird before ________________.

Ciphers were easily broken so clever coders often hid the message in layers. The first layer had been based on a Roman numeral sequence. Once she identified it, the code was broken, bringing the true message to the surface. But the last part of the code was hidden by a second cipher and they'd been banging their heads against it for days and she might have pushed the men to continue had she not felt like she was missing something important, something that doomed their search to failure.

"Resume the sequence," she said, trying to make it sound less like a command and more like a request. "We'll go just a little further and be done."

The men seemed to accept and their shoulders straightened, just enough, so that they might push on a little more.

While they worked, Heron examined the folded parchment from Apion. Dried blood smeared the corner. Heron thought of the door warden who had given his life for the book of Archimedes. The stewards of the Great Library had quietly removed the body. A death in their halls was nigh unheard of and they didn't want to spook the scholars.

War will be waged right outside its doors and the Library is concerned about one murder, thought Heron. She unfolded the thick paper and flecks of pulp broke from the edges. The paper sat in her metal hand and she smoothed out the folds.

The last part of the code eluded her. The first part had been a series of Roman numerals. The last part, the part she was missing, appeared to be Greek numbers with extra markings in them.

Retrieve the warmaster's prize in the temple of thought. She understood that part well. The warmaster was Archimedes, the scholar of Syracuse. His inventions had kept Rome from taking the city for three years. The temple of thought was clearly the Great Library and she'd seen the missing book in Apion's hands. She even had an idea of why they'd taken it, but she didn't dwell on it, focusing instead on the code.

The eagle comes so take the flightless bird. The eagle was the standard of the

Roman Legion, but the flightless bird wasn't clear. She hoped figuring out the last portion would clue her to the meaning.

Heron traced the first symbol in the second section with a chalk-dusted fingertip. A circle with a dot in the middle. The circle alone was the omicron, the Greek symbol for seventy, unless the dot was a misshapen theta and then the number was nine. The rest was less clear. What appeared to be a koppa, or ninety, was second. The message was five symbols long. Heron assumed the number sequence was taken from a commonly known calculation and by finding the source number, she would be able to determine the answer.

...so take the flightless bird before...

Before what? Why did it matter to take the flightless bird before this other thing? Was that another artifact of Archimedes' hidden in the Library? The Curiosity Rooms were one possibility and she'd thought of asking scholars to look out for Apion, but the halls were so large and labyrinthine and Library scholars were not known for their attentiveness.

The men at the counting machine were working through the last numbers. Heron tapped on the parchment, willing the symbols to change shape into something she understood. The answer eluded her. She could feel the familiarity of the sequence, but her mind, when pressed, could not conjure it.

If she knew more about Apion, she thought it might help. The Library stewards had known his name and had promised to keep watch for him, but Heron thought the act pointless. He would be long from the city by now. Back to Rome, where he lived.

Apion had been known by the stewards because he briefly studied astrology in the Great Library. Heron knew little of the practice, only that it involved the ruling of men's lives by the stars. A practice she only proscribed value to because its charting of the heavens supported the works of astronomy.

Casto called on Heron to examine the final numbers. She shook her head. There was nothing meaningful about them.

"Apologies, good scholars," said Heron. "I have led you on a fruitless journey."

Casto knuckled away his sleep while yawning. "Not fruitless entirely. We have delved in places not seen before. Our charts are more full, though are heads are empty of sleep."

Heron refrained from reminding him that without the city's protection, Rome might put an end to their practice, but they were tired and she was near her end. War would come regardless. She would speak to Agog in the morning, if only to let him know about the Roman spy.

As the scholars prepared their things, Heron stared at the parchment. Whatever message was sent to Apion, she understood the important part, at least she hoped.

"Casto," she said, stopping him before he left, one last thought on the matter creeping through her mind, "do you by chance know anything about astrology?"

Casto shook his head and she deflated. She thought she'd seen him in the astrology rooms, but she must have been mistaken.

"I know a little," offered Aristokles.

Heron held the parchment out. "Do these symbols at the bottom right look familiar to you?"

He nodded and a spark of hope formed in her chest. "They look like Greek numbers with parts missing or added."

"Plato have pity," she mumbled.

Aristokles turned his head, narrowing his gaze. "But they could also be radix numbers from the Denanic hour chart."

Heron grabbed Aristokles by the arm, using her flesh hand. "What does it say?"

The scholar scrunched up his face in thought. "I studied astrology as a curiosity, but the Chaldaean logic was too often mystifying."

"This is important. What do the symbols mean?"

"It might be Chiron in the third house. I think," said Aristokles.

Heron sighed defeated. "That means nothing, then. I hoped it might be a date, that would make sense."

Aristokles brightened. "It can be a date. We're in the third house, and the festival of Chiron is celebrated at the full moon."

"And when is that?" she asked.

"Tomorrow."

"By the balls of Bacchus!" she yelled, frightening the scholars. Aristokles shrunk away from her. She was about to pour her gratitude onto him when a huge man with swords drawn barged into the room.

The scholars froze.

"Jarngard? What are you doing here?"

He hesitated, glancing from Heron to scholar to the counting machine and back to Heron. Each time his gaze passed over her, she felt tingling in her chest.

"The King needs you on the wall and I came to bring you to him," he said.

She could see he had more to say. "Your work is complete, friends," she told the scholars. "I will report your good names to the King."

Alone with Jarngard, Heron felt the weight of her new limbs keenly. She pulled the metal arm to her chest, the gears clicking through their paces as the elbow bent.

Heron glanced at her feet and Jarngard was there, up close, his scent, musky and delirious.

"I've missed you," he whispered, his hand reaching.

"I cannot." But she wanted to.

Heron smoothed the hair away from her forehead, feeling the grime and stickiness of days-long sweat.

They stood in silence, a hands breath apart, until Heron finally remembered what she'd been doing in the bowels of the Library.

"I must see Agog. I have grave news," she said.

"He needs you on the wall. You were supposed to supervise the steam catapults," said Jarngard, icy blue eyes locked on to her. "But I need you more. The steam catapults can wait a little longer, I think."

Heron shook her head and saw his disappointment in the slight frown and downcast eyes. She held the parchment up. "The Romans are planning to attack tomorrow. We must prepare."

"A spy?"

She nodded.

Jarngard raised his head and looked away in thought. "The dust trails. The attack might come sooner than tomorrow."

Heron opened her mouth when the bells began to ring. The ringing carried across the city, every bell in every tower taking up the clarion call until the air reverberated with the message. Even in the belly of the Great Library, the sound carried its tune, bringing word, bringing the news: War comes to Alexandria.

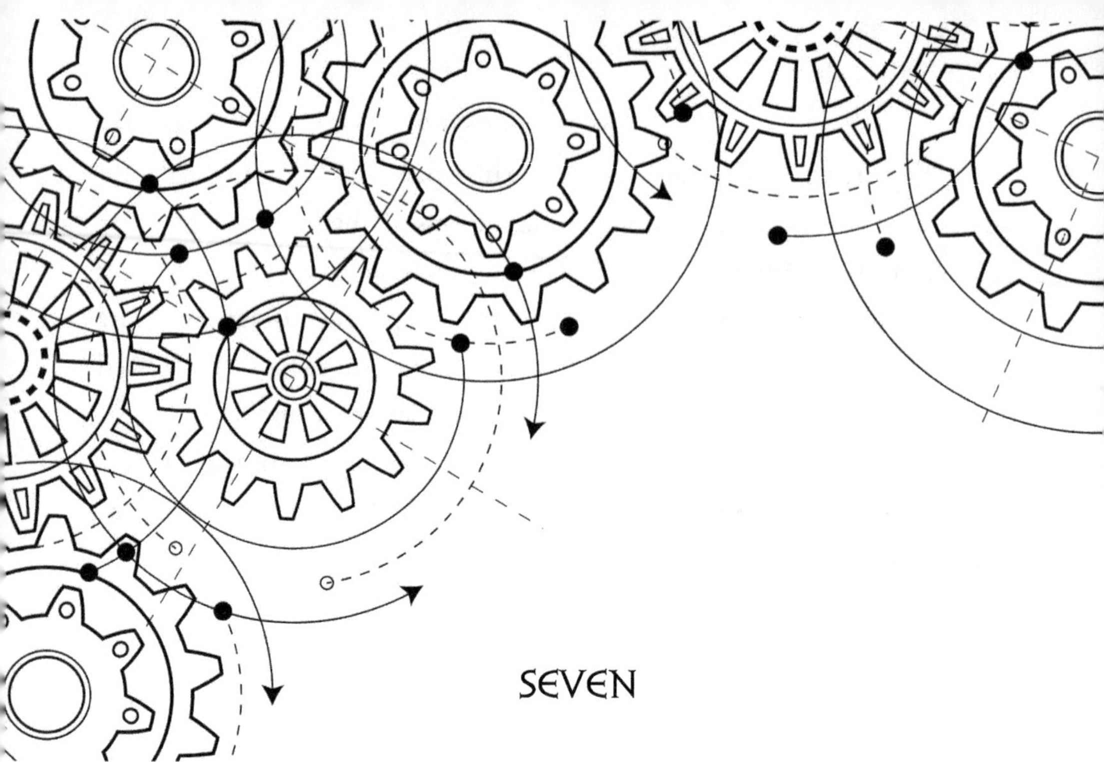

SEVEN

Dust rose above the city as a menacing cloud, brought by the invading army. The glittering mail of Parthian cataphracts reflected in the setting sun, lined up in two long rows on the sea side. The Roman cavalry made their place along Lake Mareotis. Somewhere behind the line, the throaty roar of steam mechanicals made their presence known.

Agog spit over the wall and growled slightly as he pounded his fist on the roughhewn wall. "Cursed wind is in our face. We'll be choking on dust if they attack."

At his side, Vestalis glanced behind them at the setting sun. Agog didn't bother to turn, he knew what was there: a brilliant and bloody sky.

"The sun will be in their faces if they attack now," said Vestalis.

"But not for long," said Agog.

Two sections over, near the Canopic gate, Heron was shouting at his workers, adjusting the steam catapults. Behind them, in the streets below the wall, archers murmured as they knelt in long lines, waiting for the command. Scattered coughing could be heard throughout the defense, brought on by the wind-born dust.

Agog tightened the knot in his hair until the skin on his forehead stretched tight. If he had to join combat, he didn't want his vision blocked by loose strands. He never understood how Hoth the Black fought with his hair flowing around his face. Vanity would be the death of that man.

"Tell me what you see. Censor nothing," commanded Agog.

The merciless gray eyes of the former Roman equestrian surveyed the battlefield. His jaw rippled with thought. Only the presence of Vestalis had kept Agog from taking his army on the offensive.

"The Parthian cataphracts are unmatched on an open plain or in city streets. If they get past our walls, the defense is doomed. The Roman cavalry is anything but Roman. They're a mix of Gallic, Thracian, and Numidia horsemen, as skilled as the Parthians, but less armored, so more vulnerable to our arrow launchers. The true Romans are the officers, mixed amongst the troops," said Vestalis indicating each point with an outstretched hand. He paused and broke into a fit of coughing before regaining his composure.

"They've brought at least a half a Legion of infantry," continued Vestalis, "either double backed with the cavalry, or on wagons and steam chariots. It was a bold move to rush down a strike force."

Agog studied Vestalis. His brow was hunched, partially squinting away the dust, and partially in thought. The veins on his forehead throbbed with purpose. Though the man led a vast merchant empire, he had not lost the hard muscles earned as a Roman equestrian.

"You are surprised by this boldness," said Agog, stifling a cough.

Vestalis glanced over before nodding. "It's either desperation or boldness. Rome rules by the strength of its legions and conquest is typically used to garner political power. Safe victories are the only way to ensure a profitable war. Lose too many soldiers and the profits get eaten up by retraining new men."

The rough stone wall against his thighs was not as comforting as Agog thought it should be. It was plenty thick enough, but not high enough to dissuade ladders or siege engines.

Across the battlefield, horses shifted and regiment flags snapped in the wind. There were too many cavalry and not enough infantry to stage a wall breach. He would send a message to Jarngard at the Moon Gate on the other side of the city to watch for saboteurs sneaking over the wall. Agog couldn't think of any other way they would pass their defenses

"Which do you believe?" asked Agog.

"If it were any other man besides Consul Magnus, I would say desperation, but he is not a man to court power," said Vestalis, admiration threading his tone. "I did not campaign with him, but his name was spoken often by the other officers, gossiping about who would rise to Legate or Praetor."

"He was believed to rise far?"

"No," said Vestalis. "Because Magnus was known to be reckless and bold, risking legions in unconventional tactics. That way never leads to power."

"Yet, he is the Consul."

Vestalis bore a grim countenance. "If it were any other man besides Consul Magnus, I would say desperation, but because it is him, boldness."

The scents of burning coal drifted on the wind mixed with the dust and sweat of a thousand horses. The Alexandrian steam chariots were poised along Canopic street, readied for a counterattack, but the wind was in their face and he could neither hear nor smell them.

"What is this bold strategy, then?" asked Agog. "He's brought nothing but cavalry and not enough infantry to breach the walls. Our steam catapults and arrow launchers can easily defend those numbers. Is this just a ploy to distract us? Or draw us into a counterattack? Or just to cut off trade and keep the city contained?"

The gray eyes of Vestalis held no answers. Agog looked back to the army arrayed before the walls. Even from a distance, well out of arrow range, Agog could sense the anticipation. There was a certain feeling you got before the battle was engaged, a worried, heavy thumping in the chest. Nervous glances to your fellow soldiers, wondering which would live and which would die, and praying it was not some half-formed life between. Better glory and death than slow misery.

Agog knew this because he'd been on the Roman's side countless times before. Could feel the twitch in his arms, readying to swing the great two-handed broadsword now on his back, a comforting weight. Fear was in the air, the sweat of anticipation, of armor worn for days during a hard ride.

Agog closed his eyes and felt their energy. Heard the faint shouts of preparation, the eagerness in the tone. Eagerness to bring the battle to the enemy.

If Consul Magnus had sent this army to siege the city, they would be breaking into camps. Dusk with the sun in their face was the worst time to attack. Yet, the horses shifted and whinnied and the men held their banners high and proud.

Everything about the mix of troops and the lay of the battlefield screamed to delay an attack. Even the time of day was wrong. The Romans would be better off attacking in the morning when the sun was behind them. But Agog could sense their gathering force, like an arm tensed to hurl a javelin into an enemy's throat.

"They will attack this evening," said Agog finally.

"I concur," said Vestalis, coughing slightly. "I feel it in my bones."

"Are we ready?" asked Agog.

"That depends on the *Michanikos* and his warmachines, half of which have never been tested," said Vestalis.

Agog recalled the time in the workshop when the first steam mechanical exploded, nearly killing them; or the many explosions later when the workshops put the technology to use. A faulty anti-siege weapon at the wrong time could spell disaster for the defense and that was why Agog hated defending. A good offense only had to win once where the defense had to win every time.

"Let us put Heron and his machines to the test. Better now than during the thick of battle," said Agog.

Soldiers on the wall saluted as they passed. Heron fretted over some parchments when they approached. As the inventor turned, Agog steeled himself from reacting. He still wasn't used to the metal limbs that functioned like flesh ones: bending and articulating, even grabbing the thin paper between pinched fingers.

"Why weren't my catapults given the locations I requested?" spat Heron. The inventor's voice was muffled behind a piece of cloth tied around his face. Strange round pieces of glass were fixed over his eyes, held by copper fittings. Heron looked more fantastical by the day.

"What are you wearing?" asked Agog.

"A moist cloth to keep the dust from my mouth and goggles from my workshop for protecting the eyes," said Heron.

That was when Agog noticed the catapult crew was all wearing the same. Agog got the impression of metal bugs climbing over the brood mother.

Vestalis cleared his throat, looking almost sheepish. "Apologies, *Michanikos*, but the locations requested were needed for the archers."

The deference in Vestalis voice surprised Agog. Possibly, he was unnerved by the strange appearance of the inventor.

"The locations on the seaside wall would have given me range on the whole army. From here, I can only hit half," said Heron.

"You can hit half?" asked Vestalis incredulously.

Heron didn't even look to the army arrayed in battle. "Half, maybe slightly more."

"Let us show them a little fear, then," said Agog.

Heron stared back, but Agog couldn't read the inventor's mood. Not that he could read it much before. The man was as impenetrable as granite and the machine-like limbs only made him more so.

"Don't you want to save them for a surprise? Won't letting them know what we're capable of give them information?" asked Heron.

In other circumstances, Heron might have been right. Now, he just wanted to know what the Romans were planning. A few volleys might spur them to action.

"As long as that information comes with a little death and fear, that's my command."

"Requested location?"

Agog squeezed back a cough. "Hit a banner. Might get an officer if we're lucky."

Without acknowledging the request, Heron went into motion, tapping on the parchment before shouting commands to his workers.

A heavy stone ball that took two men to load was placed into the iron tube after being wrapped in oiled cotton. The steam catapult was brought around, using gears and wenches, and the long tube angled upwards until Agog could no longer touch the opening, even if he tried.

The workers adjusted levers on the bronze tubes as the steam mechanical thrummed into life. Agog was enraptured by the preparation, until Heron tapped him on the shoulder and pointed to a location away from the steam catapult. Agog got the message and moved to a safe location.

When the mechanical had been chugging at full for a least a half-dozen breaths, Heron looked to Agog and tilted his head. A request to fire.

Agog swung his arm down, like swinging a sword. When the catapult erupted, he felt the thump in his chest, like he'd been hit with two heavy hands. Agog wasn't sure what he'd been expecting, but not what happened. He was used to catapults that moved, rotating with tight force and then flinging their charge at the enemy.

The steam catapult did not rotate. Nor did it move, except in reaction to the stone ball flying out of the front in a cloud of steam. Agog didn't even see it, really. Only felt it in his chest and then heard the screams of men moments later in the ranks of the Romans. Calvary scattered away from the impact and the whole line crept backwards, horses turning.

"Impressive," whispered Vestalis.

"Again?" asked Heron.

Agog nodded.

The workers leapt into action, bringing the iron tube low to load another stone ball. The speed of reloading bothered Agog. He only had five steam catapults arrayed on the wall. Their use would be devastating, especially to any siege weaponry, but the enemy was mostly cavalry. Not a siege tower or battering ram in sight.

Bells in the city started ringing unexpectedly. Agog turned to see the crimson glow of fire across the city in at least three different locations.

"Saboteurs," said Vestalis before shouting orders to a pair of runners, giving commands to rally fire fighters. The city districts should be able to handle the distraction, but they didn't want to let anything get out of control, especially with the brisk winds.

The enemy was in motion when they turned back. A group of around one hundred cataphracts burst into the open area before the walls, but not headed toward the city. Instead, they curved around, running parallel to the wall. A dust cloud streamed like banners from each hoof beat, rising from the earth and filling the air with noxious dust. The wall vibrated from the thundering cataphracts.

"What is that?" asked Vestalis.

The dust cloud from the Parthian cavalry was flowing over the northern portion of the wall, on the opposite side of the Canopic Gate. Behind the cataphracts, was a line of horse-drawn wagons, following the path of the cavalry. Agog had an urge to send a volley of arrows after the wagons, but he wanted to see what they were up to first.

A thicker white dust, like a cloud shaken free, flowed from the back of the wagons. Men on the wagons dumped bags of powder into the air and the wind carried it up, turning the air to white mist.

"What sorcery is this?" asked Vestalis.

Agog watched with a breath caught in his throat as the pale cloud reached the northern section of the wall. Screaming came right after and suddenly, Agog felt exposed on the wall as the cloud moved swiftly toward them.

As the dust enveloped men, the screaming grew. Soldiers on the wall fell like reeds cut with a scythe, clawing at their eyes and rolling uncontrollably across the ground. Agog thought about leaping from the wall but his escape would only incite chaos in his troops and he wouldn't be able to get away from the swiftly moving cloud, anyway. The archers behind the wall moved cautiously back with bows in hand.

Before the whiteness reached him, Agog took a deep breath, filling his lungs with dusty air that almost made him cough it all back out. His eyes began to burn immediately, even before he realized the dust had reached him.

He squeezed them shut. Pain came in waves, centered around his head at first. Even his ears burned. It was as if someone had dumped hot oil over him. Men screamed as his heartbeat labored.

Agog fought the urge to take a deep breath. His lungs burned with effort. Someone grabbed his arm. He pushed them away.

The whole world had turned to fire. Beneath the pain, he knew they had lost. There was no one on the wall to defend. The Romans could put ladders on the wall at their leisure. The defense had been bunched up along the point of attack. There was nothing they could do. Agog didn't know how it could have happened so fast, but it was done. The war was lost. The Romans would take Alexandria.

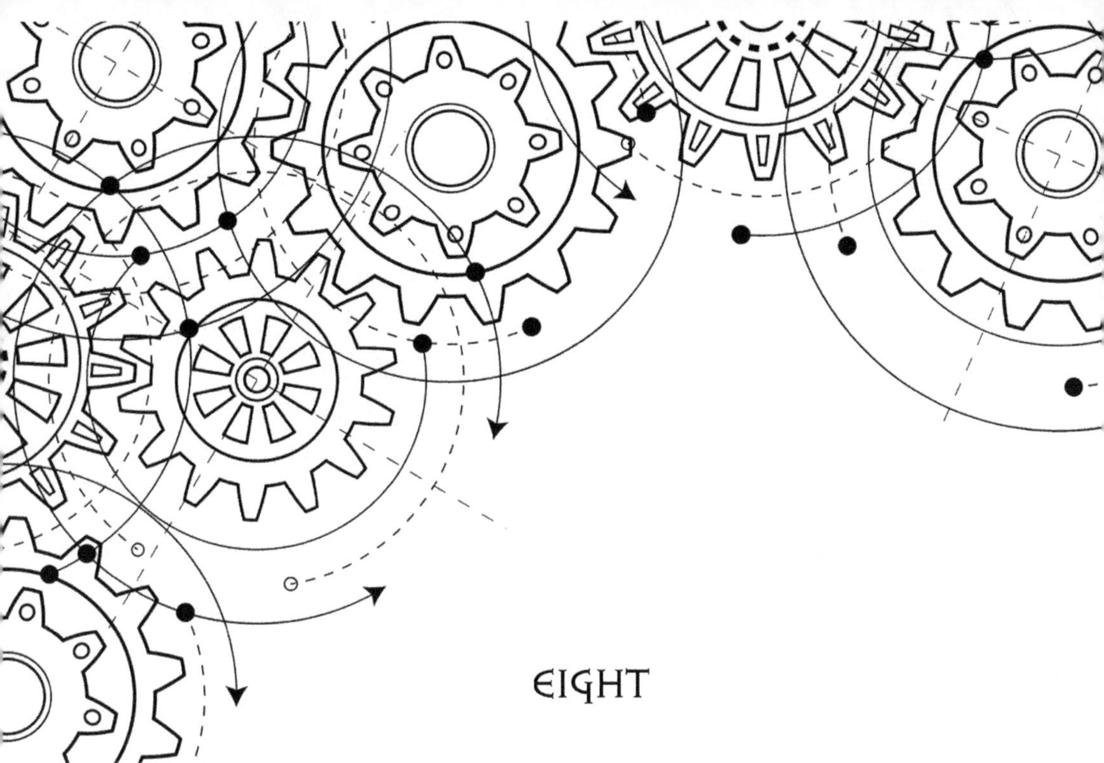

EIGHT

$\mathbf{A}$gog found himself on his hands and knees. The rough stone of the wall was almost comforting compared to his eyes and nose and ears. Even his arse and cock burned. He wanted nothing more than to douse himself in a pool of cool water, but he didn't even know if that would save him.

Who had ever heard of a white powder that burned? How could he have even prepared?

Men screamed all around him. Even below, where the archers had been staged, they howled in pain. A man nearby whimpered, and between each seething breath, he called out the gods names and begged them for mercy: Zeus, Jupiter, Set, and so on.

Agog's chest ached until he could hold his lips clamped no longer. He took a sputtering breath and regretted it instantly. The fire went into his lungs and belly, poured down his throat like hot lava.

He heaved, vomit passing his lips and splattering his forearms. Someone touched his head and he wondered if it were a Roman soldier.

Time felt meaningless. They could have breached the walls. A soldier could be lining up a sword-blow as he waited.

A wet cloth was pushed against his face and his hand was placed against the cloth. He held it over his mouth and took a tentative breath. This one felt better, but the fire still smoldered in his chest.

Cool objects were placed against his eyes and then a strap of leather pulled tight against his head, right under his hair knot. When the heavy object bumped against his head, Agog knew it was Heron.

Agog tied the cloth around his face and then the pieces of glass held by a leather strap. He dared to open his eyes and though they still burned, he could see.

The world through the glass was misty gray and fuzzy. Vestalis stood next to him, wearing cloth and goggles. Heron had returned to the steam catapult and was preparing another volley.

Vestalis patted Agog on the shoulder and pointed to the wide plain before the city. A pair of steam chariots with a huge ram suspended between them sped toward the gate. The cavalry lined up behind the ram.

Agog glanced around him. His army was in tatters. Men rolled across the ground, moaning and crying, cupping their eyes. A few stumbled to their feet, spitting, but not enough. They were too few.

The world was muted. The dust had damaged his hearing, though it burned less, now. He muttered a few curses and even through the wet cloth around his face, his throat ached with each breath.

The cloud had passed. The buildings behind the wall were coated in a fine powder. From a distance, it appeared to be light snow.

The chariots neared. The huge trunk was bound in iron like a piston, ready to demolish whatever it hit.

Agog grabbed Vestalis by the shoulder and pulled him toward the gate. Nothing else mattered now.

He ran past Heron. The steam catapult was being repositioned, but it would be too late to stop the ram. Every breath was a knife in the chest. His vision was bleary, tears pooled in the corners. Agog leapt over an Egyptian soldier, his polished bronze skin dusted white.

When the ram hit, Agog was knocked from his feet. Thick timbers reinforced with iron splintered outward, killing the fallen men behind the gate. What remained of the wood was buckled and a chariot sized hole remained.

Thunder filled his ears as the Parthian cataphracts streamed toward the breach. The Roman attack flooded toward them like the sea unbound.

A pair of arrow launchers guarded the wall near the gate, but the men meant to operate them were incapacitated. Agog leapt on the platform and aimed the weapon. The mass of bronze tubes filled with arrows normally took two or three men to turn, but Agog grabbed the sides and growled as he repositioned it.

On the plains below, ringed mail armor gleamed crimson in the dying light. Arms were raised skyward, weapons readied. The curved backs of the horses rose and fell by the hundreds, legs churning toward the gate like hounds on the hunt. The spear of the Roman army thrust toward Alexandria.

Agog aimed the arrow launcher at a spot directly in front of the gate. The mechanical that powered it puttered listlessly until he pulled the lever initiating the gearing that fed air to the tubes.

He was familiar with the design. Heron had created smaller versions his men called Manticores. The wall mounted weapons could be larger and didn't have to withstand the impact of the uneven ground traveling around on the back of a steam chariot.

Those versions shot a single arrow, one after another until the weapon was empty. Agog expected much the same when he diverted air to the tubes by turning a lever. What he got was a hailstorm of death.

Each second, a full row of arrows blasted out of the tubes to a repetitious *thump*. Each volley slammed into another wave of riders. The ringed mail of the cataphracts could have been wet papyrus for all it did to protect its wearers; and for the horses he hit, they went sprawling into the dirt, flinging riders from their backs. The terrible power of the launcher made him feel like a fledgling god, dispensing death with a thought.

When air hissed out of the tubes, announcing the weapon was empty, Agog shut the lever. He'd decimated the first wave, though a few riders had gotten through. A new round sped toward the gate and there was no one to load the launcher.

Distracted by the incoming riders, Agog didn't see the Roman horseman lining him up until the bow twanged. The arrow grazed his arm, leaving a line of crimson.

While the horseman pulled back another arrow, Agog searched for something to throw. More riders approached the gate and the weapon was still empty. The riders who had made it inside the gate were removing the iron chains that held the way closed. Soon they would be able to swing it open.

A blur flew by and the earth exploded, throwing horses and men like toys. Heron had fired his steam catapult, delaying the assault and giving Agog precious moments to act.

As a younger man, Agog might have leapt from the wall onto the Roman soldier with a bow. He was at least the height of a three-story building and would have made the jump even five years ago, but age and injury had taught him wisdom.

Agog grabbed a shield the moment before the arrow was released. The arrowhead stuck between the planks of the shield, not far from his face.

Throwing the shield away, he moved to the ladder and slid down, jumping the last length. The cloth fell from his mouth, but he had no time to fix it. With the great sword drawn from his back, he charged the horseman.

The man was a Thracian by his dark hair and square-cut jaw. He spurred his horse and sped toward Agog. The seal of the Roman Empire displayed on the barding thundered toward him.

Agog meant to step out of the way and cut the rider down, but he'd forgotten about the strange pieces of glass on his face. When he swung, he found the horse much closer than he'd planned and the thick chest of the beast slammed into him.

He had just enough time to square his shoulder for the impact, but it knocked him back a few paces and stunned him. Spots formed in his eyes and the breath had been knocked from him. The world rotated but he kept his feet.

The horse reared on its hind legs, turning. The soldier had been thrown onto the neck of the horse and scrambled to get back on.

Agog shook his head, dispelling the spots, and bore down, taking three loping steps toward the Thracian before swinging. He nearly cried out as the heavy blade soared through the air, pain ripping through his shoulder, but he held tight and took the soldier's arm clean off.

The chains on the gate were almost unloosed, the Roman soldiers yanking on the thick links, clanking through the iron hoops. The gate would be open soon.

Agog checked around him. He was surrounded by dead bodies. Where was Vestalis? Had he abandoned him? He couldn't see Heron or his crew on the steam catapult, but he could see more horses headed toward the hole in the gate.

His hearing had come back. There were shouts. Agog moved toward the soldiers, sword dragging in the dirt, while he ripped the glass from his eyes. Each step brought a grimace, his shoulders, his lungs, his chest. The soldiers turned. There were three of them. Two pulled swords, short gladii, and hefted metal bucklers to defend. The soldier behind them almost had the chain completely free from the loop.

Agog had no time to parry. He lifted the tip of the blade from the dirt, turning his body and grabbing the hilt with his other hand, fingers wrapping tightly around, leaning into his hips, bringing maximum speed to the heavy blade.

The wide-eyed soldiers lifted their feeble bucklers, cringing away from his strike. The blade tore through them, ripping through the first shield, and arm, and into the chest of the second man. Agog kicked out, sending the man sprawling and brought the blade around for the killing blow.

Agog bit his lip, the shoulder had worked itself loose and his left arm hung uselessly by his side. He hefted the sword onto his right shoulder and calmly strolled toward the last soldier who was struggling with the chain, wide-eyed, and watching Agog approach.

Agog nodded toward the opening and spoke in commoner's Latin, "Flee while you can."

The soldier, a Gaul, probably, dropped the chain and practically tripped over himself escaping. With the soldier gone, Agog dropped the sword, feeling his limbs tremble with exhaustion, and pulled the chain back on the hook, which took longer than he wanted because he had to use only one arm.

"Now I know how Heron feels."

Behind him on Canopic street, there were signs of soldiers returning. The screaming and crying had lessened. Whatever effect the white dust had on his army, it was fading.

Moving to the center of the street, he called out, "Vestalis?"

An answer came from the north side of the gate. Vestalis, looking like a desert bug on stilts with cloth and copper-bound glass still around his eyes, stepped to the edge.

"Here."

"By the jarls, why are you up there? I could have used you."

Vestalis pointed over the wall. Through the hole, a new pile of horses had been formed, the arrows facing north rather than south.

"They took the ram back," yelled Vestalis.

"What?"

The chariots had been smashed on impact. Agog didn't understand until he looked through the gap. In the distance, a team of horses dragged back the huge iron-wrapped trunk toward another pair of steam chariots.

"By the cold winds of the North, our gate can't withstand another hit and those arrow launchers won't slow them down," said Agog.

"It looks that way," said Vestalis.

Behind him, Alexandrian soldiers were reloading the arrow launchers. Coughing echoed mutely over the walls. His soldiers stumbled to their posts, spitting and holding their eyes, some with only one eye open.

"Maybe Heron can hit it with his catapult," said Agog. "He is the miracle worker."

Vestalis shook his head. "Heron left the gate."

Agog sighed. Nothing was going right. "I'm sure he has his reasons. Let's rally and get this gate reinforced. Direct some men down here and I'll put them to work."

Vestalis moved away and began yelling orders. Glancing back, Agog tried to ignore the smoke hovering over the city. The earlier fires weren't raging unchecked, but they certainly weren't under control.

He surveyed the damage as men climbed the ladders. The thick iron supports that held the pivots were cracked. He was surprised the whole thing hadn't come crashing down already. Even if the chariot-ram didn't hit the gate cleanly, it would open a hole big enough to bring the whole army through.

Holding his shoulder tight against his body, Agog called out orders, instructing the soldiers to clear the dead and bring new timbers to set against the gate. Through the hole, he watched the Romans resetting the ram, willing his men to move faster. It wouldn't be long before their defenses would be tested again.

"I should have attacked," he muttered, shaking his head. "I should have attacked."

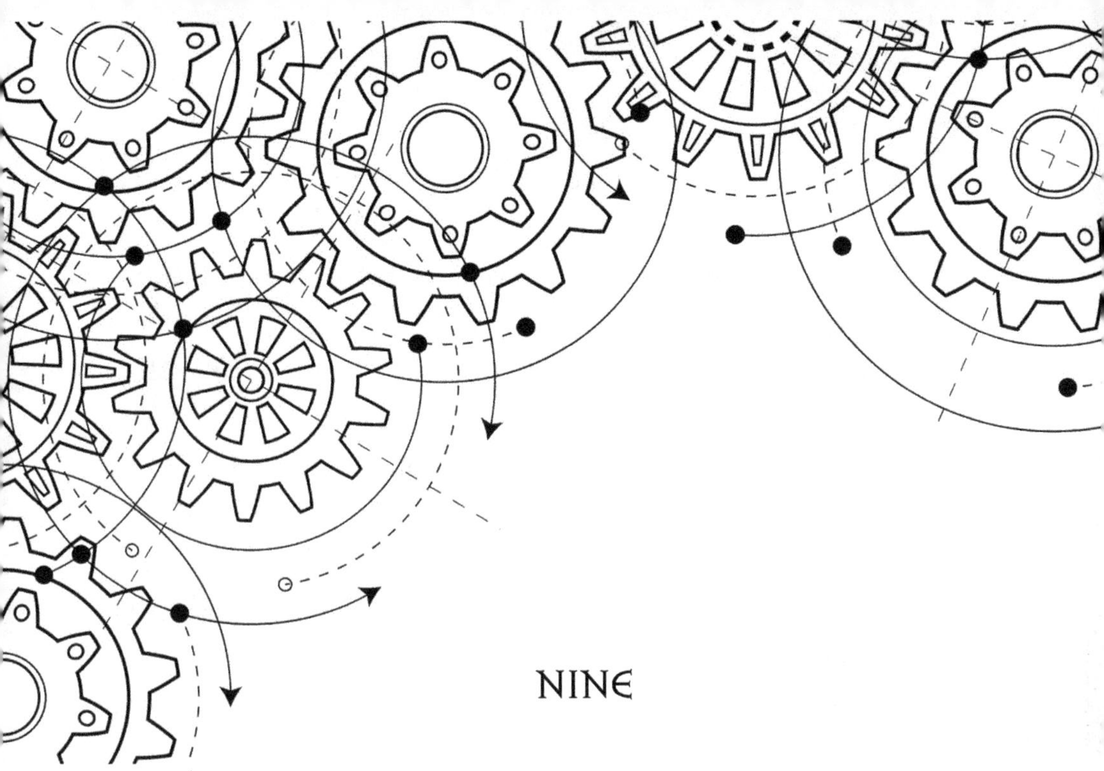

NINE

As soon as she saw the mass of riders peel away from the main force to circle Lake Mareotis, she knew she had to come to Jarngard's aid. Once the attack on the Canopic had been stopped, Heron found a chariot and instructed the Greek soldier at its helm to give it to her. The chariot wasn't configured for her metal limbs and she fought the steering as the craft sped toward the Moon Gate.

There were a mix of Parthian cataphracts and Roman cavalry, along with a pair of steam chariots headed around the lake, mail glinting in the dying light. Heron wondered if the chariots were ones she'd crafted, or if they were Roman made. It wouldn't matter. Either way, they could be used to destroy the Moon Gate.

Rather than head straight to the Moon Gate, she detoured to her workshop. The defense of the western gate needed more than just troops.

Back in her workshop, Heron limped through the array of scaffolding. Her workers were probably away in the city, helping put out fires. She needed at least one other person to help gather equipment. Heron moved toward the warm glow of the foundry, finding Punt tending the banked fires.

Punt gave her a strange look. Fine, white dust clung to her tunic. She knocked some loose with a swipe.

"No time," said Heron, "we need to get the water pump to the Moon Gate."

"But it's empty," he said, scratching the tuft of coarse hair on his chest.

"Good, then we won't have to drain it."

Punt wanted to say something, but quickly changed his mind. He helped her connect the pump wagon to the steam chariot, and then they loaded extra sacks of fuel. Punt steered the craft to the western side of the city while Heron tinkered with the equipment.

Jarngard greeted them when they approached. He commanded a token force at the western gate. Agog planned to utilize the steam chariots for support should the Romans split the attack, since the defenses weren't completely in place, but the first assault had changed that.

Atop the wall, two steam catapults' bases had been bricked in, but there was no weapon to fire. She did see an arrow launcher from a cannibalized Manticore on the wall, but that would do little versus a determined attack.

Jarngard looked past her to the empty street. "I hope you have more coming. A mixed *alae* regiment of cavalry approaches. The defenses won't last ten minutes."

She shook her head. "Just Punt and I. Hopefully, it's all you need."

He hesitated, glancing once to Punt. The blacksmith was stone-faced, a grim darkness haunting his gaze. Jarngard nodded.

"Tell us what we need to do," he said.

"I need that water pump as close to the wall as possible. On top, if we can manage," requested Heron.

"It's too heavy to lift, not with the short crew we have here," replied Jarngard.

"As close as you can, then."

Jarngard shouted commands, and a trio of men came running. They pulled the wagon with the water pump to the wall. As the soldiers grunted with effort, a lookout yelled, "Another minute!"

"You know there's no fire here," said Jarngard perplexed.

"There will be," she said, wrestling with a fuel box. "Help us bring these boxes over. Hurry. And light torches, as many as you can."

Dust and the sounds of riders flowed over the wall. The steady thrum of a steam mechanical echoed outside. One of her children was being used against her.

Arrows flew over the wall. Men fell. The Manticore unleashed its volley and was spent.

Jarngard climbed onto the wall and directed the defense, shouting and occasionally ducking behind the crenellations. Metal hooks in the shape of griffon claws landed on the top of the gate.

"Cut the lines! Cut the lines!" shouted Jarngard.

On the other side of the wall, steam mechanicals growled, pulling the claws tight. Heron stoked her fire, watching for the mechanical to churn.

"Punt, dump that coal dust into the water chamber," she commanded and he went right to work. The question that was on his lips would have to wait until after the battle, though she suspected he wouldn't need to ask once he saw what she was going to do, assuming they survived its use.

While the mechanical was gathering steam, Heron collected the long leather tube that extended from the tank. Plutarch had called the device a pregnant elephant the first time he saw it. Heron couldn't disagree.

She tucked the hose under her mechanical arm, and began climbing the ladder on the wall. The sounds of men dying was all around her. There were too many Romans and Parthians outside the gate and not enough defenders. The Manticore was abandoned. If the Romans had brought infantry and ladders, they'd be over the wall already.

"Jarngard, get me that torch! Quickly!"

The gate buckled from the pulling force of the steam chariots. Heron hoped the top of the gate would snap off before taking the whole structure with it, but the iron-clad wood appeared stronger than the supports.

She reached the top and pulled the slack from the hose, keeping a low profile. The chariots churned in the dust, spitting dirt onto the gate. Three more hooks were thrown onto the wall, connected to teams of horses. The gate would break soon.

"Is the tank full?" she yelled down to Punt.

"Not yet, Master Heron!"

"Hurry!"

With the hose held against her hip she crawled to the edge of the wall where the gate began. The hose didn't quite reach. She sighed and looked down at the wagon. If someone moved it another length, she could hang the hose over the wall, but there was no time. Two more grappling hooks had been thrown over and the iron bands on the wood cried.

"No more time!" she shouted down. "Latch the chamber and start the pumping."

Heron positioned herself as close to the gate as she could. The Romans had stopped firing arrows, most of the defenders were dead.

She glanced around. Where was Jarngard? She needed that torch if this was going to work.

When the pump engaged, the flexing of the hose almost ripped it out of her hands. The hose reacted like a thrashing serpent. Black dust sprayed from the end and she caught a face-full as part of the stream reflected against the wall. Most went over, forming a black cloud that the wind caught.

The soldiers reacted instantly to the new threat. Bows fired in her direction, arrows whistling past her head. The main support on the gate snapped, bending the gate outward even further. The whole structure groaned.

"Jarngard!" she yelled.

Mysteriously, he was on the ground below, on the sea side, a sputtering torch in his hand. He wouldn't make it up to her in time. The gate would be broken.

"Jarngard! Throw it over!"

He didn't have to be told twice. Jarngard launched it over, spinning flame whirling through the air. Heron feared for a brief moment that it would go out and it appeared to as it fell through the cloud. Heron was certain nothing was going to happen, that her idea, born from the Roman's attack on the eastern gate, had failed.

The explosion knocked her off her feet. Flames licked past, heat rising up like the sun had fallen on her. Lying on her back, the hose pointed skyward, spewing black coal dust straight up, a geyser of deadly fuel.

Heron knew she should get up and point the hose over the wall again, but she couldn't breathe, or move. Half the cloud was being blown out of the city, but the heavier particles fell. If the dust caught, she would be immolated.

Her ears rang from the force of the explosion. Men screamed from beyond the wall. Heron tried to get onto one elbow, but her body wouldn't move.

Punt appeared above her, pulling the hose from her hands. He pointed it over the wall again and a second smaller explosion sent a fireball into the air.

Heron crawled to her knees and peered over the crenellations. Her fingers were a mix of black and white dust. Hair on her hands had been singed.

The Roman and Parthian regiment wheeled away from the Moon

Gate. Flames engulfed the two steam chariots and charred corpses hung half off the platforms. Burning flesh was thick in the air.

Gouts of flame sputtered from the hose until the pump finally failed. When nothing but air came out, Punt threw the leather tube away. Jarngard appeared by her side, his arm comfortably around her. She leaned into him, still partially stunned from the explosion.

"And why have you been saving this surprise?" Jarngard chuckled grimly.

"Coal dust explosions have always been a danger in the foundry," she said as Punt nodded agreement. "The trick was just making a cloud of it." She glanced east, toward the Canopic and said wistfully, "I just wish it would stop a chariot ram."

Jarngard and Punt followed her gaze and as if the words summoned the reality, a great thunderous impact echoed from the far side of the city, shaking the ground slightly. Heron felt it acutely in her mechanical leg and sighed. Nothing was ever easy.

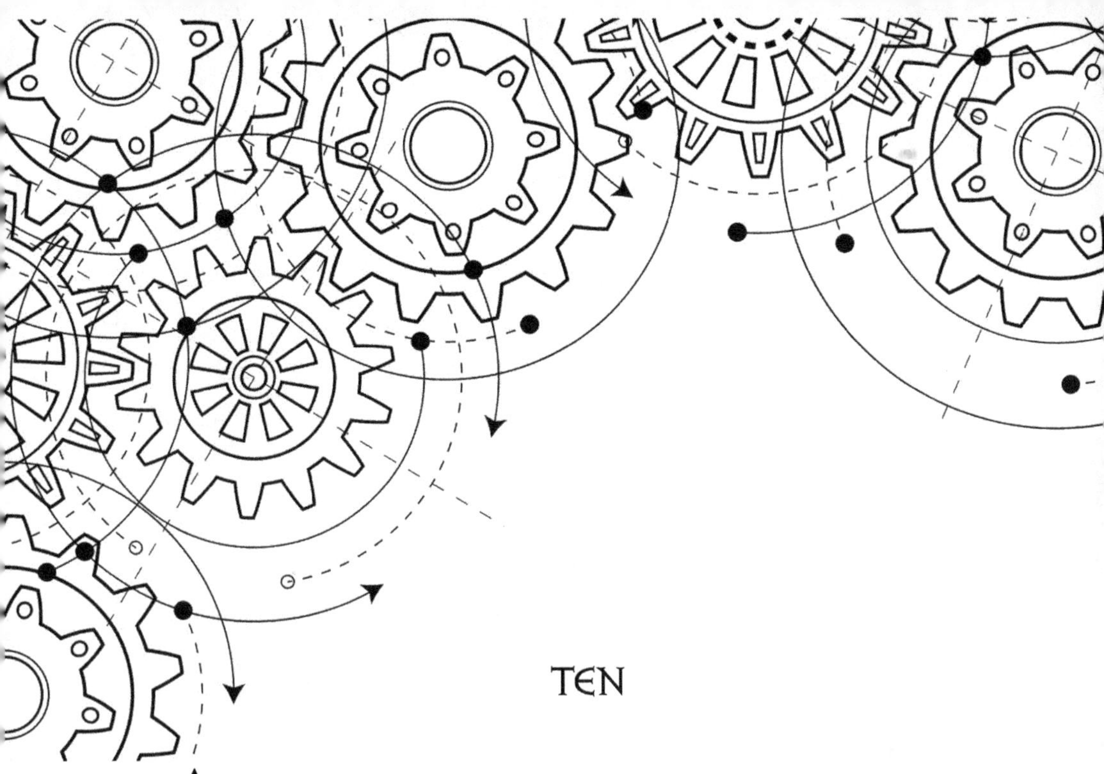

TEN

Agog loved battle. Get him drinking around a group of soldiers, it didn't matter the nationality, even the Romans would be fine drinking companions in the right circumstances, and he could trade stories until the world serpent came back to claim the earth again.

It wasn't that death didn't scare him. It did. That's what made the press of battle thrilling.

But it was more than that. War was an art, a passion, and a science. Agog had studied the world's greatest strategists and tacticians: Alexander the Macedonian, Caesar, Hannibal Barca, Epaminondas of Thebes, Phillip II. He knew every battle, every line formation, the weapons used and the terrain the battle was fought over. He'd been born a warrior and his instincts forged in the Germanic wars.

Yet, he stood on the chalky, white walls of Alexandria, light fading and endless coughing echoing, the corpses of his enemies outside the gate stuck through with arrows, a badge of the first battle victory, and his bones ached with frustration.

"I *hate* defending," Agog growled at Vestalis.

"I've heard you mention it a time or two," said Vestalis dryly.

"I feel like a wooden dummy, lined up for sword practice," said Agog, tugging at his beard. "Battle is a dance and we're nothing more than shadows of the Roman's movements, reacting, hoping to make the right move."

Vestalis regarded him with humorless gray eyes. If sternness was a virtue, then Vestalis was the god of it.

"The chariot-ram will be ready soon," said Vestalis finally.

Agog checked down the line of the wall. The light grew dim, but he saw well enough to know his men were weakened by the first attack.

"By the gods, how does one withstand a siege," said Agog. "The waiting would kill me."

"That's the point," replied Vestalis.

Agog paced along the stone path on the top of the wall, stretching his shoulder. His left arm still tingled numb from the earlier battle. "They're all watching the ram being assembled. They know what it means. It's like being tied to a stump by a horny sheep herder and waiting for him to stick it in."

Vestalis gave him a look.

"It gets cold and lonely in the north," grinned Agog.

"It's good you can enjoy humor ahead of the battle," said Vestalis without a trace of it.

"Who said it was humor?"

Outside the wall, the enemy shifted ranks. They were preparing the attack. He could taste it, smell it, mostly in the fear of his own men.

"They caught us taking a crap in the woods," said Agog. "The troops Queen Amanitore promised aren't due for another week and Hoth and a quarter of our Northmen are out hunting Romans on the sea, not to mention the patrols and scouts that missed an army rushing to meet us."

"We have the steam chariots," remarked Vestalis.

Agog slapped the stone, and grimaced, regretting the action as it reverberated into his shoulder. "An advantage nullified by this cursed wall."

"Then attack."

He dug his fingers into his beard. "I would, but once the ram destroys the gate, they can just ignore us and break into the city. Once we're fighting street to street, their superior numbers will beat us. When I took the city, it was a surprise and then when I beat Flaccus, it was because he was an idiot. This Parthian, Khusra, the one who leads their side, he's no Flaccus and has shown cunning."

Vestalis gave no counsel, so Agog stared at the dead bodies. If there were enough of them, the ram wouldn't get a straight line at the gate. But that would only slow the enemy down. A lane could be cleared under suppressive arrow fire. A temporary solution at best.

"My victories have trapped me in Alexandria."

Vestalis stared back as if he'd said the most uninteresting thing ever in the history of conversation. The man was a master at it. Agog shook the tingles from his arm and gruffly sighed.

"How is your shoulder?" asked Vestalis.

Agog raised an eyebrow. The man was a treasure trove of surprises, even at the cusp of battle.

"Feeling concern for your King?" Agog grinned.

"Can you fight with it? You seem to favor it," said Vestalis.

"Fight?" barked Agog incredulously. "That shoulder's been knocked loose dozens of times. I put it back in its place." He paused and then fired off one final retort. "And I can still take a man's head off with one hand if I please."

"Good then," said Vestalis dispassionately. "I assume you want to lead the counter attack?"

"But the gate."

The upper lip of the old Roman equestrian twitched with what could be called mischievousness, if Agog knew the man, and he thought he did, enough to trust him with the care of his army.

"Some day I want to find out what the Roman Empire did to get you to turn on them," said Agog.

"It's not what they did," said Vestalis. "It's what they didn't do." He paused. "*Your Grace*, do you want to counterattack or do you want to stand behind this rather unimpressive wall and whine about the field of battle."

Agog chuckled, rubbing his belly. "If I were a stricter King, I'd have you whipped for insolence. But since we're short on time, I'll join the chariots and trust whatever it is you're planning."

Vestalis bent at the waist in a crisp soldier's bow. "You might want to line them up on Prosody Street along the wall. The gate area will be less than hospitable soon."

Time was short and Agog made the chariots after a short jog. The shoulder was a source of discomfort, but he held it stiff for his soldiers.

The lead steam chariot was helmed by a lanky solider with skin the color of cobblestone. He could feel the men's spirits lift as he joined them, his pains disappearing like smoke. Tormod greeted him upon the platform, twin axes strapped to his back.

They clasped forearms. "This better mean we're goin' on the attack." And after a pause, Tormod added, "Your Grace."

"Walls were made for holding up roofs, not cowering behind," said Agog. "Yes, we're going on the attack. Fire 'em up and we're moving."

Cheers erupted behind him, the news traveled fast. And then the throaty growl of over a hundred steam mechanicals roared into service. As they wound to the assembly position, Agog closed his eyes and let the rumble soothe his impatient heart.

When he'd taken the city from Flaccus, they'd only had fourteen Manticores. The steam chariots outmatched the Roman infantry, lunging forward to spray arrows before circling away. After frustration set in, Flaccus kept his legion in quad formation, shields interlocked, but the force of the arrow launchers penetrated the gaps and eventually the men broke. Winning that battle had been frighteningly simple and even at the time, Agog had wondered if war would ever be the same.

This time, he had nearly one hundred and fifty steam chariots of various sizes and weaponry. The one he stood upon had a thick, curved shield on the front with a gorgon head stamped into its bronze surface. The majority of them were Manticores, but Heron and the other inventors had devised cunning, but untested, variations on the steam mechanical. How they would fare against five times their number of cavalry and an equal number of infantry, he would soon find out.

High above the city, the glare of the Lighthouse burned brightly while daylight faded from the air, replaced by a thousand wavering torches as the wind scooped dust from the trampled plains and flung it in the air. The sky was a blood red cloud.

Lined up along the wall, two or three abreast, the steam chariots belched smoke upward. The vehicles were ungainly beasts, full of piping and gearing, pistons churning awkwardly, nothing like the sleek lines of a stallion bred for war, but they were his metal beasts and he planned to forge their use in battle.

A signal came from the wall command. Vestalis warned them that the ram was incoming. Soldiers nervously bunched around the gate. Agog couldn't imagine they were bracing the impact as one might from a ram carried by soldiers under a turtle, but two teams stood behind the iron-wrapped timber gate as if they were.

Agog set himself, stabbing the massive blade into the wood and hooking his sandaled tan feet into the foot holds that had leather straps connected to the floor boards. Tormod smashed his axes together, loosing sparks.

"You'll dull the edges, brother," said Agog.

Tormod gave him a skull-like grin. "They'll split a man's face, yet."

A commotion erupted at the gate. The word treason came to mind as the soldiers pulled on thick chains, swinging the gate open. His knuckles cracked, squeezing the hilt, and heat rose to his cheeks.

His disbelief quickly turned to understanding as the chariot-ram blew through the gap. Vestalis had preserved the gate by opening it at the last moment and the chariot-ram was moving too fast to steer away. Agog scolded himself for entertaining a concern of treachery.

An explosion of rock and dust made him duck. The chariot-ram had hit a building. The signal was given and the chariot driver engaged the mechanical and they lurched forward. Unbalanced, Agog nearly toppled off, grabbing the rail.

"Nearly fell off," Agog called to Tormod, "would have been a good start to the—"

The sudden acceleration ripped the words from his lips. The steam chariot wheeled around the corner, wooden floorboards creaking in tension, and burst through the open gate, speeding faster than the fastest horse he'd ever ridden.

The brilliance of Vestalis' counterattack was clear when they found the enemies' flank exposed. The Parthian cataphracts, confused by the lack of a destroyed gate, had turned north, parallel to the wall. The price of the old Roman's loyalty seemed cheap now, and Agog promised to give the man a great bear hug when the battle was over.

With the wind snapping the loose strands of his hair knot against his neck, Agog lifted the heavy blade with one hand. The pain in his shoulder was distant and the rush of acceleration brought laughter to his lips. The sword was poised in the air like a scythe ready to cut wheat. The blade itself was unimpressive: a plain, dull-gray sword with a bright edge, a gnarled guard that would have blanched Punt's face, and a grip notched with hundreds of dagger blows so Agog could grasp it tightly without fear of it slipping from his fingers, even when they were soaked with blood. It wasn't a work of art, but it was long and heavy, a blade that made the muscles in Agog's shoulder and arm ripple with effort.

On the eastern side of the city, the ground was drenched in shadow. Distant torch light glittered the ringed mail of the cataphracts. The steam chariots hit the Parthian cavalry like an avalanche of metal lions.

Agog ducked when their craft clipped the back end of a barded stallion in full gallop, slaver whipping off the beast's muzzle. The impact shook Agog's bones, making him bite his tongue, bringing coppery blood. The rider skipped off the shielding and there was a muffled scream behind as the trailing chariots bounced over him.

A spray of arrows felled a clump of Parthians. The chariot banked hard, avoiding a field stone. Another chariot hit the rock and a helmet flashed over. Agog hooked Tormod around the waist before he fell off, and an elbow caught him in the shoulder.

Riding amid the enemy cavalry, surrounded by screaming Parthians, Agog reached out and chopped a man off his mount before he could bring his bow around. They'd been separated from the main force. Agog tapped his driver on the shoulder and pointed to the other chariots to their left.

Tormod screamed. A shaft poked from the meat of his shoulder, and he dropped both axes. One skipped off the floorboards and got lodged beneath the mechanical while the other was lost to the darkness.

They peeled away from the main force of cataphracts, but a group of five riders followed. Agog ducked behind the churning pistons as arrows sung through the air overhead. The chariot was pointed at the hippodrome, the old chariot racing field the city used before the stadium was built.

The steam chariot rattled across the stony ground, forcing Agog to clamp his jaw together or risk biting his tongue again.

They sped through a field in the darkness, high grass whipping the shielding. Agog imagined more large stones hidden in the darkness, waiting to crush a chariot wheel and throw them to their deaths.

It was a glorious ride.

The cataphracts were catching up. The war-trained mounts threaded the dangerous field, while the riders fired bows. The chariot couldn't go as fast on the soft, uneven ground.

Agog got onto his knees, the chariot threatening to throw him off at any moment, and fished out the axe beneath the mechanical. Tormod sat against the shielding, grimacing as he held the arrow shaft sticking from his arm.

"C—can you, t—tell him to find some flatter ground before I stab this arrow through his neck," growled Tormod, eyes bloodshot and sore.

Agog stood and flicked the axe at the nearest rider, taking him in the face. The man flew off his horse into the darkness.

"For Alexandria!" shouted Agog, laughing.

The bulk of the hippodrome was distant and still they sped forward. The sound of battle was far behind and though four cataphracts followed, their bow shots had only hit earth or the metal shielding.

Agog opened his mouth to taunt the riders when the chariot lifted into the air. The King grabbed the railing as a gap formed under his feet. The impact sent a knife of pain through his shoulder. Tormod cried out. Something in the chariot's gearing snapped, but the craft didn't slow.

"I'm going to kill him. I'm going to kill him," muttered Tormod, leaning on his side, holding the bloody shaft. "I'm going to put it in him and break it off."

Agog checked back with the cataphracts to find them strangely slowing. The city seemed far away now, the flickering lights just pale oranges. Only the lighthouse high above seemed to shed any light. The cool sea air whistled by, drying the sweat from his brow. They were so far from the battle, no sounds reached them over the thundering mechanical.

"Driver," Agog shouted, "steer us back to the action. My brother, Tormod, wishes to kill some Romans."

"Curse you, Agog. I want to kill him for poor driving. This is why I hate horses! Especially metal ones."

The driver was hunched over the steering lever. Agog touched him on the shoulder and he fell to the ground. Dark, blood covered his front. An arrow had passed through his throat.

"Freda's tits, he's dead," said Agog.

"I'll shed no tears for that torturer," muttered Tormod.

Ahead, lights flickered in the distance, a strange sight since the city was on their left and not ahead. Agog tugged on the steering lever. Nothing happened. The steerage had been snapped.

The wind was cooler now and the lights bobbed in the distance. Agog realized that they were almost too late.

"Ship lights!"

As he grabbed Tormod with one hand, the other still holding his great blade, Agog leapt from the steam chariot. Tormod tried to hold onto the shielding, but Agog yanked and the two tumbled to the earth.

There was a horrible snap. They bounced across the ground. Agog lost the sword when his shoulder hit first and pain seared his vision, turning the world to bright oranges and vivid, breathtaking blues.

The chariot, only seconds after they jumped, sped off the cliff and soared through the air into the jagged rocks below. Agog never heard the crash, because he blacked out, or because of Tormod's screaming, when the arrow in his arm broke off.

Agog was lying on his back, steam slipping from his lips, when he came to. Above, the sky glittered like jewels and he almost forgot why he was out on the plains outside the city, when the pain in his shoulder returned, making him gasp.

Tormod groaned a few paces away. Agog rolled over onto his hands and knees, favoring his right side. He spit dirt and blood from his mouth, coughing out another lungful of dust, which caused shards of pain at each convulsion.

Kneeling erect, Agog breathed deep, sucking in the cool, night air, before punching his left shoulder as hard as he could. He nearly fell over onto his hands again, but was able to stay conscious, enough to know the shoulder was back in place, tenuously so.

Agog prepared to climb to his feet when the riders approached. His ears still rung from the steam mechanical and he didn't hear them until they were right there. Not that it mattered, neither he nor Tormod could have moved very far or very fast.

Even in the dim light, the ringed mail armor of the Parthian cataphracts glittered. Dust from the horses washed over Agog and Tormod.

One of them spoke in tortured Latin, clearly spoken for their benefit, "I told you they survived. I heard their pig, Northman screams."

Agog stayed silent and without turning his head, glanced around for his blade, though he knew the chances of finding it in the darkness were slim. And even if he could find it, he had to get to it and kill four Parthians before they could kill him.

He'd been in worse situations.

The Parthian cataphract spoke again, "Get up, pig Northmen. I want to see your faces before we kill you."

Or maybe not. Agog glanced back to the distant lights of the city and almost missed the safety of the walls. Almost.

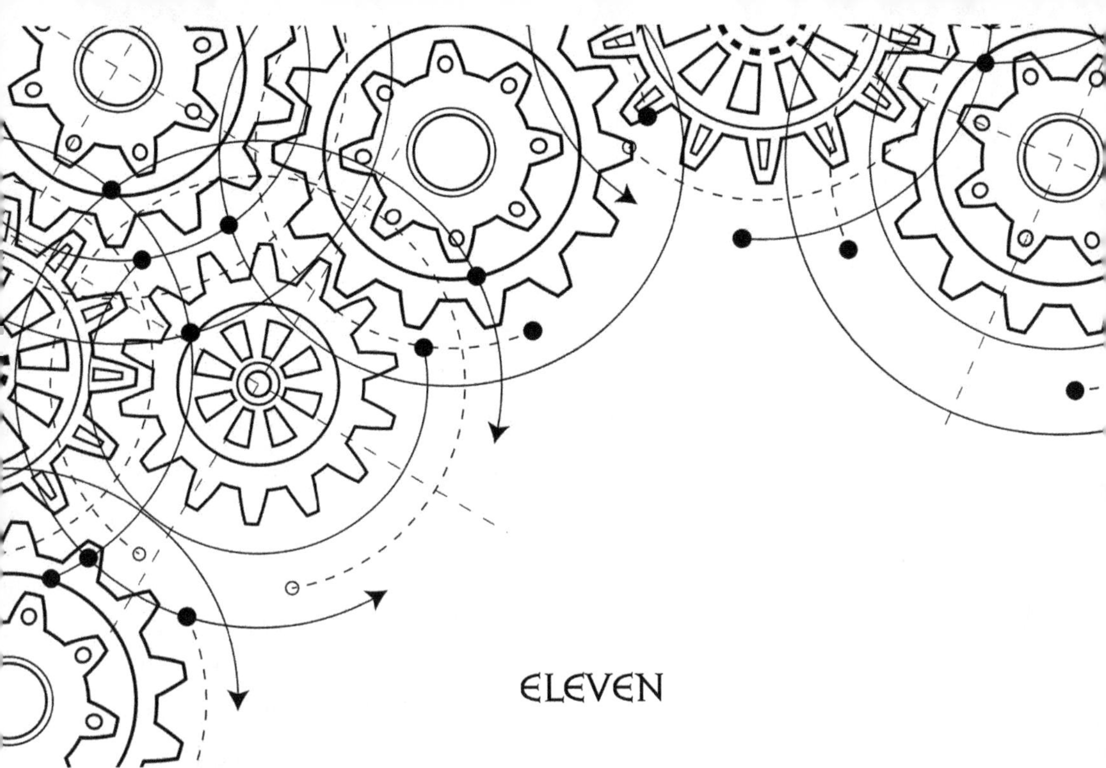

ELEVEN

Only two of the Parthians had their bows drawn, one aimed at each of them. Agog stood, holding his hand out so they knew he wasn't going to attack. When he didn't feel the impact of an arrow, he considered his options, circling slowly.

"My friend cannot stand," said Agog. "Surely you have better things to do than to kill a couple of wayward barbarians."

The rush of waves smashed against the cliffs below, louder than the ringing in his ears from the steam mechanical, and he thanked the gods he had leapt off in time. Agog took a step toward one of the riders and the bowman pulled the string back slightly. A frown warned him away from another step.

The Parthian who seemed to be the leader of their group spoke again, "Kill you sitting or kill you standing, it's all same to me."

When he nodded, Agog threw his hands up. "Wait! Wait! I'm more valuable to you alive than dead."

That got their attention. Bows dipped.

"Speak and speak quickly," said the Parthian. "I want to get back to the fighting."

He hadn't wanted to say this, but capture was better than death. "I'm King Wodanaz. The one who took the city from the Romans," he said.

Laughter broke out immediately. Agog risked a glance at Tormod, who was bent onto his side. He'd bleed out soon if they couldn't get away.

"You? You look like black bear I fucked in woods once. Maybe was your mother?" said the Parthian. "King that take city not so dumb to get lost in battle."

In the silence right after, Agog heard a chuckle, but it wasn't the Parthians. It was Tormod. And he was right. Love of battle had seduced him into stupidity and now he was caught, him and Tormod both, the driver dead, and they'd be soon to follow. Tormod maybe first, by the look of him.

If he only could locate his sword. And a shield. Agog squeezed his eyes shut until shapes formed against his eyelids. He needed any advantage he could get, even if it was better night vision.

"Aye," he said. "Dumb. Stupid. Enraged, too. That cursed powder burned my eyes and ears and throat. Made me want to chop the head off who ever thought of that."

The Parthian shrugged. "A Roman trick. We Parthians do not need such tricks. Kill you in battle, just like kill you now."

"—but more valuable alive." He was, but the enemy soldier didn't seem to think so. The bows raised a little. He needed more time and more advantage. He was bare-handed, bloody, and bone-shaking tired, and his shoulder felt like an ice jarl had been punching it all afternoon. The riders circled slowly and Agog's back itched with the promise of an arrow.

He pointed to the Lighthouse, but kept his eyes downcast. "See the Lighthouse of Pharos? I'm worth as much as that. Even if your commander doesn't want to sell me back, they'll reward you for my capture."

They each looked to the Lighthouse, and Agog clamped his eyes closed again. Before they looked back to him, he glanced around for his sword. He needed a weapon and soon, he didn't think he could delay them much longer.

The Parthian scoffed. "That's what I hate about royalty. We soldiers spill our blood for free, but nobles earn their lives back with gold. Our gold. I think my reward would be just the same for a King's corpse, even if you are a King, you pig Northman."

The leader's horse sauntered along the cliff. As Agog scanned the ground, he caught a glimpse of shine. It could have been anything from the steam chariot, maybe a gear, or a broken axle, or maybe it was his sword. He smiled thinking about his friends laughing if he lunged for the bit of shine, ready to take a man's head off, only to come up with a tube of bronze.

"What is funny, pig Northman, who says he is king?"

Tormod coughed, a wet gurgle that marked the nearness of his death. Agog let a grin stretch across his face until his cheeks hurt.

"The Lighthouse," said Agog, still grinning.

The Parthians glanced upward, but warily, clearly not trusting.

"Lighthouse? What do you speak of you fool?" asked the Parthian.

Agog let his grin turn grim. "I'm going to kill you with that Lighthouse."

The Parthian laughed nervously while looking at the crimson glow of the beacon flame. "I always heard you Northmen were crazy, sleeping in house of ice and worshiping trees, but this will be great story. Pigman who thinks he's king threatens me with a Lighthouse, too far away. When we take the city, I should have you thrown from it, show you what it takes to kill a man."

"Yes," said Agog, "you see that Lighthouse. Do you want to know how I'm going to kill you with it?"

The leader shrugged. "If you feel you must, it is worth a laugh before you die."

"Every time you look at the Lighthouse, you ruin your night vision and so will miss with your bows. Me? I see well enough now to know where my sword is."

The Parthian opened his mouth to speak right as Agog leapt forward taking two powerful steps before dipping his shoulder, the good one, and driving it into the flank of the horse. Feet dug into the sandy soil and the horse, confused by the impact, reared up and Agog lowered his shoulder and flexed his thighs, extending himself until the horse and rider began to fall away, over the cliff.

The two with bows hesitated, not wanting to hit their leader, but as the screams disappeared into the waves, they hesitated no longer. Agog dove forward and the arrows barely missed him. He rolled once, grimacing as the bones in his shoulder ground together, and came up with his sword.

Like a bear ambling through a river, Agog crouch-ran under the chest of the nearest stallion, using the rider as a shield and swung his blade around, cutting cleanly through, warmth hitting his face.

Grabbing the reins, he ran along side, keeping the mount between him and the two bow men. Rather than head away, he circled around until he'd tangled his horse with another. A whoosh went by his head. Agog jumped and pulled the rider over the first horse and slammed him head first into the ground, bringing the snap of a neck breaking. The body flopped like a sack of flour into the weeds.

Agog prepared to do the same trick on the last rider when the horse reared up and kicked him right in the shoulder, not his good one. His vision turned to searing blue light and the world disappeared beneath the pain.

He was on his knees, held up by his sword that was stuck into the ground, when he could see again. The shoulder hung uselessly by his side.

"Three times," he muttered.

Astride his horse, the final Parthian lined him up with his bow. There would be no escape. Agog wasn't even sure he could stand up without passing out from the pain.

The man's grin was final and resolute. He pulled the bow string back to his ear. Agog waited for the punch to his chest and then the sight of his heart's blood running onto the grass. He would die staring at the Lighthouse.

When the arrow loosed, Agog clamped his eyes shut expecting pain. There was no pain. Only gurgling.

Standing next to the rider was Tormod, a slim shaft stuck into the neck of the Parthian. Agog looked for the arrow in Tormod's arm. When he realized it was missing, he knew how the Parthian had died. Tormod had killed him with it.

Agog fell onto his right hand and after taking a breath, slammed his shoulder into the ground, popping it back into place. He tried to muffle his scream, but he was sure the whole city had heard him.

He caught Tormod before he fell over. His friend was covered in sticky blood and trembled like a leaf in the wind.

"Let's go back," said Agog. "I'll throw you on a horse and you'll be drinking cups of heady wine before you know it."

"I hate wine," said Tormod.

"Great. More for me. Beer, then."

Tormod spit and blackness fled from his lips like a shadow. His black teeth shimmered in the dim light. He was bleeding on the inside.

"No beer, either," said Tormod. "A nice rest, though. I think I'll sleep. Might do some good for this ugly mug."

Agog held his weakening friend up, trying not to squeeze too hard around the middle. Tormod wheezed at each breath. Agog knew the signs. He'd buried friends like this before.

"You rest," said Agog. "You deserve it. And when you wake again, I'll be there with you, in the night lands."

Tormod spoke softly, almost a hiss, "I would like that."

"I'll guide you home, brother. Be not afraid. I'll see you soon."

Tormod was a warrior, built of gnarled muscle and spit, and heavier than a jennet carrying a load of rocks, but when the last breath exhaled, he was as light as brushed silk. Agog gently put him on his shoulder and then laid him across one of the horses. With a hand to steady, Agog threw his leg over and pulled Tormod's body onto his thighs, ignoring the aches of his bones, and tendons, and memories.

He rode back to the city slowly, almost forgetting that there'd been a battle and that he'd led the counterattack. It was his city, after all. Torch lights bobbed across the entrance to the Canopic gate. If it were the Parthians or Romans, he didn't care.

He was almost run through by the first Alexandrian to see him as he appeared out of the darkness, but once the soldier realized who he was, he escorted Agog to the gate. Vestalis greeted him with sober eyes.

"Did we win?" asked Agog.

The old equestrian narrowed his gaze at the body briefly, before his lip twitched. "Aye, but for a price."

Agog nodded and nudged his horse towards the gate. "Yes, for a price. There's always a price."

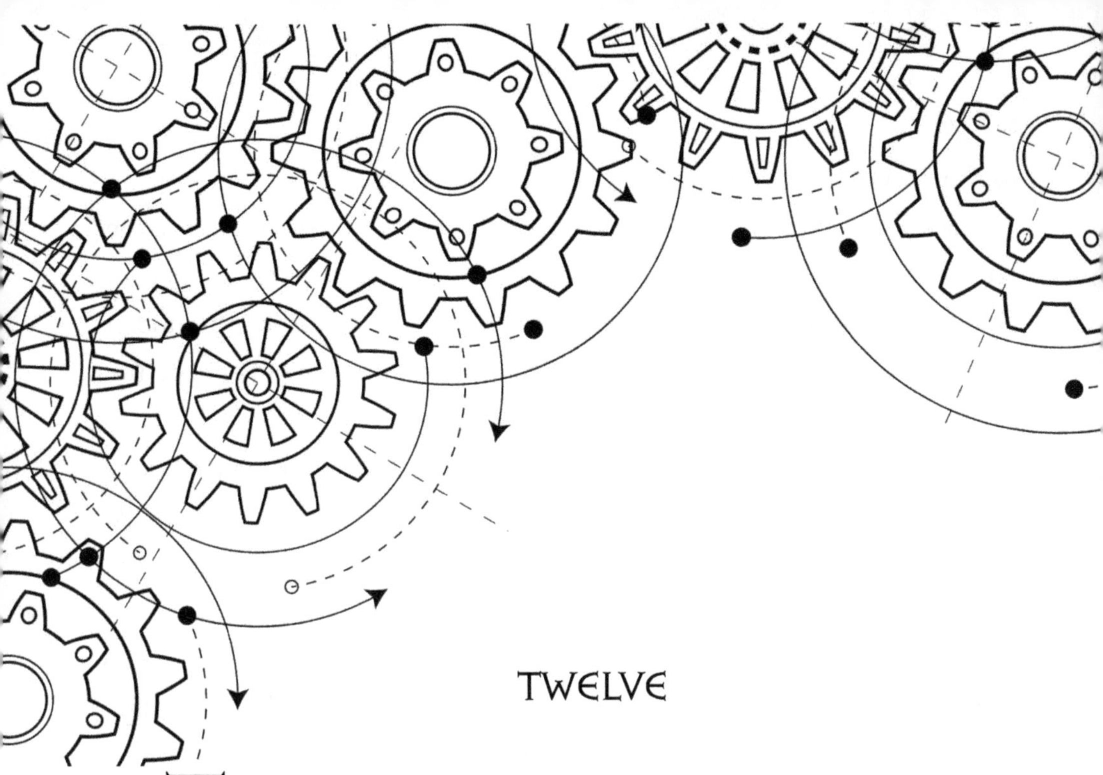

TWELVE

There were no gilded halls in the North. No mahogany tables, polished to a glassy shine, the work of a thousand upon thousand slaves. Maps may have hung on walls, in the war councils Jarngard had attended, but they were crude, hand drawn affairs, not woven tapestries from floor to ceiling and wall to wall, details down to old trade roads and piss-water villages.

Servants did not wander through with trays of sweets and cups of wine—strong, strong enough to make the muscle at the base of the jaw clench with tartness. No, men drank whatever they brought, in gut-sewn pouches, or pewter mugs with handles cast into the shapes of animals of the North: elk, fox, wolf, bear, or salmon.

The air was smoky, wood-brought smoke, clean and fresh with pine, not greasy oils from whale or wherever they found it and burned in oil lamps. And there was a certain grim laughter that hung beneath the surface of every word, as war plans were made, not a veiled silence that amplified every step on the marble floor when a servant arrived with more food to sit untouched upon the table.

Jarngard stared at the map on the far wall, as they waited for the King to arrive, and fantasized about the lands sketched vaguely in the east. Details on that side of the map were few, only major rivers and mountain ranges were shown, along with an elephant to represent the people of the Indus valley.

Heron sat three to his right, but he dared not look at her. The battle at the Moon Gate had been enough for him. What would he do if she were killed? So he kept his gaze averted, fearing Vestalis would see the desire for Heron in his eyes.

On Vestalis, the silence in the room rested comfortably. The old equestrian plucked grapes from a tray and slipped them past his thin lips while his gray eyes studied the map. Despite the summer heat, the room was cool, and Vestalis seemed at home in it.

When the King arrived, Vestalis and Heron stood, while Jarngard stayed seated. The others sat when Agog took his position at the end of the table. Hoth the Black came streaming in after the King unexpectedly and swept into an empty chair next to Heron.

Agog rapped his knuckles against the table and glared at Jarngard. "I don't care a lick if you actually respect me or not, but the next time you stay seated when I come in, I'll have your feet." Agog pointed a meaty finger at him. "We can't beat the Romans if we're not going to act like a real army. This isn't the North and it's not the Gauls we're fighting."

Jarngard ignored the sun-sized smirk on Hoth's face. "Yes, Your Grace."

"Good, that's settled. We've got some planning to do," said Agog, sliding a copper tray of spiced figs to his seat. "Vestalis, what of the army you beat? Do our scouts still have them?"

"North and north. Toward Damascus they flee, but not too rapidly." He paused and the corners of his lips stretched. "They limp quite carefully and I think they want us to follow."

The eyes of the King were as green as the sea before a summer storm and Jarngard's gut knotted in response. He knew that delirious gaze, and had seen it last before Agog had left for Alexandria from a snow-peppered beach along the North Sea.

"I would hate to disappoint them," said Agog. "Where do you think they're trying to lead us?"

Vestalis pushed away from the table, and the chair squeaked along the marble, before he took station at the map, crossing his arms and leaning back to gaze at lands around the Mediterranean Sea. Despite the man's dour exterior, Jarngard knew him for a master of the stage. The old equestrian had been staring at the map for a good, long time and he knew damn well where he thought the Romans wanted to trap them, but he took his time, playing out the moment.

If it'd been Jarngard, he would have marched up to the map and jabbed his finger into the lands east of Antioch, right in the valley before the Tigris exited the mountains. The rough lands would nullify the steam chariot advantage and the mountain passes would make for safe retreats should the battle go against the Romans, as unlikely as that was.

Jarngard stole a glance at Heron to give her a secret smile, but she was staring at Vestalis. Hoth, on the other hand, caught his gaze and gave him a questioning look. Jarngard was saved by Vestalis clearing his throat.

"My spies report that the Legions are still in Rome and won't make the Black Sea until early fall. So the most logical and opportune location for defense would be right south of the mountains; giving them the field advantage. The garrisons at Antioch can cut off our supply trains and Tyre and Damascus, both cities under the Roman control, will be at our rear."

Jarngard drummed his fingers against the table. "No wonder the Romans lost Alexandria, are all members, or former members of the Legion this ponderous? A simple tap on the map would have worked, we all know where they want us to go."

He wasn't sure what led him to say it, but the scouring look he received from Agog could have tanned leather. Jarngard crossed his arms and sunk a little lower into his chair.

A smile toward Heron was left unanswered, the inventor was studying a leather-bound book, and Hoth raised his eyebrow. Jarngard grabbed a mug and noisily slid it across the table.

"How many Legions will they bring against us?" asked Agog.

"Eight."

"Eight?" laughed Agog incredulously. "They took Briton with only five. And that doesn't include the Parthians. They're equivalent to another two Legions, maybe more with engineers and auxiliaries and the cataphracts are generally intact. Most of their losses at the Canopic gate came from the Roman cavalry, inferior to the Parthians."

Vestalis placed his hands behind his back. "When Alexander beat Darius on the great plains, he was outnumbered three to one and crossing difficult terrain. We'll be outnumbered ten to one, an unwinnable situation, especially if they can pick the location for the battle."

Jarngard was expecting Agog to question him further when Hoth the Black spoke up, "It's worse than that."

The sea captain cricked his neck. A quip would have been more appropriate from Hoth, but he matched Vestalis seriousness.

"The envoy to the Greeks were captured. I found Agnar's ships, even the iron boat, half-sunk a day's sail from Athens."

"The iron boat?" Agog slapped his hand on the table. "That should be our advantage. We need that rebellion to keep at least three Legions from the battlefield. How was it taken?"

Like Vestalis, and most commanders Jarngard had known, Hoth was a performer. He let them wait in silence until they were supposed to be wrought with questions, but Jarngard stared at the map instead. There were a lot of unknown lands to the east and northeast he would like to see.

"By some sorcery, as far as I can tell," said Hoth the Black. "I found a body, eyes burnt and lips crusted with scabs. I had to keep the details of the sailor's death secret from my crew or they would have mutinied."

"Explain," said Agog.

"The attack had come days before we arrived on the scene. The Romans lured the three ships into close proximity and somehow overtook them. The wood and iron in the water showed signs of burning, and the sails smoldered when I arrived."

Agog grumbled, rapping his knuckles on the table. "But the body?"

The perfumes Hoth wore finally reached Jarngard and he wrinkled up his nose. Heron appeared to be lost in thought and Jarngard wasn't sure she was listening as she smoothed her good hand across the leather bound pages, eyes flickering from the book to the map and back. The other sat limply in her lap.

"He cut his own throat." Hoth scowled and looked away. "What drove him to such extremes has bothered me the whole way back to Alexandria. That and what caused the fires that left black marks on the iron."

"Quicklime," said Heron softly and the others leaned toward her. The inventor seemed almost surprised that she had spoken. "Quicklime, I just realized what the substance was that the Romans used to blind us. It must be the same that they used on the iron ship."

"What is this quicklime?" asked Agog.

Her metal arm thudded onto the table, causing Heron to cringe. "A form of limestone. We use it to make stone blocks for the pyramid. The substance reacts with water to create heat and along with crushed stone and volcanic ash, makes wonderful building blocks." An awkward smile turned flat. "But it burns in the eyes or ears or mouth, reacting to the wetness there. Archimedes believed it was part of the weapon called Greek Fire, though it works just fine as a weapon by itself, if used properly, as we saw on the wall."

"What do you mean?" asked Hoth. He had not been there during the attack and had not seen firsthand like the rest of them. Jarngard had only come late to the scene, but had seen the wounded. A few, not many, had lost vision in one eye or the other, or at least it had not returned yet.

"They scatted quicklime into the winds and it blinded the defense," said Heron.

Hoth nodded. "That explains how they took the ships. A single vessel dead in the water might have lured in the three, maybe marked as an ally, or important enough to divert from their task."

"Blind, yes," said Heron, "but that would not explain the burnt marks on iron. That can only mean they've learned the secret of Greek fire."

"A wild guess, *Michanikos*," said Vestalis, setting himself opposite of her. "If the Empire had kept such technologies, I would have known."

"They only recently discovered it," she replied.

"And how could you know such a thing? My spies have heard nothing," said Vestalis plainly.

"I encountered a spy in the Great Library. He killed the door guardian and took a book, the journal of Archimedes, and I found a note in the aftermath of our struggle," said Heron.

Hoth chuckled, "Did you stab this assassin like the others?"

The hint of a smile formed on Heron's lips, but did not crack the heavy thoughts there. Jarngard was annoyed by the blossom of jealousy in his chest.

"Not him, but I killed his brother, Philo over a year ago. But this was Apion and I found a message on him: *Retrieve the warmaster's prize in the temple of thought. The eagle comes so take the flightless bird before the full moon.*"

Agog grumbled. "Speak plainly."

"The warmaster's prize was the book, Archimedes' journal. The eagle was the Roman army and the flightless bird was the trader *The Red Ostrich.*

I checked the dock records after the battle and the boat had already left. A man fitting Apion's description was seen boarding."

"Why is this book so important?" asked Agog.

"Archimedes is the greatest inventor of any time and his warmachines kept the Roman army from Syracuse for three years. Only treachery took the city and eventually his life, despite the Roman general wishing it spared. During this time, he devised many weapons, including some that were never recovered after the siege. It seems there are a trio of secret technologies that were hidden after his death by his apprentices. Greek fire is one of them, though it could be a formula of his making and not the stuff of legend. Archimedes was a master of turning thought to action," said Heron wistfully.

"And now Rome has this technology," said Vestalis. "If these other two are as effective as the Greek fire, then we are lost."

"The other two are yet to be found," said Heron. "That's why Apion was sent to Alexandria, to retrieve the journal of Archimedes. The clues for the other two are contained within its pages."

"But you say the book is taken? If so, then they can find them at their leisure, or at least keep us from them," said Vestalis, clearly distraught. "This only gets worse."

Jarngard found himself staring the soft curve of her neck, despite the serious discussion. How could they not see that she was a woman?

Using the mechanical arm, which ground and clicked as the elbow bent, until her metal fingers were near her face, she wiped an errant strand of hair aside. The fingers moved, and Heron blushed. Jarngard was distracted by the contradiction of the woman.

"Don't despair, my friend," said Agog. "I can see the mind of the *Michanikos* working. He has some plan behind those curious eyes."

"More than a plan," said Heron. "I have the book. The journal of Archimedes."

There was a stunned silence, so Heron continued, "I've read his journal countless times and the words are imprinted in my mind. I transcribed the pages last night so that we might have another copy."

"So we could send someone after the remaining two mysteries?" asked Agog.

Heron nodded. "I was hoping that could be me. I can think of no other for the job."

Agog sighed and scratched his black hair, green eyes flashing with mirth. "I've promised myself a dozen times I would not send you from the city again, for fear of losing you, but here I am agreeing to it once again. Name your companions and I will round them up."

Slunk in his seat, Jarngard brightened, and sat tall, waiting to hear his name pass her lips. What better adventure than the two of them after a dead man's secrets.

"I can only think of one that I must name right now," said Heron. "The others will have to wait until I have discussed it with them."

Jarngard readied his acceptance of the task, the words right on the edge of his lips.

"I would take..." she began, "Hoth the Black."

Jarngard choked on his disapproval. The others looked to him questioningly.

"Do you disagree?" asked Agog sharply. "The choice seemed obvious."

Jarngard opened his mouth to suggest himself, but he realized the room was weighted against him. The strange look on Heron's face felt like betrayal.

"Yes," said Heron. "I will need his fastest iron boat and his wit, though hopefully not his sword arm."

"Where will you go? Does the journal tell you that?" asked Jarngard more forcefully than he intended, receiving a second tilted head from Heron.

"Syracuse," she replied.

It was Agog's turn to choke. "When I agreed to you leaving the city, I didn't think it was to head right into the arms of my enemy."

Heron shrugged. "The journal suggests that's the place of the next secret. We'll find out when we get there."

"It's settled, then," said Vestalis, "we'll double our efforts on the defense of the city while you find these ancient secrets. Once they're safely in our grasp, we'll have months to put them to use. The Romans will be foolish to attack then, even with their numbers."

"We're not waiting," growled Agog.

Vestalis seemed genuinely surprised. "We're not?"

The King shook his shaggy head. "We're not. Once the Kushites get here, we're taking the bait and taking our army North. If I have to stand behind another wall, I'll put my fist through it."

Vestalis brow knotted with concern. "The Legions will overwhelm us with numbers and superior soldiers."

Agog grinned. "You can't win an empire sitting behind a wall."

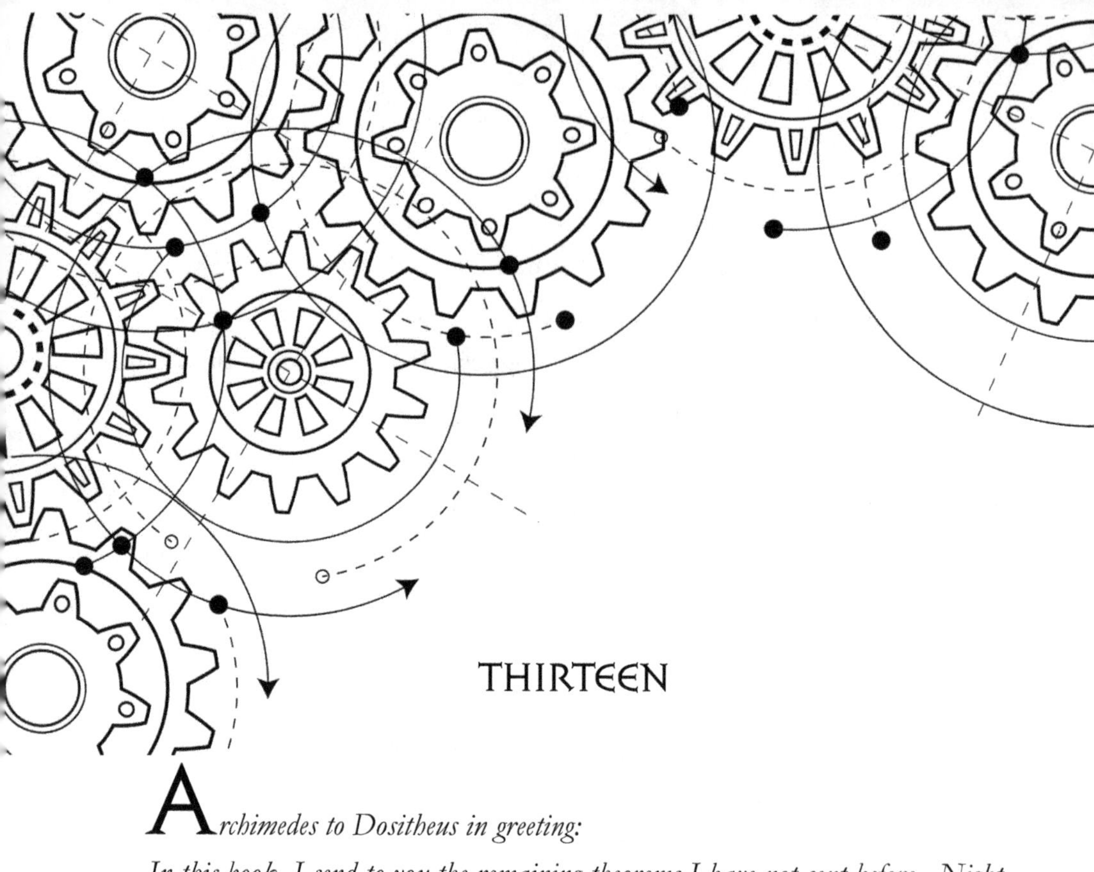

THIRTEEN

A*rchimedes to Dositheus in greeting:*

In this book, I send to you the remaining theorems I have not sent before. Night descends on Syracuse, and with it, Rome's blockade. I fear I will not have the opportunity to wander the olive groves until this war is over. The King has beseeched me to devise a defense, but my theorems will suffer, suffice it to say, though I cannot deny him and part of me relishes the act of putting the designs of air into earth and fire...

Waves slapped against the dock on the far side from the book houses. Even from a distance, the thumping of runners loaded down with scrolls carried through the wood. The beast on the hill, the Great Library, had an endless hunger and the ships brought its meals in the form of knowledge.

Heron cinched the cloak around her, warding off the night chill, careful not to expose her metal limbs. Leaving the city was meant to be secret and she was unmistakable, so she had ridden down with Plutarch and let him take her mount back. She waited by the small craft for Hoth to arrive.

The one-mast boat bobbed lazily in the black water. Lights from the city reflected in the bay, will-o-wisps floating across the surface. So beautiful, but so deadly. One slip on this trip and she'd sink to the bottom of the sea, dragged down by her limbs.

Heron hoped the iron boat would inspire more confidence. Their real ship had been loaded with gear in the royal harbor, along with Sepharia, disguised as a sailor. They would meet it a day's sail north and transfer to the iron boat. For fear of Roman spies, they had planned this subterfuge, since no spy could watch every boat in the great harbor, especially in the middle of the night. Heron thanked their luck that cloud cover hid the pregnant moon.

The edge of the wool cloak was soothing against the tips of her fingers as she rubbed it. Heron was afraid bringing Sepharia was a mistake, but the metal limbs made it impossible for her to keep up the disguise. Punt had been an option, but his talents were needed in the workshop and he would be demeaned by the job.

Sepharia was the better choice all around, except in Heron's heart, which feared the worst for the trip. Heron paced a few steps before standing still again, the tell-tale thump of her metal foot echoing too loudly across the water.

A shape materialized out of the darkness and Heron gripped her cane tightly. The cloaked figure stepped across the wooden planks without sound.

"Hoth?" she whispered.

The figure approached and her heartbeat rose until she could no longer hear the slapping of the waves. There was movement beneath the cloak. Heron steeled herself for action.

"Ada," the whispered name released the tension from her breast.

Jarngard stood close, close enough for his heat to touch her hands, still gripping the cloak tight. Reflected lights etched the details of his face.

"You shouldn't have come," she said, even though she was glad he did.

"I had to."

She sucked on her lower lip.

Jarngard pushed a hand out of his cloak and his fingertips caressed the back of her hand, sending shivers through her.

"Why didn't you ask for me?" he asked, the hurt evident in his tone.

"I need Hoth's ships and Agog would never give you up. He needs you for the battle."

Jarngard growled. "I'm not a general. I'm a killer, and sometimes a thief, maybe a warrior, but not a general."

"Agog thinks otherwise," she said. "He said as much before, and the Roman's strategy, you saw it the same as Vestalis."

He did not answer and seemed to be thinking. Heron guessed at the reason he had come and it wasn't just to see her.

"I can't leave," said Heron. "The city needs me. Agog needs me. Maybe after the war we can run away and be adventurers, but not now."

"This war will ground us both into dust."

She turned her hand so his fingertips trailed across her palm. "I can't go."

"It's not the city, or the war," said Jarngard with grit in each word. "You want Archimedes' secrets, his legacy."

The lust that ached beneath the bindings, and fake limbs, dissolved. His accusation was more painful than a slap across the cheek, mostly because it was true.

"He is the master inventor," Heron whispered forcefully. "He saw things that no one else could, or has since."

His fingers stopped and eventually pulled back into the cloak, leaving her hand cold, empty.

"I thought you didn't like making warmachines? That you wanted to free the slaves with your contraptions, or some such nonsense," he muttered.

"I don't and I do," she said breathlessly. "But if we don't get his secrets first, the Romans will use them to continue their domination. With mine and Archimedes' inventions, Rome could take over the rest of the world, as far, and farther, than the Indus river. There'd be no place to run. And it's not just the warmachines. His writings have always hinted to other inventions that no one has found since, I hope these secrets contain other knowledge, other books, other ideas."

"You're going, then," he said, most pathetically.

"I'm going."

He shifted, and Heron thought he might be turning away, but the hood slipped away from his face, so the edge hung on the crown of his head. His winter-blue eyes searched hers, and she wanted more than anything to push against him, feel his warmth, press her face against his chest and inhale.

"Before you go," he said softly, "just one kiss."

The dock they stood on was far away from the regular traffic, which was light due to the time of night. There was no one around, not a single soul, but she hesitated, the barriers of a lifetime keeping her guarded.

"Just one," she said and started to lean forward, waiting to taste the mint on his breath on her tongue, feel his body against hers, if only for a moment.

"What are you doing here?" came the whispered question as Hoth the Black appeared out of the gloom.

Heron pulled away from Jarngard, heat rising to her face. They hadn't heard him approach.

"A message for Heron from Agog," said Jarngard.

"Quiet," Hoth seethed. "No names, you fool, and I just came from him, so why would he send you?"

Rather than answer, Jarngard shrugged and started to walk away. Hoth grabbed him by the arm, and Heron noted how much larger Jarngard was than the sea captain.

"You shouldn't have come here," said Hoth.

Jarngard yanked his arm away. "I know." He trudged into the darkness, soles shuffling across the wood.

Hoth appeared by her side. "What was that about?"

"A message, as he said," she replied.

Hoth didn't seem to believe her answer, but he moved to the boat. He held out a hand to help her in.

"Stay to the center if you're worried about falling in," he said. "I'd prefer not to have to fish you out in the dark."

The seat was cold and the water smelled of fish, while the boat knocked against the dock, until all the ropes were loosed. Hoth kicked away and the boat slid smoothly into the harbor and soon he'd caught what little wind there was and they propelled toward the open sea.

Glancing back, Heron thought she saw a shape on the dock, looking out, but it could have been her imagination. She faced forward and set the metal arm in her lap, trying to forget about her conversation with Jarngard, but she couldn't, and was afraid that she never would.

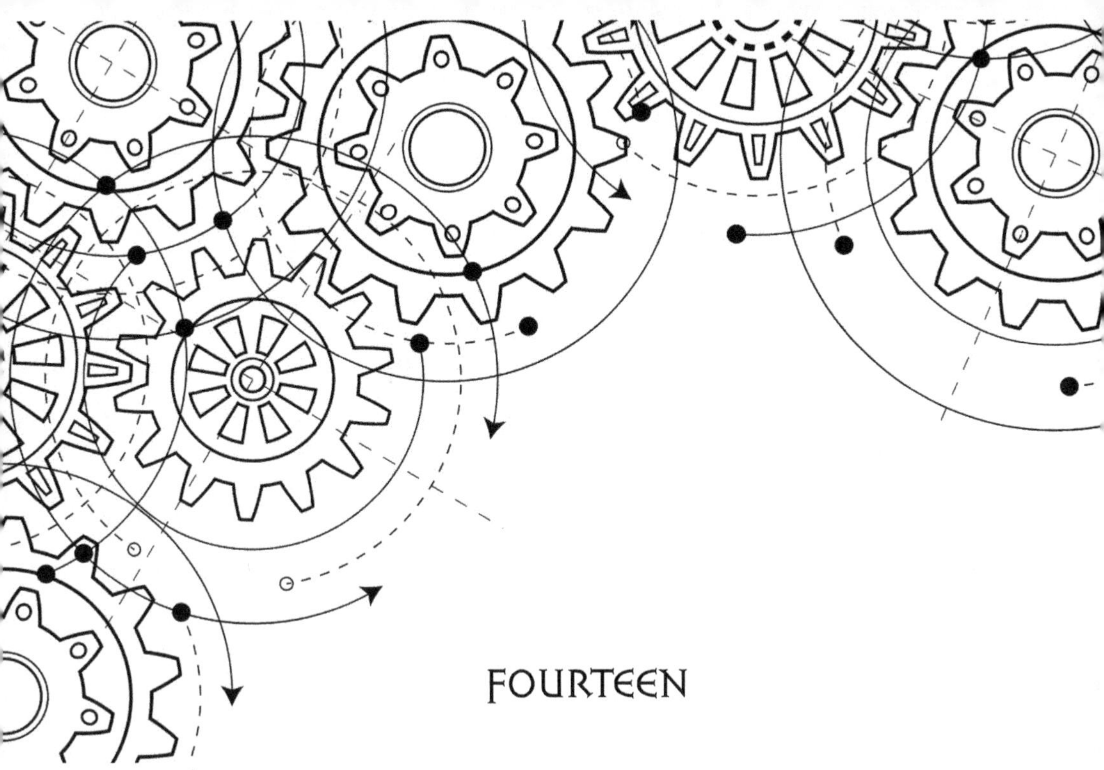

FOURTEEN

Agog leaned into the saddle as the procession of soldiers left the Canopic gate. This was not the army of Alexander the Macedonian, a well-trained fighting force, or even of his Northern army when he battled the unruly Germanic tribes.

Passing through the heart of the Roman Empire on his way to Alexandria, Agog had observed the Legion performing maneuvers on the Elysian fields. Those soldiers moved like a machine, lock-step, like oiled gears connected to ten-thousand boots, and shields that rippled like scales on a dragon.

He'd seen them in action when his army was routed, but it'd been the end of a long campaign and he'd been more worried about Aurinia than watching the Roman soldiers slaughter his people. So as he watched the jagged lines weaving into the distance, a train of shuffling steps that seemed more appropriate for a line of prisoners rather than an army, Agog sighed.

A horse sauntered next to him. "You were never going to beat them straight up, army to army, anyway," said Vestalis.

Agog grunted a short laugh. "Can you see inside my head now like Heron?"

Vestalis allowed himself a brief smile. "I see it the same as you, Your Grace. It's not the army that's going to beat the Romans."

"Then what are we bringing them for?" laughed Agog. "Let's just leave the soldiers and take the steam chariots and cavalry."

Vestalis squinted into the distance and his forehead wrinkled. "Because, Your Grace, if you don't look too closely, it looks like an army, and the lands we conquer will respect it."

"A shrewd man. A shrewd man. I'm glad you're on my side," said Agog. "I suppose we can take the chariots on the offensive and leave the army behind."

"A wise idea."

Agog laughed. "And one you've already thought of." He rubbed his beard and adjusted himself in the saddle. He could tell his muscles had lost their riding shape. It would be a sore start to the journey.

"Where is your steam chariot, Your Grace?" asked Vestalis.

"After the battle, I decided I was not meant for those bone-jarring vehicles, though it did give me some ideas I gave to the workshops for improvements."

"Good," said Vestalis, suddenly, surprising Agog. "Yours was one of the few we lost. I can't repair a steam chariot that's been driven over a cliff."

The old equestrian stared with cold, gray eyes. A hint of a grin trickled to his lips before Vestalis stared back into the distance.

"You're in a good mood," said Agog.

Vestalis nodded crisply. "I missed the march of war, the smell of horseflesh, the matching of wits."

Agog nodded in agreement, though it wasn't as enthusiastically as it might have been in years past. His shoulder still wasn't right from the multiple dislocations and he'd lost another tooth in the back and his tongue had been worrying at the hole since.

"Where are the steam catapults?" asked Agog, nodding toward the broken stones on the walls above the gate.

"Packed for battle. I have a few ideas on how we might use them," said Vestalis.

"The supply trains?"

Vestalis sat tall in his saddle and despite the warm sun bearing down, seemed as comfortable as a man sitting in a fountain enjoying a cool lemonade.

"I borrowed a few scholars from the Mausoleum to keep our stores in order," said Vestalis.

Agog let his considerable surprise show. "Borrowed? I thought the Library stewards tried to stay out of taking sides."

"I presented it as a mathematical problem and had twice as many volunteers as I needed."

Agog slapped his knee and the horse shifted slightly beneath him. "Scholars are drawn to problems like Hoth is to whores."

"Or we are to war," said Vestalis coolly.

Agog nodded. "And the Kushites?"

"They went straight up from Memphis. We'll meet them south of Tyre," replied Vestalis.

"Tyre," Agog tasted the word in his mouth like a piece of grit. "We can't let them sit at our rear and wreak havoc with the supply trains. An army is only as good as its belly. But that cursed city is near impregnable. It took Alexander almost a year to take it and we don't have time to siege. I want to make it to Antioch before the Romans pass the Black Sea."

"Give me a week and I'll have the city," said Vestalis.

"I don't have a week to give you. We'll just leave a garrison outside the city and keep them contained. Put our army to use," said Agog.

"Three days," replied Vestalis.

"Three?" Agog raised an eyebrow. "Two and the bulk of the army keeps marching."

Vestalis fell into a meditative silence. Amid the morning heat, horsetails swished and hooves stomped, while sandaled feet shuffled into the distance, kicking up clouds of dirt. Agog hoped for a bit of rain to keep the dust down, but he knew it was wishful thinking, unless the gods looked favorably on his war efforts.

"One."

When Vestalis spoke, it startled Agog. He thought the old equestrian had given up on the siege of Tyre.

"Are you familiar with the arts of negotiation?" asked Agog, smirking. "Typically, you demand looser terms, not the opposite."

"One," said Vestalis with purpose. "I will take the city of Tyre in one day."

Agog narrowed his gaze. "Are we speaking of the same city of Tyre? The city on an island with only a causeway the width of two wagons to reach it? I saw it on my way down to Alexandria because I was curious. The walls are fitted with anti-siege equipment and our navy is busy keeping the sea clear for Heron to reach Syracuse, they'll be no amphibious attacks."

"The same Tyre," said Vestalis.

Agog wanted to ask him how, but he could see the old Roman would not let him in on his secret. Whatever the strategy was, pride oozed from the man's pores as he sat tall on his stallion.

"One day?" asked Agog.

Vestalis nodded comfortably.

"One day," said Agog. "I'll hold you to it."

"Accepted."

And with that, the siege of Tyre was planned.

"One day," said Agog. "I'll hold you to it."

"Accepted."

And with that, the siege of Tyre was planned.

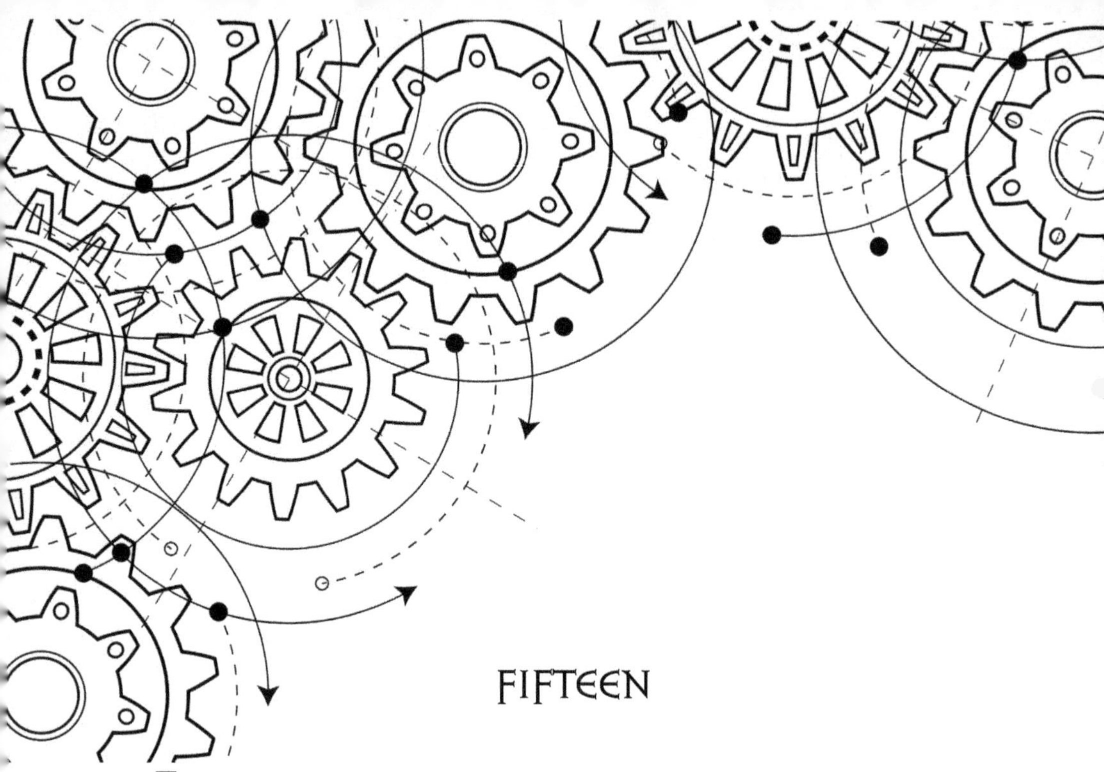

FIFTEEN

It was a bloated whale, or at least that's what the sailors called it. Hoth thought of it as a woman in full, well-fed, maybe a few months past squeezing a child from between her thighs, but as desirable as a maiden in flower.

He ran his fingertips along the steering mechanism, polished wood, silky as a woman's bare ass, and humming with faint vibration. Nektam's shipyard had outdone itself, taking every suggestion and improving on the designs of previous ships.

Had the ship been wood, rather than a shell of iron, it would have taken a crew of six to work the lines and sheets. This beauty - without a white sail on it - could be crewed by one if he didn't mind a lack of sleep.

Chalky-black smoke trailed from brass tubes, marking the ship's passing, a sign to friend and foe alike within sight of the horizon. The coal burned hot and Hoth was glad for the sea air that diluted the noxious fumes. But what a trivial price to pay for speed and maneuverability.

On the foredeck, a towering arrow launcher - without a mast to interfere with its sightlines - surveyed the sea. A crew of three could ambush a much larger ship; one to steer, another to shovel coal, and a third to load and fire the launcher. There were three of them and he wouldn't mind if a Roman trireme found itself in the way when they neared Syracuse so he could test its capability.

A sweet scent caught his nose: the inventor's daughter stood at the foredeck, hair waving in the breeze, wearing a man's tunic and boots. The wind pressed fabric against her shape, leaving Hoth to muse what a difference it would be if it were only the two of them and no war to fight or secrets to uncover.

Heron was below, inspecting the steam mechanical that churned the massive 'oars' on the back of the boat, two cylinders spinning, spitting droplets into the air, and kissing the back of Hoth's neck when the wind shifted. Hoth guessed the *Michanikos* was adjusting the levers and gears, as the pipes coughed different shades of black from time to time.

Or possibly, Heron was checking on the materials he'd brought with them. The huge box that had been loaded onto the ship in the Royal Port was not suggestive to the cargo inside. Heron only indicated it might help them find Archimedes' third secret, but stated he hoped they wouldn't need it.

And like a god, Heron seemed to answer his thoughts by appearing on the deck, the click-thump of his automata leg announcing his arrival well before he was seen. On approach, Hoth marveled at the delicate features of the *Michanikos*, a contradiction to the hard man he knew.

"Hail, Machine Man! The sea welcomes the thrust of the *Grey Cetus*, spilling white foam on its brow!"

Heron soured, his mechanical arm clamping to the rail. "Your pushing it too hard, I adjusted the pressure release so you don't blow the chamber."

"Better to blow it now with no one in sight then when the need is upon us," replied Hoth. "I need to know the capability of my ship, especially if we're going to raid so close to Rome."

With the nudge of a button to release the fingers, Heron lifted his metal arm. "A steam mechanical explosion would sink the boat and I wasn't a good swimmer even in the best of conditions."

"Fair enough," smirked Hoth and he pulled back the lever a smidge, decreasing the rotation of the cylinders. Once the vibration settled into a lower pitch, he pushed it back to full and the boat lurched in acceleration, the hum making his back teeth ache. "The rest did the mechanical some good, now I think it's ready for more speed."

The *Michanikos* regarded him with half-lidded eyes, olive skin already pink from sunshine. "I thought you were bothersome on land, but it seems I was mistaken. The sea is your natural habitat and it brings out the fool in you."

"You might be the great inventor on land, but as you said, this is my habitat and as your captain, I must know the capabilities of my ship," explained Hoth.

The pinkness traveled to Heron's cheeks and the words frothed at his lips: "A machine is not merely a horse to whip and assess. When it breaks, it breaks for good, and we have no other means of locomotion, if you haven't noticed. And you might be a sea captain but you don't know a thing about my inventions, or what they're capable of."

Hoth almost responded immediately, the spike of anger was brief, filling his face with heat, so he paused, letting it deflate until he could speak with resolute calmness.

"I am not made from machines like you, so I know nothing, nor can I learn, unless I push the boundaries," said Hoth, "a maxim I have heard uttered from your lips on more than one occasion."

Before the furious response from Heron could erupt, Sepharia was there, like a bolt of sunlight, her eyes crinkling with a smile. "Father.

Hoth," she said, running her hand along the curve of his elbow. "We're not a day and a half from Alexandria and already you fight. Can't we talk about the task at hand, instead?"

Hoth found himself suddenly agreeable to her opinion, noting the softness of her touch and the delicious curve of her neck. Heron was staring, not hot like before, but a cold, penetrating gaze that made Hoth reach for the lever and adjust the speed down.

"There," said Hoth, "the vibration was putting my teeth on edge and how could we have a conversation with such noise?"

Heron spoke with forced emphasis, "The vibration was the mechanical being pushed—"

Sepharia put a hand out, stopping her father, and Hoth took a second look at the inventor's daughter. Despite the plainness of her garb, Sepharia had collected wisdom on her cheekbones, and her eyes sparkled with clarity. He'd wanted her before, as he wanted all women, but his desire for her doubled upon seeing the value of the prize.

He let a cautious smile rise to his lips. "A truce. I shall not push the ship until the need is there. And your lovely daughter is right, we should discuss the task at hand. You've given little details about where you believe Archimedes' secrets are hidden."

Heron relented and cradled his metal arm with the other, for it appeared the weight of it bothered the inventor. "We sail—" Hoth raised an eyebrow at her. "—or churn through the water, toward Syracuse, the city on the southern island. I have maps that should help us find a suitable cove from which we might strike off to the royal necropolis near the palace. The site is on the eastern side of the city, along the plateau, and we should find enough cover to keep hidden, or travel at night to avoid Roman soldiers."

"A cemetery? Did Archimedes bury his secrets with him?" asked Hoth.

"I don't know," said Heron, "it's the epitaph on his grave I wish to see."

"Don't keep us waiting," smiled Hoth.

"Upon the stone is an etching of a sphere inside a cylinder, the mathematical proof that Archimedes is famously most proud of, or a clue to the location of the second secret," explained Heron.

"You inventors are strange folk, putting shapes on your graves, rather than words." Hoth paused, a question forming. "Won't Philo's brother, Apion, be waiting for us? Or have guards at the tomb?"

"Apion cannot guess that we are following, so we should not expect him unless there is a spy in our close counsel. Otherwise, only the book would lead us to the tomb and he has the book," explained Heron. "Still, when we near, we should take suitable precautions in case he has, or lingers near the site, or maybe he has not read the signs correctly."

"What is that?" asked Sepharia, arm outstretched indicating a spot on the horizon.

Hoth squinted. "A trireme and in our path, we'll circle wide and examine it at a distance."

"We should let it go by and not give it sign of us, even a well-meaning trader can give us away," said Heron.

"It does not move and we would lose too much time in keeping secret, since there are no islands to hide behind on this vast empty horizon," explained Hoth. "A volley from the arrow launcher will solve any disagreements should we need it."

The inventor frowned, glancing at the ship in the distance. "Why engage what we can avoid?"

"It's not moving. It might be one of ours, damaged." He held up his hand when Heron tried to speak. "I'm the captain. I want to see this ship."

"You want to play with your toys," remarked Heron before clodding to the front of the ship. Sepharia stayed nearby, despite the glance from her father that clearly expressed his expectation that she would come with him.

"You like to aggravate him, don't you?" asked Sepharia sweetly.

The answer appeared on his lips though he knew he should be silent. "Your father always believes he is right and rarely listens."

Sepharia shrugged playfully and the tunic slipped away from her shoulder, exposing endless olive skin. "He has a busy mind and does not suffer fools."

The softness of her gaze led him to believe that Sepharia did not think he was a fool, but Hoth suspected she had her own agenda.

"Care to steer the *Grey Cetus* a while?" he asked.

Hoth gave her the opportunity to step into his arms, but she deftly brought her leg around, leveraging him away from the steering column and grasped the lever confidently.

"Problems?"

She winked and Hoth buried his lust, because the immobile boat was nearing. He gave Sepharia an impish smile and joined Heron on the foredeck.

The wind had picked up, turning the waves choppy, white triangles of foam spilling over. The sails on the ship ahead were noticeably unfurled and it appeared the deck was empty.

"Maybe you were right," said Hoth, leaning on the rail, "we should have gone around, this feels like an ambush."

"We still have time," countered Heron.

Wind swirled whipping hair into his eyes. He tamed the mess and continued speaking, "They've seen us now, better to play out the trap and deal with them appropriately."

"Is that wise? We're not here to keep the sea lanes free."

Hoth nodded. "Better than leaving them to follow, or set others on our path. There are few iron boats on the sea and Rome would want to know why we ventured so close." He paused. "And we know their trick with the quicklime. I plan to approach from upwind."

As the ship neared, Hoth noted the details he could not see from afar. This was a modified trireme, once the primary warship of the Mediterranean, but now its chief trading vessel. The two rows of oars, which normally stuck from the sides like two sets of ungainly thin arms, were not present.

Hoth did not recognize the ship from the port in Alexandria and he had an eye for the slender curves of a sea-going vessel. It floated low in the water, spray passing through the oar holes. The whole affair was odd and his stomach doubled over.

A motion to Sepharia at the helm directed the line he wanted to take, not as close as he first planned, since the placement and condition of the ship made him uneasy.

"Are you a scholar of ship designs as well as mechanicals?" asked Hoth.

Heron quietly shook his head.

"A shame," said Hoth, "for I'm certain this is an old Greek design I haven't ever seen before, but I have nothing to base it on. It's presence here without oars drains my desire to see it up close."

"Let us pass it from afar," said Heron, "as I've said from the first."

The inventor stared him down with an unblinking gaze.

"Maybe a little closer."

Hoth focused ahead, ignoring the inventor. It appeared a great cloud of darkness in the water surrounded the ship and the foam was bubblier, rolling like white balls between the waves.

"Do you see that?" Hoth pointed and the inventor followed his outstretched arm.

"There's something spilled into the sea. Do you smell it?" asked Heron.

"Like burnt wax it smells, but worse."

Heron frowned. "We should move away. I don't like it. Whatever it is, we're almost in it."

"A little further," he said, "I want to know this mystery."

A bit of movement on the trireme caught his attention. Something moved behind the oar holes.

"Go closer!" he yelled back to Sepharia.

Heron clamped the metal arm to his forearm, and Hoth yelped in pain. "Steer away," said Heron, as Hoth tried to pull his arm out.

"Get this cursed thing—"

The words fell dead in Hoth's mouth, as he saw the flicker of flame from the trireme. A man stepped to the deck and Hoth tried to move to the arrow launcher, but Heron's tenacious grasp kept him at the rail.

Heron did not see the man with the flame, he seemed appalled that he had clamped his metal fingers and was busy trying to loose his grip, but kept missing the button. Hoth realized the man on the other ship had a bow in his hands.

"Steer away!" he yelled to Sepharia over his shoulder.

The bowman on the trireme pulled back his arm, the flame hung from his arrow, dripping fire onto the deck. The arrow sputtered through the air and Hoth prayed to the winter gods that it would go out, but it arched over the iron boat and into the water, for as soon as he saw the flaming arrow, he knew what the substance in the water had to be, though he'd only seen it used once in a village on the eastern steppes.

The metal fingers released his forearm as a fireball lifted from the sea, surrounding the *Gray Cetus* in a fiery embrace. The world had been cut from the sky and replaced with heat and pain. Hoth rolled to the deck, swatting out the fire on his tunic.

The heat, mercifully, only lasted seconds as the iron boat sped through the flaming sea and the cool air was a balm on his lungs and eyes. Heron was bent over coughing and Sepharia clung to the steerage, keeping them headed straight.

Behind them the sea burned and on the horizon a line of white sails appeared. With the trap sprung, the hunters swooped in to collect their prize. Either the Romans had changed their tactics or he'd been wrong about how the other ships had been taken.

His relief was quickly replaced with concern when he realized the *Gray Cetus*, despite the high whine of the steam mechanical thundering in his ears, was steadily slowing. Sepharia had left the steerage and stared at the cylinders behind the boat, which Hoth hoped were still whirling.

Almost as soon as he reached the back, a heavy thud jarred him from his feet, knocking him to one knee. A gush of steam burst from below deck, right after which Heron hurried down to attend to the mechanical.

Hoth leaned against the rail, hair and eyebrows singed, face hot with effort. The once whirling cylinders that powered the iron boat were immobile, the *Gray Cetus* drifted to a dangerous calm. The ships on the horizon, Roman quinqueremes if he knew his sails, rapidly approached.

"Ready the launcher," he said, tasting noxious oils on his tongue, while the sea behind burned bright like the sun.

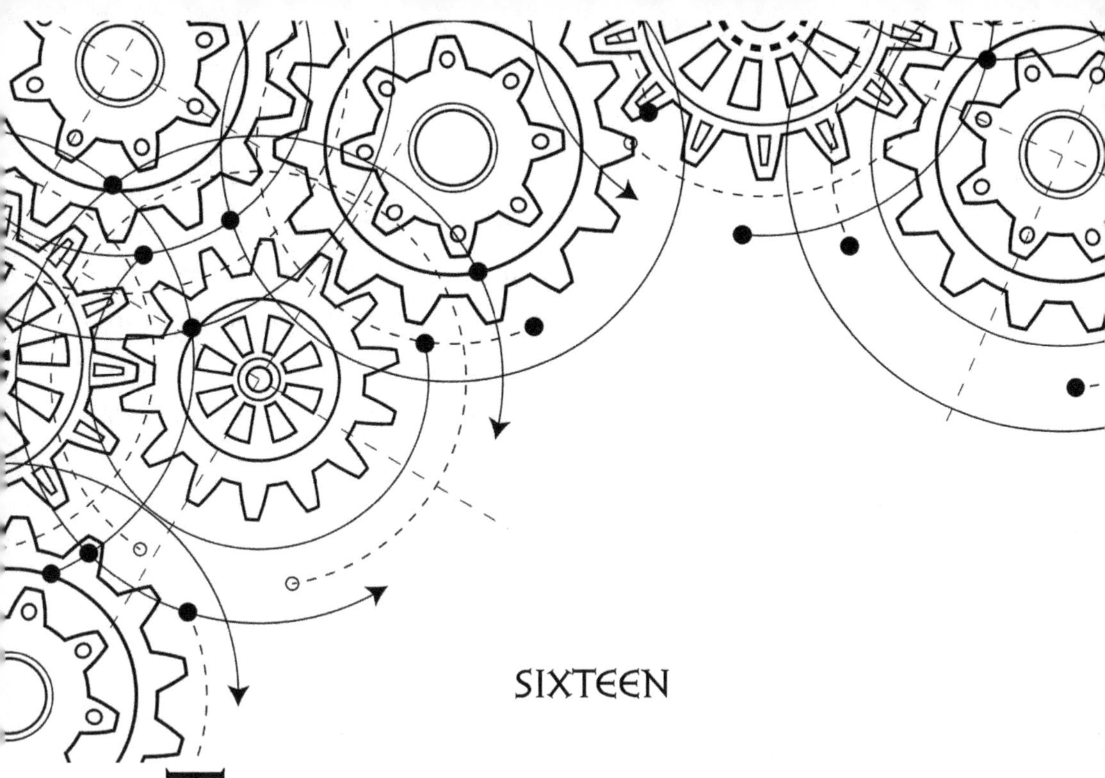

SIXTEEN

The Alexandrian army rested in the craggy hills south of Jerusalem, beside the ancient gravel road that had carried the fruits of the Nile for millenniums. Alongside the rocks and scrub grass, chunks of broken pottery, chicken bones, and other discarded refuse, lay on the sandy soil.

Dagi, a volunteer soldier in the fourth regiment, fidgeted with the buckle on his shield. The brass clasp had rubbed a blister onto his wrist. He was used to training with the buckler, but not carrying the round wooden shield for leagues on end.

Yesterday, he'd ridden a steam chariot, the mysterious carts that were pulled across the ground by what he'd thought were invisible horses. Each regiment took a turn riding with the chariots. When he moved to climb on, Dagi had circled around front, expecting to run into a beast hidden from sight, but upon making the other side, he decided it was true what his friend Usa had said about the stinky, smoke-puffing vehicles: the *Michanikos* had enchanted them with the essence of dragons.

The whole ride, Dagi touched the brass belly of the beast, searing the tips of his fingers with black marks that he kissed for fortune. He watched deep azures pass like clouds across the surface of the brass. The driver, a noble-born, who'd bought his way into the officer corp, said the changing color was from the boiling water inside. Dagi spit on the surface once to watch it sizzle, only to decide the dragon might be cross with his disrespect, so he stayed to his corner of the platform and watched the steam lick from the pipes and leap into the air.

Dagi ripped a piece of discarded cloth he found behind a bush when he was making water, making it small enough to wrap around the buckle so it wouldn't rub into his wrist, when one of the giant-men, the ones from the North, appeared like the Colossus.

"Ave, soldier," said the giant-man, as he hunched onto his heels, demon-blue eyes peering into Dagi's soul.

Dagi gasped and nearly choked on his own saliva. The giant-man tugged the buckler away and examined the strap, while Dagi gawked.

Dagi had seen a crocodile up close once when he was a boy in Memphis. Fetching water from the Nile was always a dangerous job and he was usually vigilant, but a dragonfly had been particularly distracting and he'd lingered too long at the edge of the water. Only a spooked catfish that had been lying in the shallow muddy waters warned Dagi of the approaching crocodile. He remembered the rippling power of the beast, the lumpy scars on its snout, the overwhelming presence. Mesmerized by the possibility of death, Dagi barely made it out of the water, wading out only as it splashed mud on his backside.

The Northman was like the crocodile in his own way: faint scars littering his arms, nose tilted slightly to the right, earned in battles Dagi could only imagine, a presence that made him feel like a mouse in an open field.

"Tie this around your belt," said the Northman in thick Greek. The breath of the man was thick with wine.

Dagi took the cloth and made a loop around his belt. The purpose was clear, it would hang and not bother him during the long march.

As the Northman watched, waiting, Dagi realized who this man was: one of the King's own men, not just a soldier. This was the one the other soldiers called a name, a name that came unwanted to Dagi's lips, for his sense had fled.

"Geri."

He was also called Jarngard and that was the name that he should have said. Jarngard grabbed his tunic, bloodshot eyes filling his vision. "Why did you say that name?"

Up close, Dagi drowned in wine-soaked breath. An uncontrolled battle-rage simmered right beneath the surface of the Northman. Dagi could sense that if he said the wrong thing, the man would tear him in two.

"By the light of Ra, I repeat name only. May Osiris strike me down and give my eyes to the Nile should I be lying," said Dagi, trying unsuccessfully to hide the quiver in his voice.

After a moment of consideration, which took the length of two breaths, the bloodshot anger seemed to fade from Jarngard's eyes. The grip loosened and the quiet murmuring of nearby soldiers could suddenly be heard.

Much to Dagi's surprise, the Northman unceremoniously plopped onto the sandy soil next to him, crushing an unlucky scrub brush in the process, though the Northman didn't seem to notice it under his massive thigh.

Though Dagi had seen the Nile rise and fall fifteen times, he felt a boy next to the Northman. When Dagi had volunteered for the army, it was for the meals and the promise of gold and glory. The bargain seemed weighted in his favor, since he could just as easily die in Memphis as in battle.

Seeing the shattered beast of a man next to him staring blankly at the ground, Dagi realized there was a third way, to survive the fighting, but to be broken inside.

"Apologies," said Dagi in Latin, hoping it was the proper way, as he'd heard said by the higher born, "I will never speak that name again."

The light which had fled from the man seemed to return, and Jarngard looked up, and Dagi thought he saw what a desolate place the North was through the cold, blue eyes, stark with the frozen rain he'd heard of that had to be an invention of the underworld.

"A man who survives and earns a name in battle shouldn't be surprised when it passes through his ears," said Jarngard sullenly.

A horn blew nearby, announcing the continuation of the march. Dagi stood, ready to escape the Northman and return to his regiment gathered on the other side of the road. A callused hand grabbed his arm.

"When the fighting comes, and it'll come sooner than you think, and the fear bites at your heart like a ravenous beast," said Jarngard, "stay with your squad mates and fight as one. Together as brothers in arms, you will survive."

Dagi nodded, daring not to speak another word. The Northman named Jarngard, one of the King's own men, left, wandering back along the road. Dagi quickly lost sight of him, as they marched over a hill.

The soldier Yota, a fellow Egyptian as he, marching alongside, remarked as Dagi kept glancing backwards for one more glimpse of the Northman, "Was that the King's man? The beast they call the *Geri*?"

Hearing it from Yota's lips, Dagi realized the word was alien to their tongue, a name brought south with the barbarians. Yota shared an eager smile.

"Do not speak that name," lectured Dagi, louder than he intended, drawing the notice of the soldiers marching around him, "or he will visit you on the battlefield and send your soul to Osiris."

Yota laughed it off, for Dagi had found his fellow soldier brimmed with laughter. "I'm not afraid of the pink-skinned barbarian and we won't be fighting. I heard from an officer that we're just going to march for a few weeks and then they will trade gold with Rome and we'll go home."

"He said we fight soon," said Dagi, tasting the dust from the road. "Maybe Tyre, since the Romans hold it."

"Bah," said Yota, not laughing, but his face was in semblance of it, "Tyre cannot be taken. I heard from that same officer that we're going to go right by Tyre and leave a few garrisons to keep them from leaving. If we're lucky, we can be one of those and we'll spend this war eating cheese and bread and drinking watered-down wine."

The other soldiers seemed to like this idea, and the smiles spread with quiet murmuring.

"We're going to be fighting soon. I know it. *You* didn't talk to the Northman." The words came out of Dagi's mouth more forcefully than he intended and the smiles faded to be replaced by disappointed stares. He knew better than to open his mouth. A soldier who tempted the gods with his hubris, putting the rest of the squad in danger, could be killed in his sleep, or pushed off a cliff, to keep the others safe from harm.

Yota shrugged and Dagi felt the loser of this exchange, despite being right. If they stayed at Tyre in the garrison drinking and eating, and living out the war, it would be attributed to Yota. If it went the other way, and they fought, his squad mates would blame him and he would be the goat.

The trudging of sandaled feet filled the air as Dagi mulled his bad luck for meeting the Northman and daring to utter his name. Yota glanced down at the buckler Jarngard had fitted for him and frowned.

After wiping the dust from his brow, Dagi carefully and as inconspic-uously as possible, pulled the buckler hanging from his belt, and gripped it, matching the form of his fellow soldiers. The buckle bit into the blister on his wrist and Dagi remembered that those who rode on dragons hidden in brass machines and walked beside Northern gods should not dare to catch their notice.

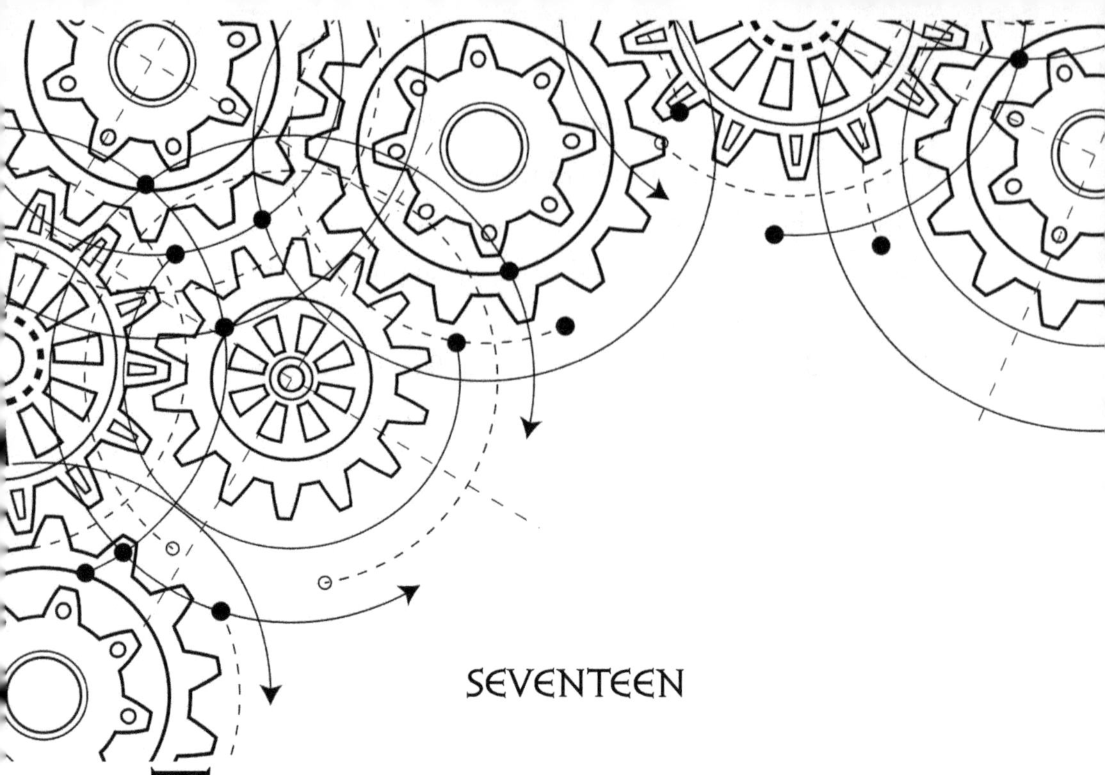

SEVENTEEN

The catapults rain stones as large as horses against the outer walls, day and night through storm and sunshine, but still they stand. Though the muck has slowed the advance of the infantry, I see the worry in the King's jaw. I relate to him my theorem that, "A solid lighter than fluid will, if immersed in it, not be completely submerged, but part of it will project above the surface," but he did not catch my meaning. Whence I explained it to our general of defense, he did not understand either, so I set them out one by one, in the manner of perceiving things, but still no understanding. They did agree to carry out the task, first pumping sea water down the slope to where the catapults rested and then pumping mixed pitch on top of the water until it flowed around the catapults. When the torch followed, they glowed like the sun and we smiled upon it.

— The Journal of Archimedes

Burning water. The Greeks called it burning water. Heron had seen the pitch springs herself on Zycynthus. The black stringy substance woke to flame, creating noxious fumes; its use never daring to supplant the use of whale oil for lanterns.

Heron had dabbled with it, using the rock oil, as it was sometimes called, to lubricate the gears and pistons of her machines, but eventually, it grew sticky and the machines would not move.

The Romans must have poured a hundred barrels of it into the water. Oars appeared on the trireme and men poured from below deck. The lake of fire lay between them, but it wouldn't take long for the trireme to circle around.

Heron staggered to her feet, the smoke making her dizzy. She grabbed the rail with her good hand, steadying herself against the rocking seas and the unevenness of her mechanical foot.

The *Gray Cetus* was dead in the water and the lake of fire drifted toward them on the sea's current. Heron tasted soot as she wiped her face, leaving smeared marks on her palm.

Hoth was shouting, but the ringing in her ears kept the words distant and fuzzy. Both Hoth and Sepharia pointed to the cylinders on the back of the iron boat.

The deck rose and fell beneath her feet as she teetered to the stairs. When moving, the ship cut confidently through the waves, keeping the deck even, but now becalmed, the sea pressed against the underside of the iron hull and rocked them in rolling undulations.

She made her way to the back and saw that the cylinders were not moving. "The mechanical," she muttered, nausea making her knees weak, before taking to the stairs. Hoth nodded and moved to ready the arrow launcher, before she waved him off, it would not work without power from the steam mechanical.

The lanterns below deck had been knocked out and her vision, marked with orange spots, failed to adjust. Heron stumbled through the hallways, the swampy air thick and stiflingly warm, toward the mechanical room, using the vibration and hammering of pistons to guide her.

With her eyes clamped, waiting for sight to return enough she could find the lantern on the wall, the tortured music of the mechanical became clear. Heron imagined the steam escaping against the spinning aeolipile, driving the pistons. The energy should be converted into the gears to spin the cylinders and propel them through the water.

If the cylinders were not moving and the pistons were, then the connection between the two had been interrupted, probably by the impact of the fireball from the sea igniting. When she opened her eyes, light flooded into the room as Sepharia appeared, lantern held high.

The room was the largest on the boat, taking up what would be a kitchen on a trireme. A secondary room filled with coal was attached, but the fires were stoked and the steam belly of the mechanical hot.

Heron saw the problem immediately. The pining bolt that connected the rod to the gearing was snapped. The long rod stuck out a window on the iron boat, spinning the cylinders when moving. The pair of rods lay limply against the gears.

After a quick survey to check that the rest of the mechanical was intact, Heron took the lantern from Sepharia.

"The arrow launcher should work," said Heron. "Go up top and load arrows for Hoth."

The fear was evident in Sepharia's eyes, but to her credit, she stayed calm. "Can it be fixed?"

Heron eyed the broken connection. "Of course, but it might take some time. I need to figure a way to connect the rods."

Sepharia turned to leave, but Heron put a hand on her, the real one, she didn't want a repeat of what happened above deck with Hoth. "Pull the lever to the stop position. I can't fix it while the gears are moving."

While Sepharia went above, Heron searched for the broken pin. If enough remained, she might be able to reattach the rods.

A heavy clunk sounded above her head, causing Heron to duck, only to find the gearing disengaged from the mechanical. She wiped the sweat from her face, the moist air left her skin damp, and the action only temporarily relieved her annoyance.

Knowing the Roman trireme neared, Heron lurched around the room, searching for the broken pin, ignoring the ungainly bumps and clanks as her arm or leg impacted with the metal walls. Her heart leapt when a different set of gears whirled to full.

"Strike true," she whispered, trying to ignore that Sepharia was up there as well, vulnerable to returning bow fire. Heron just hoped the arrow launcher could outdistance the trireme, or at least make it hard to accurately return fire.

On all fours, she found the broken pin, and grimaced, for the piece of steel, the length of her smallest finger, was snapped in half and the edges mushroomed out, leaving no possibility of reuse.

Heron canvassed around, hoping Nektam had left them spare parts in case of damage, but there was nothing she could see. Getting up, Heron smacked her head against a brass pipe, bringing spots.

Shaking off the pain, Heron momentarily panicked, as the swampy air and close, dark confines reminded her of the chamber beneath the Temple of Sobek.

Chomp!

She took a deep breath and cleared her mind. This was no time to relive those memories.

A flicker of movement snapped her head around only to find it was the lantern sparking as the waves shifted the oil. Heron put her hand against the iron wall, finding it warm.

Peeking through the holes in the back, she could tell they were drifting back into the sea of fire. If she didn't fix the mechanical soon, she'd get cooked in the room.

Chomp!

Heron tried to drown the song from her mind by talking to herself.

"Two by two is four, four by two is eight, eight by two is sixteen..."

The numbers erased the feeling that Lysimachus' stump would bump into her back as he slid the noose around her neck. The song still played in her mind, but it was distant, as if children sung it from beyond a thick wall.

"...two-hundred and fifty-six by two is five-hundred and twelve..."

Side-stepping around the mechanical, Heron searched for a piece of tubing or thin rod she could repurpose. The arrow launcher had a couple of pieces that would work perfectly, but the whirling gears could not be stopped or the Romans would capture them.

With every surface of the room exhausted, Heron used her tunic to dry her dripping face. Droplets tickled her ears and even the binding beneath the tunic was soaked through. Flames licked into sight through the porthole. She was running out of time.

Then she saw the answer quite near her face. The rod connecting the buttons to her metal fingers could work as the pin. Heron tugged on the slender shaft of brass, but it wouldn't budge.

As a permanent solution, the brass shaft wouldn't hold up to the punishment, but they didn't need a permanent solution, only one that would last until they escaped the trap and reached Syracuse. Heron hated to damage the clockwork arm, gears intricately fitted and polished to a mirrored shine (though now it was smudged with oil and beaded with metal sweat, which in her eyes, almost added to the beauty).

Without time to carefully remove the arm, Heron positioned it near the spinning gears from the launcher. Using her hand to protect her face, Heron jammed the slender brass shaft between the spinning gears.

The impact threw her into the wall, face hitting first. Heron lay on the floor, cradling her metal arm, the shoulder nearly torn from its socket. When the pain lessened enough to open her eyes, she found the brass rod snapped on one end, sticking perpendicular from her arm.

Grabbing the shaft, she worked it back and forth. The bend was cracked and each time she snapped it forward, the crack grew, but not fast enough.

Flames engulfed the back of the iron boat. Each breath was like breathing through scalding water. Heron coughed, keeping her focus on the rod, levering it over and over, willing it to snap.

The muscles in her arm screamed, but she kept going, slowly moving to her feet so she could fix the mechanical when it finally broke. The rolling motion of the boat, her mechanical leg, and the dizziness from the heat and getting thrown into the wall made standing difficult. Heron lurched against the belly of the mechanical once, burning her hip, but ignored the urge to stop working the rod.

Sweat poured into her eyes, burning them with salt. She wouldn't be able to stay in the room much longer, the heat was growing rapidly. Flames came through the porthole and Heron feared the wooden parts of the boat would catch fire soon.

When it finally snapped, Heron stared dumbfounded before leaping to motion. The rod was too hot to touch, so Heron trapped it beneath her metal hand that had lost the ability to use its fingers.

When the two pieces fit together and she pushed the brass rod into the hole, Heron had a moment of panic that the rod was too thick, but her fingers were slippery and she hadn't pushed hard enough. They slid together and Heron made a silent cheer. The bend in the rod kept it from falling through the hole, so she left the connection suspended and raced upstairs, banging into every wall on the way.

The air up top was worse than below. A bank of black smoke engulfed the *Gray Cetus* and a lake of fire cradled the steerage. Hoth and Sepharia were at the launcher, firing a dwindling supply of arrows at a trireme that would board soon.

Fighting through the heat and smoke, Heron grabbed the lever and engaged the steam mechanical slowly, praying the brass rod from her mechanical arm would hold. When the smoke swirled and flames kicked up higher, Heron knew the cylinders were spinning. She steadily increased the lever, eyes nearly closed to keep the scorching smoke away.

Fresh, salty air washed past her face, like a kiss from the sky. Heron took a delicious breath and opened her eyes just in time to see them careening towards the Roman trireme. She jammed the steerage to the starboard and prayed the impact wouldn't break the brass rod.

Without the smoke to hide them, the bowmen on the trireme took shots and arrows whistled past, leaving Heron to duck behind the slender steerage. When the *Gray Cetus* slammed into the Roman trireme, the collision jarred her teeth. A world-shattering crack ripped through the air.

Heron feared the worse, but the iron boat kept going and she saw the Roman trireme was rapidly taking on water through the starboard hull. The hail of arrows ceased and the iron boat quickly outdistanced the sinking trireme.

"Father, your arm!" exclaimed Sepharia, joining her along with Hoth at the steerage.

"It can be repaired, just like the ship," said Heron.

Despite the recent harrowing events, Hoth looked like he'd stepped out of a Roman bath, the sweat beading on him like magnificent jewels rather than the sooty splotches covering her.

"What a wonder," said Hoth, "that a piece of you now powers my ship."

The realization furthered her concern that she was becoming less a person. "It had to be done."

"The Romans," said Sepharia.

Heron had almost forgotten about the other boats, the quinqueremes, the fastest ships in the Roman fleet. The *Gray Cetus* was headed directly for the three slender boats with two sets of oarsmen on each side and five billowing sheets.

"Do we have any arrows left?"

Sepharia shook her head. "Not enough to matter."

Hoth stepped behind the steerage and Heron gave him the room. His reckless smile worried Heron.

"Now we see how fast our iron ship can go," said Hoth, who seemed to be relishing the thought of racing the Romans, as he leaned into the speed lever.

Heron didn't have as much confidence as the sea captain, especially when she knew a fragile part of her arm held the steam mechanical together, but it would either hold or it would break, and there was nothing she could do about it now.

"Yes," said Heron, relieved to have the crisp sea air in her face, "let Mercury curse our speed."

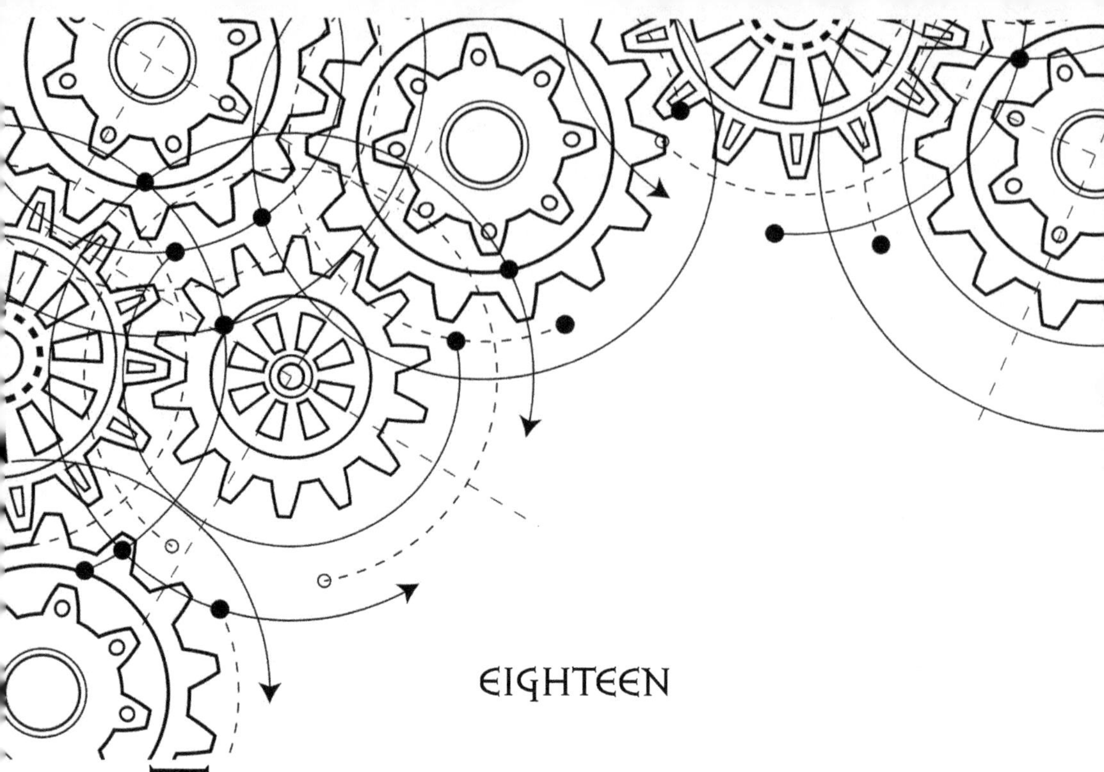

EIGHTEEN

The Roman-held city of Tyre, much like the city of Alexandria, was once an island. The difference Jarngard could see, sitting astride a chestnut mare in the cobblestone courtyard on the edge of the new city while sipping at his pouch filled with sweet wine, was that the levee leading up to the walled enclave had been built in conquest.

True to their history, the leaders of Tyre had kept their high, paranoid walls, and narrow strip of land connecting the old city and the new. The road that connected the island Pharos to Alexandria was wide enough for three wagons to comfortably pass without touching wheels, while Tyre's road could only fit one wagon, which made it obvious why the market was on the new side.

The water surrounding the island had silt lines running from the coast into the sea, upon which a dozen Alexandrian quadremes blockaded any attempted escapes. The two harbors on the island were barred and no ship could pass those gates.

The crimson arc of imperial helms stuck up behind the battlements.

The gate was a double portcullis of reinforced iron and attacking it with a ram would expose the men to heavy arrow fire and boiling oil. Nothing about taking the city would be easy, Jarngard decided, no matter what Vestalis said.

As if summoned, the ex-Roman soldier sauntered up on a warhorse with full barding, wearing a golden breastplate embossed with the Vergina sun. The Alexandrian general gave a belittling glance towards Jarngard's mount.

"I didn't realize we were going on a hunting expedition," quipped Vestalis. "Or is there not a city to be taken?"

"I don't fight in armor," replied Jarngard.

"The city needs to be taken before the day is over," said Vestalis. "We need to present an efficient face to our army. How can they perform if you're going to sit on that scrawny mare wearing nothing but light leathers and slouching in your saddle like a Thracian scout?"

For the sake of Agog, Jarngard bit back his anger. "I'm not the one that promised the King I could take the city in a day."

"I promised a day because anything more would compromise our goals and we cannot let this Roman stronghold remain at our rear, ready to cut the supply lines. An army travels on its stomach." Vestalis paused, his cold, gray stare unblinking. "Or are we too busy drinking with the common soldiers to care about the orderly function of this army?"

A retort was cut short by a cacophony of clattering like a thousand brass bells being dragged across the cobblestones. The noise echoed between the stone buildings, making it sound like a traveling circus marched on Tyre. There were multiple avenues leading to the causeway and Jarngard couldn't tell which direction the racket was coming from.

When the steam chariot appeared pulling a wide wagon, upon which one of Heron's catapults was mounted, Jarngard cracked his knuckles and watched the proceedings with interest. Except, Jarngard disagreed with the term catapult. The weapon had more in common with a soldier spitting a rock from his mouth, rather than lobbing it over the shoulder, but with destructive force in either case.

The steam catapults were not well tied and the shaking set the brass pipes and gears to rattling, filling Jarngard's head with a bone shattering noise. Even his horse danced, sideways and neighing, away from the chariots.

"Are you planning to annoy them into opening up the gates?" barked Jarngard. "By the jarls, that sound is maddening."

Vestalis appeared wholly unaffected, even smiling, if a man like that could smile. An amused stare, maybe.

"I do plan on opening the gates," he said eventually.

"You won't do it with those things," said Jarngard.

Vestalis raised an eyebrow. "Did your dice tell you this?"

Jarngard resisted the urge to touch the leather bag around his neck. It would give Vestalis too much pleasure.

"Those tell me what I need to know," replied Jarngard, "but I don't need to ask to know those catapults won't help you one bit. They practically ripped themselves out of the wall when Heron used them on the cataphracts and I've seen catapults turn into an explosion of deadly splinters when an unbalanced load was used on an unweighted base. You'll just end up breaking them if you fire them from the wagons and it'd take you days to get them drilled into the ground. You told the King one day."

"And one day he shall have," said Vestalis, all too smugly for Jarngard's taste.

Despite the judging gaze, he took a drink from his pouch and watched the men set up the steam chariots. When it seemed they would be firing from the back of the wagon, Jarngard just shook his head.

The engineer in charge of the steam catapults approached Vestalis for instruction. The old equestrian leaned over and gave a few commands, speaking lower than Jarngard could hear.

"That's double reinforced steel on those gates with two sets of port-cullis. I'm not even sure you could dent them from this distance, even with Heron's machines. The ones on the wall did so much damage because they hit flesh and blood."

"If you disagree with my plan so much," said Vestalis, "why did you not offer your own to the King? We are supposed to be enjoying equal position in his army, though it seems I'm the one doing all the work and you're drinking your way to Rome."

Jarngard tugged on the reins and directed his horse towards the pier. If the sanctimonious prig wanted to promise something he couldn't deliver, then it was his problem.

Vestalis dutifully ignored him, giving commands stiffly from the back of his warhorse. When a trio of scholars marched up leading a jennet with a wagon trailing behind, Jarngard got curious and returned to the area the catapult was being set up.

"Fifty talents," Jarngard called out.

The scholars seemed more interested in what he'd said, glancing nervously past Vestalis, but not wanting to appear unfocused, but...scholars being scholars.

"Fifty talents," he called out again, louder.

Vestalis finished his instructions to the scholars before turning his horse. The scholars led the jennet and wagon to the catapult.

Craning his neck, Jarngard snuck a peek at the contents of the wagon. Melons, it appeared, though he was confused since it wasn't the season for them.

"Is this what we're doing now?" asked Vestalis condescendingly. "Betting?"

"Fifty talents."

An eyebrow raised. "Do you think me deaf? No. Don't answer. I know the truth all too well. I always thought you barbarians were uncontrollable savages until I met Agog. Of course, he'd taken the city by then, a point to his favor. But still, I see that recklessness, that willingness to prove yourself over and over, not the slow patience of war, or politics. The King knows restraint, even the sea captain Hoth does, but you, you're a different animal. Or maybe an animal is all you are."

Vestalis smiled and Jarngard balanced his palm flat on the hilt of his sword. While the ex-Roman soldier had been the King's loyal servant since Agog took Alexandria, Jarngard didn't quite trust the man, despite all signs otherwise.

The old equestrian continued, "The King told me that you'd quit once. Twice even, depending on how you see it, and now you're busy having pissing matches over a little pride. If I were the King, and I'm not, I'd have you thrown in prison until the war was over."

Jarngard bared his teeth. "I think you're just afraid I'm right. If you really believed you could take the city in one day, you'd have accepted already."

Gray eyes stared back, followed by an amused sniff. "I did not take your bet because gold is meaningless now. If we lose the war, we won't be able to spend it without our heads attached and if we win, fifty talents is a piss in the ocean compared to the treasury of the Roman Empire."

"Tell me your deal then," spat Jarngard.

Vestalis glanced toward the wagons. "If you win, you can have your fifty talents, if that's what you want. But if I win, I get to make a request at a later date, one that you will not turn down, if you have any honor."

"I don't like the idea of making a bet that I don't know what it is," said Jarngard.

Vestalis patted the neck of his mount, the reins laid casually over his lap, as he used his thighs to control the horse. "Don't worry, I won't ask for something you would not do. I believe, if the time comes to it, it might even be something you want to do."

"I'm not..." began Jarngard.

Vestalis clucked his tongue, mimicking the way Agog made the noise. "A moment ago you were confident you would win. What's changed?"

Jarngard thought for a moment, but he couldn't see a way out of the bet now. "Agreed."

"Good. With that settled, we can watch my victory." Even stiff-backed in his saddle, Vestalis appeared as comfortable as a whore on a cushioned divan.

The soldiers finished setting up the catapult while they watched. The angle of the tube was not in the position Jarngard expected it. Instead of a low arc pointed toward the gates, they pointed them almost straight up into the air.

The scholars waited nervously by, touching the melons in the wagon and chatting amongst themselves. When the winds shifted and the flags, snapping on the walls of Tyre, pointed east rather than west, the soldiers groaned and started repositioning the wagon.

"Have you ever been to Tyre?" asked Vestalis.

Jarngard shook his head.

"A shame. It's marvelous city. The breezes make even the hottest days a wonder. I imagine when Alexander sieged the city, laboring over his mole, throwing wood and stone and whatever refuse they could find into the sea, they worked extremely hard. But in the city, with their wide porches and thatched roofs, you see, the people pride themselves on comfortable living, using hardy timber for building rather than stone, so the winds can pass through wider openings. It's all very nice, a place to visit under circumstances other than these."

The firing of a steam catapult startled Jarngard. He'd been listening and hadn't seen them load the tube. The soldiers pointed into the air, but Jarngard couldn't see anything except pale blue sky and wisps of clouds

like scratches in the sky.

When the second one went off, and then right after, the third - *thump, thump* - he did not startle. The melons rose quickly and then he lost them, but he gathered they would land in the city.

Under direction from the scholars, the soldiers repositioned the wagon, which pointed the steam catapults in a slightly different direction, but still into the city. They fired another half-dozen melons before repositioning again.

Jarngard watched quietly, trying to determine the purpose of this exercise. Vestalis whistled sharply and a scholar brought over a melon.

There was a plug on one side of it.

Vestalis held it up for Jarngard before dashing it onto the cobble-stones. Rather than stringy seed material, a piece of folded papyrus came tumbling out.

When the scholar handed it to Jarngard, the sweet fragrance of the fruit made his mouth water. He told the scholar, "I can't read that."

Vestalis took it and held it up without unfolding it. "I had them scribbling all last night and the soldiers practicing the firing of the steam catapults to determine the range. You see, if the load is light, the catapults will not break."

"And the note?" Jarngard found himself asking.

"A simple message asking the citizens of Tyre to liberate themselves from Roman rule. They outnumber the soldiers a hundred to one, it shouldn't be hard."

"And why would they do that?" asked Jarngard.

"Because," said Vestalis, "if they do not, I have a second wagon full of melons. These filled with whale oil. I will coat the city and then send in fire. A city of timber and thatch will turn to a great conflagration, fed by the sea breeze, and unless they abandon their city and jump into the sea, they will die."

The old equestrian stared confidently at the city, self-satisfaction brimming on his thin, hard lips. Jarngard stared at him, for a good long while. The firing of the melons went on until the wagon was empty and then they waited.

Occasionally, the crimson helms of the Roman guard moved across the wall. There was some activity going on, but they couldn't tell what it was from this distance and moving closer would put them in arrow range.

Eventually, Jarngard's wine pouch was empty and his mouth became dry and his throat sticky in the gathering heat, but he did not move to find water, because next to him, Vestalis watched like a great bird of prey looming over the city of Tyre.

And like a bird of prey, the man's gaze never wavered from the city, unblinkingly. So when the crimson helms on the wall began disappearing, Jarngard was not surprised.

The two sets of portcullises raised and a group of men walked out, headed across the mole. The leaders of the city, Jarngard assumed.

Jarngard turned his horse towards an exit street. He couldn't deny his thirst any longer.

"Had enough?" asked Vestalis, keeping his eyes forward.

"You won the bet."

"I know."

There wasn't enough wine in Tyre to drown Jarngard's frustration, but he was going to try.

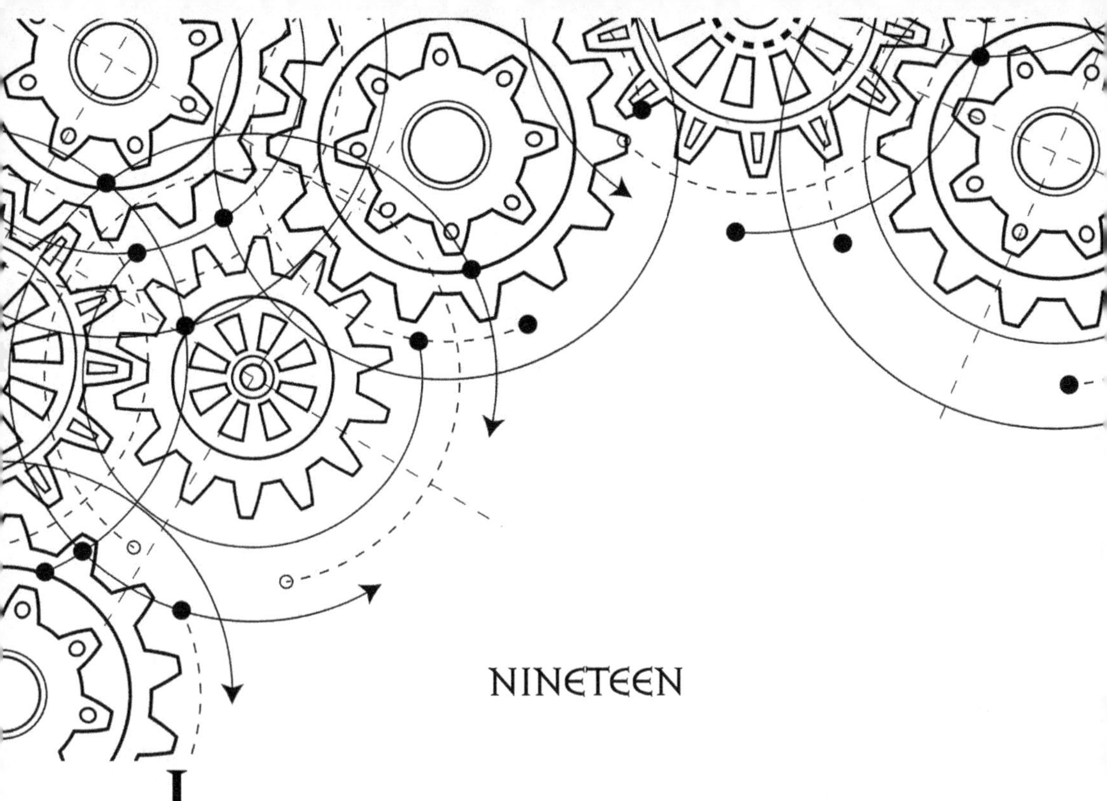

NINETEEN

fear the strain of war upon my mind, I dream of great machines that crush the Romans from the safety of our walls, reaching out like a kraken's tentacles to smash the artifacts of our eventual destruction. I would wake uneasy except for the designs that wait for me in the morning, poised on the tip of my quill.

— The Journal of Archimedes

The Roman quinqueremes were the backbone of the fleet. Even after Hoth smashed the armada, Vestalis' spies reported that Rome was putting new ships into the Mediterranean with a focus on speed. These quinqueremes had five masts instead of three and the lines were sleeker, like a hawk rather than a whale.

For Rome, the navy had always been used for carrying the Legions, so its previous ship designs were bloated around the middle, the holds large enough for two hundred soldiers. These quinqueremes had no holds and flew through the water, spray singing behind them.

Heron leaned against the rail, her now useless metal arm resting on the wood. The three Roman ships had split. One headed directly at them and the other two were making wide curls so they might run with the *Grey Cetus*.

Skipping across the choppy water, Heron wondered when Hoth would change course. If neither ship turned, they would impact head on, but Heron did not bother pointing this out to the sea captain.

On his face, a grim countenance was revealed, the danger of his name—the Black. Heron recognized the calculating stare and waited.

"You're not worried?" asked Hoth, suddenly smiling.

"No."

"We're nearly out of arrows, the ship is damaged, and we're outnumbered. Surely, this is a concern?" he asked.

Heron shrugged. "Either you get us away or you don't. Without two hands, I cannot help Sepharia load fuel into the steam mechanical and this ship needs no sailors besides yourself. I have no purpose but to observe."

Hoth laughed, his eyes brightly wild. Heron was reminded of the chariot ride to Old Babylon. "By Poseidon's cock, your purpose is clear. That piece of your arm holds us together so we may outwit these Romans."

"It's not my arm..." she muttered too quiet for him to hear. A pause. "Outwit? Should we not outrace? I thought the *Gray Cetus* faster than any wooden ship?"

"It is," he replied, "but we near Syracuse and I do not want to give our purpose away, especially when we leave such a bright beacon to our presence." He nodded toward the line of smoke trailing into the sky.

She slammed her metal arm on the railing, grimacing from the impact to her shoulder. The iron boat lunged to the right and Heron scrambled to stay upright.

The Roman quinquereme was upon them. The main deck of the opposing ship was a great height above them, since the iron boat ran low to the water. Heron noted the lack of adornments, no scrollwork or gilding, the Romans had built it in haste.

Arrows flew limply into the water, the passing speed too great a challenge for their archers. Hoth graciously waved at the ship as if they were pleasure barges passing on the Nile. Sailors on the quinquereme shouted commands to draw the lines and adjust the sheets, the sounds of their efforts quickly fading beneath the choppy slap of the iron hull on the waves.

In the distance, the other two boats had finished their turns and headed parallel to the *Gray Cetus*. Slowly, the ships narrowed the gap.

Tapping her fingers on the rail, Heron stared at the sea captain, who was humming to himself. His smugness overflowed like a child who'd just stolen golden eggs from Zeus' chickens.

Normally, the boastful sea captain would have explained the plan, but she began to realize that he expected her to figure it out. Heron surveyed the sea, two quinqueremes running with them, one trailing behind. Using the sun, drifting lower in the afternoon sky behind them, she put them headed east.

Closing her eyes, she felt the hum of the steam mechanical in her chest and most keenly in her stumps. The pink flesh was sensitive to irritation. The pitch of the mechanicals had lowered and Heron thought she knew why.

"You're leading them to Greece," she said.

"That took you longer than I thought it might," he said.

"I didn't realize we were playing this game."

Hoth fixed the strands of hair flying loosely around his face. "There's always a game and anyone not playing it is either dead or poor." He paused. "Is that all?"

"No," she said, annoyed by his subtle taunts, "you've reduced our speed so the Romans will stay with us, though not much as they have a brisk tailwind judging by the crests on the waves. I seem to recall you once saying that which is pursued just out of reach drives one to be ruled by their passions."

"I was speaking of lovely ladies, trying to teach you a thing or two," said Hoth. "But as you say, your work is your woman."

Heron ignored him and continued, "Once it's safely night and the darkness hides our smoke trail, we'll turn back for Syracuse, reaching it by early morning."

She didn't wait for him to acknowledge that she was right and headed to the lower deck to get some rest. Hoth was whistling as she went by.

The darkness of the lower hold consumed her and she fell into a deep sleep only coming out when a change in the mechanical's pitch woke her. Fresh sea air cleared her lungs from the stuffy confines of below deck and on the horizon, a nimbus hovered there, a harbinger of dawn. Heron could not recall the last time she had slept through a complete night.

She heard giggling and found Hoth and Sepharia at the steerage, her daughter comfortably in Hoth's arms as they adjusted the levers.

"I heard the mechanical slow," she told them and much to her annoyance, neither flinched.

Heron stood to the side. Sepharia nestled against the sea captain, leaning into his weight. Heron regretted her long sleep, though another part cheered her daughter's resilience after the horrors of the Parthian prince. In addition, Heron knew about Sepharia's deep infatuation with Cleopatra, a fact that both worried and comforted Heron, as the Egyptian queen had learned to manipulate men to her designs, but in the end had died for them.

"We near Syracuse," said Hoth without a trace of shame. "We slowed our speed since the noise of the iron boat can carry far." He nodded ahead. "You can see the cliffs north of the city."

Her vision was well adjusted to the darkness, but ahead the stars disappeared into nothingness. Hoth took them closer, whispering occasionally in Sepharia's ear. The cliffs were not vertical as she first thought upon approach. The plateau had a slow rise and climbing would be strenuous, especially given her mechanical arm.

Hoth found a secluded cove, one he thought less likely to attract fishermen, which they had already seen signs of: lanterns floating across the water on small ships like aquatic will-o-wisps.

Standing on the shore with overland supplies at their feet, Hoth crossed his arms. "I've gotten us to Syracuse. Now how do we get to Archimedes' tomb? You're not expecting us to just march up there, the three of us?"

Heron threw the sack she'd been holding at his feet. The contents crashed together like a bag of horseshoes. "I brought disguises for us. We're going to be a Roman patrol."

Hoth began laughing. "Are you mad? I look nothing like a Roman, or haven't you noticed my long, pale hair? Or Sepharia's for that matter, or her tits, which protrude most noticeably from the front, a spectacular feature, I might add."

Sepharia only smiled in his direction while she gathered up her equipment. Her daughter was well acquainted with disguises and knew this part of the plan.

Heron produced the razor sharp blade that she'd been holding behind her back. "My daughter's tits, as you say, can be hidden beneath armor, but the hair...tsk, tsk...we'll just have to make it a little more Roman."

The open mouthed stare was nothing short of pure shock, and Heron almost felt bad for how good it made her feel. She could tell by his reaction that a blade hadn't touched his hair in many years.

"My hair..." It was the only thing he could seem to get out.

"Yes, yes. As you say, you look nothing like a Roman, right now. But a little cut and some dye I brought with us and you'll look the part of a Legionnaire," she told him.

When he didn't respond, Heron stepped close and held the blade before his eyes. He fixed on them, wide-eyed.

"Shall you cut it or shall I?"

TWENTY

The stench made Dagi want to retch, but all eyes were on him, so he picked up the helmet, a curved cap of steel with leather straps and a woolen pad where the head would seat, and marched to the water's edge. Mounds of shit steamed from the bowl of the helmet and when Dagi neared the river, he dumped the foul material into a bush.

The tributary came from the mountains east of Damascus. Dagi plunged the helmet into the brisk water, surprising a school of finger-length fish that darted away. The shore was rocky enough Dagi could crouch on the river's edge without fear of falling in, though he stayed aware in case Yota or one of the others from the squad might take the opportunity to push him in.

The shit washed off the metal easily, but not the leather or wool. The regiment had started marching early and had reached the camp first, after which Dagi had been sent to the supply wagons to bring back wood for their fire, punishment enough since the load took him three trips, but he'd wanted to prove to his squad that he could be an asset. The supply wagons were across the camp and it took him the afternoon to complete his task. By the time he returned, foot-sore and doused in a thick coating of sweat, the shit had been sitting in his helmet for hours in the hot sun.

Dagi wondered how the others could have stood it. When he finally returned, he smelled it before he even got near his belongings. At least they'd not tampered with his sword or buckler.

After a final splash of water, Dagi sniffed the leather, finding the smell had soaked in. He trudged back up the slope to the camp and set his helmet upside down to dry in the remaining sunlight.

Yota was staring, his bushy eyebrows furrowed. "Better you got lost getting wood. Maybe join another squad."

The fire crackled, wood snapping. The other soldiers shuffled their feet against the gravel.

Dagi knew why Yota had spoken in halted Latin rather than Egyptian. It was the only common language they shared and Yota wanted it to be known he did not approve.

"You can't know the mind of the gods," replied Dagi.

Yota spit in the dirt. "Since you spoke to that cursed Northman, we always get early march, and they skipped our turn on the chariots. The *Geri's* curse has tainted you. We must rid of you before we all die."

Dagi looked around to see if the others were on Yota's side. The Egyptians tended to share Yota's opinion, glaring at him with open hatred. The true Alexandrians, a mix of Greek, Roman, and Egyptian heritages, weren't making eye contact, which wasn't comforting.

He took a deep breath. Either he had to stick up for himself now or he'd find a dagger in his belly when he was sleeping. Dagi stood and Yota immediately matched him.

"If an early march is cursed then you must be like an *ebien tikr*," responded Dagi.

The collective gasp from the Egyptians was followed by Yota marching angrily over, fists clenched by his side. Dagi had called him a 'poor eunuch' which was the worst thing for Dagi to call another man, or at least a fellow Egyptian.

Dagi stood nose to nose with Yota. He could practically taste the man's last meal, he was so close. The crack of a large stone landing in the fire, scattering sparks and coals and ashes, startled them both. Standing at the edge of the camp, the Northman Jarngard watched them with half-lidded eyes.

"Who's the captain of your regiment?" asked the Northman.

No one answered, so Dagi pointed to the reed-brown tent on the flat part of the rise. Jarngard began to leave, but stopped and spoke to them briskly.

"If you're going to fight, do it quickly, I'm taking this regiment on a little mission," said Jarngard before continuing his march to the tents.

Yota's nostrils flared in victory. "I told you, you were bad luck." He spit on the ground and walked away, gathering his equipment.

The grumbling from the squad increased and the other soldiers shot nasty glances at him as they put on their light armor and adjusted the straps on their shields.

Dagi found his shield and weapon damp and a careful sniff told him it was piss. After a quick rinse at the river's edge, he fixed his gear and prepared to march. The helmet he carried rather than wore.

The captain of the regiment led them through the camp. Dagi didn't see Jarngard, so he must have gone ahead. If he'd time, he wanted to ask why he'd picked their regiment, rather than one of the others, but he knew it was doubtful he could muster the courage to speak.

About twenty steam chariots waited, making the rally point a noisy and stinking cloud of burning coal. When they loaded on, Dagi made a point of mixing with soldiers from outside his squad, since only five or six could fit on each chariot and there were twenty in the squad.

At the head of the line, Jarngard stood on the back of his chariot. His muscular arms flexed as he held the shield post, leaning off, and grinning at the regiment.

"Ave, fellow Alexandrians. We have reports of a group of Romans that fled ahead of our approach carrying Roman gold. They've taken harbor in a town not far from here, a place called Hanabi. Our task is to raid the town and take the gold back. A denarius for every soldier once we're done!"

The soldiers cheered and Dagi found himself looking for the others of his squad so he could gloat, but their chariots were on the far side of the group. Before he could find them, the vehicles took off down the rocky road, leading east out of the mountains.

The ride to Hanabi was much different than the slow march north. When he'd gotten to ride before, the chariots kept pace with the soldiers and the road was smoother. The road they bounced across now was a boulder infused goat path that forced the chariots to go single file most of the way. A short distance into the trip, Dagi was coated in dust, digging clods from the corner of his eyes frequently.

The foothills they passed through were steep and ravine-filled. A herd of sheep crossing delayed them at one point, which only made Dagi hungry. Past an ancient settlement of mud huts, long abandoned and overtaken by scrub, the town of Hanabi came into view.

The town, like most in the Mesopotamian valley, was built on top of a hill. Even from a distance, Dagi could tell the steam chariots would never fit through the narrow arch leading into the town.

They left the vehicles at the base of the hill and marched up on foot. Otherwise, they would have never gotten them back down since the path to the town followed a steep cliff.

Reaching the arch, Jarngard stopped them, forming them into squads. Based on the glares from his squad mates, the promise of a denarius hadn't improved their moods. Someone stepped on his foot as he moved into position.

The Northman, the one they called Jarngard to his face, and *Geri* behind his back, looked at them with hungry eyes from the top of the trail. The dull, laggard gaze from the day with the buckler was missing. His muscles flexed in readiness and he nodded slowly.

Dagi ran with the regiment, a loping climb, for as he ran, the flush of battle rose in his veins and he flexed his limbs at each step, knowing that he longed to meet the Romans and hoped they had already fled in the same breath.

The Romans must have known they were coming because the streets of the walled town were empty, though Dagi found it odd that the gate was unbarred. The captain, Jarngard, didn't seem to care and sent them in three groups, one along each wall and the others straight through.

Dagi and his squad went with Jarngard. The time for petty fighting was gone and stone-silent eyes made agreements for truce and brotherhood. Even Yota's dark-lidded eyes, the kind Egyptian women thought desirable, failed to signal thoughts of revenge.

"That cup of steel works better on your head than under your arm," said Jarngard who was suddenly by his side. "Unless you like the insides of your head on the outside."

The desecration of his helmet seemed unimportant now and even the thought of shit-stained wool didn't keep him from slapping the armor on his head. Rather a little stink than his lifeblood leaking out his skull.

Dagi stayed close, running at the heels of the Northman. The helmet slipped on his forehead and sweat stung his eyes. He gripped his weapon tightly, watching Jarngard for signs of worry. The building passed in a blur and Dagi didn't realize the battle was joined until he heard his squad mates cry out.

The twang of crossbows made Dagi duck. A soldier around his age fell to his knees, a bolt sticking out of his neck. The street felt claustrophobic, Dagi searched around, but death flew through the air. The Romans had set a trap for them.

A heavy hand grabbed his shoulder. Jarngard kicked a door open and dove through, pulling Dagi with him.

Inside the house, a woman screamed. Dagi expected the bite of steel. He tried to blink away the darkness, but saw only spots, reflections burned into his vision, from the glint of Roman weapons in the sunlight.

Jarngard stood in the doorway. At least fifteen soldiers lay dead in the dirt and the others had scattered or fled. On the other side of the street, huddled in a cubby between two buildings, Yota and two soldiers from his squad hid behind their bucklers.

The Northman calmly surveyed the scene. Dagi crawled up to the doorway. A group of Romans had taken position behind a flipped over wagon.

Peering out the doorway, Dagi checked behind to make sure some old woman wasn't creeping through the dark house to put a dagger in his calf. The screaming had stopped at least, which Dagi marked as a good thing, until he realized that when the woman was screaming, she couldn't sneak up on him.

The Romans, having reloaded, were aiming their crossbows at Yota in the cubby. Even a poor shot wouldn't find it hard to miss.

Dagi was lifted to his feet by Jarngard. The barbarian pulled his long blade and glared at Dagi, nodding his head to the right once.

When the Northman lifted his blade, Dagi thought he'd gone mad. He dove to the side as Jarngard split the door from the hinges.

He picked the door up like a shield and looked down at Dagi. "If you want your friends to live, follow close. Cowards with crossbows always die quickly."

Without a word, Jarngard burst through the doorway, right as the Romans began to fire on Yota. Surprised, Dagi scrambled to catch up, regretting his bravery instantly as the Romans turned on them.

Bolts punched through the wooden door and Dagi wasn't sure how they missed Jarngard's arm, or even how he continued to carry it while holding his sword. Jarngard ran straight at the wagon, a war cry bellowing out of his lungs. The Northman threw the door against the wagon and sprung up it, leaping into the middle of the Romans, who were busy reloading their crossbows. Weapons whirled through the air and men screamed. The Northman was death and the soldiers fell to his touch.

Dagi wasn't entirely sure what happened next. Jarngard's blade swirled around him like steel leaves and Dagi, inspired by his courage, ran around the wagon, only to find himself squared off with two Roman soldiers, larger and wearing scale armor.

The first slashed his weapon forward and Dagi barely blocked it with the feeble buckler that only covered his forearm. The two Romans hammered at his sword and shield and Dagi could only block and block and block, his shoulder ringing with impact.

Dagi didn't remember tripping, but suddenly he found himself on one knee, a blade coming over his buckler and hitting him squarely in the forehead. He fell into the dirt, tasting blood, feeling wetness on his face. The second Roman soldier followed the first and all Dagi could see was the blade, plunging directly for his chest.

He hadn't expected to die so soon.

TWENTY ONE

If it were that each problem presented itself in a neat fashion, and I might solve them, like cows lining up for the slaughter, but the Romans come like the tide, and my sleep breaks like the walls. Still, I find inspiration, and my papyri are filled with such destruction that I consider burning them. My apprentices beg me not to and though they do not tell me, they scheme on their own...

— The Journal of Archimedes

"You look more Roman than the Romans," said Heron, smirking at Hoth, who kept touching his clipped black locks. "Except for the pouting and grumbling, that puts you off the disguise."

Hoth threw the last sips of his wine into the bushes. A nearby bird startled and burst into the early morning sky. Stars were still bright and the day only a hint of glow on the horizon. But for the insects and small creatures, their day had begun.

"What good is my disguise if you cannot hide your machineness? I should have never let you cut my hair."

"Don't worry about my limbs, I'll take care of that." She threw him a scroll that he caught deftly with one hand. "While Sepharia helps me with my armor, memorize the contents of that document. We might need to bluff our way past real Roman soldiers."

He stared distrustfully at the rolled papyrus. "What does it say? I might look like a Roman now but I don't sound like one and my Latin is terrible."

"Magnus Julius Severus, the Consul of the Roman Army, keeps special envoys and units for his own purposes. They're given liberty to do as they please in service to the Empire. It's not unheard of for a Thracian to rise in the ranks of these special forces."

His brow hunched in thought. "But I'm not Thracian."

"No," she said, "but there are no barbarians of the north in his army and Thracians are the closest thing to a Roman barbarian. Most true Romans are too enamored of their empire to learn about other cultures."

The gentle smack of waves against the hull of the iron boat reminded Heron they were alone on Roman soil. They'd found a scraggly inlet, scraping the sand bars and rocky floor to hide the boat in an area they hoped wouldn't be frequented by local fishermen. The thick, tangled vegetation put off an earthy scent. Heron hoped it wouldn't be too dense that they couldn't climb out of the inlet and make for the plateau.

"How do you know so much about this Roman General? Or is that required study in the Library?" asked Hoth.

"Vestalis told me everything he knew about the man and his spies forged those documents for us."

Hoth glanced at the scroll as if it were a snake, holding it with tentative fingertips. "We're trusting our lives to that man? How do we know he's not a plant for the Romans? It was curious that the trap had been set on our path and only a select few knew about our trip."

"Trust or not, we're here and if you don't like the man, then you shouldn't have come," she said.

"So you trust him?" he asked.

Heron shrugged. "The time for those thoughts have passed. If he sold us to the Romans then we shall soon find out."

When Sepharia appeared in full Roman scale armor over crimson tunic and leather loincloth, Heron didn't recognize her, though the light was still dim. Sepharia pulled out the second set of armor and began helping Heron don it. Arm and leg guards hid the majority of her mechanical limbs and a semi-circular shield, painted in the colors of the Empire, crimson and gold, would hide the rest.

"Not a very imposing pair of Roman soldiers," scoffed Hoth.

Sepharia produced the gladius and held the tip to Hoth's throat. "I can still push this through your neck."

Hoth slapped the weapon away from his face. "The two of you can barely hold your shields up. If we encounter a patrol, they'll never believe us."

"I'm expecting you to be your normal, annoying self, and that if we do run into a patrol, they won't be able to take their eyes off you."

"Great." Hoth rolled his eyes. "I thought we had a real plan."

They gathered their gear and began the march up the steep hill, using the rocky ravines to avoid the thickest vegetation. By the time they reached the summit, Heron was drenched in sweat and leaning heavily on her shield. Hoth said nothing, only shaking his head and sipping from his water pouch.

The inlet was further from Syracuse than planned and the glow on the horizon strengthened. Covered in leather and overlapping plates of polished steel kept her from enjoying the cool sea breeze. Whenever they stopped, she pushed her helmet up and gulped at the fresh air.

Halfway across the plateau, they found a goat trail, making their journey slightly easier, though Heron cursed the dreadful weight of her armor each time they stopped.

"How does one fight in this?" asked Heron.

"I don't," said Hoth. "Armor only slows a man down. It's not meant for marches through the forest either, typically soldiers keep the heaviest gear on their horse until battle nears, but I didn't choose your disguise."

Heron grumbled, knowing the comment was revenge for cutting his hair. He'd certainly known this when they set off from the hidden cove.

When they reached the edge, a place of waist-high bushes and pale grasses that waved in the wind, Syracuse lay below them, still draped in shadow from the plateau. Lights bobbed on the sea, outnumbering those in the city.

"The necropolis lies on the eastern edge," said Heron, pointing down the slope, feeling a mess of knots and aches where the steel plates from the armor pressed into her muscles. "Plato have pity, it shouldn't be much further, or you might bury me there when we arrive."

Vines and untended bushes smothered the boundary of the graveyard. The iron hinges on the gate screamed in protest of their entrance. The hair on the back of Heron's neck went up, but not because the place of the dead unnerved her. As she stepped onto the stone path, weeds poking through the cracked slabs, Archimedes' voice, the one she imagined as she read his journal, returned to her, whispering the greeting she so desired.

"Where is the tomb?" whispered Sepharia, starling Heron from her thoughts.

The layout of the necropolis was etched into her heart. Heron raised her good arm and stretched it out until one finger indicated a marble building set into a small rise. Behind the grassy knoll was a scaffolding under which a construction was underway, though currently unmanned. A drilling of some sort, if Heron guessed correctly.

Heron sighed both reluctantly and in utter anticipation. The weight of the armor seemed less punishing now, almost buoyant.

"Archimedes lies entombed there," she said reverently.

"Soldiers guard the way," said Hoth.

"Really?" She squinted. "How can you tell? I see nothing."

His jaw was hardened with purpose. "They are there."

Hoth led them to the tomb, walking leisurely across the path as if he were strolling down Canopic street in Alexandria. Heron gripped her shield tightly, muscles aching from the long march.

"By Claudius' balls," called out Hoth as they neared, startling Heron to flinch, "who lurks there? Show yourselves."

A lantern sparked to life and orange light flooded the space between the dark entrance of the tomb and a tangled copse. Three soldiers stepped forward, hands on gladii, seal of the Empire stamped proudly on their leather chest armor.

"For the Empire," said the first soldier, saluting.

Heron raised her arm to reply, but when Hoth did nothing she clung to her shield. Sepharia glanced askew for guidance and Heron discreetly shook her off.

"Where's your wineskin?" asked Hoth drolly, "I thirst."

The soldiers glanced at each other. The first stepped forward, thrusting his chest out. "What's your rank, soldier? What Legion do you report?"

Hoth picked at his teeth with fingernail and flicked something into the bushes. Heron wanted to kick the sea captain, he wasn't acting like a Roman soldier at all. The soldier in back had a loaded crossbow at his side. Even the steel plates she wore wouldn't stop a bolt at this range.

"I said, where is your wineskin? I thirst." Hoth spit at the man's feet.

Heron closed her eyes momentarily. If it came to blows, she'd barely be able to lift her sword. Holding the shield took every effort already.

The first soldier pulled his sword and held it toward Hoth's chest.

Hoth eyed it dismissively.

"I wouldn't do that," said Hoth, "unless you'd like to be sent on the next northern campaign."

The soldier didn't seem as confident as he first was when he pulled the sword. He looked to his fellow soldiers for support.

"Wineskin. Now," said Hoth.

The soldier swallowed. "First, tell us who you are."

Hoth gave a dramatic sigh and threw the scroll at the soldier's feet. The man leaned down, keeping his gaze and sword aimed at Hoth the whole time. The soldier handed the missive to the one behind him after he'd picked it up.

When the soldier gasped, Heron knew he'd gotten to the part revealing Hoth's position. Most soldiers didn't interact with the special units.

He handed the document back and disappeared behind the trees, returning momentarily with a wineskin and threw it to Hoth. The sea captain snatched it out of the air and squeezed dark liquid into his mouth, spilling some on his chest.

The first soldier had let his sword drift to the ground, but he did not look pleased by their presence. Hoth cricked his neck and spoke, "This is the tomb, right?"

"The tomb?" said the first soldier, dumbfounded.

"Archimedes, you fool."

The soldier appeared to not know what to make of being insulted, frowning. "Yes?"

"Yes?" said Hoth, mockingly. "You're not sure. Is it, or is it not?"

"Yes, it's the tomb of Archimedes."

Hoth made an exaggerated sigh. "By Jupiter's balls, thank the gods. I tire of these errands."

Hoth smacked his lips and crossed his arms, looking at the soldiers with abject disgust. "Well?"

"What?" said the first soldier, clearly off balance from the sea captain's constant verbal assault.

"Get out of the way." Hoth threw his hands aside.

The soldiers backed away and as Heron lifted her shield, the first one cleared his throat. "Apologies, I must ask a question. Master Apion instructed us to not let anyone into the tomb, he is worried there are spies about, but clearly, you are not them. But I will need to tell him you came to the tomb and why."

Hoth stared at the soldier with half-lidded eyes. "*My* master wishes a first hand account of the tomb. He cannot understand what all the fuss is about, so I was roused from my more pressing duties to ride out here and investigate. While I've been assured this is some very *important* work, it looks like worthless scholar business."

The soldier nodded and they made their way toward the entrance of the tomb. Hoth was passing beneath the stone arch when the first soldier cleared his throat again.

"Where are your horses?" he asked, and then added after a moment of thought. "You said you rode horses, but I did not hear any, nor do I see where you tethered them."

Heron swallowed deeply, unsure of what they could say, while Hoth's confusion was evident on his face. He'd said they'd ridden out to investigate, but no horses. If Apion guessed they were coming, he would know they would be on foot and give his soldiers proper warning.

Hoth glanced at Heron, his mouth half-agape, clearly searching for an answer. The soldier stepped forward, lifting his sword higher.

"The scutums," said the soldier, indicating the shields they carried. "Why do you need them to investigate a tomb?"

The other two soldiers that had been standing back passively, completely accepting of the disguise, twitched in thought and stepped forward, joining the first soldier. What had first seemed like an easy entrance was now quickly moving toward a fight. Heron looked to Hoth, hoping he was as good as he said with a sword, because neither she nor Sepharia would be able to help. The soldier with the lantern held it higher, peering into their faces as if he saw something.

"You must tell them, commander," said Sepharia suddenly, using a lower voice.

Hoth did not hide his surprise. "I must?"

"Yes, commander, tell them."

Heron's whole body tensed and the only thing she could see was the soldier's sword, pointed directly at her chest. Hoth turned to Sepharia and scrunched up his face.

"If they have clearance enough to guard this tomb," began Sepharia, "then I believe they can know about what we rode."

Heron got her meaning a moment before Hoth did, the realization flickering into his eyes.

"Yes, I suppose you're correct," he said.

"What are you talking about?" asked the first soldier angrily. "Make yourself clear."

"A Roman made steam mechanical," said Hoth. "But this is a secret. We don't want those Alexandrian scum to know we've mastered their technology."

The soldier's eyes went wide with amazement. He glanced back the way they'd come. "May we see it?"

Hoth smiled. "Of course," and when the soldier took a step past them he continued, "but after we've investigated the tomb. I want to get this over with. I promise we'll be quick. Then we can show you the wonder of the Roman Empire."

The soldiers seemed to accept this new reality and let them go in, even giving them a lantern to light the way, their mistrust turned to anticipation. Even the first soldier smiled as Heron walked past.

Relief flooded into her limbs as they stepped beneath the arch and that feeling turned to elation and not for the encounter with the soldiers outside. The stairs were stone-cut and plain, the opposite of the last tomb she'd entered. The walls were clean and smooth, unlike the weeping stone of the hallway before the Demetarium. As they descended into the earth, she found her breath shallow and the armor and mechanicals on her limbs weightless. At the end of the passage, Heron stepped into a wide room, her eyes nearly glazed over with the realization that she was standing in the tomb of her mentor, a man dead for over two hundred years, the inventor Archimedes.

TWENTY TWO

Greasy lamb stew. It seemed like an odd thought to have in the last moments before death, but there it was—greasy lamb stew. Maybe the gods were visiting him with irony as the sword blade, shimmering like glass through the air, flew towards his neck.

Dagi had only eaten it once, almost a year ago, when he'd signed up for the Alexandrian army and taken his bonus. The coins were time-worn, the face of Cleopatra only a smudge of lines, but the café had taken it and Dagi had sat in the shade of a sycamore tree along Canal Street and scooped the greasy water with lamb chunks and spiced roots and greens into his waiting mouth. It was the best thing he'd ever eaten and now he was going to die for it.

He clamped his eyes shut, tasting the greasy broth, and fell backwards. Men screamed and inexplicably, he remained alive, turtled on his back. Tentatively, he opened his eyes to find Yota standing above him. The Roman soldiers were dead. Yota and his mates had slain the Romans before they could do the same to him.

Yota offered a hand and helped Dagi up. The Egyptian soldier with the painted eyes squeezed his shoulder and nodded. "Many thanks for your bravery, Dagi. May the beasts of the Nile find you repulsive."

Dagi smiled in response. "And may the pharaohs find your eternal services unnecessary."

Around them, dying men moaned. The smell of blood and shit was thick, the Roman at their feet had pierced bowels from a spear thrust. He would die soon. Jarngard strolled around the wagon with blood splattered on his chest and face.

The remnants of the squad gathered. They'd lost half in the ambush. Disembodied cries echoed from other parts of the walled town.

"The Romans set a trap for us," said Jarngard. "Gather your weapons, loot the Romans if you want, and I'll double your bonus if we capture the gold."

Two denarius was quite a sum for a soldier of his rank, but no one cheered. They were all just glad to be alive.

The Northman stood at the end of the street, looking deeper into the town. Dagi joined him, tentatively opening his mouth before speaking.

"May I ask a question?"

Jarngard's eyes had a far-away look to them, pensive. Dagi wasn't sure if he envied the warrior's stoic nature or pitied him.

"You've earned it."

Dagi's chest tightened in anticipation. "What does *Geri* mean?"

The Northman's eyes flared with pain. Dagi could see old battles and towns on fire in that gaze.

"You haven't earned that," spat Jarngard, his jaw pulsing with anger.

Dagi squeaked the word out, "Apologies," and shuffled back to the others.

"Wait."

The word froze him in his tracks, head down, hunched, ready for admonishment from his superior. Dagi turned slowly to find Jarngard facing him.

The old warrior sighed. "It means Ravenous One, a lover of war and death and killing."

Dagi wanted to ask why but the question was lodged in his throat. The Northman's eyes were bloodshot, matching the splatter across his chest. Carefully, Dagi nodded and turned away.

With the bodies looted, Jarngard formed them up, evidence of his pain hidden behind a warrior's mask, but Dagi could see what it was now, and the revelation made him question his joining of the Alexandrian army.

At least his rewards of friendship had grown. His bravery had earned him Yota's trust. His fellow Egyptian smiled now whenever they met gazes and the others called his name fondly, adding the nickname *Jabari*, which meant Brave One.

The nickname made it to Jarngard's ears, earning Dagi a glance and a nod, an approval he wasn't sure he deserved. He'd killed no Romans, only charging into overwhelming odds, which in a place of reflection felt more like foolishness.

But he did not argue his new nickname, enjoying the familiarity that his squad mates said his name, almost a badge.

"...did you see the way Jabari leapt into the fight!"

"...Jabari fears nothing! Not even ten Romans against two!"

Dagi smiled and as they left the square, Jarngard motioned them to silence. Swords drawn and shoulders hunched as they jogged, they made their way through the streets toward the sounds of distant battle.

Ahead, Jarngard led them, and Dagi saw the name Ravenous One in his gaze, forward and merciless. Dagi took position at his right, earning more approving nods from his squad mates for the acknowledgement of his new nickname.

There were shouts and cries of agony two streets over. They doubled their pace and Dagi gripped his sword tightly, realizing he'd left his buckler back at the previous fight. At the corner of the next street, the crimson and gold armor of Roman soldiers flashed into view.

Jarngard screamed a battle cry and Dagi found his voice adding to the din as blood pumped gloriously through his veins. They ran and the Romans reformed, shields locked, a wall of steel and muscle.

Strides ahead, Jarngard leapt, feet coming down squarely on the metal boss of the center shield. The impact broke the wall and Dagi followed in behind, barely dodging the thrust of swords and swinging with abandon.

The battle was joined and it wasn't at all what Dagi thought it would be. With the shield wall broken, the fight turned into a dozen individual skirmishes. Dagi found himself matched off with a Roman soldier unused to fighting by himself. Without a shield to hinder him, and buoyed by the spirit flowing through his limbs, Dagi hammered away at the opposing soldier, until the man tripped over another.

A sword thrust pierced the gut between two steel plates and Dagi was left to stare into the soldier's frightened eyes as he tumbled backwards. The Roman held two hands across his belly and dark blood pumped between his fingers. His jaw quivered.

"Help me," said the Roman soldier.

Around Dagi, the battle raged. The others were locked in combat, so Dagi was left alone. The dying soldier wasn't much older than he was, just better equipped and trained.

Looking up, he watched Jarngard dispatch two Romans with ruthless efficiency, beating back their sword blows and then cutting them across the unarmored neck. The Northman caught him watching him and gave a grim nod.

The Roman soldier was dead, eyes glazed over and blood leaking from his lips. Only steps away, Yota was engaged with a much taller Roman with arms that bulged through his armor. The overhead swings shot sparks between their swords. Yota could barely keep his guard up.

Dagi took two steps and shoved his gladius into the Roman's side, finding a gap in the armor when his arms were raised. His death was frighteningly simple and Dagi nearly dropped his sword in surprise.

Out of breath, Yota patted Dagi on the shoulder. "My thanks, Jabari."

His fellow Egyptians ran toward the other fights, leaving Dagi alone. They outnumbered the Romans now and the last few were hunted down.

After it was over, a soldier from his squad, one of Yota's friends, found the missing gold when he went to sit down on the wagon. Two large chests were hidden under sacks of grain. The remaining Alexandrians, less than half that had come to the town of Hanabi, gathered around Jarngard as he gave out three denarius to each.

Three coins for two lives. Dagi tucked them into a pocket and tried to look at anything but the dead bodies while his squad mates searched the Romans for more coinage.

Dagi found Jarngard lounging against a post gulping down dark liquid from a pouch. The Northman was bleeding from a cut along his jaw and thick blood dripped from his chin.

"Is it always this hard?" asked Dagi.

Jarngard frowned and wiped the blood away with a rag he pulled from a pocket. "It only gets easier." And then after a pause, "but that's the worst part."

A few cheers sounded behind him. Yota and his mates had found a stash of wine amongst the sacks of grain. They cracked the wax seals and poured the drink into their open mouths, not caring if it splashed across their chests.

"Jabari!" they called his name, encouraging him over.

Dagi looked back to Jarngard.

"Go join them," he said. "It'll be good for you."

Dagi jogged over to the welcoming embrace of his squad mates, letting them pat his back and ply him with warm wine that made his head spin. In short order, he was a little drunk and the numbness from the battle a distant memory. Before they gathered up the gold and fallen equipment, Dagi decided he would buy another bowl of lamb stew the next chance he got, to celebrate the victory and this time he'd have money left over to save for after the war.

TWENTY THREE

King Hiero the Second sent a force of men to counterattack the Romans, who had begun building a great siege engine. I admire the King for sending these men to their death, knowing their sacrifice was for the good of the city. The men took it well, and they were feasted and sang songs of valor all night until the appointed time. We kissed them and bid them the luck of the gods, for it is our luck too.

— The Journal of Archimedes

The weight of the armor became unbearable, suffocating even. The warm, moist air of the tomb caught in her throat and Heron clawed at the metal gorge. Before her was the tomb of the greatest inventor she knew and despite her adoration, she found herself suddenly claustrophobic.

Heron stumbled down the last few steps, dropping the shield to clatter on the ground and leaned against the carved wall, ignoring the geometric lines criss-crossing the stone. With her good hand, she clutched at the buckle at her side that held the two halves of the armor together, while Hoth watched curiously.

In her haste, she jammed a fingernail on the corner of the buckle, a shot of pain ran up her forearm, but the clasp would not budge. Heron yanked on the leather strap until Sepharia calmly took the buckle from her and began removing the armor. Before Sepharia could get the last pieces off, Heron was sliding out of them, pushing them to fall on the floor.

"Get this cursed armor off me," said Heron. "I'm sick of being someone I'm not."

Heron, standing in a sweat-soaked tunic, watched the glances between Hoth and Sepharia. They thought her mad, she decided, but let them think that. She eyed the useless metal limb once before deciding it was too much trouble to remove.

"Are we done with disguises?" asked Hoth with an eyebrow raised.

Heron froze, at first thinking he meant her gender, but then she realized he was just speaking of the armor. "I'm not carrying that shield a second longer and without it they'd know who I am. I'm sure Apion has given them my description."

"May I take my armor off?" asked Sepharia, resulting in a nod from Heron.

Wiping the sweat from her brow, Heron sucked greedily at the water pouch, not caring if it spilled on her chest. The bindings were soaked through to the skin already.

"What is this place?" asked Hoth. "It's like no tomb I've ever seen."

Heron surveyed the room, realizing for the first time that the walls were curved. Lines carved into the stone criss-crossed, making geometric patterns like a stone-spider had let its web dissolve into the stone, except the distribution was not even, and the spaces between not equidistant. A swirling spiral was formed into the stone on the other side of the sarcophagus. Heron let her eyes follow the lines until she got dizzy and gave up. Sepharia was standing before the sarcophagus in the middle of the room running her fingers across the front. The lines did not touch the stone coffin.

By Sepharia's side, Heron reached out, tracing the inscription on the stone. The hair on her arms raised and a shiver went down her spine.

"What is that?" asked Hoth from behind them.

"A sphere inside a cylinder," said Heron quietly.

Hoth scoffed. "You speak of it like a mother does her baby."

Heron spun on him, nearly toppling due to the mechanical leg and her exhaustion. "This man changed the course of history more than any other inventor. These pure calculations did not intrude directly on the vulgar aspects of life, though it reaches them later at a tangent, informing those who came after to build on what he had done. I am nothing without Archimedes."

"We're not here to worship at his altar, but find this weapon he devised," said Hoth. "So get to finding. I'd rather be quick about it. Our friends up top probably can't wait to see our non-existent steam mechanical."

Heron circled the room slowly, finding the beginnings of an excavation on the far side. Apion had tried digging through the stone, but the hole had filled with water. Heron found this odd as the necropolis was situated on the crown of a hill further up from the city and the tomb should be well above the water table. It'd been rather dry lately as well, so it was doubtful that it was a result of storms. She decided they'd poured the water in to test the constitution of the stone.

"The tomb has been opened," said Sepharia, peering under the edge of the massive lid. "The seals are broken and the edges chipped where they reset it."

"Then the weapon isn't in there," mused Hoth.

"I would have never looked in there," said Heron. "Whatever had been done, was done *after* his death. Putting it with his body would be too obvious."

Leaning against the sarcophagus, Hoth struck a casual pose. "Then what *are* we looking for?"

"A good question," she said, sensing that he was feeling peevish and she hadn't the energy to spar with him. Carrying that armor up and over and down the plateau had drained her. "A text in some form. Vestalis' spies report the first weapon was found in a papyrus scroll."

"How did they find it?" asked Sepharia.

"By accident," she responded. "They were rebuilding a part of the royal Palace when a worker fell through a hole. Part of the text indicated the other two weapons and the importance of his journal."

"So the papyrus was found out of order?" said Sepharia, running a hand through her short, black hair.

"Yes," responded Heron, noticing how fierce a woman Sepharia had become. The events with the Parthian Prince had changed her, made her more wary. Standing there in her Roman soldier tunic with a gladius at her side, she could be a warrior Queen.

"What are all these cracks?" asked Hoth, crouched onto his heels, running his fingertips along the smooth stone.

"They're not *cracks* and I wish I knew," she replied. "I see shapes in the spaces between the lines, trapezoids, parallelograms, triangles, and all manner of other designs, but not the reason for them. There's even a spiral on the far side of the room. I fear they will require measurement and a proof to divine their purpose."

"That sounds lengthy," said Hoth.

Heron crossed her arms, surveying the designs. "I'm afraid so and I didn't bring anything to measure with, though I suppose we could use a bit of cloth to mark a standard distance and convert it."

"Eventually those soldiers will become curious," he said. "If we're going to spend that much time down here, I'd better sneak up and kill them."

Heron sighed. She thought it'd be easier than this. Every word of his journal was firmly imprinted in her mind. She hoped upon seeing the tomb an important phrase would illuminate itself and lead them to the weapon.

"Not if we can help it," she said. "I'd rather leave without Apion knowing we were here."

"He won't suspect our cover?" asked Hoth.

"Even if he does, he won't know for certain. Even a hint of doubt will throw confusion into his plans."

"Find it quickly," said Hoth, patting his hilt with a hungry look in his eyes.

Heron circled the room twice more, touching the walls and shapes, tracing lines, and crouching on her heels to peer at the shallow etching in the stone. Despite the dry weather, the room had a musty scent, though she dismissed that thought eventually, after all, it *was* a tomb.

The etching on his sarcophagus bothered her. She knew the theorem was his proudest legacy, but even she, a famed mathematician and inventor, could not completely agree with this source of pride. True, the ratio of three to two helped connect other pieces of geometry. Her own *Geometria* owed a debt to this formula without which it would not stand as an important mathematical document.

But in her eyes, he had more important discoveries and inventions, like his theory of hydrostatic forces, which made her water-powered inventions work, or the water screw with which to move water efficiently, needed for large ships and gardens. The Heavens Mechanism, upon which her counting machines were based, provided all manner of important insights into gearings and levers and the calculations with the natural world to make them work.

Heron sighed. Archimedes had many writings that she thought more important than this simple theorem: *Liber Assumptorum, The Method of Me-*

chanical Theorems, On Floating Bodies, On Spirals. Standing with her back to the steps of the tomb, Heron surveyed the room, trying to see, but not see. She knew she was missing something important.

"The clue must be in the room," she whispered. "The room, the room. What do the lines mean?"

"Maybe the lines mean nothing," answered Hoth.

Heron glared. "Of course they mean something. Be quiet and let me figure this out."

Hoth shrugged and meandered around the tomb touching surfaces at random. Heron blocked him out of her mind, he wouldn't be able to find the solution. Only her, only she knew Archimedes, her mentor, though they'd never spoken.

Heron closed her eyes and let the images from the room dance across the surface of her eyelids. She played with the shapes, spinning and twisting them, putting them back together again. Was it a dissection puzzle, or tangram as the Romans called them?

Archimedes had written a treatise on them called *Ostomachion.* The geometrical game used a 14-piece dissection puzzle forming a square, usually made of bone. Heron had played the game with her twin when they were children. The name even meant bone-fight and the shapes could be made into other objects: an elephant, a sword, a barking dog, or a tower.

Heron tried to match the shapes of the puzzle against the shapes in the room, but only a few pieces were similar. Around and around her head, the shapes turned and rotated, matching and not-matching. The muscles in her forehead knotted with effort.

"Heron?" asked Hoth with an annoying lilt.

The shapes fumbled, interrupted by the maddening sea captain. "Not now," she fumed.

"*Her*-on." Her name came out sing-song with an underlining amusement that shattered her thoughts.

"What, you imbecile?" she rebuked Hoth savagely, eyes still closed. "Can't you see I'm trying to solve this puzzle."

Hoth chuckled and she felt a stab of anger run through her. "I have a question?"

"A question?" she sighed.

"Yes."

Heron opened her eyes and looked over the sarcophagus at the sea captain, his shoulder dipped and his arms crossed, scratching his chin absently. He was glancing upward at the center of the ceiling. Heron followed his gaze, but saw nothing of importance except an intersection of lines.

"What is it?" she said, the questions squirting through her teeth like forced water.

"I'm not a scholar, nor a mathematician, but isn't this room a cylinder?"

As soon as the words left his lips, she grew dizzy and nearly stumbled over. How had she missed it? She'd just thought the design of the tomb an odd shape and had been so focused on the lines that she couldn't see the most important shape before her.

Limping to Hoth's spot, standing still so long had numbed her good leg, she saw what he was looking at. The lines intersected on the floor and the ceiling right where an imaginary sphere would touch the cylinder. Another line went around the middle of the wall. Heron wasn't sure if she wanted to hug him or kick him.

With a smirk rivaling a boastful god, Hoth made his comment: "An apology wouldn't be completely unnecessary."

"No time, remember," she said, kneeling on the cool stone, her mechanical leg making a *tink* as she set it down. After a moment of quiet examination, though she could swear she could hear Hoth grinning above her, she found the little triangle at the bottom of the sphere.

"Interesting," she said and noticing where Hoth was standing. "You might want to move."

Hoth looked at his feet before stepping to the side. He'd been right on the center of the spiral.

Using her thumb, Heron pressed on the little triangle but it didn't budge. She looked around again, confirming her suspicion.

"Hand me your sword and that rock by the watery hole and then I'll need both of you."

Heron set the rock on the triangle and balanced the sword across it. "I'll need you each to step on one side, Sepharia, you on the blade, and Hoth, you on the hilt."

"What are we doing?"

She let a little laughter bubble to her lips. The old inventor had a sense of humor. "Archimedes wrote in his journal 'Give me a place to stand on, and I will move the Earth.' I thought only that he was speaking of the importance of levers and maximizing force, but in this case, it was a clue to solve. Step on this two-sided lever, please."

At first, when Hoth and Sepharia put their weight upon the sword, nothing happened. Then a faint *click* could be heard beneath them and the little triangle of stone slipped into the earth. A moment later, a grinding sound echoed through the ground and the stone spiral fell away.

"By a jarl's balls, what is that?" asked Hoth, staring into the darkness of the hole.

"A staircase," she said, climbing to her feet with Sepharia's help. "An apology wouldn't be completely unnecessary, you know."

Hoth grunted and grabbed his sword and the lantern. Heron resisted the urge to grin.

"Let's go see what Archimedes left us."

On the walk down the spiral staircase, using Sepharia's shoulder to keep steady, the hair on her arm raised, partially due to a cold wind escaping from below and partially because of what she thought they might find.

"The air smells too fresh and cool for this to be just another room," remarked Hoth from the front.

Heron didn't know how right he was until they stepped into the chamber, a full fifty steps below Archimedes' tomb. The orange light from the lantern seemed meager compared to the vastness of the chamber. Hoth lifted the light high and still it did not even brush against the ceiling. A light squeaking sounded from somewhere above, bats, or mice even.

The rocky earth curved away from them, any steps forward would require leaning back so not to fall. A sheen of wetness formed on the stone, turning it a rich, glossy black and making it slick, a treacherous path even if she had two good feet. A patient dripping echoed in the darkness and Heron did her best to push away the choking fear that rose up in her throat, memories of the Temple of Sobek.

"There's water ahead," said Hoth before sitting on his rear and sliding down the brief incline until he reached a flatter spot. Heron matched him, coming up sore when a rock bounced off her bottom.

"Come on, Sepharia," called Hoth playfully, "I'll catch you."

Sepharia crossed her arms and replied, "I'm sure you would, but I'm going to head back up. I didn't think the stairs would go this far and I forgot the knapsack with our scrolls and writing utensils."

"Hurry back," said Heron. "We'll get started while you're gone." Then to Hoth. "Do you think this chamber goes anywhere?"

"Let me see." Hoth started fussing with the lantern, adjusting the oil and opening the slats on the other three sides until the ball of light expanded to cover the complete bottom of the bowl.

"Plato have pity," she whispered upon seeing what was in the center of the room.

"What is it?" asked Hoth.

"I don't know," she replied, "but it looks similar to the Heaven's

Mechanism, except bigger."

The Heaven's Mechanism was a device for calculating the positions of the stars and it could be placed in the back of a wagon easily. Her counting machines were much larger, but this dwarfed even those and Heron estimated it was as tall as she was with her hands stretched upward and a similar width, almost the same size as one of her pyramid blocks.

The machine, and it was clearly a machine, by the brass gearing reflecting light through the mold smeared glass case, was connected to a series of iron rods that reached up to the ceiling. Heron hoped the mold was only on the outside of the glass or the whole contraption's use might be in jeopardy, though that could be a good thing because she didn't like the placement of the rods, which were as thick as a sailor's rope and as long as four steam chariots front to back. There were six of them, one for each side of the hexagonal machine.

"What does it do?" asked Hoth breathlessly.

"Gives us the Archimedes weapon I hope, though it looks like it could bring the ceiling down on our heads by the positioning of those rods," she replied.

"What do we do with it?" he asked.

"I mean to find out," she said, realizing an immediate, but minor problem. The whole room was one big sphere, rough and natural, but the dripping water had collected around the base of the machine. A stone stair, stacked and mortared by whoever had created this place (she imagined hooded acolytes performing the work in secret, scuttling to and fro through the necropolis disguised as grave tenders), allowed one to climb to the top of the machine, where Heron assumed some way to interface with it would be found. Except Heron couldn't easily go through the water without getting her mechanical leg soaked.

"I need you to carry me over the water," said Heron.

"You're not serious, are you?" he asked.

Heron slowly shook her head. "I'm about as excited about it as you are, but just do it, unless you want to carry me back to your ship when my leg gears seize up."

"First, my armor goes. I dislike this Roman-make and it unbalances me."

In a few smooth maneuvers that made Heron jealous, the sea captain unbuckled his chest plate and shrugged off the bulk to unceremoniously clatter onto the ground. He put his arm out and Heron stepped close. He lifted her easily, one hand under her knees and the other supporting her back. His musky odor tightened her nipples against the binding, but she tried to remember all the ways he annoyed her so it would go away.

As he strode into the water, he remarked, "What are those straps around your thighs and waist?"

"The crocodile," was all she said, but it was enough, he nodded and foraged ahead. Thankfully, the water wasn't deep, maybe up to his knees and she was on solid stone before long.

Rather than risk falling, Heron crawled up the stairs, her metal leg skipping off the stone each time she lifted her thigh as the straps didn't support that direction well. When walking, the motion of the leg felt smooth, or at least not as bad as a wooden leg, but crawling, the leg felt like a weight was tied to her foot.

By the time she reached the top, her hands, knees, and feet (one flesh and one mechanical) were covered in a brownish-green slime that gave off the faint aroma of vinegar. Heron barely started to clean off her hands when she spied the top of the Archimedes machine and gasped.

"Now what?" asked Hoth as he climbed the steps.

"It's an ostomachion puzzle, or primarily a treatise on combinatorics involving dissection puzzles," she said, remembering her thoughts from above.

"By a jarl's balls, speak plainly."

"A little known mathematical sect from Archimedes' writings, that I fortunately am familiar with, though faintly through his journal." She put a hand to her chin thoughtfully. "He wrote briefly about a particularly vexing problem which he never said if he solved, but I suppose I shall have to determine as such."

A male voice, booming in from the entrance, startled them, "Then we're quite fortunate, because I know nothing about it, but I do have something to motivate you to solve it."

Standing at the entrance, holding a squirming Sepharia with one arm around her waist and a knife to her throat was Philo's brother, Apion. Stepping into the chamber behind him were six soldiers including the three they had fooled above.

TWENTY FOUR

The trail of dust followed them through the low-set and ravine-filled hills, appearing as a brown mist snake rising into the afternoon sun. Jarngard, back against the vibrating iron box of the mechanical, watched his raiding party fade behind them.

He'd charged one of the ex-Romans to lead them back, going slow enough that the horse-drawn wagons filled with the fallen could keep up. He'd also instructed them to leave those bodies and make for the Damascus camp. While there'd been no signs of the Parthian cataphracts, Jarngard didn't trust them not to hit a small band like theirs.

The gold was safely on his steam mechanical. Agog would welcome the funds, since they were low, and had borrowed heavily from the Kushites to keep the steam mechanicals in production. Every day a new one rolled into camp, though they were running out of capable nobles to pilot them.

Cresting a hill, the line of black smoke from Damascus came into view. The siege was either underway or over. Jarngard prayed to the northern gods it was over since he hated going over walls or up cliffs, head exposed to enemy rocks or burning oil the whole way.

When he reached camp, Agog was coming to greet him in the yards. The King had a jovial smile which either meant the siege had gone well or Jarngard was about to be sent on another task.

"Lose something?" asked Agog, as the cooling steam pot ticked.

Jarngard rocked the chest and coins clinked together. "Figured you needed this more than that city up there and it felt like the Parthians were going to show up at any moment."

"The city's mine now," said Agog. "They tried to call Vestalis' bluff only to find out it wasn't a bluff. Not sure I've ever seen a gate crumple away like that before. Looked like the world serpent had hit it with its tail."

"Remember, Wodanaz, I've never seen the world serpent," said Jarngard.

Agog nodded, his eyes twinkling with the mention of his other name. "I forget that sometimes. I'd like to forget it myself."

Jarngard hopped down, dust springing up from the impact of his heels in the dirt. He held an arm up to block the reflection of sunlight on the copper shields at the fronts of dozens of waiting steam mechanicals.

"Iron boats. Ghost-driven wagons. Metal throats that spit fire and earth." Jarngard shook his head. "What kind of war do we wage now?"

"The winning kind, I hope," replied Agog and Jarngard took a second look at his friend, his King. He had a hungry look, not a dog with ribs showing hungry, but hungry like a beast in the woods draped in shadow.

"I heard a name recently," said Agog.

Jarngard nodded. "I've heard it as well. Did it fly here on raven's wings?"

Agog gave him a grim smile. "A man who earns a name in battle shouldn't be surprised when it reaches his ears."

"*Geri*. It has such an ugly ring to it."

"I rather like the old tongue. Would you prefer Ravenous One?" asked Agog.

"I would prefer to leave this war behind me and head to parts unknown. I weary." Jarngard touched the leather bag around his neck, which drew a creasing of the eyes from Agog.

"You've said that many times, my friend, but this time I believe you mean it. What changed? Have you met a woman?" asked Agog earnestly.

Jarngard couldn't help but smile. "No," he lied, thinking of Heron's relentless mouth against his, "but maybe I will on the road." He sensed another question so he asked one of his own. "Where do we go after Damascus?"

"North and then north again. We'll follow the Euphrates until we meet the mountains near Karkemish."

"Isn't that where the Romans want us?"

Agog nodded. "Unless we can reach that ground before them. If not, we'll head west and sack Antioch to keep them from flanking or attacking our supply lines. With the spoils of Damascus added to our treasury, we should be able to sustain the war until then."

"What if we reach Karkemish and find the Romans waiting for us, ready to smash our lines?" asked Jarngard.

Agog rubbed his beard absently, grunting with thought. "We must keep them in the north. If they make it much further south, they can flank us and head for Alexandria. If we can beat them there at first clash, then we can march on Rome and have their empire by spring."

"You would risk a winter mountain march?"

"I would risk everything," replied Agog.

"And they call me Ravenous One."

The heavy thrum of Manticores stopped them, arms raised to block the glare, while the officer Jarngard had left in charge hopped off the mechanical and jogged up and saluted them crisply.

Jarngard noted the fresh blood on the officer's arm. "A fight?"

A nod. "Ambushed by Romans with crossbows. The Manticores made short work of them."

"Any losses?"

"Just a few of the volunteers, no one of note," responded the officer.

A terrible knot formed in his gut. "Take me to them."

The officer hesitated, before nodding and leading them to the steam chariots in the back where the rest of the regiment was filing off the vehicles. Jarngard tasted dust and coal, spitting twice, while Agog gave him a careful look as he followed behind.

Jarngard recognized the shield strap hanging from the belt upon approach. One eye had been knocked open by the bouncing vehicle, so Jarngard smoothed it closed with his fingertips, resting his hand on the Egyptian boy's forehead when he was done. It was the young soldier that had dared to call him *Geri*.

"Too young," whispered Jarngard.

"As young as we were for our first battle," replied Agog. "The only difference is we survived."

"We survive and survive and survive, and leave behind a great field of bodies," said Jarngard, still touching the boy soldier. "You're right, O' King of Kings, I've earned my name. Earned it a thousand times over on the backs of dead soldiers like this one."

"You'll earn it again soon enough," said Agog solemnly. "We march north in the morning."

TWENTY FIVE

Friend Conon, should this message reach you, know that I placed your friend-ship in the highest order, and your advice among the greatest of thinkers, including yours upon last message to not despair...

— A Letter to Conon of Samos from Archimedes

"I wondered if I'd see you again, *Michanikos*," said Apion, still gripping Sepharia by the shoulder. The point of the dagger nicked her chin and a rivulet of blood ran down her neck, bringing chills to Heron, who not-ed Sepharia's hardened eyes and wondered what sort of things happened while she was a captive of Prince Vima. Heron grit her jaw and promised herself that wouldn't happen again, though she feared she would be unable to keep that promise under the circumstances.

"I guess it's fortunate that I didn't kill you in Alexandria since this tomb has vexed me for quite some time," continued Apion. "Though it might have soothed my brother's ghost to do so. He always hated you."

The resemblance to his brother, Philo, wasn't as strong as she remembered, but he did have the same Roman nose and simpering grin that put an ache in her jaw.

"I did nothing to him," responded Heron. "He was jealous of my designs."

"In his letters, he would tell me it was the other way around," said Apion. "I can only assume you had a part in his death when Alexandria was overthrown, so now these circumstances give me great pleasure. When we're done here, I'm going to make sure you live a long and painful life in Rome."

"It's not going to help. I won't give you the Archimedes weapon no matter how much you torture me," said Heron sticking her chin out. "I don't fear that any longer."

Apion handed Sepharia to a soldier, cupping her short hair appreciatively and wiping the blood away from her neck with his thumb, taking his time, while Sepharia watched him coldly.

"You're quite inventive," said Apion. "Cutting the hair of the Northman and your daughter. Hiding your metal limbs behind armor. I'll have to admit it was chance that brought us here at this time. Frustrated by the lack of information in the journal, I thought I might commune with the dead, you know, read the book in the presence of his old, desiccated bones."

He turned back to his soldiers and the trio from above dipped their heads in shame. "I would have thought the *Michanikos* easy to spot. Our spy in Alexandria gave precise descriptions of this group which in turn, I gave to my soldiers. I applaud your ingenuity." He clapped his hands lightly, inclining his head in their direction.

A knot formed in her stomach at mention of the spy and that the leaving of Alexandria had not been as secret as they thought. She could see Hoth fuming already and knew the name on his lips: Vestalis. Heron still trusted the ex-Roman soldier, but she promised herself, should they get out of this situation, that she would be more wary in the future.

"But torture you?" asked Apion. "No. I wouldn't do that. The tale of your survival, including the horrific loss of your limbs has reached even Rome. How the people marvel, speaking even at the parties our dear Claudius has thrown, about the Machine Man, and the wonders of his inventions and the man himself. No. Claudius would have me killed for harming you, not that I would anyway." He held his hands up to the room around them. "Though what irony it would be to do so in the tomb of Archimedes, the last great inventor to die mistakenly by a foolhardy soldier?"

He winked. "I do not suppose I could break you even if I tried. For whoever did that to you and then tried to feed you to a crocodile, they failed, if by the gods' intervention that they were not done with you yet."

Though it didn't change her situation, she noted the lack of Rome's involvement in her capture by Lysimachus. He was truly mad as she believed at the time, mad for his crocodile god.

Apion glanced back to Sepharia and her heart sunk. She knew what he was going to say next. Hoth must have guessed too, because he moved down one step and rested his fingertips against the leather wrapping of his hilt, the muscles in his arm rippling like a cobra.

"I wouldn't," said Apion, shaking his head at the Northman. "No. I cannot kill or injure the Machine Man, even if the gods would allow it, but I do have the next best thing. His daughter. How long can you sustain her screams until you give in?"

Apion whirled around, slicing his hand through the air in a wide arc until it connected with Sepharia's cheek. The impact echoed through the spherical chamber and bats squealed from their homes, flapping and disappearing down some ancient unseen crack.

The dead look returned by Sepharia was unnerving. She spat a bloody wad at his chest and he hammered her again, this time using the back of his hand. Each slap made Heron ball her fist, ghost fingers on the missing hand aching with the need to wrap around a throat.

When Hoth took another step, Apion pulled a blade from the nearest soldier and rested the razor sharp edge between her breasts.

"I'm sure you're a fearsome fighter in the North, whoever you are," said Apion to Hoth, "but no man, no matter how skilled, is a match for six soldiers in armor. Throw down your weapon or I'll plunge this into her gut."

Hoth glanced back as if to apologize and set his blade on the last step above the water.

"Now that we have that out of the way," said Apion quite emphatically, "let me tell you how this will unfold, as it seems the gods have seen fit to lay you at my feet and I shall not want to disappoint them. Your daughter's well-being here is the price for your knowledge. Unless you'd like to see my men rape her repeatedly while you watch, I suggest you busy yourself on Archimedes' puzzle. *When* you are successful solving it and somehow receiving this second mystery weapon, I will give back your daughter unharmed."

Heron shook her head. "How can I trust you not to kill us after the exchange is made?"

The simpering grin returned and Heron knew she wouldn't like the answer. "You shouldn't trust me at all. I plan on killing them and taking you captive once we've traded your daughter for the weapon, but our deal will be concluded and it'll be as a fair of fight that you can deserve. If this *barbarian* can win against six seasoned Legion soldiers, so be it."

Hoth turned and she knew by the look in his eyes that the deal offered was the best they could get. Heron took in the whole chamber, the rods reaching up to the ceiling and the Archimedes device behind her, inhaling the contradictory smells of fresh water and mold, pushing away the despair trying to leech into her bones, realizing her best chance was to solve the puzzle. Maybe she could figure a way to turn the situation to their advantage by then.

And part of her, though she felt a bit of shame for even thinking it, relished the idea of matching her wits against a puzzle of her mentor's making and if the battle came first, she would lose out on the chance before she most likely died.

"I accept your deal," said Heron. "Now leave me be."

"Grand! Oh, I cannot wait to tell the Senators and nobles of Rome, how I watched the great *Michanikos* tackle the wit of Archimedes."

"Your silence is requested," growled Heron as she resumed her spot at the top step.

Hoth joined her at the top step and whispered under his breath: "Can you figure this?"

She glanced askew and raised an eyebrow. "Can you beat six?"

"The terrain favors me, but the one in back has a crossbow," he said. "I can't dodge that."

"If it comes to fighting, use me as a shield. They want me alive to keep as a pet in Rome," she said. "Though I hope to figure another way out before then."

From over her shoulder she heard Apion call out, "I'm waiting."

Hoth took his spot at the third step and Heron poured her attention into the scene before her: a flat surface with a collection of shapes, mostly triangles, long and stretched, and short and squat, etched into the brass. Part of the device was obscured by the brownish-green slime. Heron dragged a finger through a section, the substance was cool to the touch, and it came away easily, though filling the underside of her fingernail like a shovel in wet mud.

"May I have a cloth from the knapsack," she called back to Apion. "It's covered." She held up her finger as proof.

Apion directed one of the soldiers to bring the requested item and once she had the section of cloth, Heron wiped the grime from the surface, careful not to disturb any hidden buttons or levers, which was fortunate because once she was done, she realized there was a series of tumblers by her knees. On each tumbler, and there were four of them, a Roman number was stamped into the face. Peering through the glass on the side, she could see other numbers and she assumed she could designate the answer by adjusting the tumblers in a way similar to her counting machine. If she got the answer right, she would receive the weapon, if not, she guessed the ceiling might fall on their heads, judging by the rods.

The challenge of combinatoric puzzles was not like most puzzles, simply finding the sole answer. In this case, she must determine the number of ways the answer could be found, which meant there would most likely be more than one. The tumbler went up to ten-thousand, which meant that she had only ruled out the numbers one and zero, leaving too large a number to just guess.

But combinations of what? On second glance, she found the answer. On the front of the device, right above the last step of wet stone, a simple square was etched into the front. Careful not to trip any tumblers or knock the lever that put the machine in motion, Heron crawled across the front and made sure there were no other shapes on any other sides.

Content there were no other aspects of the puzzle, Heron cleaned the remainder of the grime, feeling like a priest attending to an altar the whole while. Curious, Heron crouched over the steps and peered into the glass for sign of the weapon and to confirm her expectations for the device. As she suspected, the lever was connected to the rods by way of a stepping gear, pulling them from their positions in the ceiling.

"Hold the lantern up," she directed Hoth.

When the light kissed the ceiling, her guess was confirmed by a wetness around one of the rods. A patient dribble ran down the length of the steel that appeared once coated and now the corruption revealed itself as a thin orangish line on the underside.

"Problems?" asked Apion and she caught the hint of worry in his voice as he glanced upward to where she'd been looking.

"Failure would appear to be quite catastrophic." She nodded upward. "Any mistake will bring the ceiling on our heads."

The soldiers collectively took a step backwards and Apion, after a moment of introspection, did the same, looking almost apologetic for his cowardice.

Heron let a smile trickle to her lips as she returned to the puzzle. She wasn't sure how her little lie would help quite yet, but it didn't hurt to plant some seeds. The ceiling would not fall as she said, but instead, the rods would remove plugs holding back a great aquifer and flood the chamber. One of them had worked loose already.

Heron suspected that was the source of the water in the tomb excavation. Outside the tomb she'd seen scaffolding. Apion probably thought to dig around the tomb to find any hidden chambers, but only found water.

It didn't change their situation much, but water rather than a hill full of rocks on their heads seemed more inviting.

Heron took one last look at the machinery inside the box. Though it was hard to see, the opaque glass hid much, it appeared something rested in the center of the machine. Following the connections of the gears, she determined that once she actuated the lever, the machine would grind through its paces and either pull the rods or reveal the weapon, hidden comfortably in the center. She considered bashing through the side and bypassing the puzzle, but she figured that might bring the rods down, and she relished the idea of the solving it. Brute force was not her way.

"How many ways can I make the square shape from those triangles?" she whispered to herself.

"What?" asked Hoth from behind her.

"Nothing," she said. "Wait. While you stand guard, look around the chamber and see what you can see."

"What am I looking for?"

"I don't know," she replied. "But if it's important, you'll know it."

Kneeling on the last step, Heron leaned over the puzzle, imprinting the shapes into her mind. She rested one hand, palm down and flat against the cool brass surface. The other, the metal one, couldn't provide support, especially if the delicate rod in the middle was missing, so she let it hang uncomfortably by her side.

There were fourteen pieces total, all but three of them triangles in a collection of different shapes: isosceles, oblique, obtuse, scalene, rights, acute, and an equilateral. The last three were four, four, and five sided.

Heron stared at the shapes, thinking of the difficulty of her task. Even with the proper equipment: a writing table, measuring devices, plenty of papyrus on which to work through the theorem; it would take weeks or months to solve this problem. Just rotating the shapes in her mind and finding possible solutions wasn't enough and that was the challenge with combinatoric puzzles. The underlining theory had to be understood so all possibilities could be calculated.

A quick glance told her Apion wouldn't wait that long. His foot tapped impatiently while he picked at his fingernails.

She had to find a shortcut, or a clue in his writings. She didn't have to figure out the answer, if he'd written it down, but despite her thorough knowledge of everything Archimedes, nothing came to mind.

Closing her eyes, the shapes floated into view, like wooden versions floating on a pool of black water. As a child, her twin was better at the game that she was, always making humorous shapes out of the pieces. Her mind's eye pushed the pieces around, floating and drifting, occasionally connecting. She saw a few shapes after some effort: elephant, sword, and domus; though none of those were a square, the shape necessary to solve the puzzle.

In the darkness of her mind, the patient, time-keeping drip of water from the rod into the small pool surrounding the machine, woke something inside her. No longer was she busy at solving Archimedes' puzzle. She was back in the chamber beneath the Temple of Sobek, breath catching in her throat, darkness invading her skin and the wet, scraping shuffle of slow feet.

The sensation of a great scaly beast rising out of the water tattooed itself on her back and she flashed her eyes open and gasped, heartbeat thudding through her like escaping feet on shifting earth.

She wasn't back in the Temple, she told herself, though the primal part of her said otherwise. She was in a different chamber and though her mortal life was in danger, death would be relatively quick and the chance for escape, however small, was still there.

The puzzle. She had to solve the puzzle. But how could she solve the puzzle if the darkness brought fear? Or if trying to calculate the answer would take too long?

Staring at the shapes, she saw them form into a crocodile. She heard Lysimachus' voice, taunting her about the power of fear to spur creation.

She shook away the vision, pieces snapping back into their places and tried to reform them into a square. Surprisingly, she found a possible combination, though she had no way to test, since the pieces were only in her mind, but the number one, was something she already knew, if only by logic.

"Puzzles," she whispered. "Why this puzzle?"

The initial anticipation she had for this dilemma had turned to frustration. Why would Archimedes want this puzzle to protect his second weapon? It seemed nigh unfigurable, or was it just her circumstances that brought on this anguish?

"I won't wait forever," called Apion, his voice echoing through the chamber. "If you can't solve it soon, I'll just kill the girl and Northman, and haul you back to Rome. I'm sure a team of Roman scholars would solve it quickly enough."

"Quiet!" she yelled out. "You're disturbing my thoughts and I am close to the answer."

She didn't bother looking to see Apion's reaction. She remembered Philo's tendencies well enough to guess. He probably had his arms crossed with a creased frown on his lips.

"Are you?" whispered Hoth.

"Not unless you've found the answer within the chamber..."

Her mind whirled with sudden possibilities, an answer, though perilous if she was wrong. She barely heard Hoth speak, quickly deciding it did not matter, yet.

"I found one thing, but I'm not sure how it will help us," said Hoth.

"It can wait," she said, trying to decide if she was deluding herself.

She closed her eyes. "Apion."

"There'd better not be a delay," he replied.

"The first weapon," she said, ignoring the threat. "How did you know to visit his tomb?"

Apion was quiet and she decided he was thinking about whether or not he wanted to tell her, but she knew the lure of the second weapon and praise from Emperor Claudius would prevail.

Finally, he spoke, bringing a secret smile to her lips. "The text in the other chamber mentioned instructions for his death. That's why I went to Alexandria to get the journal. How did you know to come here?"

"I guessed," she replied honestly. "Though it felt right and the instructions in his journal always seemed odd to me. I just didn't know why until the knowledge of the three weapons came to light."

"Since when does the great *Michanikos* rely on his gut feeling?" asked Apion.

She thought about telling him that she was Alexander the Macedonian's true heir and that she'd learned from him that in times of peril, the gut, built on a foundation of skill and knowledge, was the only thing to go on. She'd learned in his temple in Old Babylon that too much thinking often led to the wrong result, mostly because it was couched in fear rather than reason. The gut knew nothing of fear. But that information was secret and she planned on escaping so it was knowledge she didn't want to give.

"I didn't," said Heron. "I calculated it based on the information at hand. Just like I've calculated the answer to this combinatoric puzzle, as well as the method of our escape."

The soldiers laughed nervously, while Apion's brow knotted with furious thought.

"Your humor is not appreciated," said Apion, while the rest looked on. Even Sepharia and Hoth gave her strange looks, not understanding the hopeful chain of events flowing through her mind.

Rather than answer, she turned to the tumblers and clicked the rightmost two until they showed the numbers she believed was the answer. Then with no more flourish than a craftsman hammering a nail, she pulled the lever.

Apion clearly had not expected her to be so quick about it and the sound of boots scrambling toward the exit bounced around the chamber. Gears inside the machine ground together, long unused, the lubricants long since dried up. Heron wondered if the machine would work at all when the whole platform vibrated from something unstuck.

Water came more freely from the one rod, the long drips turning to a stream. Heron wondered if her correct answer was doomed to the age of the machine, but she didn't have to wonder much longer when something popped and gearing clacked through its paces.

To Heron's surprise, a door on the top flipped open, and a piece of bronze, etched with Latin, rose out of the machine. Apion gasped from the edge of the chamber, and Hoth whistled in amazement.

When the machine stopped, the final gear making an audible and slightly vibrating *clack*, Heron let her breath out.

"What was the final answer?" asked Apion softly. "And how did you figure it so quickly?"

"Twenty-three," she said, but she hadn't figured it at all. The answer, as she'd first suspected, had been given by Archimedes and was displayed prominently on his tomb in the form of 2:3, the ratio of the sphere and cylinder. As a mathematician, she had automatically read it as 2:3, rather than the number 23. Had it been a slash between them, the typical notation for division, she might not have guessed it, but the other symbol was used in other affairs than mathematics and sometimes denoted important information.

"I'm afraid my methodology is not easily explainable to anyone but maybe Archimedes himself," she said.

"It doesn't matter. Only the second weapon matters. Bring it to me and I'll give back your daughter," he demanded.

"I'm afraid I cannot," said Heron, "for the plate is connected to the machine, but if you throw me the knapsack, I can place a parchment over the letters and give you a suitable charcoal etching."

Apion nodded to one of the soldiers, the one who'd distrusted them above, and Heron's stomach briefly flipped. The soldier grabbed the knapsack unceremoniously, marched to the edge of the water, and threw it over, much to Heron's relief. Hoth deftly caught it and handed it to her.

Heron pulled the paper and coal from the knapsack, leaving it slightly open with a simple latched container at the top. It was filled with dust, but not the dust she dined on regularly. This was a different powder, one she wanted to experiment with on their journey.

Smearing coal onto the parchment to transfer the words took too little time, and Heron only briefly mused on the importance of the information, not quite understanding since her mind was on what would happen next, but the hints of giant, segmented machines that snaked across the earth drilled firmly into her mind, ready to birth ideas later, when she had time.

With the information transferred, Heron rolled it up and handed the scroll to Hoth.

"We're ready to exchange," said Heron.

While Hoth moved to the bottom step, Heron feigned at imbalance and steadied herself on the lever. The soldier with Sepharia, after sliding down the slope, pushed her near the edge of the water and reached out his hand. The pool was wide enough that Hoth had to slide the scroll over his sword and hang it out. Once the soldier grabbed the scroll, Sepharia leapt into the water, and started wading through to their island.

Apion gave a nod to the soldiers and they began to move down, using each other to traverse the difficult terrain. The one in back with the crossbow lifted it, carefully sighting them.

Apion shrugged and stepped to the passageway. "Kill the girl and the Northman."

While the exchange was being made, using her sandal, Heron adjusted the tumblers, changing the number. She wasn't entirely certain this was going to work since she couldn't fully see the internal pieces of the machine, but she guessed enough that it might.

With the numbers changed, Heron threw the lever, which froze the soldiers in their advance, gladii pointed in their direction. Nothing happened at first and then she felt the machine shudder like a great weight was being dropped. Somewhere below the machine, there was a splash.

The crossbowman hesitated while everyone, including Sepharia and Hoth stared at the ceiling. The five soldiers near the water started backing way. Heron used the opportunity to grab the box from the knapsack, unlatch it and toss it over the heads of the first soldiers to hit the crossbowman directly in the chest.

She couldn't have made a better shot. The box exploded dust in his face and in seconds, he began to scream. Heron, intent on experimenting with the quicklime, had brought some.

When the first rod fell away, some of the soldiers dropped their swords and they began scrambling up the slope. Sepharia had made the island and was climbing up the steps with Hoth's help.

Nothing happened from the first rod and Heron wondered if she'd misguessed their purpose, but when the second rod fell away and a torrent of water came streaming out like a river unleashed, Heron knew she was right.

But when a slab of stone fell into place at the entrance, narrowly missing Apion, who dove back onto the stairs and into safety, she realized pulling the lever might have been a mistake.

TWENTY SIX

It is my humble shame that the origin of my great discovery on buoyancy came when my apprentices threatened to leave my service unless I took a bath.
-- The Journal of Archimedes

The spray of water was a hailstorm of needles blasting into the unprotected flesh of her good arm and face. A bone-freezing chill from the water long hidden from the sun rattled its way up and down her spine. Heron clung to the lever, her sight obscured.

The screaming Roman soldier still went on, his voice barely piercing the thunderous waterfalls. The hole above her had been pinched by a rock or some obstruction and the water fanned out, covering the whole bottom half of the spherical cavern. The second hole was larger and a pillar of water connected the floor to the ceiling. Already the water was waist deep around the mechanical cube.

Sepharia scrambled up the slippery stone steps, clinging to Heron as she stood upright, holding her arm over her face. A gash in her tunic was dyed red, though it was quickly running pink.

"Your side," shouted Heron.

"It's fine," Sepharia put her lips near Heron's ear and shouted, "I fell on a rock."

Through the battering cacophony of waterfall, steel made bright noises like flashes of lightning. The unencumbered sea captain danced across the slippery floor - looking like the barnacled back of a whale - slicing and slashing with a deadly glee.

The Romans, unused to wet rock and wearing heavy scale armor, hobbled around laying their swords out only to have them knocked away. Heron couldn't see well, but she saw enough to know the Romans were doomed.

Hoth scampered around the bowl, leaping rocky upthrusts and bands of screed, before doubling back and slipping his blade through feeble weak-wristed blocks. None of the soldiers bothered with Heron and the only scare came when the screaming Roman was finally able to wash the powder away enough to lift his crossbow again. Hoth froze, but when the string broke, he threw his dagger into the man's neck. The quicklime, reacting with the water, had weakened the string.

The last soldier, the one wearing the heaviest armor, Hoth pushed into the pool surrounding their perch and nothing more was seen but the occasional flailing arm breaking the surface and then nothing.

"Your limbs," shouted Sepharia. "You'll drown."

Heron cursed her immobility and began unbuckling the straps and ties that held her mechanical limbs in place. The water had swollen the leather and she struggled to unlatch them with slippery fingers. The water crested the edge of the platform as Hoth climbed up.

When they were suddenly plunged into night, Heron felt fear escape her lips. The water had risen above the edge of the lantern and snuffed out the flame.

With vision gone, the darkness reigned, bringing the memory of stumbling through the water in the Temple of Sobek, the great jeweled Nile crocodile on her heels. She froze, no longer unbuckling and swayed against Sepharia, expecting the sheer of jagged teeth to close around her thigh. Her ribs felt exposed, her neck felt the warm breath of Petsuchos, even though the water was ice.

The water was at her waist.

Hoth shouted something, but the words couldn't penetrate. Sepharia was diving beneath the water, still working at her mechanical leg.

When it fell away, bringing the cold bite against the pink flesh at the end of her stump, she was reminded of her brokenness. Of the violence against her. The pain of precious limbs being snipped off like dead leaves.

Water tickled her chin.

Sepharia was tugging at her arm. Heron considered opening her mouth and letting the water rush in. Letting it consume her before the great scaly bulk that she *knew* was in the water, found her and set its teeth to her ribs.

The arm fell away. She felt it bounce off her leg and then to where, unknown. Lost, as she.

She couldn't see. The cascade of water drowned out all attempts to communicate with her. The water should have felt icy and maybe she realized her distant body was shivering, but instead she felt drowned in a delirious warmth.

When the water passed her lips, there was a tug upward, or to the side, she'd lost sense of direction in the darkness. A hand pulled at her tunic, splashing through the water, until they stopped.

It was quieter there. Her head bobbed against the stone.

Heron pushed away, ducking her head under the surface of the water, but stronger hands held her fast.

She knew the muscular arms holding her were Hoth's, but part of her wished they were Jarngard's, so she could die in his grasp as the water filled the chamber.

Heron knew she should fight, but it seemed that spark was quenched. The despair from the Temple, the months she was in its sucking womb, came back in full, demolishing her solid walls until she was as she'd been there, wishing for death.

Giving up was cathartic. She felt the weights of existence lift from her limbs, there and not-there. The agonizing ever-vigilance of hiding her gender, puff into hoary smoke. The grind of fighting for her vision, of pushing and pulling and yanking, dragging others along whether they wanted to come or not, fade to dust.

Death made a home in her heart.

Freed of the worries of mortal existence, Heron found surprise at her response. Though she had despised the gods and all their trappings, Heron had harbored doubts that she could face the end without wishing to call upon their might for eternal life in whatever strange lands they promised to lord over.

No.

Their hooks and barbs were not pressed into her skin. She'd seen the inner machinery of the temples, the greedy priests and the constant press for coin. Their truths were not her truths.

Set apart, Heron wondered at her feelings for Jarngard. She loved and lusted for him, to feel him inside her, wrapped around her, to embrace her femininity. Yet. These feelings did not pluck at her strings, playing a tune that would rouse her from the cold embrace of the grave. She was content to have loved and only regretted that each of them didn't have a second lifetime in which she might fly away with Jarngard to lands unseen.

The real pluck and barb was in her machines. Not as gears and levers and pullies, but as solutions to society's burdens. And that's where her spark had hidden, not quenched, but compressed.

Even as the water sapped heat, she felt the spark kindle in her chest. So many challenges yet unmet. So many problems, clinging to civilization like a cancer of Gordian knots.

And in that moment, as Heron realized the deafening sound of water no longer filled her ears, she took a deep and cleansing breath. Like a finely tuned machine that had a burr shaved from a central gear, making an audible *tick*! as it restarted, Heron felt consciousness flow back into her limbs. Parts of her that had been scrambled before, had been realigned, and what that meant, she could only hazard a guess.

"We're alive," Heron breathed.

"Most importantly, you're alive," said Hoth, from behind her. "Though we weren't certain for a while there."

"I'm glad you're back," said Sepharia, and the pain and worry came through her daughter's voice.

A hand touched her shoulder, and Heron squeezed it.

"I..." Heron paused and an essential truth of her welled up in her chest she wanted to tell Hoth the truth of her gender. "I'm sorry to have scared you."

The words were cowardly, but she couldn't quite do it. Yet. Heron reoriented herself using their voice. She found the wall with her good hand and clung, though Hoth kept his grip on her tunic.

"The chamber didn't fill completely," she realized out loud.

"And it drains slowly," said Sepharia, "though we don't know how."

She remembered. "The bats. There must be a crack in the stone."

"Hopefully big enough to let all the water out, otherwise we're trapped here," said Hoth.

"We'll freeze to death before long," shivered Sepharia. "I'm so cold."

Strangely, Heron was numb and that worried her. Maybe the missing limbs affected the feeling of cold somehow. She left her observation unsaid so not to worry them.

"Can you cling to the stone alone?" asked Hoth. "If so, I can circle the edge of the water looking for where it escapes."

"With Sepharia's help, I can. You go. I'll manage," she said.

When his hand left her, Heron bobbed into the water, catching a mouthful. She hadn't realized how much he'd been holding her up until he'd let go.

Hoth wasn't gone long and when he returned, he sounded despondent. "The crack isn't wide enough for us to fit through, though it does go down to the floor, or at least near the floor. It's hard to dive in the dark."

"We'll wait."

Sepharia's teeth chattered and Heron hoped they could wait long enough.

As the water receded, they worked themselves down the wall. Heron was tired, and the cold turned her muscles into rocks. If they hadn't the wall to cling to, they would have succumbed to the depths long before the water went down.

When it seemed it would drain no more, or was draining too slowly for them to notice, they edged along the wall until they found a ledge to stand on. Hoth went exploring again and came back after a long while.

"I think we can get out. The stone door cracked when it came down and I kicked it a few times and it moved. A little more work and we may escape," said Hoth.

Sepharia made a little noise and Heron grabbed her by the shoulder and shook, which unbalanced her into the deeper water. After a moment, with Sepharia's help, Heron clung to the wall again.

"I'm fine," said Sepharia, but Heron didn't believe her. They had to get out soon or the cold would get them.

It took a few minutes for the sea captain to break through the cracked stone. Heron was thankful that Hoth was so adept in the water, since the pair of them could barely swim under the best of circumstances.

"The hole is big enough to fit through, though you have to dive into the water," said Hoth, teeth chattering a little.

"Your limbs," said Sepharia. "They're in the water still. We'll need them."

"The water has damaged them. They probably won't move again," said Heron.

"I'll get them," said Hoth. "Maybe you can work your sorcery on them and get them working. We'll have time."

There was a heavy splash as Hoth dove towards the center.

"Let's go through while he finds them," said Heron, worried.

Sepharia didn't protest and helped Heron scrambled down the wall to the hole. With only one hand to maneuver, Heron got stuck momentarily, causing a bit of panic, but eventually she was able to kick through the hole and into the warmer air of the stairwell.

Heron climbed onto the steps and waited for Sepharia to appear. Sitting out of the water was almost colder and when Sepharia joined her, they both set to shivering.

She got worried when Hoth didn't appear for a long time. Sitting in the darkness made time drag out and when finally he splashed into the chamber, Heron breathed a sigh of relief.

He had her metal limbs, as useless as they probably were now, but she put that out of her mind and with Sepharia's shoulder supporting her, hopped up the fifty or so steps to Archimedes' tomb.

They didn't bother taking the armor they had brought with them, leaving it on the etched floor, and went straight out, after Hoth checked for guards.

Worried about patrols, and too cold to stop moving, they stumbled through the necropolis, and up a path until they found a section of grass and fell upon it. Lying there, they caught their breath and watched as the sun slowly came up.

A night. A whole night in the darkness.

They greeted the sun with exhausted smiles, too tired to continue. They were off the main path, but well in sight, but they couldn't move. A cramp seized Heron's calf around the same time Hoth reached for his thigh.

It wasn't until they were bathed in sunlight, warmth trickling back into their limbs that they felt well enough to move, the spasms having subsided, or having been banished by light.

Preparing to move, Heron began the laborious process of putting her mechanical leg back on. It wouldn't work like before, but would keep her from falling over or having to hop all the way back to the iron ship.

"By Freya's frigid tits," cursed Hoth suddenly.

"What?" asked Heron and her daughter simultaneously, looking up from the buckles.

"The weapon," said Hoth. "Apion has Archimedes' second weapon and he'll probably know where to find the third. We've failed completely."

For the first time in a long while, Heron felt a smile christen her lips. "Not completely, my friend. Not completely."

"How?" he asked.

"You *have* heard of my famed memory, right?"

TWENTY SEVEN

"War breeds ambition, Praetor Scipio."

Flags overhead snapped in the autumn breezes. Magnus cupped his hand to guard against the sun, surveying the Taurus mountains, chopped out of the sky and dotted with pines. The narrow valley wound into the distance and a line of troops marched beside the river like a twin made of glittering armor.

He'd been studying the maps for weeks and he knew the contours like the back of his eyelids. The Cilician gate led to the Cydrus river and beyond the plains of Issus - the very place Alexander the Macedonian took the world from Great King Darius - were the last of the mountains before the Mesopotamian valley.

His forehead was sore from countless nights with only flickering candles as companions, reading ancient texts written by passing scholars. He felt he knew the fields better than the shepherds, roads better than the smugglers, and the mountains better than the goats.

"What do you mean, Consul?" asked Scipio, stiff-backed as always, his dour face frowning away the sunlight, too rigid to raise a hand to block it.

"Ambition. Like flies on a field of corpses. The Legates desire - no, no, hunger for it - and will not be satisfied until their bellies are bloated with glory so they can retire in Rome and turn their ambitions to the Senate," explained Magnus.

Scipio stared back, unblinking, the creases around his eyes absent of any sun-earned glow. Magnus wasn't sure how the Praetor had kept his pale complexion on the months-long march east, but there it was, plain and white as a cow's milk. He'd taken him in hopes of loosening up the Praetor, that the dust and sunlight might break him in like a stiff saddle. He'd also taken him because of the Praetor's lack of ambition, a viewpoint that had its drawbacks, since even a modest amount of it would provide a buffer between himself and the Legates.

So instead...

Magnus sighed and continued, "By Jupiter's balls, the Legates are annoying the days from my life's thread. Especially Tiberius, that prig spends more time letting his seconds faun over him than performing as I requested. In his last message, he reported that he left the safety of the mountains and moved south to Antioch with his two Legions. I'm sorely tempted to put him over my knee, swat his bottom like an unruly child, and send him back to Rome without a command."

Even the Praetor's normally stoic façade couldn't hold back his concern. "But Tiberius is the Emperor's cousin. Claudius might take your command away."

Magnus studied Scipio's indignation, wondering if it were directed at Tiberius for putting him in this situation, or for himself, voicing such an unpolitcal maneuver. Scipio lacked ambition, but he lived by the rules of the game, including the unspoken ones, which was why he'd made it as far as Praetor, but would never go any further.

"That might be the best course for me," said Magnus. "If these Legates can't do as they're told, the whole war plan falls apart. Maybe I'll just retire on one of the Empire's islands and live out my days until the war is won or lost."

Indignation turned to horror, and Magnus flashed his second a smile to let him believe he wasn't serious. Turning away, he labored across the hardpack, trying his best not to limp, the mountain air brought out the weakness in his wounds, though it'd been his choice that brought it. The Praetor had wanted to set up camp in the valley, but Magnus preferred the view and the clean air, a polar opposite to the stifling oppression of Rome's smoky, ambition-drenched streets, even if it meant his knee ached the whole time.

"Since we both know that's not an option," continued Magnus, glancing back at Scipio. The rod in the Praetor's back seemed to have loosened slightly, which meant that it wasn't so stiff it was going to snap under its own tension. "It appears I must deal with the impetuous Tiberius, who believes this war is nothing but a parade for glory."

"Shouldn't the Legate's two Legions be enough to defeat the barbarian?" asked the dour-faced Praetor.

Magnus snorted. "Haven't you been listening to me, Praetor? The *barbarian*, as everyone seems to love to call him, has won every battle. He turned back the forward thrust of the cataphracts and steam engines through ingenuity of his own, defeated Tyre in a day - a city that resisted Alexander for nearly a year - and Damascus in a month. I have the commander in Damascus to thank for the precious time we have even now. Had he let the Alexandrians win in only a day like Tyre, they'd beat us to the mountains and Karkemish, leaving us poor second choices of terrain. The pass north of the city is not the place I want to fight my battles, but by Jupiter's own luck, Damascus was held, and we have our moment. I just need to fix this Tiberius situation first."

Magnus cast about, ignoring the pain of each step as his boot pivoted in the rocky soil. Praetor Scipio gently cleared his throat, an odd noise from an inflexible man.

"Yes?"

"Can't you just order him back to his position?" asked Scipio.

Magnus didn't so much as smile, but let his relaxed pose and silence relay the naiveté of the question. Scipio, though rigid and overly serious, was not unintelligent, and eventually came to the point Magnus wished him to.

"If you do," began Scipio, who was working through the logic as he spoke, "then Tiberius will blame any failure in battle on your orders. But if you don't, then won't the battle fail?"

"It might," said Magnus, "if I let it."

And this was the difference between himself and his peers—the Legates and those who came before him, only saw the political measure of any move, while he saw how those political ambitions could be used to benefit his strategy while not giving up his own positions.

There were times that Magnus wished he didn't have this foresight. It'd be much easier to go ignorantly into these things, relying only on his skill as a strategist. This was one of those times. While it would give him no end of pleasure to thwart Tiberius and teach him a lesson that would be clear as a bell to the rest of the Legates, he knew such a lesson would come with great loss from the legions.

That was the burden of his position. Breaking the Britons in short order so they could turn their attention to the Alexandrian uprising had resulted in too many losses. It'd been political as much as strategic. Without a victory in Briton, the Senate would not support more levies for troops to fight the Alexandrians. He sacrificed thousands of men so he could in turn, throw thousands more at their southern enemy.

Magnus rubbed his knee, the ache throbbed and it set his jaw to pulse. He knew what he had to do, he just didn't like it. Because of another glory-hunting Legate with Senatorial ambitions, he was going to have to sacrifice thousands of men.

"The Legate stuck his head out, so I'll use him as bait," said Magnus.

"Bait?" asked Scipio.

"Yes, bait. I suspect Tiberius moved to Antioch because he's heard the stories about the city, its history, its renown, and he believes a win there will capture him enough glory to return to Rome with full honors," explained Magnus. "Little does he know, the reason there are so many stories about Antioch and glory is because the city is frighteningly easy to conquer. The terrain favors the attacker and its citizens would rather not prolong a siege which usually leads to looting and raping when the siege is won, so they keep low walls and inferior defenses. Far better had he stayed in Issus or at the Amanus Pass."

"How will you use him?" asked Scipio, stepping forward, an uncharacteristic curiosity on his face. It hung there uncomfortably, as if those muscles were long unused.

Magnus tapped on his chin as he spoke, "Their Northern king, the man Agog, he will see the split of the Roman legions at Antioch as a mistake and will rightfully pounce. I will further this ruse by placing the remnants of the Parthians and one Legion near Karkemish. He will think them vulnerable without our reinforcements. The temptation to split his forces and take both armies will be strong; and I suspect a bold man like himself will want to end the war then and there before the remaining legions can impact the field."

"What will your legions do?" asked Scipio in rapt attention.

This would be the tricky part. Timing, as it always was in war, would be everything.

"Take them over the Pinarus Pass right between the two Alexandrian armies, and smash them, one, two, before turning south to retake the city for Rome." The words tasted like sweet victory in his mouth, but he choked away his anticipation, for war and men made a mockery of plans.

"But Consul Magnus," said Scipio, confused, "there *is* no Pinarus Pass."

"In war, the terrain can mean everything. Pick the right location and the outcome is almost assured. Be surprised by anything at your chosen location and watch victory turn to bitter ashes," said Magnus. "King Agog will believe that there is no way for our legions to come between the two halves of his army. He will believe that because the maps will tell him this and my scholars have assured me his maps from the Great Library are the very same we have in Rome."

"Then how do you...?" asked Scipio.

"Not every map lies in Alexandria and I have found one from an ancient scholar who was want to avoid soldiers in the old city of Khalab near the pass," said Magnus.

Scipio had lost his normal stiffness, caught up in the strategy. "You trust this map?"

"I trust it like no other," said Magnus. "It's the work of a man from Alexander's time when he returned to Greece after a falling out with Alexander. A man keen to avoid Alexander's notice."

"One of his generals?"

"No," said Magnus, smiling, "the man was Aristotle."

TWENTY EIGHT

*M*y *greatest joy, and terror, is seeing my ideas made flesh. Before the war, I could relish the discoveries in ignorance, now I watch as my success culls the Romans from the field like a bloody scythe...*
— *The Journal of Archimedes*

The air bladder stretched out across the trampled grass looking like a misshapen whale. Its waxy surface glistened in the morning dew, bubbling outward, the vast cavity filling with heated air. The scents mixed together - coal and onion grass and sea salt - creating an industrious tang that made Heron feel like she was in the workshop of the world.

"It looks like the kraken ready to give birth," said Hoth suspiciously. "And I still don't understand what we're going to do with it."

Sepharia looked on, eyes wide with curiosity. Her daughter was used to such oddities, born of the workshop, but even this one seemed to stretch Sepharia's acceptance. Behind her questioning gaze was a worry that tugged at the corners of her lips and knotted her brow.

"We're going to ride it," said Heron, scarcely believing it herself.

"How?" asked Hoth. "The Mediterranean goes no further east and I see no wheels on it. When you opened the crate, I expected a chariot."

"It's a sailing ship," she replied.

Hoth frowned. "That's no ship I've ever sailed."

Heron indicated the sky with her outstretched hand. "We're going to sail those seas up there."

The cocky swagger that was always present right beneath the surface of the sea captain drained until he was a motionless husk. Heron wasn't sure she wouldn't have gotten a worse reaction if she'd told him she was going to cut off his legs and ride him like a sled.

"By the gods of the North, I will not ride the sky," said Hoth, perfectly still.

Heron crossed her arms, the stump on her left side making her feel uneven. "Then you can take your iron ship and sail back to Alexandria. The third weapon lies that way—" She pointed to the east. "—and if we're going to beat Apion then we need to take this air ship and ride the winds east."

"But how do you steer? That woven box has no rudder and there are no oars that I can see," complained Hoth.

They were good questions, questions Heron had asked herself. She knew the design worked. Ever since the Temple of Sobek, when Lysimachus had attached her nipples to floating bags of hot gas, she knew she wanted to make a larger version.

She'd tested smaller versions at the workshop with Plutarch, at night or away from the city to not cause a panic. The air bladder rose into the sky, though not with any passengers, and as soon as she saw the tugging on the anchor rope, tugging in the direction of the wind, she knew it had limited controls. Up and down, at best.

This version hadn't yet been tested, except for the strength of the bladder. She'd meant to do so before the Romans attacked. She brought it on the trip as a last second measure, knowing they would be deep in Roman territory. She believed it would work. But when had her inventions ever worked the first time?

These were things Hoth didn't need to know, so she propped up a smile. "It works and that should be enough for you."

Hoth shook his head as if he had a mane full of hair still attached and the motion looked awkward. Heron still hadn't gotten used to the short-haired sea captain, though it appeared Sepharia had, by their nightly nuzzling on the deck of the *Gray Cetus*.

"If you can't tell me then I'm not getting in the cursed thing," said Hoth, glancing at the sky. "Who knows what gods might become jealous by our invading their realm."

"When has knowing ever stopped you?" asked Heron, trying to stand in the oratory pose of the Library, but the stump left her frustrated so she put her good hand on the remaining upper arm of the other. "Did you question a ship captain about the laws of buoyancy before you boarded his craft?"

"Ships have been sailed for thousands of years," retorted Hoth.

"And birds have flown in the sky for longer," she said. "Sepharia, tighten those anchor lines, we don't want our ship to sail without us."

The bladder was beginning to appear more roundish, the skyward side reaching upward as if it were a living thing waking to the sun. It'd been unnerving the first time she'd seen it and she was not a superstitious person.

"I'm not getting in it. I don't trust it and I don't like high places," said Hoth, staring at the air bladder like a venomous snake.

"I thought you Northerners were afraid of nothing and I think I recall a story or two about you scaling high cliffs to attack a few towns," said Heron.

Hoth paced away, putting his back to them. The waves slapped against the rocks where they'd moored the iron boat. It'd taken them a day to find a place they could haul their equipment on shore.

"Before I was captain, if I was made to be the lookout, I spent my time with my eyes closed in the eagle's nest," said Hoth, face drenched in memory. "And when I climbed those cliffs, I did so at night, so I couldn't see if I were to fall."

"But Sepharia's rescue?" asked Heron. "You climbed then."

"Fear." He shrugged. "I had no other choice. *Here*, I have a choice. I'm not getting in."

Frustrated, Heron tried another tactic. "You'd watch Sepharia ride in the basket while you stayed on the ground? I thought men were supposed to be superior to women."

Anger snarled his mouth. "She only rides because she's your daughter. You lend her your strength as a man, as her father."

Heron ground her teeth and resisted the urge to stomp her foot, for it would probably only lead to falling. She ran a hand through her short, black hair, feeling the grit and grease layered from months on the sea.

Going without him wouldn't do. She needed Hoth for the final leg of the journey. They'd been delayed on the sea outrunning Roman ships and had to forage for fuel on three occasions, one lasting two days while they stayed hidden in a Greek cove. Apion had plenty of time to beat them to the third weapon unless they could leave now. Once there, she didn't know if she'd need a sword arm to help claim the last prize.

Heron took a deep breath, the memory of revelation from the pit of water back in Syracuse flowing back into her mind. She knew a way to goad him, to convince him to join her in the air ship, and the admission would serve to loosen the rusty chains on her heart. Before she could reconsider, she let the words rush from her lips. "What if I said that I was really a woman?"

"You jest," he said, but his eyes said something different. A flash of recognition.

Sepharia was shaking her head behind him, while she mouthed denials too late.

"I never jest."

She could see it. That slow creeping recognition, but he kept shaking his head.

"You can't be a woman, you're too..." The words trailed from his lips.

"Strong? Intelligent?" she offered. "Are these the words you're looking for?"

He narrowed his eyes at her. "Manly. The lower passageways are narrow and those aren't woman parts between your legs. I've even seen you pissing off the side of the deck."

Heron lifted her tunic, exposing the wooden genitalia held by straps. Hoth marched over and grabbed it, palm up, the confusion creasing his face.

He let go and stepped back, his mouth opening and closing like a dying fish. He nearly said something two or three times before finally matching her gaze, his former incredulous disgust softened to a tortured understanding.

"I knew this," he said, "I think. I always thought it was your scholarly ways that confused me." Hoth grabbed her wrist. "Such thin, slender fingers." He touched her face and she did not flinch. "Your voice, the way it cracks high sometimes." He paused. "But your breasts...? Ahhh... the bindings. The trip to Old Babylon and your injuries. Punt knew, didn't he."

She shook her head. "He learned on the trip."

Hoth paced away, glancing back at her and to Sepharia. His brow rippled with thought.

Next to them, the air bladder had lifted from the ground, its sagging weight slowly reaching upward. Heron stared jealously at the air ship, for even its creation, a miracle by the standards of her day, could not draw away the sea captain's attention. Her path, should she choose to keep following it, would only get harder.

"Who else knows?"

"A few."

"Agog?"

She shook her head. "No."

"Jarngard?" His eyes widened even before she said. "Yes, he knows, doesn't he? I wondered why he looked at you that way. Why he was so angry that you choose me over him for this trip. You're lovers."

Of course, he would guess correctly. She blushed, feeling out of place for a moment. Only Sepharia's cheering smile kept her grounded.

"Only Sepharia, Punt, Jarngard, and yourself know, though I suspect Plutarch does as well, though he would never say anything," she said.

"So much makes sense," said Hoth, with a hand gripping his dyed black hair, showing faint lightness at the roots.

Heron stepped forward. "You can come to terms with it on our journey. We should get moving before this craft draws notice."

Hoth nodded absently and returned to their pile of belongings on the shore. The bladder was filled and straining at the ropes with the modified steam mechanical sending hot air into it. It was much quieter than the chariot version since it had no parts that slammed together and Heron was thankful, because they would ride right beneath it.

They gathered their equipment and climbed into the basket after throwing torches onto the deck of the iron boat. The deck had been coated in oil and it caught flame quickly. Heron loosed the anchor ropes and the basket lifted from the ground.

The woven bottom stretched beneath their feet and Heron clamped down on the panic flooding through her veins, thinking they would fall through. She leaned away from her mechanical leg, the weight of it keen to her senses, feeling like a lodestone pulling her down. The air bladder lifted higher in the sky and each of them clung to the sides, not trusting the stretching material at the bottom.

Quickly, they rose higher than the smoke, curling and crackling from the iron boat, bright sparks spitting into the water.

Her stomach fled and a wave of nausea passed through her. Hoth looked worse than she, with fingers digging into the basket edge, eyes wide in fear and skin pale with a greenish tint. Of the three of them, Sepharia looked most unaffected, wide eyes gazing outward, not with fear, but with wonder. Sepharia even relaxed her grip on the side after testing the strength of the weave by pushing with her foot, proving that it would hold, but also eliciting strangled gasps of concern from Hoth.

So focused on the roiling humours of her own body, Heron scarcely had time to realize how high they were, until she looked over the edge to see a distant mud house looking like a piece of cheese fallen from the table. She was no stranger to heights, having spent countless hours at the top of the Lighthouse, but this was altogether different.

On the Lighthouse of Pharos, she had the strength of stone beneath her and an architect's mind to know it would hold. While her calculations and experiments proved her air ship should work, it was as untested as her early steam mechanicals and those had been prone to exploding.

With each shift of her foot, Heron felt like she was going to slide through the gaps in the weave, even though she knew it wasn't possible. So she stopped looking down that way, finding that peering over the edge was much less terror inspiring.

Using considerable willpower, Heron unclenched her fingers from the crackling weave and wished that Sepharia had done more than lock her mechanical fingers into place, forming a claw, and had given back some function, so she could use that arm to hold herself tight without straining.

Once her emotions had calmed, Heron took a deep breath and took in the scenery. The clouds were suddenly right there above them and they passed through a layer and she felt the cool, wispy kiss on her face.

The absolute silence was unnerving. Not a rustle of leaves or bird twill to disturb the eerie quiet. Except for Hoth's incoherent mumbling, there was not another sound in the sky.

Heron couldn't keep her gaze from the earth, the blanket of green appearing to be a bed of moss rather than a vast forest. Rivers were twinkling, silvery lines snaking through the landscape. Distant mountains rose from the haze, feeling like airy companions rather than faraway destinations. Villages were no more than brown blotches in the landscape, and individual houses mere chips of gray or black amid the verdant rolling hills.

Concerned that the air ship was rising too high, Heron adjusted the speed of the air entering the bladder. The design was similar to her water pumps and more compact. The bladder rippled with the adjustment.

A slight lurch sent her stomach to flutter, eliciting more mumbling from Hoth. The air ship seemed to have settled at a particular height and Heron wished she had a parchment to make notes upon, but most of her supplies had been lost in Archimedes' tomb.

"By all the gods, old and new," said Sepharia, "it's so beautiful."

Heron smiled and squeezed her daughter's hand. Behind them, they heard a noise. Hoth was leaning over the edge of the basket, looking like he had something important to say.

Then he vomited.

TWENTY NINE

Jarngard chucked the empty wineskin into the river and leaned back in his saddle, letting the sunlight dance across the surface of his closed eyes. He couldn't remember what the tributary was called, only that it blocked the way north as the fjord was swollen with rain from the western mountains. He opened his eyes in time to watch a massive tree, ripped from some distant bank, bob through the brown, swirling waters.

He searched the saddlebag for another skin. "I thought there was another left," he mumbled to no one in particular.

Jarngard squinted behind him to see if he'd dropped it, but the thick underbrush grabbed at his mount's calves and would have swallowed anything fallen.

The scent of some nameless flower, sweet and bitter all at once, brought back memories of a tangled evening in the reeds of the oasis.

Jarngard thought about the time later in his tent, her teeth gnashing against his shoulder, her thighs, slick with sweat, squeezing and grinding. Heron's short hair had spiked and her eyes had glowed with a primal ferocity.

The memory was more urge than vision, bringing heat to his face, but he was too drunk to get a hard on. He whispered curses as his mount wandered through the brush, barbed limbs scratching his ankles until his sandals were wet with blood.

Heron had chosen *him*. It didn't matter that he'd forgiven Hoth, that was between the two of them as brothers of the North. But why hadn't she said his name? Or why not the both of them on the journey to Syracuse? Couldn't she have used two sword arms?

He knew what she would say, that she couldn't trust herself, but those words cut like jagged rocks. He would at least be there, protecting her, keeping her safe. For all he knew, she was at the bottom of the sea, her dead body being picked apart by crabs and sightless fish.

He checked the saddlebags again. He needed a drink, badly, if only to wash his shame away.

And she didn't need him, that much he knew. She was tougher than any man he'd ever met, surviving the loss of her leg, bitten off by a massive Nile crocodile.

She didn't need him, and that's what hurt most. Because he needed her. Felt for her like he had no other. Otherwise, he would have left Agog's side long ago. Only Heron kept him with the Alexandrians, in hopes that she might go away with him.

Ahead, the sounds of hammering rung through the air, above the steady rush of the flowing water. Alexandrian engineers were building a floating bridge across the water. Ropes had been strung between two sets of pillars, one on each side and men dangled from them, feet bouncing only a cubit from the surface of the brown, bilging water.

He found Vestalis standing with a group of engineers, pointing into a parchment and glancing back to the rope lines. Jarngard started to wonder why he'd never noticed that flecks of gray had been creeping into Vestalis' hair, but then he realized he didn't care.

"West, I said. Take the army west where the trade routes swing. We'd be over this cursed river by now if you'd listened to me," said Jarngard.

The engineers suddenly found a reason to leave, striding away quickly while rolling the parchment. Vestalis fixed him with his gray eyes, eyes as desolate as the clouds over the frozen north.

"That way might have been blocked, too, and if we're going to build a floating bridge, this is the better spot," said Vestalis.

"I think you want to delay us," said Jarngard, "make us late to the field of battle."

The words tumbled out of his mouth faster than he could rein them in, but once said, he decided it was better that way. They had to get these things out in the open before they festered. Jarngard swung his leg over the saddle and marched over to the ex-Roman soldier.

"Always this," said Vestalis, "no matter how many times I prove myself to Alexandria, you question my motives. If I wanted to delay or hinder us, then why did I take the city of Tyre in one day?"

Tongue loosened by an afternoon of drinking, Jarngard let it wag. "I don't know the devious mind of a Roman pig. I just know we should have gone west."

Vestalis' jaw practically popped out of place, he squeezed it so hard. "If you spent more time at our war council meetings than drinking, we might have gone west. Your opinion went missing while we planned."

"It's not easy making sure there's no wine for the soldiers to drink," said Jarngard. "I'd hate to see them drown crossing this bridge."

Jarngard had expected a searing look, he hated to admit it to himself, it was what he wanted, but he didn't get that. Instead, Vestalis looked at him, or *into* him, like his skin was made of glass. The tension released from his peppered jaw and he smiled, like a crocodile about to bite into a fallen antelope.

Jarngard squeezed his fists trying to make the feeling go away, whatever it was that Vestalis was doing. Jarngard steadied a sway and stared back at the ex-Roman soldier.

"You've been in many battles, haven't you?" asked Vestalis, his lips curling into a grimace.

A blast of sunlight burst through the clouds, forcing a hand up momentarily. When the brightness faded, Jarngard nodded.

"More than I care to count," he replied.

"Then you'll know that there are three types of soldiers." Vestalis broke eye contact and faced the raging river. "Men who fight, men who flee, and men who lead."

"Which one are you?" asked Jarngard.

Vestalis didn't look back. "It's obvious, isn't it?"

No witty reply came to Jarngard's lips, so he stayed silent.

After a pause, Vestalis asked, "Which man deserves our admiration the most?"

Jarngard answered quickly, "Men who fight."

Vestalis watched the river and settled his arms behind his back like a general watching his troops parade by.

"It's the man who flees for he is the bravest amongst them." Vestalis paused, letting the words sink in. "No sane man wants to die, yet because their brothers go screaming into war, they feel the keen cut of their honor go slipping by their throats and rush in after, not because they are brave, but because they are a coward.

"The man who flees must withstand the hatred of his brothers, but does so to preserve his life. Bravely stands for himself rather than get caught in the riptide of battle frenzy," said Vestalis.

"And what is a man who leads?" asked Jarngard.

"A smart man," replied Vestalis and after a moment of reflection and glancing once over his shoulder, he chuckled to himself. "Do you know what you are?"

"No," said Jarngard, trying to flex his hand.

"Before I tell you," said Vestalis, "I want my favor now. The one I won at the siege of Tyre."

"Fine," growled Jarngard. "You can ask, but I'm not promising anything."

"I want you to be brave and leave. Go east like you want to and have tried to do twice before." Vestalis cut him with his eyes. "Be brave, not a coward."

"No." It was the only thing he could get out, and as he said the word, he thought of Heron.

"Tsk, tsk. You know what you are, Northman? Not brave enough to flee, not willing to fight, and too stupid to lead."

Jarngard's fist connected with Vestalis' face, knocking the stern soldier to the dirt. He heard a shout and Vestalis was looking up at him, blood dripping across his teeth in a grisly smile.

Striding across the field, as dozens of engineers and soldiers looked on frozen, was Agog, looking like a thunderhead about to bring down lightning.

Jarngard really wished he had a drink.

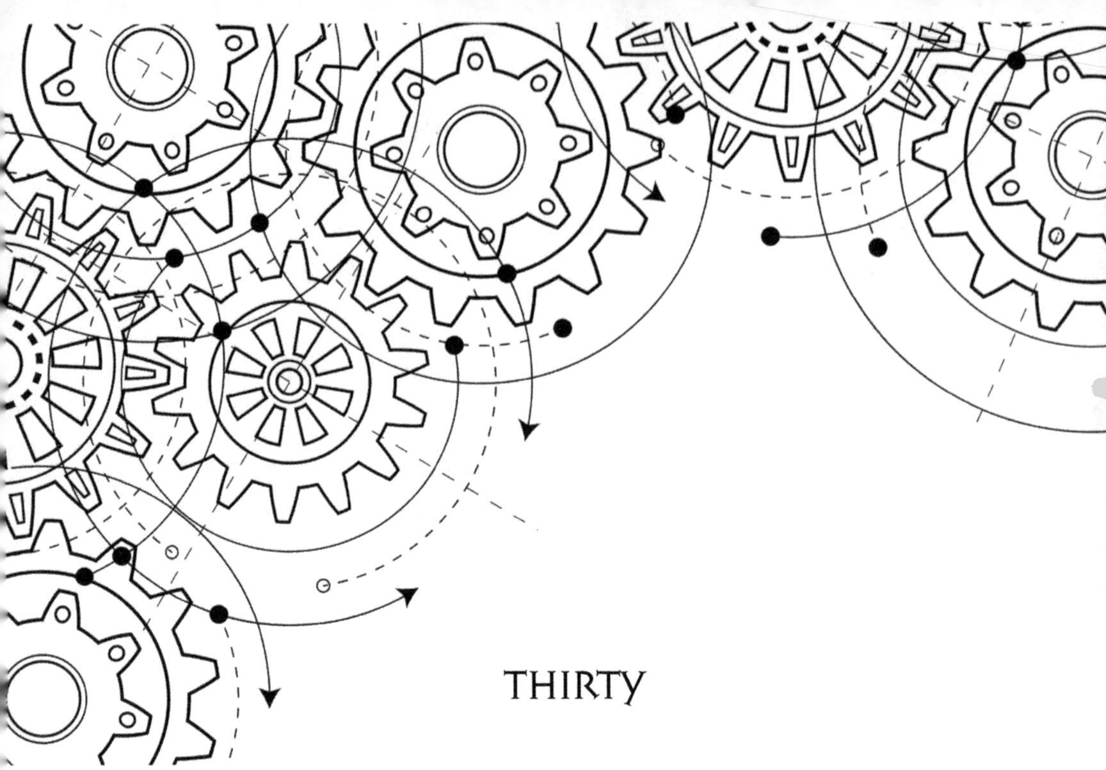

THIRTY

If Qq be the base of any segment of a parabola, and P, the vertex of the segment, and if the diameter through any other point R meet Qq in O and QP (produced if necessary) in F, then the relationship can be discovered. A straight line between points is much faster, of course.

— The Quadrature of the Parabola

"How do we steer?" asked Hoth, standing meekly at the edge, hands perched on the edge of the basket looking like a child on his first trip to the observation level of the Lighthouse of Pharos.

Heron hid her smile, not because she didn't find amusement, but because their journey into the sky had been an undertaking for the sea captain. After vomiting over the side a few times, he'd curled into a ball at the bottom of the basket, eyes clamped shut and shivering like a fevered prisoner.

She couldn't help but silently cheer the look of disgust from Sepharia. On the *Gray Cetus*, the cocky swagger of the ship captain had drawn her daughter like a magnetic stone to north. Now, with hair shorn and pride dashed against the infinite sky, he was less desirable.

"We don't," she said. "The wind takes us where it goes."

Hoth recoiled in horror. "We are but driftwood in the sea of the sky."

In the distance, clouds painted castles, great towering pillars crushing whiteness into ominous gray. Heron guessed they might encounter storms further east as evening sunlight shaded pinks and oranges across the upper cloud structures.

To the north, mountains clawed their way up through the earth like jagged fists. When the sun had been higher, the rivers cutting through the distant valleys sparkled like a silvery ribbon, but now they were drenched in shadow, filling with blackness that would soon spill onto the plains below, much as the Romans would when they reached the Mesopotamian valley.

"The lesser scholars of the Great Library," began Heron, not caring if Hoth was listening, "catalog endless parchments about weather patterns. It was easy to determine that these wind patterns would be useful to travel east to Agog's army."

Hoth sucked carefully on a water pouch, pausing occasionally to belch. "I thought we were headed to the third weapon."

"This task is one and the same," she replied.

"Were you planning on enlightening us, or we're you just going to drag us through the air in this cursed ship of yours until the gods threw us back to the earth?" spat Hoth, who seemed spent for the effort.

"There was time on the boat, but you seemed busy with other tasks," said Heron as Sepharia blushed.

Hoth opened his mouth to speak but the basket dropped a length, clacking his teeth together. Heron fumbled at the basket, forgetting her mechanical hand had no function, feeling for a moment she would be tossed over the side. The lurch, while sudden, was only one, so Heron paused and glanced around for the source.

"Did we fly into a bird?" asked Sepharia, to shrugs from Heron.

She checked the burner and the ropes again, inspecting for frays, but everything seemed in order.

When she turned to Hoth, he was paler than usual, which was saying something since his skin somehow negated the sun, a feat Heron found near impossible, given his profession. Most sailors were burnt a deep umber. She decided it was either a trait of his Northern kind, or a result of his woman-loving inclinations keeping him in his cabin, or both, she supposed.

Hoth didn't seem ready to hear her explanation, so she craned her head past the edge of the basket, letting exhilaration fill her chest like a great welling of air. She wondered what Archimedes would think of the air bladder sailing through the sky. Before, she had conquered earth, and fire, and water, and now, air. Mistress of the four elements, they might name her, and though she knew hubris was often punished, it was hard not to gaze upon the distant earth, hills like verdant lumps and forests just tangled carpets far beneath her feet, and not feel a spring of pride bubbling up.

A thrumming vibration moved through her, starting at the base of the spine, and climbed upward until she felt like a tuning fork struck on the keystone of the world. What couldn't she accomplish given enough time and resources? What problems could she not conquer?

She felt power over all, except death, but how long would that door stay shut if she should turn her gaze to it? Heron briefly wondered if the steam pump had sprung a leak and some gas tainted her thoughts. She knew the gas-sniffers of the Great Library were prone to hallucinations and flights of delusion, but the mechanical seemed in working order.

Heron found the other two staring at her oddly. "What?" she questioned them.

"You looked like you were about to fling yourself from the basket like a baby bird," said Sepharia.

"And why should I not feel this way? We're the first to fly through the air of our own power," she said.

"It's not the flying but the landing that excites me," mumbled Hoth. "Though for now, I would prefer to hear about this task before you lose yourself to visions again."

Heron frowned, only enough to show her displeasure at being disrupted from her thoughts, since the exhilaration was still a light buzz across her skin. "The third weapon lies in the Temple of Fire, in the mountain town of Zeruas, a place not far from where I hope to land," she explained.

"Archimedes gives some hint to the weapon in that it is a child of fire."

"She speaks of landing!" Hoth threw his hands to the sky like a mystic. "Maybe she will actually do it soon."

Heron peered over the edge again. "Yes, I would land now, but I do not know how far east we have traveled. We've passed the extent of my knowledge. I thought we might know the Euphrates and land then, but each river looks nearly the same from this height."

Sepharia spoke up, quiet, but intent. "Will this third weapon be more useful than the second? This steel serpent you described makes no sense to me."

She nodded, knowing what her daughter spoke of. The weapon described in the etchings was a long, metal vehicle that would ride down a metal road, starting at the highest mountains, so the momentum would carry it over the next, and so on, until it reached its destination.

It was not the weapon she thought it would be, nor why he chose to hide it, except that Rome kept its Empire through the strength of its roads and he didn't want to offer another advantage, for only a great empire could build such a monstrous iron road.

There were problems with the design, of course, things she saw almost instantly, even as she handed the papyrus to Apion. The iron serpent would never have enough momentum to make it over the next mountain. But it wouldn't matter if they used a steam mechanical. Using steel roads, they could keep the track smooth and straight and clear, and the mechanical could reach great speeds carrying troops, and people, and goods quickly across an empire.

All these things she thought in an instant and answered almost right away. "It's a weapon only an empire could build, so it matters not until we are that empire. This third weapon, however, I suspect will be immediately useful and could impact the war."

"The war, yes..." Its mention seemed to sober the sea captain from his terrors. "What will we do about this secret uncovered?"

"We will say nothing, or they might kill me," she barked.

Hoth flashed an impish smile. "Not that secret, by all the gods old and new and by the wetness between a woman's legs, I promise to keep your secret." Then it faded and was replaced by a soldier's face. "I speak of Vestalis, the spy."

"We don't know he's the spy," replied Heron.

Sepharia spoke up, "We don't know, but it seems likely."

Heron sighed. Both of them believed Vestalis had betrayed them, and she couldn't completely disagree with them, except that he had done nothing but support Alexandria's rise.

"We know nothing to implicate him," countered Heron. "Apion mentioned spies in Alexandria, but did not implicate anyone. Our secret flight from the city could have been spotted. Unlucky but possible."

Hoth pulled himself up from a crouched position. "Agog is about to clash against the Romans with Vestalis, an ex-soldier of that army, at his side. How can we not tell him? Warn him of the possibility? Look what happened with Ramses the exile."

Sepharia nodded along with the sea captain and her siding with him put a weight on her heart.

"Agog must keep his focus at this critical juncture. If he must alter his tactics for fear of betrayal then we are already lost," said Heron, feeling a froth form at her lips. "Can't you see that such concerns are too late? If the proof had been stronger, maybe, but it wasn't. Instead, we must band together, no matter what our differences or fears, and fight the Romans and tear down this empire of enslavement."

A broad smile formed on Hoth's lips, and she steeled herself from his pithy reply.

"That was quite the inspired speech. Are you sure you're not a man?" he cracked.

Heron punched him in the arm, forgetting it was her metal one, and the sea captain rubbed his shoulder, laughing.

"I'll throw you over—"

The basket dropped again, and the three of them with it, sending her stomach into her throat.

The hair on her arm raised and a flash of blinding light filled the air, followed by a deafening bang that shook her very bones.

Heron looked up in time, and through great purple blotches on her vision, to see the bladder bulge, whipping the basket to the side, and throwing them together. Wind slammed into them, bringing with it tiny shards of rain.

"The storm!" shouted Sepharia over the blast of noise. "We flew into the storm!"

Hoth clung to the basket, face pressed against the weave as he lapsed into his native tongue.

Another gust swirled them around, slamming Heron into the side as she tried to reach for the mechanical.

"We have to go down!"

Lightning streaked across the sky below them. Too close for Heron's comfort, leaving more purple outlines. The thunder shook the basket and added to the ringing in her ears.

The wind turned the rain into stinging needles and Heron, trying to adjust the mechanical, had to hold her forearms across her eyes so she could see.

"The storm is here!" shouted Sepharia.

A great billowing bank of gray wrapped its tendrils around the air bladder, pulling it into the cloud.

Heron, stunned by the seeming aliveness of the storm, could only watch in horror as a whiteout washed over them.

Hoth looked up to her, eyes red with fright, "The gods punish us!"

When they entered the cloud, Heron expected total blackout, but instead, the air pulsed with energy from distant and not-so distant lightning.

Shaking off the hesitation, Heron tried to reduce the speed of the pump, but it was stuck in the fully open position. Not only were they not going down, but they were climbing rapidly.

Heron watched as a tree of lightning seethed through the mist right above the bladder, kicking sparks off the surface. If one hit directly, it could tear a hole in the side and they'd plummet to the earth.

The storm battered the air ship, tossing Heron into the side of the basket as she tried to fix the mechanical.

When she realized she didn't have the strength or leverage to unstick the lever, she grabbed Hoth by the hair and pulled him standing.

"I need you to fix it!" she shouted in his face.

Spit formed on his lips as he mumbled and shook his head.

Heron pointed up. "Pull on the lever! Or we'll die."

The sea captain glanced up, as the strobe of lights flickered across the mechanical suspended above them. The bladder yawed to one side and he clung to the basket like a barnacle.

"Pull it!"

He put one arm, half-heartedly above his head, fingertips not even scraping the bottom of the mechanical.

"Do it!"

Heron pushed at him, hitting him in the chest. The violence seemed to waken something in him, but right when he raised his arms, a gust tossed the air bladder and basket through the air like an ice giant had thrown them.

They clung to each other, Sepharia on her leg, fingers grasping on the basket. A lifetime of thoughts went through her head in that moment.

"Hold onto me!" shouted Hoth.

Heron grabbed him by the midsection and Sepharia by the legs. He lifted his arms, pulling them back once when a gust hit, but then grabbing the lever with both hands and hanging on it.

Heron wasn't sure something hadn't been irrevocably damaged and that they wouldn't be able to stop the bladder from taking them higher, until she heard a snap and the lever came down like a guillotine.

The air bladder didn't begin to fall at once, or she couldn't tell, given the strobing whiteout around them, but they huddled in the basket, waiting for what seemed like certain doom.

When mist fell away and the bottom of the clouds, dark and ominous, appeared above them, then rapidly retreating, Heron realized they'd lost too much air and they would probably die upon impact.

Released from the mist, the stinging rain returned. Heron levered upward easily, finding that the connection had been broken. The mechanical was barely putting out air and the bladder was deflating as it fell.

Through the weave at her feet, the earth grew darker, and she assumed closer.

"Lift me!"

Hoth grasped her around the middle and pushed her upward. Heron shoved her fingers into the gap around the lever connection, hoping to move the rod there, but without leverage, it didn't want to go.

There wasn't enough time to explain it to Hoth, whose finger strength was much stronger, so she summoned her will, and strained against the rod. Her fingernail caught and ripped, bringing blood, but she shoved her hand back into the hole and kept going.

When the rod finally moved and the mechanical thrummed to a higher pitch, Heron almost breathed a sigh of relief, but for the rapid approach of the earth.

The bladder bulged slightly, a result of more warm air, but would it be enough?

The three of them stood against the walls of the basket facing each other, hands gripping into the weave. Glancing over the side, the hills were now almost even with them, and gaining height.

As they raced earthward, the wind whipped Heron's hair into a frenzy. Darting rain kept her eyes half-closed, but it was enough to see the ground approaching.

Her only warning of the impact was the canopy of a tree line rapidly passing by the edge of the basket. They hit with the force of a charging stallion, throwing the three of them to the floor of the basket.

Heron found herself tangled around Hoth's limbs, too stunned to move. In the intervening silence, she realized that she could only hear the sound of rain. The steam mechanical that fed the bladder had been knocked silent and the canvas bag above their heads was slowly deforming onto them.

With a shift of weight, Heron knocked the basket onto its side and led them out by way of crawling. Away from the air ship and getting steady soaked by rain, Heron collapsed in a heap and let the comfort of the earth hold her.

Not far away, Hoth mumbled, "Oh, mistress of the sea, I will never again stray from your watery arms."

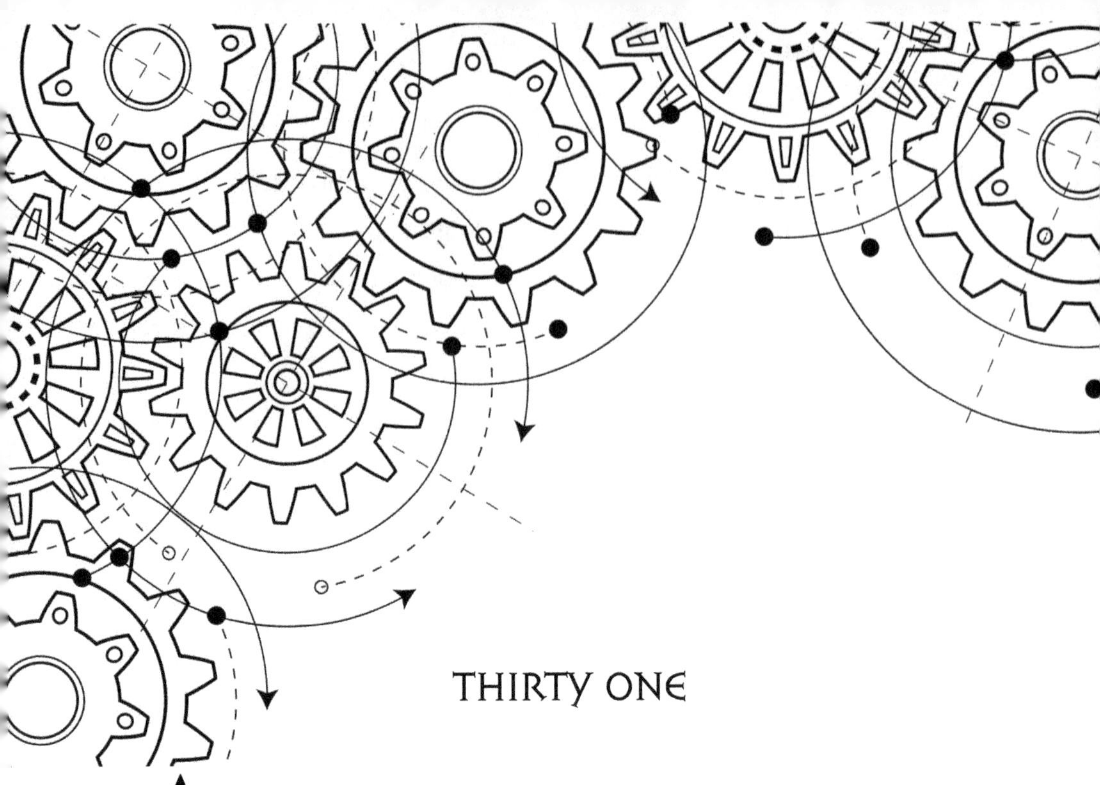

THIRTY ONE

Agog crouched amid the dying embers of a campfire, the soldiers already drilling in the plains below, distant shouts carrying through the humid morning air.

He poked the wood with a stick, ignoring the ache of his knees and the straining in his back. He hoped that whatever happened in the next few weeks was the end of the war.

Aurinia.

How she would laugh at him now, like she did when they first met, him standing beneath the hut on stilts, her at the edge, barefoot and looking down with raven-like hair forming a cloak around her face.

She'd laugh at him for overreacting, a deep and wondrous voice with a thousand smiles in it, overreacting like he did when she sent him away to prove himself for her, subduing the killing spirit of the forest to his will when she only wanted a token.

Agog pushed himself standing and stretched his back until it popped. Wars were for young men.

The potato-cloth tents rustled lightly in the morning wind. A storm had passed through last night bringing cool air, a break from the relentless heat of late summer.

Even from the camp, he could smell the spiced breads from the nearby town of Beroea. He could have slept there in a comfortable bed, but he didn't trust the way the Romans had abandoned the town and with the great battle approaching, he wanted to sleep amid the army.

There was also the matter of Jarngard, who was sitting in the jail. He pushed that thought from his mind. He had a battle to plan.

"Your Grace, I've been looking for you."

Vestalis marched up the hill sternly, his breastplate gleaming in the morning light. Too quickly the thoughts of Jarngard returned.

It seemed like his whole army had seen Jarngard strike his fellow commander, and if wouldn't have been for that, he would have dismissed it as pre-battle nerves and moved on.

Which bothered Agog, since it removed Jarngard from his service. Was Jarngard just a drunken idiot as he first thought or had Vestalis purposely taunted him?

"It's a good thing we didn't fight the Romans right away," said Agog. "When we first left Alexandria, our soldiers were undisciplined and unorganized. Now they set up clean camps and drill every morning, even before a march." Agog fixed his gaze on Vestalis. "I have you to thank for that."

"It's my duty," said Vestalis with no more emphasis than if he were commenting on the weather. "But it's not the soldiers who are going to win our battles. It's the Manticores. Each one is worth a hundred Roman soldiers."

Vestalis cleared his throat. "But I did not come here to tell you that. I came here to tell you that the Romans have taken the town of Antioch."

He looked to the northwest as if he could see the town perched there on the horizon. "Antioch? Are you sure?" Vestalis nodded. "And the Parthians are still at Karkemish?" Another nod. "Is this a mistake or a trap?"

"My spies tell me the legions at Antioch are led by Legate Tiberius," said Vestalis.

Agog scratched his beard, which had grown more unruly in the passing weeks. If he had a gold coin for every time that Vestalis began a sentence with 'my spies tell me...' he'd be a rich man.

"Is something amusing, Your Grace?" asked Vestalis perplexed.

"No," said Agog. "Do you know anything about this Tiberius? Or why they took Antioch?"

"Before, when I was..." Agog motioned for him to go on. "I'd heard of Tiberius. He's an ambitious up and comer. He desires power and glory as much as a Phoenician desires gold. The word is that he took this forward position against Consul Magnus' wishes, in hopes of securing the victory himself and returning to Rome as its savior."

Agog sighed, wishing he had at least one of his countrymen with him, and when he saw Vestalis' eyes widen in surprise, he turned to find a travel-worn trio tramping up the hillside led by Heron. The two with him, poorly-equipped and mud splattered soldiers, he did not recognize.

"By the jarl's balls, what are you doing here? I thought you were in Syracuse? And where is Hoth and your daughter?"

"Right here, Your Grace," smiled the taller soldier wearily.

Agog took a second look. "Your hair? The both of you? What happened on your journey? Did you find the Archimedes weapon?"

He felt a moment of elation in his chest. Maybe the inventor had brought him a new weapon, one that would easily win the war, but when he saw the heavy disappointment in their eyes, he knew it hadn't gone well.

"I cut their hair as a disguise and we found the second weapon, but it's of no use," said Heron heavily.

Much had happened on their journey, he could see it in their eyes, and by the bruises and cuts across their arms and faces. Sepharia's right eye was nearly swollen shut, and Heron held her good shoulder against her side.

There wasn't just one thing wrong with Hoth, but clearly something had wounded him deeply. He was a shadow of his former self, the shine knocked off him like armor after a bloody battle.

Agog caught a brief glare from the sea captain directed at Vestalis, and general confusion whenever Heron spoke. He'd sent out a warrior and gotten a beaten peasant in return.

"How did you get here so quickly? And without getting caught by the Romans? They hold the coast west of here," said Agog.

Heron was about to speak when Hoth cut him off. The delirious laugh that slipped from his lips bordered on madness.

"Oh, no. You will not speak of that journey. At least not in front of me. Tell him later if you must, but living through it once was enough. I will never look at another bird in the sky the same."

Agog was about to speak when Vestalis cleared his throat again.

"Your Grace, should we retire to your quarters and continue our discussions?"

"War plans?" he asked. "Here is fine. There are no spies about and we need more opinions than our own."

He could not help but notice that on the word 'spies' all three of them looked at Vestalis. Had they learned something on the trip? Is that what strangeness he detected?

Vestalis glanced unapologetically at the others. "Fine."

"Bring them up to speed," said Agog.

Vestalis gave them a terse explanation of the situation, thoroughly lacking in detail, so Agog pulled a stick from the edge of the fire and drew a rough map in the dirt.

"There's a proper map in your quarters," said Vestalis.

"This will do. I've made many a map in the dirt. Sometimes, they're the best kind." He glanced conspiratorially at Hoth, but the sea captain was too busy glaring at Vestalis.

"So, here are the Taurus Mountains, forming the last barrier before the Mesopotamian plains," said Agog, pointing to an arc along the top left side. "And this is the Euphrates river, which forms a wall on our right side, the east." He tapped on a snaking line going south. "The Mediterranean forms the western barrier, leaving the field of battle this misshapen box."

Agog looked to each of them for understanding before continuing. "The Parthians, with the remnants of the attacking force, are waiting at Karkemish, which is at the edge of the Euphrates and the Taurus, which sits at the northern pass, in the top-right corner of the box, one of the few ways past the mountains into the plains."

Then he tapped on the city near the coast at the edge of the bottom left, or western, curve of the mountains. "Here is Tiberius' army, three Legions worth, at the city of Antioch, which guards the western route, or Amanus pass."

"Where are the rest of the Legions?" asked Hoth.

"Good question," said Agog and he almost began with 'Vestalis' spies tell us...' but thought better of it. "We have reports that Consul Magnus is moving to the northern pass, to reinforce the Parthians, which we think was the original plan until Tiberius took Antioch."

Agog could tell that Hoth could see it as well, as he glanced around the map, at first his brow hunched in confusion, and then relaxed in understanding.

"This Tiberius overreached," said Hoth, to nods from Vestalis.

"And Magnus is moving slowly through the mountains," said Vestalis with uncharacteristic glee. "We beat him north, despite the siege of Damascus. There have been some unknown delays in the mountains. The gods are on our side."

"Mountain travel is always treacherous," said Agog.

"Where is Jarngard?" asked Heron suddenly. "Why are we discussing war plans without him?"

The inventor seemed distraught when no answer was given right away. Vestalis stepped away from the dirt map, leaving Agog to answer.

"He is under arrest. He was overcome by madness and struck another officer of this army. It appears he no longer wishes to contribute," explained Agog.

The hungry air turned to quiet contemplation, until he tapped on the map again, summoning them back. Heron seemed heavily distracted, implications he would have to consider later.

"So, our enemy is divided into three parts. One in the west, one in the northeast, and one behind the mountains, and each is too far away from the others to offer support," said Agog. "In this, the Romans have made a crucial error."

He tapped on the map, right where he'd marked the town of Beroea, the town they now camped at. "We're within two days of each army, and though they outnumber us three to one, we have the superior army. I shall take the strength of the army west and destroy this Tiberius and his three legions at Antioch, while Vestalis takes a smaller force to Karkemish to keep them in check until I can return."

Hoth spoke up, "But won't the cataphracts overrun any token force? They're the better cavalry."

"I'm giving him half the Manticores and all our cavalry," said Agog.

Vestalis nodded approvingly. "I'll harry them at the edges, never engaging, until you arrive."

"Good, because the terrain is terrible for the Manticores," said Agog. "All jagged hills and rocky."

"Where is the town of Zeruas?" asked Heron.

When Agog didn't know, Vestalis pointed to an area west of the northern pass.

"The third weapon lies there at the Temple of Fire," said Heron. "I wish to go to it."

Agog shook his head. "It's too close to the Parthians and I can't spare any soldiers."

"But Apion is on his way there," said Heron passionately. "If he gets the last weapon, they may have an overwhelming advantage."

"They already have an advantage, but if we strike quickly and hard, we won't need this weapon, no matter how powerful."

Agog expected Heron to argue, but instead, the inventor seemed to draw into himself, leaning heavily on his mechanical leg.

"I will go with Vestalis," said Hoth, looking a bit more like his former self. "His operation sounds more like my kind of battle."

Agog had to agree so he relented. Hoth took his leave to find food, a bath, and new clothes. The ones he wore were about to fall off him.

The others left, except Heron, who stayed behind. He caught the inventor's glance at Vestalis' back and expected what she had to say to be about him. He had to admit to himself that he trusted the ex-Roman only because he must, and because the man had been loyal so far, but he knew he could never trust him like he did his countrymen.

On the eve of battle, this became even more important, and before Heron spoke, Agog decided that if they had questions about the loyalty of Vestalis, he would replace him with Hoth, and put Vestalis in a cell alongside Jarngard.

"I have something important to tell you," said Heron, his face screwed up with concern.

"Good," said Agog, "I was expecting this, and maybe it's for the best."

Heron recoiled, giving Agog pause. "You did? You know?"

"I don't know," said Agog. "It's only a guess. But it seems you suspect him as well."

Heron shook his head, glancing at his feet. "Suspect him? What?"

"Are we speaking of the same thing?" asked Agog. "It appears not. Strike my words from your mind then and tell me what burdens you."

Heron put a hand to his chest and a look of need was perched on his face so fraught with danger, Agog had to tilt his head.

"I need to tell you..." Heron looked away. "I am..."

"Yes?"

Heron opened his mouth, paused and Agog saw a decision made in his eyes.

"I need," began Heron, almost disappointedly. "I need to go to the Temple of Fire."

For a brief moment, Agog thought the inventor was going to say something else. It was as if the gods had laid his soul out for Agog to see. It was something important, but whatever it was, Heron wasn't going to say.

"You know I cannot spare the men," said Agog. "And I need you to stay in Beroea. I'll leave a token force along with the wounded and broken Manticores. Maybe you can fix them and send them to Vestalis. Any additional steam mechanicals will help."

"That's all you need me for?" asked Heron.

Agog nodded. "It may not seem important, but it is. I have so few men I can trust."

A word seemed to catch in Heron's throat and then he turned, a pivot made awkward by the mechanical leg, and he walked away, as slowly as a mule pulling a plow. At each step, Heron hauled the metal leg forward rather than making a smooth step.

The inventor seemed like a broken man. There would be more of those before the war was done.

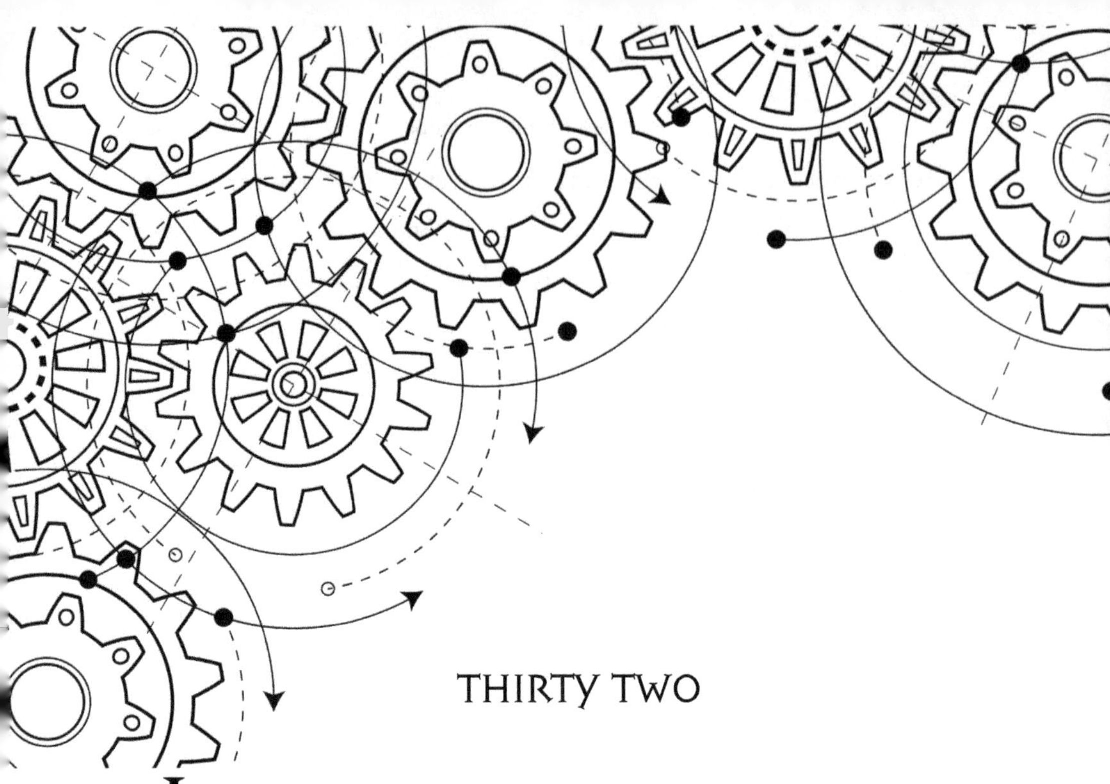

THIRTY TWO

Jarngard did not want for food. His goaler brought him ample portions of roast lamb, spiced tubers, and turnips. Nor did he thirst, not even for wine, of which they allowed him a cup with each meal.

Of all the prisons Jarngard had ever spent time in, this was the most luxurious. Yet, of all the prisons, this was the one that he most wanted to escape.

His cell window faced the southern hills and the day before, he had watched the Alexandrian army throw a great dust cloud into the sky as it broke camp.

He kept expecting to see Agog at the bars demanding an apology, one that he would freely give, before his captain would bring the goaler forth to rattle keys in the lock, until the rusty hinges screamed open, and he rejoined his companions a little more humble.

It'd been a long night in his cell, waiting for a visit that never came.

By the morning, he felt anger so thick it seemed to choke in his throat like smoke billowing from a pyre of the dead.

Agog had left him.

A few times he convinced himself that Agog was teaching him a lesson and would soon appear. He hated himself each time he thought it, feeling weak for doing so.

The tray of food sat untouched. He spilled the wine onto the gritty broken stone floor before it tempted him and not because his day of drink had gotten him thrown in the jail. He refused to drink because it eased his pains and he wanted to know them in full.

Shame.

Jarngard yanked the leather pouch free, relishing the cord snapping against the back of his neck. The dice spilled onto the stone in the far corner, thrown in anger, and then ignored in practice only.

When Heron's hand and leg had been taken off, they'd made mechanical limbs to take their place. There were no mechanicals that could soothe his ache.

Alone in his cell, his mind went from anger, to shame, to loathing, and then back to anger, like the world-serpent eating the tail of its emotions.

Jarngard was slumped against the bars when he heard the uneasy gait, punctuated by a metal heel on stone. He dismissed it as his imagination, until the apparition persisted. He was turning when he heard his name, spoken softly, familiarly.

"Jarngard."

He struggled to his feet and nearly pulled her against the bars until he saw the goaler at the door and even then he almost did it anyway.

"How did you get here?" he asked, noticing the pink stump rather than the mechanical hand.

"The wind."

He pressed his lips together and frowned. "It's not kind to jest."

"I'm not," she replied, her eyes searching him. "Are you well from your madness?"

He placed his hand against her fingers, the ones wrapped around the bar, but she pulled them free and crossed one arm across her chest.

"Madness? Is that what Agog told you it was?"

"To strike Vestalis and give no reason sounds like madness to me," she said.

"Then why are you here?" he asked.

"I need you."

The words hung in the air and it took all his effort not to pull her against the bars and force his mouth on hers. He needed her just as much, maybe more. Having her so close reminded him how much he'd missed her, maybe even loved her.

She smacked her lips and continued, "...to help me get the third weapon."

"What?"

"The third weapon," she explained with excited breath. "It's not far from here in the town of Beroea. I can't let Apion get there first."

"You want me to help you?"

She became irritated. "Of course, what else would I mean? Hoth left with Vestalis. I don't think it'd be safe for just Sepharia and me. I need your help. I can't chance that Apion gets the weapon. It's too important. I know it is."

"And if I don't help you, you won't let me out?"

Heron hesitated, and then clearly she realized she'd hesitated and tried to speak quickly, but the damage was done.

"I will release you," and then she added, "if you are mad no longer."

Jarngard leaned his forehead against the bars with his eyes closed. The metal was cool.

"You need me to get the weapon."

"Yes."

He could hear the nervousness in her answer.

"Just the three of us?"

"I thought it safer that way. We could use one of the steam mechanicals."

He shook his head. "No. Too obvious. We'll ride horses."

"So you'll do it?"

He opened his eyes. He'd do it if it let him spend more time with her. Even if she'd asked him to march on the gates of the Underworld.

"Of course, I will."

Heron waved the goaler to the door and he expected her to wait and walk with him, but as soon as the key was in the goaler's hand, Heron marched away.

Without looking back, she said, "Eat and gather the horses. I'll get Sepharia. We leave as soon as you're ready."

She left him with the goaler and an open door. Jarngard sighed and walked through.

THIRTY THREE

If it was said that Rome was the heart of the Empire, and Alexandria - before it was taken - was its mind, then the city of Antioch would be its cock.

Even from the lower hills of Mount Silpius, the place where Alexander the Macedonian burned an offering to Zeus on his way east after Great King Darius, Agog could easily see the colorful streamers of Antioch flap lazily in the seaward breeze from the multitude of spires and towers, like an army of giant spearman with mismatched banners.

It was a festive place that Emperor Caligula had visited often to sample its many wares. The city's pleasure houses were said to contain slaves trained for every desire. If only Caligula was still at the head of the Roman Empire, then its conquest wouldn't be so difficult.

But here he was, standing on the doorstep of such a victory, despite the enormous challenges.

Agog shook his head and cupped away the bright sunlight. The fool Tiberius had ignored the shelter of the city walls, as meager as they were, and camped his legions on the southern plains. But an enemy eager for glory was not always an easy opponent. Boldness counted for something, even if it usually led to failure.

Agog knew this lesson well. His boldness had cost him Aurinia.

He shook his head again, clearing the past from his thoughts while tugging on his tangled beard. Staring at the three legions lined up between the hills and the river, one of the last major battles between him and marching on Rome, made him realize that tearing down the Empire wasn't going to ease the ache he'd been carrying with him for far too long.

His side looked comically small. Ragged parallel lines opposed the Romans, looking like they were set there by drunken captains.

If it weren't for the seriousness of the situation, the promise that many men would die on both sides, and that many more would begin their journey to the underworld depending on the outcome of the battle, he might have laughed.

But it wasn't the thin lines of his side that would win the war. Those cobbled together regiments wouldn't even stand up to half a legion, let alone three set in motion by a bold commander.

It was the hundred and fifty steam mechanicals sitting on the infantry's flank where the mounted men would normally position themselves that gave him confidence. One hundred and fifty versus fifteen thousand.

The start of the battle was waiting for one commander or the other to give the command. Agog wasn't sure what he was waiting for, his plans were set, the flag crew stood patiently nearby waiting to give the signal, and the terrain was as favorable as he could hope for.

Agog wasn't worried about trickery from Tiberius. Vestalis had pegged the man as a glory hound, desperate to push into battle and declare victory for Rome. It was why he hadn't bothered sitting behind his walls.

Scouts had seen lights from distant lanterns flicker on the southern slopes of the Taurus mountains as the army marched through the night to reach Antioch. Some of his men called them will-o-wisps and others dismissed them as herders bringing sheep in for an autumn slaughter and Agog was inclined to agree with the second, though it amused him to hear such stories existed in the south as the north. He also knew it was possible they were scouts for Tiberius, but it wouldn't do the man any good, he would see them soon enough.

Agog wasn't sure why he hesitated to give the command. Even his signalers knew it was time. They waited patiently, looking over their shoulders at him, but trying not to be too obvious.

On the southern walls of the city, residents in colorful garments packed the battlements to watch as if it were a festival. He imagined if Rome was victorious, there would be a great party, and orgies would spill into the streets. And even if Rome lost, he thought the city might open its gates and legs and cheer their victory, if only to have reason for festiveness.

Agog turned his head, thinking he heard music drifting from below, or maybe it was just the beating of his heart, and the wind teasing through rocks acting as the melody.

With the heaviest of sighs, Agog looked to the signalers and slowly brought his fist down like a hammer. The enthusiastic waving brought snaps and crackling from the crimson cloth and Agog felt the rumble of steam mechanicals coming to life in his balls.

One hundred of the metal beasts broke loose and sped forward between the gap, keeping the river on their left and a Roman legion on their right.

There was a great shout, and the clanging of shields, as the Romans matched the flanking of the steam mechanicals with defensive measures. Their voices, five-thousand men as one, brought back memories of the Germanic wars and put doubt in his plans.

For a brief and terrible moment, he remembered the press of his countrymen as the legion surged forward, thrusting spears. Men panicked and fell, the scents of blood and pierced bowels thick in the air. The Romans had tightened like a noose around them, until men were stabbing each other as much as the enemy. Agog remembered stepping into another man's guts and falling to his knee and then taking a pommel to the spine so hard it made his left leg go numb.

Agog's face was hot and he felt the trap surrounding him, much as he had on that day. Confused for a moment, he almost gave the signal for retreat, feeling like the Romans had baited him into an unwinnable battle, just like they had in the north.

But that was Germania and this was Antioch, and this Roman legate had overstepped.

Near the hills, the third legion began to advance, looking like a block of ice sliding across the earth. The ragged lines of his troops broke and in segments they fell back, exactly as he had commanded.

Another army would have surged forward to rout the enemy, but the Romans were more disciplined than that and they stayed in formation, just as Agog predicted they would.

On the river side, the lead Manticores had reached the back of the legion. Agog gave the signal and the steam chariots unleashed a hailstorm of arrows. He gave the Romans credit, the barrage was quite lethal and soldiers did fall, but the holes disappeared quickly as men shifted to take their place.

The Manticores stopped firing and circled behind, while the two legions not advancing shifted into a shimmering wall of armor with shields facing both directions. The third legion was in pursuit of the Alexandrian infantry that was still falling back.

In any other circumstances, letting his cavalry force get trapped behind the enemy while his infantry retreated was a recipe for absolute defeat and he knew his opponent would be eager to crush him should the opportunity be presented, so present he did.

He'd been there before, confident of victory, certain that well-thought plans would carry the day, only to have the enemy turn those plans to dust.

If all went well, Tiberius would feel that today.

His steam chariots weren't ordinary cavalry, even though he'd placed them in the spot his mounted soldiers would normally be positioned. Agog set them there because he wanted Tiberius to think of them as ordinary horse, or even chariots, and the tactics for fighting such enemies were well known.

The enemy commander Tiberius was reacting exactly as he'd planned, almost too well, as if it were only a preplanned exercise and not a full fledged battle.

When the two legions, extended across the gap between river and hills, began marching to crush the steam mechanicals against the wall with javelins held at the ready, Agog made a second clenched fist and held it to his forehead.

He only had eyes for the fifty steam mechanicals in reserve, even as the saffron banners snapped in the early morning air.

With Vestalis, he'd sent the fastest of the crafts (and the steam launchers,) but these fifty were the opposite of those vehicles, some that had been tested in the arena's steam chariot races. From the battle at Alexandria, Agog had learned about the vulnerabilities of the steam mechanicals. Mostly, that the pilot was unguarded and a lucky javelin throw could disable the fearsome machine.

Though the motions were anything but crisp, the clanging of steel shielding being set into place made his heart soar. Agog had made them leave the metal plates that created a barrier on the floor of the mechanical and drilled them in reforming the shielding day and night until they could do it in less than a minute.

He wanted the transformation to be a surprise.

Thirty craft, a mixture of Rhinos and Porcupines (names given by the soldiers training on them and quickly accepted by the army at large,) rumbled toward the two legions advancing on the Manticores. The other twenty in a similar mixture headed towards the single legion, these more sluggishly.

"Quad!"

The shouted word was a thunderclap. Agog's own jaw clenched with the ferocity of it.

The legion condensed into a square, shields interlocking on all sides and top with spears forming a prickly defense.

Agog knew this formation. When his mounted forces had attacked a similar legion on the northern plains, he'd expected them to break like infantry did when run down by screaming horsemen.

His mount, partially lame and bleeding from a gash in the flank from early skirmishes, had kept him at the rear of the charge. When the lead horsemen surged up and over the field of shields, running across the inter-locking metal and wood, and held up by ordinary men, Agog remembered his shock and dismay.

In their confusion, his countrymen had ended their attack until the horses nervously pranced on the back of the legion. Agog had stopped his charge, yanking on the reins until the horse had reared up.

Then by what Agog could only assume was a silent count, holes opened in the roof of the legion, leaving man and horse to fall through and die quickly by a dozen thrust gladii. Agog counted himself lucky that day he did not share the fate of so many.

That lesson was impressed into him as he watched the twenty steam mechanicals race toward five-thousand men. He saw the front of the shields dip, ready to accept the momentum of the steam mechanical and propel it onto its back. Like a great metal beast with ten-thousand legs and five-thousand scaly backs, the legion prepared to accept the invaders.

But these were no ordinary mechanicals. These were powered by their strongest mechanicals, not for speed but for carrying weight.

When the first Rhino hit the edge of the shields, Agog feared he'd miscalculated. The wheels ran up and over the edge, just as it would hitting a mild slope.

The legion held and the craft made it a good twenty paces before the shields rippled like a stone thrown into a pond and then broke and the Rhino fell into them, still plowing forward through the soft flesh beneath the legion's armor.

Maybe it was a sudden burst of fear, or that the first mechanical hadn't been as heavily loaded with stone and steel like the others, but when the next wave hit, they scattered men like dust thrown from a shovel.

All morning, Agog had instructed his men to overload the mechanicals, putting every piece of scrap metal onto the crafts. Even over protests from the army's blacksmiths, who treated their anvils like newborn babes, he had them loaded up.

The twenty craft, like massive bulls charging through a field of wheat, broke the legion. Then Alexandria's four-thousand ragged infantry changed directions to engage the routed enemy.

Agog turned his attention to the other battle. He could see the lines of Roman soldiers tensing on the approach of the steam mechanicals. In a tactic taken from Alexander in his battle with Great King Darius, Agog knew they would leap aside and let the steam chariots charge through, throwing javelins at their backs.

The tactic would have worked if they'd continued their charge. Instead, the steam chariots banked hard and turned to run parallel to the two legions.

He saw the shimmer of doubt in the wall of shields and the Romans were right to feel that way. When the Porcupines extended their metal rods, thick as a man's arm and reinforced to withstand heavy impact, the crafts leaned into the line of men, ripping through steel shields as if they were wet papyrus.

The will of the legion broke immediately and once the Roman soldiers put down their shields to run, the Manticores unleashed their arrows and men fell like rain.

What had looked like defeat turned to slaughter.

Agog turned away from the battle, looking on the southern slopes. Upon a sycamore, staring at him with black pebble-like eyes, was a raven.

He did not smile at the sentinel bird. Nor did he frown. They watched each other as the din of battle continued behind him.

He closed his eyes when the bird flew off, a parting *caw* as it flew overhead. The rumble of steam mechanicals played on his back and his ears prickled from steel clashing with steel. And somewhere in the depths of his gut, through his thighs and calves into the soil, he felt a steady marching rhythm.

When he concentrated, the beat disappeared, so he dismissed it as his imagination. Turning back to the battle, he saw his side was winning. The first pass was done and now they fought in small groups, steam mechanicals churning through men, some running, some clustered in defense.

He searched the sky for the raven, but it was gone.

He closed his eyes again.

Aurinia.

"It'll have to do."

THIRTY FOUR

"Care to warm my bed tonight?" called Hoth from the back of his steam chariot to the young woman on the side of the ravine-filled road. "Afterwards, you can brag to your friends that you slept with the Scourge of the Seas, the man who beat the Roman armada with fishing boats, the Master of the Mists, the infamous Hoth the Black!"

The dirt-smeared young girl with a chicken under her arm stared back dumbly, her eyes never wavering until they'd gone around the rocky outcropping.

"Curse the inventor for cutting my hair," said Hoth to the steam chariot pilot, a man whose name he'd already forgotten. "We could have fooled those Romans without putting a knife to my head."

Hoth leaned against the metal casing that protected the riders from the churning pistons. The vibration rattled his teeth and the steady thudding beat a rhythm into his chest. He pulled an apple from his pocket and bit into it, sheering the crisp skin, and a sharp sourness exploded from the fruit that made his jaw clench.

"Bah!"

He threw the apple at a passing tree, bursting the unripe fruit into a white smear.

Three days. Three days they'd been circling the foothills south of the Taurus mountains, passing unnamed villages, playing games with the Parthian side.

Three days of dust and constant foraging for fuel. They'd raided every blacksmith shop in the area for coal. At least horses could forage for themselves.

It wasn't that he disapproved of the tactics. Never engaging the enemy unless it was on his terms was how he'd earned his reputation in the northern seas. But the roads were as rough as a crocodile's back and his brain had been rattled into jelly. At least on the trip to Old Babylon with Heron, the roads had been relatively flat.

It was the dust, too. No matter how many times he sucked on his water pouch, his throat felt dry, so much that each swallow felt like his throat would never reopen.

Hoth tapped on his pilot's shoulder. "Take me to Vestalis."

The general was at the head of the army, a word that barely fit their band of only one-hundred craft and maybe three-hundred total men. Hoth thought of it as a raiding party.

He tugged at his short hair. At least it was cooler, he decided. He hadn't realized how much heat it held in until it was gone. But there were advantages, too. What was the point of regularly risking your life if it didn't get you into soft beds with even softer and hopefully wetter women?

Sepharia. He'd have liked to have taken her to his room on the *Grey Cetus*, but not with her father, or mother, or whatever, on board.

He ground his teeth thinking about Heron. How she'd fooled him, fooled everyone for that matter, still bothered him. But now that he knew, he could *see* her.

Maybe it was her gaunt cheeks and intense hungry eyes that seemed like they were devouring the world that kept her secret. Sepharia had more shape, and a softness - steel too - but softness that was much different than Heron.

But for all his desire for Sepharia, he would not act on it now. The gods were fickle folk and he'd been witness to Heron's rebuke in the sky. Hoth counted himself lucky to have survived the fall through the clouds.

Vestalis was stopped at the crown of a hill. Stone-stacked walls formed a ring around trampled and chewed grass. The sheep shit was old, maybe a few days, but it put a tang in the air.

Hoth was about to remark how the hill looked like Vestalis' bald head when the general turned and speared him with those gray eyes and his remark fell dead in his mouth.

"The Parthians have proved more cleverer than I thought," said Vestalis. "They won't take the bait."

"A meager bait you're offering," said Hoth. "This force tasted defeat at Alexandria. They know the capability of these steam chariots."

A nod and Vestalis' eyes creased. "Truth."

He gazed across the plains, east toward the Euphrates. The fertile land was ripe with green, a verdant strip marked by deeper browns, even as the season moved through autumn.

Vestalis spoke, "Khusra wishes to trap us against the river. The soil is soft there and our wheels will find it hard to get traction."

Hoth smirked. "It's almost a shame Sepharia killed the older son, Vima. He would have taken the first scent of bait and this battle would be done."

"We would have crushed that fool at Alexandria," said Vestalis.

While the older man gazed at the distant river, Hoth took stock of him. He'd come to this steam cavalry expecting treachery only to find unquestioning loyalty and a cagey battle mind Hoth wouldn't want to be on the other side of.

Maybe Heron had been right. There were other ways that spies could have infiltrated the Alexandrian side. It didn't have to be Vestalis.

Vestalis surprised him with a question while he was considering the weight of the man. "Did you really ride through the air in a sky ship of the inventor's design?"

The man's gaze had an uncharacteristic twinkle.

"By the gods, I did."

"Not by the gods," said Vestalis, "but by Heron."

Hoth shuddered. "Please do not say such things. I fell through the sky in that craft of hers. A punishment from the gods, I can only assume, for treading on their territory."

Vestalis' eyes creased again, and after a long and thoughtful pause he said, "The *Michanikos* might just be a god, for all we know. His inventions seem like miracles and magic at times."

Hoth had rarely spoken with Vestalis, except on matters of war, so he knew little of the man. But by his words and the near smile on his face, Hoth decided that Vestalis had joined Alexandria's side partially due to the inventor.

"I cannot argue," said Hoth. "But do not ever ask me to ride in another air ship."

Vestalis chuckled lightly. "I would like to do such a thing."

Hoth's gut clenched in memory of the harrowing ride.

The light mood disappeared as Vestalis sighted a line of dust in the distance, well to the south and not where they expected the Parthians to be.

"Curse this Khusra, he slipped behind us again. We'll need double time to the mountains," said Vestalis, shaking his head. "We can't get trapped here."

"It'll burn our fuel supplies low," responded Hoth.

"We can forage when we get there. Better to use wood than nothing," said Vestalis.

Hoth nodded, knowing the truth of it. "I'll let the men know."

Vestalis gave him an approving nod before turning his gaze back to the south. Hoth's steam chariot turned to head back through the line. The road was wide enough, or at least sections of it were, so he could pass back and notify the pilots to stop conserving fuel and to head quickly to the rally point near the mountains.

After a glance back, the memory of a word he'd used came back to him. He'd said *her* instead of *him* in regards to the inventor. Hoth didn't recall any recognition from Vestalis, but the man was nigh unreadable under the best of circumstances. Hoth decided that his mistake had gone unnoticed and that Heron's secret was still safe. He'd just do a better job of watching his tongue in the future. They had more important things to worry about, like a Parthian force ten times their own hunting them through the northern edge of the Mesopotamian valley.

He hoped so, anyway.

THIRTY FIVE

Far to the East, there are men who labor at the designs of the air, and conjure the demons of war from these investigations. My correspondence has opened my eyes, but shuttered my heart from the possibilities.

— The Journal of Archimedes

When Heron opened her eyes she saw fire.

It wasn't the stuff of campfires. It was a raging multi-tongued beast flickering at the clouds, trying to pull the sky down onto it. Brilliant yellows streaked through the base, burrowing up into darkness like living things.

The nighttime journey had brought them high into the mountains and she felt weakened by the nearness to the sky. Low clouds slipped over the town of Zeruas, moving quickly and whipping the bonfire into a blazing frenzy.

The heat brought a flush to her face, even from across the square as she sat propped up in the back of the wagon. Dancing impossibly near the bonfire, figures jumped and weaved snake-like, details beyond their shape blackened by the light.

Jarngard slid off the front of the wagon and approached the back at a languid pace. At her feet, Sepharia roused herself from the blankets, yawning and scratching her neck.

"The temple of fire," mumbled Jarngard.

"Signs of Apion? Or any Romans?" she asked.

Jarngard crossed his arms. "How am I supposed to know? You took Hoth with you to Syracuse."

Heron ignored his tone. "I think you'd know what Roman livery looks like, but either way, it doesn't matter. We have to find the weapon."

Sepharia stretched, looking refreshed from sleep, where Heron felt groggy, having been unable to completely fall asleep during the last leg of the journey.

"What are we looking for again?" asked Sepharia brightly.

"The text pertaining to the third weapon said: *know that the last leg of the journey ends in the heat of the Ahura, near the bottom of the sky, so find the focus of the sun and know that once you hold my final weapon, flame is your only enemy.*"

"The *heat of the Ahura* is the temple of fire, right?" asked Sepharia.

Heron nodded. "Yes, the Zoroastrians believe fire is a purifying force. There are other temples, but this is the highest one."

"Any higher and we'll be swimming through the clouds," said Jarngard.

"What is the focus?" asked Sepharia. "Should we wait until morning when the sun is out? *Find the focus of the sun* seems like we should."

"We can't wait," said Heron. "There were too many delays on the *Gray Cetus* already and we're probably better off searching in the dark while the locals are busy with their festival."

The only answer from Jarngard was a grumble as he walked away.

Heron rubbed the skin-chipped stump and resisted the urge to pick at the scab that had formed on the end. Wrestling with the mechanical arm brought Sepharia's confident hands to help.

Once the straps were tightened, Heron tested the weight of it.

"It feels lighter?" she asked Sepharia.

She nodded. "Since the fingers no longer work, I took out the guts while you were sleeping. You were favoring that shoulder. I thought it could use the lightening."

Heron touched her shoulder. It was sore. "Thank you. I guess without function, it feels more like a burden."

Sepharia looked up, a serious question lurking on her lips, and the oranges of the fire playing across her eyes. She glanced to Jarngard, who stood a few paces away.

"Did you and he?" whispered Sepharia.

She didn't answer right away and that was all the confirmation it took for Sepharia.

"I knew it," said Sepharia. "I could see it in the tension between you two."

"There's no tension," said Heron flatly.

Sepharia opened her mouth to speak, before closing it. She squeezed the good arm before climbing out.

Outside the wagon, Heron gave instructions. "We're looking for a statue or an engraving or something."

"How will we see it in this darkness?"

She looked back to the festival goers. "Some carry torches. We have one lantern. The other two can use torches."

"We're splitting up?" asked Sepharia worriedly.

She paused. "We have to. I just don't trust that Apion hasn't made it here yet."

"Then why are we splitting up?" asked Jarngard, his imposing frame blocking part of the bonfire heat.

"It's dark. We'll be safe. And it's the only time I can search without being seen. I'm a bit obvious with these." Heron held up her arm for effect. "We'll rest during the day and search at night. I'm wide awake now."

"Take this cloak at least," said Jarngard pulling it from the back of the wagon. "It'll hide your metal limbs from a distance. Otherwise they reflect."

"Thank you," she replied. "Here, the fire is warm, but further away, it's chilly. These mountains are high and autumn is half over. Better that we blend into the locals that way."

When they split up, Heron took the lantern, only because it was easiest to maneuver with one hand. Her metal knee still hadn't fully recovered from being submersed in the cavern, so she had a noticeable limp, where before it'd been slight. She hoped there would be no stairs on her search. Heron kept the cloak up and round her head, letting the lantern stay low to the ground.

Noises from the festival carried away from the center, bouncing off the walls and making it appear there were multiple parties, but it wasn't hard to keep her bearings because the bonfire reached high above the buildings, forming a red eye on the bottom of the rushing clouds.

Away from the square, Heron pulled the cloak tighter. The wind stole the heat from her fingers sticking out of the cloak.

A noise startled her from ahead. Heron froze and she thought about how stupid she was to split them up in the middle of a strange village.

Heron slowly turned the lantern until the pale light shown against the source of the noise.

Lying against a large stone, a mangy mud-clumped dog, curled up against the cold, was wagging its bushy tail. Heron sighed relief and leaned down on one knee to pet the dog. It nuzzled against her hand. The fur was matted together so she stuck to scratching the dog's ear.

Heron was about to stand up when she realized the dog was lying at the base of a statue. She lifted the lantern to the height of her head so she could see who the statue had been modeled after.

Breath caught in her throat when she realized it was Archimedes. She knew it by the scale in his hand.

Heron had assumed that he'd hidden the third weapon in the town without the villagers' knowledge. The presence of his statue indicated that at least during the time of his death, they knew of him.

She searched the base for markings but found none. The rest of the statue was devoid of letters or notations.

Standing with her back to the statue, she tried to see where Archimedes was looking, but it only pointed toward the center of town. Behind the statue was a stone building with Zoroastrian markings on the door, while the far side of the street was filled with a blacksmith shop.

Heron examined the statue thoroughly before moving on, feeling like she was missing something. The street curved away and the previously joyous noises from the festival, warped by the low clouds and strange angled houses, turned to cackles of sharp sounds in her ears.

As she hobbled on through the dark, she couldn't help but cringe away from each scuffed sandal, while her heartbeat labored in her ears.

The streets made for a confusing nighttime adventure. She was used to the perpendicular travels of Alexandria, streets criss-crossing at predetermined intervals. This village of Zeruas seemed less than planned.

It wasn't quite haphazard, buildings askew at every angle. The streets did flow and even the walls conformed to the shape, but they curved, which made seeing much more than beyond the light of the lantern difficult.

She did enjoy that the bonfire kept to her right, almost always at a perpendicular angle, at least on the back end of the village.

Her earlier worry faded away as the search became a little monotonous. Unlike Syracuse, where she'd been immediately confronted with the clues from the tomb, Zeruas in the dark was lacking information for her mind to scratch upon.

Pausing at a side street, Heron realized her bladder was pressing heavily against her gut. She hadn't encountered anyone on the street yet, the villagers were all clearly celebrating in the square, so she didn't think anything of moving behind one of the houses, pulling back her cloak and letting her water go out the special genetalia she wore.

She didn't miss that, at least. Urinating while crouched over a hole. Men had it right on the matter of relieving oneself.

Heron was about to hobble back to the street when she heard the sounds of two men chatting softly. The voices were growing louder so she assumed they were coming her way.

She crouched down and made sure the shutters on the lantern were tight, hiding the device behind her cloak and using the wall to steady herself.

It didn't take long for her to figure out they were speaking in Latin. She tilted her head around the corner and listened intently.

She couldn't tell what the first man was saying, because he was speaking to the other and his voice carried away and details were lost by the wind noises. But when the second spoke, his words flew through the air, almost as if by zephyr, and settled into her ear like hot ash.

Heron's jaw clenched. She knew that voice.

It was Apion.

THIRTY SIX

His knees knew the Romans had arrived before he saw them.

The battle below on the plains south of Antioch had disintegrated into mixed skirmishes. The remnants of the three legions, hunted by the circling steam chariots, engaged with the Alexandrian infantry to survive. The Manticores and other vehicles wisely stayed out of the fray, or risk killing their own side.

A hazy smoke hung over the field like a black blanket, tearing into shreds and drifting west in the brisk wind. Agog was watching, wondering how best to force the Romans to surrender, when he felt the reverberation in his knees.

His gut soured immediately, followed by a taste of bile, and his thoughts ran to Aurinia. Fear for her, but it was too late.

"She's already dead," he mumbled to himself, squashing the errant memory.

The banner men had already turned to look and Agog knew what he was going to see, even before he followed.

Marching up the road from the south, around the hills, armor gleaming like silver fish swimming energetically through a mountain stream, the other Roman legions advanced on Antioch.

The words stuck in his throat. There were no curses strong enough to relieve his anger at himself.

"They're not supposed to be here."

Just like that day when Aurinia died, the Romans had shown up where they weren't supposed to be, where he knew they couldn't possibly be.

The answer came to him immediately. The lights on the Taurus mountains. The Roman general had found a hidden pass and instead of moving to support his Parthian allies, had turned west to trap him against Antioch.

The banner men stared at him, but Agog wasn't ready to give commands yet. He had to work through it.

They'd trapped him right against the city. There was no time for a retreat. The river to the west would keep them from escaping with the steam chariots. It would be a slaughter.

He believed Consul Magnus had at least four, maybe five, or possibly six Legions with him. From what he knew about Magnus, he was no Tiberius, clearly from the cunning of his attack.

Agog shook his head. Magnus had used the bold and reckless Tiberius as bait, risking the lives of those legions to trap him here. Most Roman commanders fought for glory, but this Magnus seemed to be fighting for absolute victory.

Even if he lined his steam chariots up into a wedge, they couldn't break through that many legions. They didn't have enough arrows for the Manticores and Agog didn't think Magnus would fall for the same tricks that Tiberius did.

For all Agog knew, Magnus had scouts watching the whole battle. It was more than possible. They'd waited until the absolute best time to attack. Agog was sure of it, which boded ill, since Magnus had sacrificed the younger Tiberius for the cause.

There was still distance between the advancing Romans and the battle below him, but not much. His side hadn't yet noticed, and when they did, he feared they would rout.

Agog looked at the city, and back to the Romans, and then the battle. It probably wouldn't work, but it was his only shot at surviving.

He marched to the men holding the banners. "You three, can any of you pilot a steam chariot?"

None of them nodded at first, until one, a soldier with a pock-marked face, cautiously nodded. Agog cuffed him on the shoulder.

"There's no time for caution now, speak soldier."

The soldier spoke in broken Greek while his eyes watched the advancing Romans. "I—I...I help pilot one, once. I—th—think I can."

"Good," said Agog, squeezing his shoulder. "You two ride with him, he's your captain now. I want the three of you to take my steam chariot over these hills, it's specially made for rough terrain, avoid the Romans and head east, about two days, and find Vestalis and the other steam chariots and tell them to head here immediately and attack the Roman's rearguard. Destroy their auxiliaries and food wagons. Do you understand?"

The pock-marked soldier nodded, still watching the Romans.

"Don't delay, move!"

The three of them scurried toward the steam chariot, looking behind them as if they were being chased, or that he was going to change his mind.

It occurred to Agog in that moment that the three soldiers might decide to leave his army, taking the steam chariot with them, or selling it to the Romans.

It was a chance he was going to have to take.

Agog took one of the soldier's mounts, the largest one, which wasn't saying much. It was a slender roan with spindly legs and Agog wasn't sure it wouldn't buckle as he kicked its ribs for more speed.

He barreled down the hillside, scrub whipping his legs. For a moment, a giddy laughter frothed to his lips, as he raced the legions. He wished one of the others was with him to share in his mad flight. Hoth, or Jarngard, or Agnar, or even Heron.

His laughter died when his horse stumbled onto the plains, nearly throwing him, and the screams of men dying could be heard above the hoof beats.

"Retreat to the city!" he yelled as he circled the battle, hitting the stone road.

The Alexandrian soldiers were surprised when they saw him astride the horse, screaming, but then it was usually enough for them to notice the advancing Romans.

The battle had turned to skirmishes, clumps of Romans fighting off the advantaged Alexandrians, so it was easy for them to disengage.

Agog made the waiting steam chariots and shouted orders to the first Rhino he saw.

"Ram the gates! We must get in the city!"

The men on it hesitated, but only for a moment, and turned it toward Antioch.

From below, the citizens on the walls looked even more colorful than from the hillside. He could see golden cups of wine held in outstretched hands. Giggling and chatting, even over the thunderous steam chariots. The men and women, it was hard to tell the difference, pointed slender arms toward the incoming legions, watching them as one watched a theater performance rather than a real war.

When the wedge of steam chariots burned towards the gate, the casual ambience of the people on the wall turned more urgent, fleeing even. They couldn't move fast enough to get away, dropping trinkets and goblets over the wall in their haste.

The lead chariot hit the gate, splintering wood like straw. Agog had expected more resistance, but the barrier was more for show than actual resistance. Which would make their task harder since they wouldn't be able to block the Romans from storming through the gate.

Right outside near a statue of Dionysus, Agog waited, encouraging his men to move faster. The legions, unleashed by Consul Magnus, ran screaming after the Alexandrian troops, who were already worn from battle.

Inside the city, a barricade was being constructed from wagons and steam chariots too damaged to use. A row of Manticores backed up, facing their arrow launchers outward.

The air was thick with confusion, shouts and screams. Alexandrians manned the inside walls, slaughtering fools in silken togas still trying to watch the battle.

The crimson and steel tide of the Roman legions absorbed the Alexandrians too slow to make it to the city. Agog, busy cheering his fleeing men, almost waited too long to gallop inside the gate. He slapped his mount's rear and climbed over the wagons only moments before the wall of soldiers rushed into the gap to be met with feathered death.

But even the hailstorm of arrows couldn't hold back the Romans, and men climbed over the wagons, crawling under, or somehow making it through. Agog neatly chopped a helmet right from the head of a Roman coming up from beneath a chariot.

Steel clanged and men died beneath the gate, falling like wheat cut with a scythe. Agog swung, and swung, his body in perpetual motion. He tasted salt and grime splattered into his right eye, forcing him to fight with one eye clamped.

The sea of Romans felt never-ending and Agog was certain they would be overrun, when suddenly there were no more Romans to kill. Trumpets flared and they watched the Romans take up positions outside of the city.

Agog climbed the stairs to the top of the wall, ignoring the mound of bodies in the shadow of the gate, the moans of dying men, and the black shapes circling in the sky.

Outside the wall, the Romans drew up their legions. When Agog realized how few men they had actually killed, his heart sank, and doubly when he saw how many legions Magnus actually brought to bear against them.

Nine legions. They stacked up three abreast and three deep. The skirmish at the gate had killed a few centuries, but almost too few to even notice in the overall formation.

Even from the low angle of the wall, the Romans appeared to be a quilt of crimson and steel. The eagles of the Empire were displayed valiantly over the field of battle.

Nine legions. Even when Vestalis arrived, it wouldn't matter. Nine was too many, even if they could last long enough for those scouts to make it east, and return with the hundred steam chariots.

Agog wiped the sweat from his face, ignoring the stinging gash on his forearm still dripping blood.

Nine legions.

"Your Grace!"

An Alexandrian soldier, one whose name he couldn't remember, saluted. "The captains want to know what the plan is."

Agog grumbled as he realized what he was standing on. A wall, an immobile stinking wall that might be the most indefensible piece of dung he'd ever stepped foot on and it was the only thing standing between them and nine legions of the Roman Empire.

"By the jarls, we hold the wall. We hold the god-cursed stinking wall."

THIRTY SEVEN

Hoth neatly hopped over the stone-stacked wall before the bull noticed him.

Down the hill, he could hear the men calling to each other, foraging for wood to burn for fuel. They'd spent the night avoiding the Parthians, only narrowly, by keeping to the back trails through the low hills.

The muscle in his thigh ached from pushing a steam chariot through the mud. The moment before the wheels broke free, he felt a pop in the meat of his leg.

Hoth picked the dirt from his fingernails and continued looking for a safe place to shit. His leg kept him from just crouching behind a bush. He needed something sturdy to lean on and thought he'd found it, until he noticed the bull.

There'd been fighting in the night, but it'd happened at the back of the line, when a group of twenty cataphracts happened upon them. The battle was brief and deadly, the enemy was upon them, jumping onto the backs of the chariots and making the arrow launchers useless by fighting hand to hand.

By the time Hoth had gotten there, limping through the darkness, cursing his leg more than once, and feeling a twinge of sympathy for Heron in her awkward charge, the battle was over. The Parthians fled, having only lost a few men, but having killed a dozen Alexandrians.

They took men from the other chariots to keep them all running. After the skirmish, Hoth found Vestalis and explained what had happened, and together, they decided they needed to set an ambush, one deadly enough to keep the Parthians from pursuing so close.

Scant trees, knobby bare-leafed loners, dotted the crown of the hill. Hoth found a fallen log that he could lean against in a copse filled with low scrub, and thorn bushes.

It was the best he could do, so he sighed and scrambled in, removing the offending thorns from his legs and arms as they pricked him.

Settled comfortably against the log and enjoying the peaceful solitude and shade of the copse, Hoth prepared to complete his task when he heard the rumble of a steam chariot.

Peering through the trees, Hoth saw a familiar balding man climb from the back of his vehicle and march steadily to a place not far from his location.

Hoth thought the general might be taking a moment of rest and prepared to call out a feigned animal noise when he heard the rattling of scale armor and the thump of hoof falls on soft soil.

"Ave, Vestalis," said the rider in Latin. "How goes the chase?"

"Get to the point, Juvenes, I cannot be away very long, nor be seen talking to you," said Vestalis crisply.

"It hasn't been easy to find you, scurrying about the hills, avoiding the Parthians. You should have a care to greet me with a little more warmth," said Juvenes.

"I don't pay you for warmth," said Vestalis, his voice seething. "Now out with it."

"Apologies," said Juvenes sarcastically. "Remember, I can always be bought by a higher bidder. Rome is full of jangling coin purses."

Hoth's injured leg began to cramp, but he feared to adjust and make a noise. He wanted to hear the rest of the exchange.

"If you think someone can pay you more, I will double it," said Vestalis.

"And what makes you think I already haven't been paid double, or more," said Juvenes. "Maybe Emperor Claudius has given me a seat on his council, or one of the Senators has offered me his daughter, or an estate near Palatine Hill."

When the taunt was returned with silence, Hoth craned his head to see through the bushes. He wanted to see the face of this spy who had stolen the voice from Vestalis.

He wanted to see him, and also, he was worried. This Juvenes named powerful Romans, strange words for a spy, making Hoth realize the man might not be a spy at all. Hoth had begun to trust Vestalis, seeing the worth of the man through his actions, but now he questioned that trust, and remembered the ambushes on their way to Syracuse. Hoth rubbed his cramping thigh and concentrated his hearing.

"By Jupiter's cock," exclaimed Vestalis, "I'll deal with your threats later, but for now I have a trap to spring."

"Wind your spring, wind your spring, but who are we springing it on?" cackled Juvenes.

"Betrayal suits you, *Longknife*," said Vestalis. "How many men have you poisoned?"

"Only those that deserved it."

Vestalis must have turned, because his voice seemed fainter. Through the trees, it was hard to tell if he was faced away. "The trap will spring on those that least expect it."

The words twisted in Hoth's gut. He was sure the man was speaking of the Alexandrian side.

The horse whinnied and the pair of men moved up the hill. Their voices fading.

"...and where might this..."

"...a canyon, not far..."

"...the sign..."

Legs screaming, Hoth pushed himself standing, cringing from the prick of thorns against his head. With Vestalis and the spy gone, Hoth scrambled out of the copse, and limp-jogged back down the hill, feeling the blood rush back into his thighs until they tingled.

Are we betrayed?

Truthful to himself, Hoth didn't know. His gut screamed that Vestalis was selling them to the Romans, but Agog had been quite trusting of the man. Should he confront Vestalis and suss an answer from him? It would be foolish. If he were going to betray the Alexandrian side, he'd just lie about his intentions.

No, the only thing he could do was watch and wait. He would know the time of the trap, he heard enough about some canyon. Hoth could guess where, based on the maps they studied together.

He decided he would watch and wait, and until then - Hoth doubled over from cramps - he needed to find a bush to shit behind.

THIRTY EIGHT

I *conceive that these things, King Gelon, will appear incredible to the great majority of people who have not studied mathematics...*
— *The Sand Reckoner by Archimedes*

"For four days, we've searched this piss-water village and for four days we've found nothing," said Apion from around the corner.

Heron crouched in the cubby on the side of the building, trying to make herself as small as possible. Apion and his companion had stopped less than a length away. Heron felt like she could reach out and touch the other man's shoulder. If it'd been Apion, and she had her cane, she might have put a knife in his back.

"Are you sure this is the place mentioned in the Archimedes text?" asked the other man in a strange Latin accent.

"It has to be."

At her feet, the flame in the lantern flickered, a faint orange line glowing through the slats. It was facing in the direction of the two men. If either of them looked down, they would see the lantern and most certainly move to investigate.

"The war might be over by the time we find it and then what kind of influence will it buy with Claudius?"

"We'll find it," seethed Apion. "We'll find it. Even if the war is over, and I doubt it is, the other inventions will buy that influence."

The other man scoffed. "I fail to see the impressiveness of this steel carriage. A fool's notion that pales in comparison to a steam chariot. Only an idiot thinks it's golden and maybe that's why Archimedes hid it, he was embarrassed to let anyone see it."

Heron clenched her fist and tried to breathe shallowly. It felt like her heart was so loud they would hear it.

"A man in your position cannot see the possibilities," said Apion. "This invention could change the world again, so leave your meddling to politics."

The other man blew a haughty breath out his nose. "I see. Remember who funds your little expedition. We thought it would buy us something valuable. Something to take to the Emperor. The Machine Man would have been a nice prize, but you let him drown in that cave."

Relieved that Rome thought she was dead, Heron concentrated on the other man's accent. He was a true Roman, she decided by the halting diction, probably born and raised in the political knife-fighting of that city. He was a man used to speaking to Senators and Consuls.

She also found herself agreeing with Apion. Except for the fact that he'd tried to kill her, he might not be as bad as his brother, Philo.

"I remember," said Apion. "No need to remind me."

"Then find this third weapon and let's be done with this place. I still think we should kill all the villagers and the priests so we can search this town at our leisure. Its strange construction lends itself to some hidden mystery. Let's be done with it and get back to Rome."

Heron didn't realize they'd left until she heard the foot scuffs moving away. They continued to talk, but the wind hid their conversation. Once they were out of hearing, she let out a heavy sigh.

"This town is constructed strangely," she muttered to herself and before she could take a step, a idea formed itself from that thought.

The town *was* constructed strangely. Too odd, in fact. Alexandria was built straight and true, its streets criss-crossing in an orderly fashion, like a Roman legion. This town, no village, seemed oddly built.

The center of the town where the bonfire raged was circular. Not unheard of, but the design put buildings at off angles to each other and created streets that widened as they went outward from the center.

The other main street, the one that hugged the outside wall, curved away from the back of the village like a parabola. Heron envisioned the two streets in her mind like bright string lying on chalky papyrus.

...so find the focus of the sun and know that once you hold my final weapon, flame is your only enemy.

Every good riddle had meaning hidden within the words. Did the shape of the streets indicate something from the last text?

Heron steadied herself against the wall, forgetting for a moment the world was a real thing beneath her legs. Festival noises echoed faintly as if they were a part of a dream.

...focus of the sun...

Focus.

Focus?

She wanted to scream, the answer seemed right there before her, if she could only take that last step...

Focus!

The focus of the sun. The center. The mathematical center was the focus. But the center of the circle, was the center of the town, which was the focus, and a bonfire raged on it. Was she going to have to wait for the festival to end?

But there was also a focus in a parabola.

Heron looked back the way she had come: where the statue of Archimedes stood.

She lurched in that direction, the stump at the end of her knee aching from overuse. When she reached the statue, she carefully pulled the slats away from the lantern, letting a warm honeyed glow spread over the street.

She searched around, but found no obvious hidden entrance. On one side of the street was the statue of Archimedes, facing the center of town. His outstretched arms formed the parabola, which from the street followed, one curving each direction.

The focus would not be at the statue. It would have to be at the center of parabola, the point at which the shape was derived.

Heron closed her eyes and estimated the focus of the parabola. When she opened them, she realized the entrance would be inside the black-smith's shop.

There was no door, so she limped over the threshold, holding the lantern high and hoping the blacksmith slept in a different location, or was busy at the festival. Heron had to go back to the doorway to get the distance from the statue a few times before she knew where she needed to look.

At the heart of the smithy, at the base of the anvil, Heron got onto her knees and cleared away the loose dirt and rocks with her hand. At first, she thought she might have figured wrong, but then her hand hit something metal and smooth.

She dug around the lip, finding an iron ring and pulled. The trapdoor had been closed for a long time, she assumed, and was probably stuck, so she resumed digging, finding the edge of the door and clearing away until she could see its outline.

Heron paused before her second try, wiping away sweat from her forehead. Grabbing the ring with both hands, wedging the metal fingers around the loop and holding on with her other hand.

Heron pulled, leaning backwards. The straps at the end of her arm dug into her shoulder. Fingers cramped and her forehead felt like it was going to split wide. Heron pulled until her lower back burned with effort.

When it started to give, Heron threw every last bit of energy into the task, until the wood groaned and the door shuddered open, sending dust into her mouth.

With the trapdoor broken free, she could easily flip it up to lean against the anvil. The warm light of the lantern melted down the steps going beneath the smithy.

The air was stale and Heron wondered if the owner of the shop knew what it was built upon.

Gathering her energy, Heron carefully stepped down until her head was level with the trapdoor. Realizing the steps went much further, further than her lantern could see, she set it down and pulled the trapdoor back into place. It wouldn't keep the owner from finding it in the morning, but she didn't want it to be too easy to find for Apion, should he figure out the riddle.

Heron was halfway down before she remembered Sepharia and Jarngard. She nearly went back up to get them, but decided to go a little further and see if there was anything worth finding before getting them.

Part of her knew it was anticipation for finding the last and hopefully the best of Archimedes' secrets. She promised herself she would go only a little bit further before she would go back, but at each step, one hand holding the thin strap from the lantern, the other, the metal one, scraping along the stone to keep balance, the lure of secrets revealed pulled her forward.

At each step, the air grew colder, but no fresher. She even coughed a few times. So focused on maintaining her balance and not falling, she hadn't realized the room had opened up and the stairs had ended.

Just beyond the edge of the light, something sparkled. She felt all her senses attune to whatever it was she couldn't see. She felt poised on the edge of a grand discovery.

Heron carefully set the lantern down and lifted the hood, flooding light into the chamber.

She lifted the lantern.

And gasped.

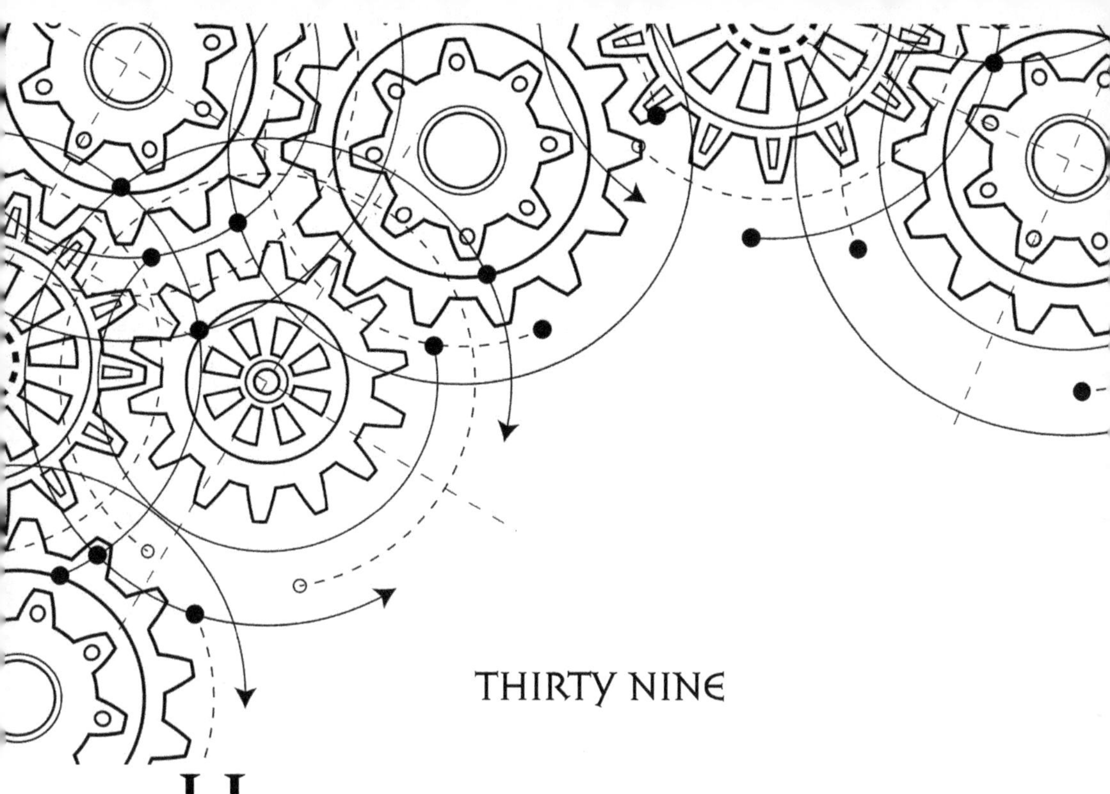

THIRTY NINE

Hoth the Black prepared to kill a man.

And not just any man, but the general of the Alexandrian army, Titus Claudius Vestalis.

He just didn't know how he was going to do it.

Hoth drummed his fingers against the shelf of rock he sat upon, feet dangling. The stone was warm to the touch and the knife-like edge pressed against the underside of his thigh.

It wasn't a simple thing to kill the general of an army. Well, killing him was easy, but surviving the murder wasn't easily done, not without a lot of coconspirators, of which he had none.

And Hoth planned on surviving this encounter. He was willing to place himself in danger, but only when he thought the gods in his favor, which usually meant that he had a water-tight plan.

But the man was a traitor. He had to be. Vestalis' ring of spies was legendary. It was how he'd gained such a sizable merchant force in Alexandria, by always knowing more than his competitors and that influence had gone all the way to Rome.

While he was *pretty certain* of Vestalis' guilt, he wasn't *absolutely sure.* Not enough to risk his life and not without a plan.

The wind coaxed gooseflesh from his arms as a shelf of gray skies slid southwest from the mountains, bringing the hint of rain. Hoth took a deep breath, inhaling coal smoke and clover.

The mountains chopped away the horizon to the north beneath the cloud cover and replaced it with a black curtain. Hoth enjoyed the lingering warmth in the stone while he considered his options.

His thoughts were broken by the unexpectedly cheery voice of general Vestalis. "Ave, Hoth the Black. Do you smell that in the air?"

He paused. "Rain?"

Vestalis clasped his hand on Hoth's shoulder, unfamiliar creases around his smiling lips. "No, victory. I've determined the location of our battle."

"And where is that?" asked Hoth, while the word *canyon* echoed in his mind.

"A canyon not far from here," explained Vestalis, the eager grin making him ghoulish. "We'll finish the Parthians, once and for all and meet Agog west of here, fresh from his victory in Antioch, with enough time to prepare for Consul Magnus."

"You sound confident of victory," said Hoth.

"I am," he replied, "with the Parthians. Of Magnus, I would not dare to be overconfident. The faster we can win our battle, the better chance we have against him."

"Do you hate this Magnus?" asked Hoth, curious.

"No," said Vestalis. "I bare no ill against him, except that he is on the other side."

Hoth nodded, matching Vestalis' smile. It wouldn't do him any good to let the general suspect.

"So what of our plans? This canyon?" asked Hoth.

Vestalis unrolled a papyrus that had been tucked under his arm and slapped it on the shelf of rock. Hoth hopped down and took his place next to the general. After placing rocks on the corners to keep the wind from destroying their strategy table, Vestalis jammed his finger into a little squiggle on the map.

"There is the canyon," said Vestalis, "barely more than a ravine, not even big enough to be named, but clearly noted by the cartographer."

"Do you think Khusra fool enough to let us trap him there? He seems canny enough to avoid such an obvious ambush location," said Hoth.

"Exactly," said Vestalis. "He's been bold when necessary and cautious when he needs to. He's done better than the father or brother could have ever done. It's a shame we didn't lock up the Parthians for our side."

Hoth shoved a hand into his short, but growing hair. The roots were blonde while the rest was soot black and it bothered him more than he liked to admit.

"You still haven't said how we're going to trap him," said Hoth.

"You're right," said Vestalis.

Hoth frowned. This giddiness was unnatural on the general.

Vestalis continued, "Hasn't he not hounded us whenever we've been stuck or made a mistake in our travels?"

Hoth nodded.

"And whenever we've erred he's punished us with a quick strike?"

"I haven't slept more than an hour straight in a week," groused Hoth. "The size of his force means he can withstand mistakes, while ours means one mistake and we're finished. Fifty chariots versus a thousand armored horse."

"Exactly. He takes advantage where he sees it. So let him see an advantage," said Vestalis.

"He'd have to think he had you trapped to go in there. The other side is blocked by a river which can't be forded in the high waters," said Hoth, staring at the map, trying to see where Vestalis was leading him. If the man was a traitor like he thought, then this trap was probably for the Alexandrian side, not the Parthians.

"And he will," said Vestalis. "I'll lead him right through the canyon and up to the water. He'll think we're defeated and take his advantage."

Hoth nodded. "The advantage will be all his side. The ground slopes toward the river, giving him speed and the ground is soaked from the rain, turning our steam chariots to mule-drawn wagons. He might take some initial losses on the first charge, but once the horse is in our ranks, he'll cut us down in close-quarter skirmishes. It'll be a slaughter, and not one I'd care to be in attendance to."

"So you think he'd take that chance?" asked Vestalis.

"He'd be a fool not to," replied Hoth, shaking his head, not seeing the advantage for Alexandria. "But why give him that? What do we gain by putting ourselves in that situation. Once we're against the river, we're corpses."

Hoth paused while Vestalis watched him closely. Was this his traitorous plan? To lure them into the canyon and let the Parthians win? Vestalis had many chances to lead them to failure so far. Why keep the farce up?

Hoth cleared his throat and continued, "If we had two hundred steam chariots, we could split them and line the others at the top of the canyon walls and rain arrows on them as they went through, but if Khusra doesn't see the full side go in, he'll never follow."

"What do we have that can do as much damage as the steam chariots?" asked Vestalis coyly.

Hoth scratched at the scraggly beard he hadn't had time to shave away and wondered why the man was leading him on like this. Why not just explain the plan? It bothered Hoth for many reasons.

"If it was drier, we might trap them in the canyon and start a brush fire," said Hoth, shrugging.

"Close," said Vestalis. "I propose we put the steam catapults at the top of the canyon. Khusra won't notice they're missing. We'll fire them into the massed cavalry after we've blocked the far end with Manticores. When they try to escape the trap, we'll chase them back out and rout them as they flee."

After a bit of thought, Hoth shook his head. "It's too risky. They'll never take the bait, and once they do, they only have to wait us out. We'll be the ones trapped."

Vestalis raised an eyebrow. "Not even if I'm the bait?"

"Maybe," said Hoth, realizing he might get his chance to kill the general after all.

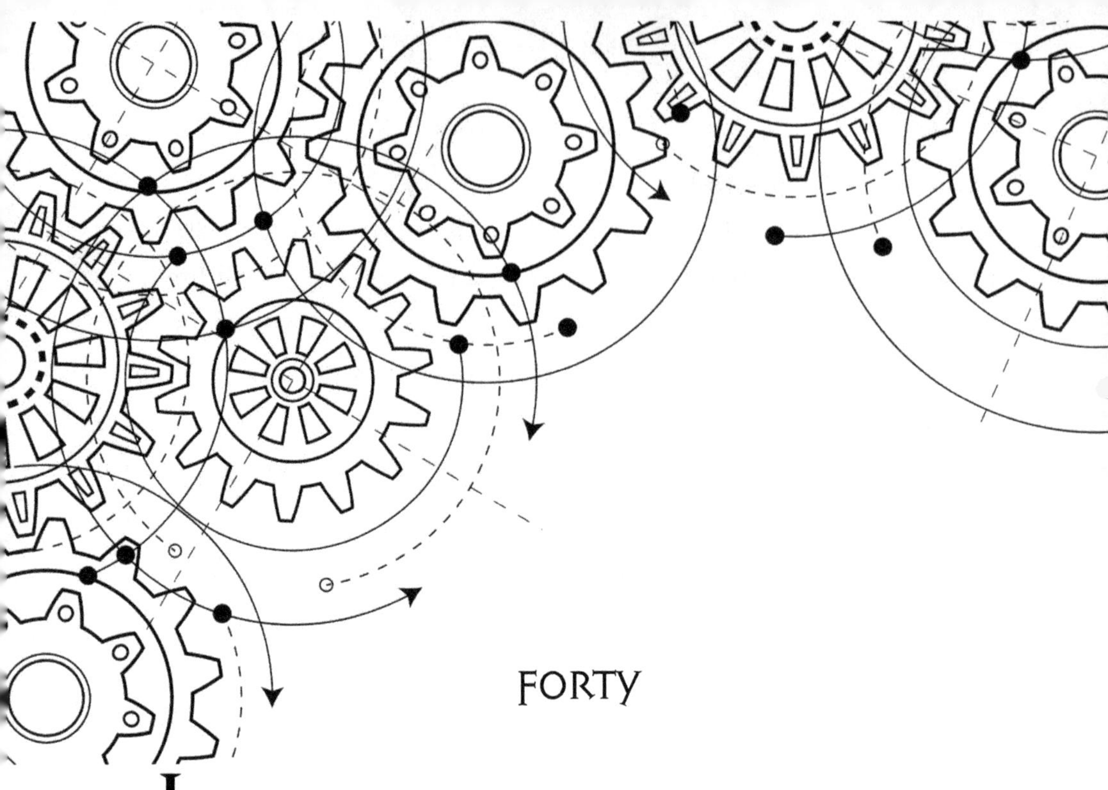

FORTY

I *think often upon the soldiers that the King sent from the safety of our walls.
Theirs was a mighty deed and I am humbled upon it. I fear my will is not the same.
— The Journal of Archimedes*

The world was not meant for such wondrous machines.

Heron knelt on the cold stone, stone that had not seen another foot-
fall for a century she guessed, and contemplated the glittering wall before
her.

Archimedes was a genius. It was such an obvious fact that even the
unlearned might know it, if only for the stories told about his life: the gold
crown, the heat ray, or any of the other tales from the siege of Syracuse.

But Heron had never been confronted with his genius on a personal
level before, not so obvious, not so interconnected, and the invention that
she gazed upon was only the barrier that kept her from the true prize: the
third weapon of Archimedes.

And what a weapon it must be, hidden behind a magnificent contraption. One he had to have devised before his death, to protect his legacy. No one else could have created it. Even the puzzle in the watery chamber of the second weapon was no match for this.

There were gears. Lots of them. A wall full of them. An interlocking wall of gears so dense it made the Heavens Mechanism into a mere toy, the aeolipile in comparison to the steam mechanical.

If she stood on her tippie-toes, a feat of balance given her mechanical leg, she might touch the ceiling, or at least her outstretched fingers would be close. From side to side, she could pace ten strides.

That space, from beginning to end, was filled with gears, and like the puzzle cube, hidden behind a glass case. This one had weathered the centuries without collecting mold and she wondered if she cracked it, the breath of those workers would come reeling out, unhindered by time.

At intervals along the wall, farther than a person's arms stretched wide, were holes set into the glass. Without even examining the construction, Heron knew exactly what they were for.

In Alexandria, she'd designed doors to capture a thief's hand, should he not address the locks correctly. And in the pit beneath the Temple of Sobek, she'd put her hand into a box, only to have it come out a stump.

Heron rubbed her upper arm absently, the memory of that moment like a grime in her mouth that she just couldn't get rid of.

Seven choices. There were seven holes in the wall, one of which would open the way to the third weapon, the others, and after a brief examination of the ceiling, would result in the collapsing of the room and her death.

Archimedes' wall of gears was a devilishly clever affair. Heron chuckled lightly to herself. If it were anyone else, but her, they would have zero chance of bypassing the trap.

The number of gears and connections was dizzying. Her mind strained at the effort of understanding. Who else but her could do it?

She stared at her mechanical arm and leg. The Machine Man. *Michan-ikos.* One machine to another.

It was not easy to determine the answer. She spent what she assumed was most of the night walking back and forth along the wall, ignoring the ache in her hip, her dry smacking lips, thoughts of her daughter or Jarngard. All of that would have to wait.

When at last she stood before her answer, an indiscriminant hole second from the left, deep enough to put the arm almost up to the elbow in, and wide enough to accommodate only one, she knew there'd been one more layer of protection added into the wall and laughed, a sharp and slightly mad cackle.

The piercing echo in the small space surprised her, forcing her to cringe momentarily. Upon pulling the lever at the end of the hole, her arm would be chopped off right above the elbow. Right where Lysimachus had taken her arm. The cunning blade was hidden behind the gears, but she could see glimmering hints of it.

Sacrifice. It was Archimedes' final lesson. Nothing in life that important can be had without sacrifice.

Archimedes had sacrificed his life in the defense of his city.

It made her wonder if he hadn't purposely incited the soldier to kill him. So he could not be used by his enemies. The presence of these elaborate hidden weapons and the plans it would have taken to make them happen gave credence to that thought.

Using the lantern, she peered into the hole. At least, the lever would be easy to pull with her mechanical arm, a sacrifice she'd already made.

But upon second examination, she realized the problem. The blade in the wall had to come all the way down and through her arm or the door wouldn't open. Otherwise, an interested party could just push a sword into the hole and snag the end of the lever to actuate it without risking their arm.

A true sacrifice. Heron stared at her other arm, the flesh and blood one, and grimaced. Even if she wanted to do it, she wasn't sure she'd survive the blood loss. She'd barely survived the attack from the Nile crocodile.

If Apion were down here and had figured out the correct hole, he'd just have one of his soldiers lose his arm, but she didn't have that luxury, and even if Sepharia or Jarngard was here, she wouldn't ask.

Heron stared at the hole and her mechanical arm for a while. There was no way to have enough leverage to move the lever *and* keep the straps loose enough so that the blade fell harmlessly between the cradle of the arm and her stump.

She was trapped by the dilemma.

For a brief moment, Heron considered putting her arm in the wrong hole and bringing the whole thing down on her head to keep the Empire from having the third weapon, but she didn't have the courage for that.

Sighing, she made her decision.

Heron carefully removed her tunic, feeling the chill air coax goose-flesh from her skin. She felt foolish, standing there wrapped in bandages, the straps and bindings that held her together apparent for anyone to see.

But it was her alone.

Using her teeth and the uncooperative mechanical hand, Heron was able to tie the tunic around her upper arm to keep the bleeding to a min-imum. If she bled too much, she would place her new stump into the lantern flame and burn it closed.

With the tourniquet in place, Heron stepped to the hole, keeping the lantern near. She took a deep and hesitant breath, feeling her lips trem-bling from the cold as she put her right hand into the hole.

The lever at the end of the hole had a light grunge on it as if the rot of time was beginning to take hold. Another few decades or a century, and the mechanism might not work anymore.

Before she could lose her nerve, she closed her eyes and pulled the lever.

FORTY ONE

Hoth the Black hummed to himself as he waited to spring his treachery on general Vestalis. If you're going to do a deed, you might as well make peace with it right away, Hoth had long ago decided.

So he sang his cheery song, under his breath and in his language, for the tale was one of backstabbing and double-crossing. A song sung on the cold seas of the North.

The melody was light and catchy, and the men stationed with him at the lip of the canyon smiled in response. Of course, that was the purpose of the melody, to sound like a tale of frivolousness.

For them, it took the edge off their nervousness. Hoth could see it in their eyes. While their mouths upturned at the corners, almost too much, like a yoke strained by oxen, the eyes were flat and dead.

While they prepared the shot for the steam catapult, one soldier threw up his breakfast into the bushes. The others laughed and joked with him, but Hoth knew they were probably jealous of the release. Nothing like a good puking before battle, though it left one shaky and hungry. A price to pay for a clear stomach.

They'd split up the three catapults to maximize the damage. Each one pointed down at a separate section of the canyon. They'd placed brush around the wagon and the port to keep it hidden until the proper moment.

Hoth commanded the third steam catapult. He'd taken the firing position, so it would be his accident that killed Vestalis.

The general planned to ride at the back of the line, piloting the fastest steam chariot, but keeping it right ahead of the Parthian force, taunting them onward. They had to be drawn forward by emotion rather than tactics.

So far, Khusra had kept his troops on a tight leash. The thrashing at Alexandria had given him battle wisdom, but Vestalis planned to break that discipline.

And that was when Hoth planned to kill the general. If Vestalis led the Parthian force into the canyon as designed, Hoth would follow his orders, and the general would live.

But if Vestalis appeared without the Parthians, proof that he'd lured them through the canyon to trap them against the river, Hoth would fire upon Vestalis to kill him.

Hoth adjusted the blades at his hip. He might need to kill a few soldiers before he escaped on the nearby steam chariot. While his motives might be noble, in the heat of battle, the soldiers on his side might see the attack as treachery and try to kill him.

Hoth was prepared to kill all five men if he had to, and he didn't think any of them were keen enough fighters to test him.

If Vestalis had betrayed them, Hoth planned to take the steam chariot over the hills, he'd picked the hardiest one for that purpose, to find his way west and warn Agog. Hopefully, the force at Antioch would have been defeated by then and they could prepare for Consul Magnus.

The remaining steam chariots would be lost; Hoth just hoped they could kill enough Parthian cataphracts to make the sacrifice worth it. He didn't think it would be, but that was just the way it was going to have to be.

Hoth wasn't foolish enough to go down with the ship, a reason he'd been a captain in the northern seas for so long. Bravery only got a man killed.

He felt the rumble of the steam chariots in the soles of his feet long before he saw them. The growling echoes bouncing through the canyon made it sound like a pride of lions fighting over a fallen antelope.

When he saw the first vehicle speeding through the gap between the mercilessly vertical walls, a tightness formed in his chest.

Which would it be? Victory or betrayal?

As the steam chariots flew by, dust filling the tight passage, he wished Heron was there, if only to count the number passing so he might know when Vestalis was due to arrive.

Hoth chanced closing his eyes to focus on his hearing. The clatter of a hundred pistons made mockery of his attempt. He could no more hear if there were Parthian cavalry behind than he could spit onto the sun. Behind him, two of the soldiers held fingers to their ears.

A motion to the soldier on the back coaxed more fuel into the fire chamber of the catapult. When Hoth pulled the lever, he wanted the steel and scrap metal to decimate whoever was in its path, be that the Parthians or general Vestalis.

Near the end of the Alexandrian line, the vehicles trickled past, more spread out than the tight formation at the front. Hoth noted how none of the men on the chariots glanced backwards. Were there no Parthians following?

Eventually, only one steam chariot passed at a time. Hoth leaned out over the edge, keeping his hand on the lever to try and see up the canyon.

A steady ringing clung to his ears even though the deafening volume had reduced.

It had to be the last few chariots he decided. Hoth wished he could see the other steam catapults at least. If they were firing, he knew the trap was safe.

The last chariot puttered into Hoth's stretch of canyon at a leisurely pace. General Vestalis stood at the steerage, piloting his craft through the canyon with care.

No hoof beats followed him. Though the ringing in his ears had reduced only slightly, Hoth swore he should be able to hear the Parthian cavalry if they were following.

The general would be in range within seconds. Hoth glanced to the soldiers on the steam catapult, noting their position in case he had to fight them. The one on the back would die first.

The general's steam chariot stopped, almost directly beneath the catapult's line of fire. Hoth glanced once more up the empty canyon before he made his decision.

Hoth pulled the lever.

FORTY TWO

Shall we not make an end of fighting against this geometrical Briareus who, sitting at ease by the sea, plays pitch and toss with our ships to our confusion, and by the multitude of missiles that he hurls at us outdoes the hundred-handed giants of mythology?

— Account from General Marcellus of the Roman Empire

Cold steel kissed her forearm, bringing wetness.

Heron leaned against the wall, her useless mechanical arm tapping woefully on the glass.

Gears sang and clattered, like a thousand bells waking from centuries of slumber.

Inside the glass case, the machinery was alive, serpentine and spinning, of metal jewels rotating in the orangish light of the flickering lantern.

Heron prepared herself for the horror of seeing her dismembered arm. The blade had gone through with such force she barely felt it, but she knew she needed to cauterize the wound quickly or lose too much blood.

When she pulled her right arm from the hole, she reeled and breath caught in her throat, while her heart tried to beat its way out of her chest.

Past her elbow, there was still more flesh and bone. There was even a forearm and a wrist and a hand. An oily substance was splattered across her skin.

With a shaking hand, Heron lifted the lantern and peered into the hole. The blade had an arm shaped space in the middle of it.

Heron leaned her forehead against the cold, hard glass. Now that she hadn't lost her arm, she wondered how she could be so stupid as to give up her flesh and blood for this third weapon.

As usual, so single mindedly focused on the task, she'd nearly sacrificed a limb to meet her goal.

She could take it as a lesson, a warning for future endeavors, but she knew herself. Knew that once she had decided something, there was no going back. It was just that this was the first time she really understood that about herself and it scared her like nothing else had really ever scared her before.

If they won the war against Rome, the danger wouldn't be over. This path they were set upon would require more sacrifice. Who else would sacrifice themselves and for what purpose?

Doubt didn't linger long in her breast, she dismissed it quickly, as she always had. Doubt was expected, as was failure. She just hoped to survive each failure with enough knowledge to keep going.

Heron pushed the sweaty hair from her forehead and looked for her prize. A door at the side of the chamber stood open. After donning her tunic, she passed through it cautiously, wondering if there were more traps.

The hallway went straight through stone, carefully cut by hand. Heron rubbed her hand across the chisel marks, wondering how many years they'd labored at this task.

Hidden by a trick of the light, Heron nearly missed the door. The stone was inset and a steel door blocked her way. A lever stuck out of the wall and rather than examine it (and drained from the earlier encounter), Heron pulled it down.

Inside the stone, gears grinded and an out-breath puffed from the sides of the door, spitting dust into the hallway. Heron pulled it open and stale air rushed past her, ruffling her hair and making her squint.

The door created a seal on the room. Heron smacked her lips. The dry air had sucked any remaining moisture from her mouth and she was dizzy from a lack of food.

Stepping inside, she could immediately sense the size of the room and lifted the lantern high, but the light only found the ceiling and not the far wall.

A chill vibrated through her, starting at the base of the spine and traveling up until her shoulders quivered. Lined up in neat rows like soldiers preparing for battle were hundreds of tar soaked barrels.

Remembering the warning from the second weapon, Heron hooded the open flame on the lantern. Heron moved cautiously to a pedestal. Engraved upon the steel was a message:

Vulcan's kiss will ignite passions only fit for a god.

Heron knew that Vulcan's kiss was flame. She assumed whatever this substance was, that it was dangerous.

Below the message was a recipe including ingredients and how to mix them. Though the terminology was unfamiliar, she recognized the word for saltpeter.

But it seems she didn't need to know the recipe, there were ample quantities in the chamber.

Behind the pedestal was a steel box. Opening it revealed glass globes filled with black powder. A wick stuck from the stoppered end. Though she was curious, she dared not test the globe, unsure of what *passions* it would release.

Also, inside the box was a scroll case. A quick examination revealed more notes in Archimedes' scrawling handwriting explaining the origins of his invention and proposed uses. It seemed he'd gotten the idea from a trader from the far east. Archimedes called the substance *spark powder*.

With limited carrying capacity, Heron chose to tuck the scroll case under her arm, while hanging the lantern from her mechanical fist and cradling a powder-globe in her good hand.

The hallway that went past the chamber had another door at the end, this one larger and with another iron seal. Heron realized the door was meant to keep people from entering the other side and she had a good guess as to where this one came out.

After a long and tiring climb up a winding staircase cut into the stone, Heron found herself at a trap door in the ceiling. Leaving the lantern on the steps, Heron pushed her way out to find the morning sun glaring down at her.

Wind blew hot ash into her face, forcing her to spit. Heron stood near the remnants of the bonfire, hot coals still glowing in the center and swirls of ash drifting past her feet. With each wind gust, she felt alternating hot and cool across her skin.

Ancient stone buildings stood sentinel around the center of the village. In the distance, towering white clouds marched across the plains.

Heron was about to turn around when she heard a voice that sent a knife into her gut.

"I should have known you'd find the third weapon," said Apion. "It's a shame you'll be giving it to me now."

Standing on the other side of the smoldering bonfire, Apion smiled triumphantly at her. Directly in front of Apion stood Jarngard, looking less than pleased.

Heron couldn't figure out why Jarngard hadn't killed the Roman, until Apion leaned to the side, exposing the *gastraphetes* in his grip. The name for the crossbow meant 'belly shooter' and Heron was well acquainted with its construction. She'd written extensively on it in her work *Belopoeica* and had based her larger *cheirobalistras* on its design.

In this case, her knowledge worked against her, because she knew that with the squeeze of the trigger, the arrow would impale itself into Jarn-gard's back, piercing every important organ along its path.

"Are you ready to give me the Archimedes weapon now?"

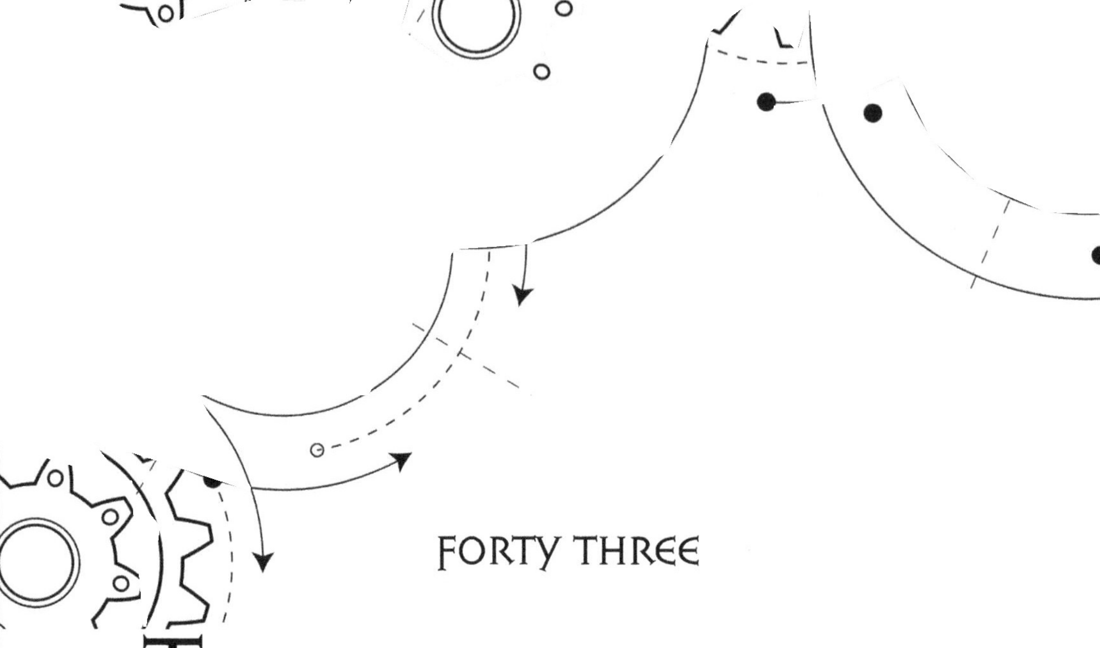

FORTY THREE

The outcome of battle often hinged on the smallest of details.

As Hoth pulled the lever, staring intently at Vestalis on his steam chariot who at that moment had glanced upward, he remembered another time and another battle.

In this other time, Hoth had been a sailor on another man's boat, still young enough not to have earned his infamous name yet. Their ship, and a dozen others, was raiding a Saxon village.

They had come upon the village nearly empty except for women and children. The leader of the raid, One Hand Vosü, wanted fresh food and supplies for a journey west and the village had provided a convenient target.

Disappointed by the lack of fighting, Hoth had wandered through the center of the village where he found the stables. After a brief investigation, he noted the gear remaining: saddle bags, bridles, and saddles; but no weapons. The Saxon men had left bare-backed, which meant that the men of the village had not ridden far and had probably gone to initiate a boy into the traditions of the village.

Hoth went running back to One Hand Vosü to warn him, when he felt the rumble in the earth. Taking a village when the men were unaware was easier than holding it when armed riders returned. As sailors, they were better fighters on the deck, or in ambush.

With the warning, most of the sailors escaped back to the ships, except for a few that couldn't pull themselves away from the womenfolk and ended the day short a head. The day was branded into Hoth's memory and before the lever completely clicked into the firing position, he remembered feeling the beat of galloping horses through the earth long before he could hear them.

Though any vibration would be muddled by the escaping steam chariots, Hoth concentrated on the balls of his feet. Almost immediately he distinguished the pounding hooves over the steady thrum. He stopped his arm motion mid-pull.

Below in the canyon, Vestalis tilted his head as if he'd noted his near assassination and then he glanced behind. The roar of stampeding cataphracts flooded through the stone walls and Vestalis piloted his steam chariot out the gap right before a group of Manticores blocked the exit.

When Hoth finally pulled the lever, the steam catapult wagon shuddered with such ferocity he bit his tongue. His men jumped to reload the catapult, motions ingrained from daily practice, but Hoth stared slack jawed at the destruction below him.

Men and horses had been blown over like leaves in a brisk wind. Hoth glanced at his feeble swords and wondered what would become of war when an army had many more of these steam catapults.

Hoth decided he'd rather head to places unknown in his ship than fight in a war that cut men down like wheat.

One of his men tapped him on the shoulder. Hoth grit his teeth and yanked on the lever again.

Even the linked chain armor the Parthian cataphracts wore did nothing to stop death raining down on them. And what he did not decimate with the steam catapult, the Manticores ripped apart with their arrow launchers.

Hoth fired the steam catapult one more time before the Parthians broke and fled the canyon. Steam chariots raced after, flinging arrows like rain.

With the work done, Hoth congratulated his crew on a successful ambush, slapping shoulders and telling jokes.

The line of steam chariots flooding after the Parthians still rumbled below them, but Hoth had no intention of joining the chase. When the war was over, and he hoped it was over soon, he had no intention of continuing with the army.

Nektam had promised him a massive new iron ship, one bigger than any made before it. Then he would have a dozen of these steam catapults placed on the deck. Once there, he would stay on the seas. Better a ship to ship battle than to be indiscriminately killed by these inventions of Heron.

That woman was changing the world.

FORTY FOUR

"*Stand away, fellow, from my diagram.*"

— *Last account of Archimedes before his death, recorded in the History of Syracuse by Plutarch*

"I won't give you the weapon," said Heron, leaning on her good leg since the other ached with the effort of the long night. Even as she tried to stand perfectly still, the straps bit into the flesh around her thigh.

Apion frowned, his narrow set eyes wrinkled in disappointment. "Then I'll kill him and take you prisoner. I'm giving you a chance to let your friend live."

Heron feigned at thought. She didn't really plan to let Apion kill Jarngard, but she didn't have a plan. Without turning her head, Heron glanced to the spaces between the buildings looking for Sepharia.

Jarngard stood as passively as she'd ever seen him. Arms hanging limply at his side. His face was drained of thought as he stared at a spot in the smoldering bonfire ahead of them.

"What say you?" yelled Apion, interrupting her thoughts. "I'm tired of this village and want to get back to Rome. With or without your friend alive."

Heron gripped the cool hard glass in her right hand. The glass was thick and it fit snuggly in her palm. She wondered if it would still work, or even what it would do. She didn't even know what the powder inside was for. Without understanding it, she couldn't use it as a weapon. As far as she knew, it was a toy like the aeolipile. There would be no time to lean down and light the wick anyway.

"I'm thinking," she shouted back when Apion shifted restlessly.

The wind blew hot air into her face, forcing her to shield her eyes with her mechanical arm.

"Come with me back to Rome," offered Apion. "The nobles will worship you and your inventions can spread like wildfire on the back of the Empire. You can even bring your friend."

In her heart, she knew she should delay and not answer, or lie to him. It would do no good to force his hand, but she was getting tired of delaying.

"I won't," she said. "Not for an Empire than enslaves its people and treats women like cattle."

Apion tilted his head curiously. "Such opinions for a man who creates weapons of death and who seeks the dangerous inventions of Archimedes. Tell me, Heron, are the weapons you found as wondrous as I hope?"

"I do not know," she answered truthfully.

Apion shrugged. "It does not matter. I'll find a way to use them. The Emperor will pour favor on me for their capture, and for yours."

"You shouldn't give it to him," said Jarngard suddenly.

He was looking directly at her, gristled jaw pulsing with thought.

"Shut up, Northman," said Apion, poking him in the back with the *gastraphetes.*

"You're not going to come away with me after this," Jarngard said to her. "You're not going to head east to parts unknown on an adventure as you said you would."

At first, Heron didn't catch his meaning. His words were a statement, not a question. He was saying what she knew deep down in her heart.

"I don't know," she replied, not wanting to admit it.

"You're not," he said. "I know it, even if you don't. There will always be another invention, another world shaking idea, another investigation into the great mysteries of the world. You'd get bored on the road."

"I wouldn't," she said half-heartedly.

Apion poked Jarngard in the back with his weapon. "Shut up."

Jarngard glanced dismissively over his shoulder. "Let him kill me and escape."

Apion scowled. "I said stop speaking."

"You don't mean that," she said to Jarngard, ignoring Apion.

"I do." He shook his head sadly. "I'm tired. Tired of war, tired of killing, tired of watching friends die."

"So you'd have rather gone back to the North on that ship?" she asked accusingly.

"No. I'm glad I stayed, that I got to love you for a little while, but it'll never work."

The weapon in Apion's hand dipped as he watched. Heron could see the slow realization on his face, the understanding born from their conversation.

"You're a woman," said Apion.

"Yes," she replied.

"Did my brother find out? Is that why you killed him?"

She shook her head. "It was as I told you before, he was jealous of my designs. I only killed him when he tried to kill me."

Apion nodded slowly. "Given your mastery of the Archimedes

weapons, I'm inclined to believe you rather than my brother's ghost." He paused, coming to an internal conclusion. "If you come to Rome with me, I won't hold his death against you. Or your gender. It's your mind the Empire needs."

"I told you, I won't be a part of your slavery," she said.

"Then I'm going to have to kill him," said Apion, shrugging.

At that moment, Jarngard caught her eye. She saw his action in the grim line of his lips, the hard stare beneath a furrowed brow. She knew what he was going to do.

She realized that she could stop it. Agree to hand herself over and Jarngard would not go through with his sacrifice. He would live even if she was imprisoned in Rome.

A deep and heavy sigh invaded her chest. A tightness squeezed as she sucked in warm, sooty air through clenched teeth.

The decision weighed on her like chains. There would always be sacrifices, even sacrifices no one wanted, especially her.

"Farewell, Jarngard," said Heron. "It was good to know you."

Behind him, Apion smiled, seeing that he had won.

Jarngard's mouth half opened and the tension went out of his body.

A cold sweat formed on Heron's back, even as the remaining heat of last night's bonfire swirled around her legs. An ache formed in her chest, right between her breasts. She clamped her eyes together briefly before opening them again.

Sacrifice.

It was the lesson she'd learned below. To truly change the world, there had to be sacrifices. Archimedes knew that when he let himself be killed by a soldier at the end of the siege of Syracuse to keep his inventions safe.

And now she knew it. There had to be sacrifices. Even if it meant going to Rome. It was the only way she knew out of this puzzle.

"I'll bury your body in the North," she said.

The confusion on Jarngard's face was brief and terrible, but then he understood. He understood and smiled. A grin filled him with such relief it hurt her to look upon it.

Apion seemed to be working through the meaning of her words, but she didn't want to give him much longer.

Sacrifice. She couldn't change the world from Rome, not unless it was Alexandria that ruled it.

Jarngard grabbed the leather pouch around his neck and yanked, tossing it into the ashes. Dust puffed up around the impact before it caught flame.

"The gods are done with me now," he said with a grin that went all the way to his toes, "but bury me in Alexandria, it was as good a home as any."

Jarngard spun around, reaching out to knock the *gastraphetes* away. For a brief moment, she thought he might avoid the weapon, but Apion shuddered and Jarngard lurched forward.

Blood bloomed against the back of Jarngard's tunic as he pulled Apion into an embrace. Philo's brother pulled out a knife and managed to slice Jarngard across the arm before he snagged it.

Breaking out of her stupor, Heron leaned down and put the end of the wick into a piece of flame at the edge of the coals. Sparks fell from the wick and suddenly, Heron didn't want to be holding the glass ball.

For fear of breaking it, she tossed it underhanded, aiming for Apion's feet. It fell short, bouncing with a large *clack* on the stone, and rolled just behind the grappling men.

When the Archimedes weapon did nothing, she turned to look for a place to run. Even with an arrow in his chest, Jarngard was putting up a fight, but she knew it wouldn't be long.

Heron looked back a moment before a bright light seared across her vision and she was thrown onto her back, knocking the air from her lungs

With her ears ringing and a bit of blood trickling into her eyes, Heron sat up. She tasted coppery salt and spit bloody mucus onto the stones.

Sepharia ran to her side and patted out the hem of her tunic that had caught fire when the coals had been blown over her. She'd been too stunned to even notice.

"Are you well?" asked Sepharia, concern rippling across her face.

Heron slapped the side of her head, trying to dislodge the ringing. She pulled a piece of glass from her forehead and stared, knowing what the implications of the destruction meant.

"Jarngard. Is Jarngard?" she asked.

Sepharia frowned and shook her head.

"He's dead."

FORTY FIVE

The ringing of the bells marked the end of the siege.

Agog watched from the Tower of Pleasure. Across the wall, a meager blood-stained wall that Agog hated with every fiber of his being, the Roman army prepared for their final assault.

In some ways, the clattering bells reminded Agog of the croaking of frogs in the deep woods of his youth. At night in the summer, lying on his furs, listening to the blanket of noise, Agog had often wondered what those frogs were saying.

He didn't have to wonder about the bells. His men had intercepted messages being passed amongst the citizens of Antioch. They would flee the city *en masse* at the signal of the bells. There were too few invaders to stop them, the message had said.

Too few. They were right by dozens. Too few and fewer all the time. Repelling the Romans had cost them too many casualties, too many men, too many steam chariots.

Agog really didn't think Consul Magnus was trying. The general of the Roman army hit them hard when he did, but he'd never brought the full might of his force against the city and Agog understood why as soon as he saw the messages.

Consul Magnus was as savvy as Vestalis had warned him. When Tiberius had forgone the safety of the walls to battle on the fields to the south, he'd left the city unprotected. By taking care of the city's residents, some that were quite connected within the Roman Empire, Magnus gained influence.

Agog had tried to capture of few of these important nobles, but defending the city had kept him from pursuing this tactic. He had a few minor nobles as hostages, but not enough to sway the outcome of the war.

The flags of the Consul were unmistakable. Agog climbed the tower each morning and evening to watch the comings and goings of the general's tent. The golden eagle flags snapped overhead, looking regal and professional, a far cry from his own side.

Agog chuckled, thinking of his Alexandrian nobles with soot smeared faces piloting strange machines that spit arrows and toppled walls. They might look more at home in a smithy these days than in war.

What would Aurinia have thought of these machines? He guessed she would have not thought them so strange, for she lived in a house that walked the wild forests and she tamed beasts better left as legends.

The distance between the wall and tent was not far. Capturing Consul Magnus could put an end to this battle, or at least give him a valuable asset to trade for safe passage from the city, but there were three legions in the way between the walls and the tents.

Every morning, the general marched three legions to stand just out of arrow range from the wall. The rest manned the sea of tents far to the south. Occasionally, they performed maneuvers, trying to strike fear into the heart of his men through their absolute professionalism. Agog had to admit the discipline and crispness of their movements was impressive, but not enough to let fear into his heart. Jealousy maybe, but not fear.

Staring at the wall made Agog squeeze his fists so tight his knuckles cracked. When Consul Magnus' legions first marched into view, Agog had wanted to take his steam chariots and load them up with as many men as they could hold and set out from the northern gate of the city to escape the Roman siege. But with so many men injured, he would have left most of his force in the city.

Now, the way was blocked. The Romans had piled wood and rocks outside the northern gate so no steam chariots could pass that way. Additionally, the two legions guarding the northern route had dug defensive trenches. There would be no escape to the north.

The ringing of the bells stopped. From his vantage point, Agog watched figures on the northern and western walls escaping from the city by scaling over the side using make-shift ropes probably once used in bondage ceremonies.

There might be a few hostage-worthy nobles among the fleeing, but trying to capture them would just invite an attack from Consul Magnus. Agog had come to respect the instincts of the general. It seemed every time his Alexandrian side tried to do anything but guard the southern gate, the Romans hammered them.

For five days they'd held the city, but Agog never truly felt like Magnus was trying to take it. Only keep them off-guard, keep them awake, keep them tired and weary.

Even Agog, who had never had much need for sleep, felt the weight of his eyelids and caught himself yawning more than he cared to admit.

On day one of the siege, they'd piled wagons and other materials at the gate to keep the Romans from marching through. Magnus had not brought siege materials with him, or if he had, they were well behind the main force, so most attacks were aimed at the gate, where the Manticores could be massed to defend.

Agog leaned on the carved pillar, ignoring that his hand rested on the carving of a naked cherub, erect and leering at a female centaur. The Tower of Pleasure was said to be a favorite haunt of Emperor Caligula before he was murdered. Agog picked it for his headquarters because the tower provided a good vantage point and because the building had tunnels below it that connected with the sewers.

Using the sewers seemed less likely with the ending of the siege growing near. Not that he could easily get away. A man of his size, and so clearly a Northman, would not go unnoticed. He wasn't ready to die yet either, even if that meant seeing Aurinia in the spirit lands.

Five days. Five days of warfare had given Consul Magnus time to construct his siege equipment. Four wide siege towers and thousands of ladders would make quick work of the wall. In Alexandria, they could have repelled the siege towers with Heron's steam catapults, but these walls were not so well equipped.

The cursed, stinking wall. Agog watched his men patrol the walkways on top of the battlement. They'd disassembled the Manticores that had broken down and moved the arrow launchers to the wall, but some of them didn't work and there were too few, anyway. If they shot flaming arrows, that might be one thing, but flying shafts of wood wouldn't keep a siege tower from rolling up close and unloading its soldiers.

A steady drumbeat rumbled up from the silence, replacing the quieted bells. Agog could hear the difference in the beat, more earnest, more determined. Even the drummers knew they would attack soon.

The sea of Roman soldiers moved into position, while siege towers glided forward, rolling on massive wheels and pushed by a gang of auxiliaries. The slow dance was performed in the deep shadow of the eastern hills, as the sun had not yet breeched their peaks.

The Roman shields, the scutums, adorned with eagle-wings, thunderbolts, and other sigils of their legion, would glimmer like jewels when the sun rose high enough. These were the jewels of the Empire. Agog had never been a man to use a shield, but he admired their use, especially as efficiently as the Romans used them.

Three legions on the attack, two guarding the northern route, and three in reserve, not counting the remnants of Tiberius' side that had been pressed into Consul Magnus' army. Agog briefly considered surrendering, saving his men the grim inevitability of death, but dismissed it quickly. While Consul Magnus was an honorable - and cunning - foe, the Emperor was not known for mercy. The nobles would be executed and the common born of the army sold into slavery. Better death in battle than that.

As the siege towers moved closer, the legions marched with them, forming a line of armored men like the tide coming in. Agog considered moving down to fight with his men, but decided against it. He'd only be one more sword on the wall, and if there was any way out of this, he needed to see the whole battlefield.

A few arrows shot from a launcher landed limply in front of the nearest siege tower. His men had flaming arrows ready, using simple bows, but the Romans had auxiliaries ready with wet furs.

The vibration from the approaching siege towers could be felt in the balls of his feet through the delicate tiles of the tower platform. Agog glanced at the scene of fornication displayed in the tile flooring, and more than once such glances had brought longings for Aurinia, but not today.

The soldiers on the wall moved purposefully, lining up with the siege towers. Agog hated walls, but thankfully, this one was wide enough to accommodate two steam chariots side by side, allowing the Manticores they'd hauled up to patrol easily. They'd prepared a few tricks for the Romans and Agog didn't want to disappoint.

When the drum beats switched to double time, heat rose to Agog's face and he regretted not being down there with his men. But it was a selfish desire, the anticipation of this moment had been weighing on him since the siege began and he wanted to banish the feeling through the ritual of combat.

Roman soldiers without shields sprinted forward, carrying ladders. Arrow launchers sprayed death amongst them, but for every Roman killed, two more took their place.

The first siege tower reached the wall, not far from the southern gate. The nearest Manticore, decked out in armor plating so that only the launcher could see out, pulled up to the spot the tower stopped. As the bridge slapped open and men poured out, the Manticore unleashed its load into the mouth of the tower, felling Roman soldiers in droves.

While the Manticore repelled the invaders, other soldiers threw flaming pots into the tower and it caught fire immediately. Smoke poured out the top like a chimney and soon the whole tower was engulfed in flame.

This minor victory was short lived, as the other three towers reached their goal, unloading their contents before they could be stopped. Agog only had so many men and so many steam chariots and had to choose wisely on where they were deployed. He could have put more on the wall, but that would only delay the inevitable. He just needed enough to keep the Romans busy for a successful counterattack. The bulk of his steam chariots were waiting by the southern gate, preparing to speed out and smash the Romans.

As more Romans climbed the ladders, faster than the launchers could kill them, his men fell back. From his vantage point, he couldn't see the gate, a church to Dionysus (one of a dozen in the city) blocked his view, but he knew they were moving the barrier out of the way by the reaction from the Romans on the road.

During the night, Agog had his men carefully rope all the broken wagons and plows and other junk they'd thrown into the gate together so they could pull it out of the way using their strongest steam chariots.

At first, the Romans had rushed toward the gate, thinking their men had opened the way. But then, the steam chariots roared out of the gate and a knot of soldiers linked shields on the road, protected by barriers of spikes and pits, thinking the rush an attempt to escape. The seventy steam chariots veered to run parallel along the wall, attacking the men on ladders, crashing through them like a sword through wet papyrus.

The flood over the walls paused, as the Roman soldiers began to realize they were about to be stranded. The counterattack struck a deep wound through the panicking soldiers. Agog could hear their confusion from the tower, seeing some trying to climb back down the ladders before the steam chariots broke them.

The Alexandrian side surged toward the hesitant Roman soldiers, overrunning them. A second siege tower caught fire while Agog held his breath.

If they could destroy all four, they'd give themselves breathing room and Consul Magnus would have to rebuild before the next attack. Agog was watching the third siege tower for flames when he saw the flicker of movement near the gate.

The counterattack was intended to be quick, out to destroy the towers and then back within the safety of the walls. It would only work once, because the Romans would take precautions next time, but any minor victory was better than a full-scale loss.

Agog had been too optimistic that Consul Magnus wouldn't prepare for this type of counterattack. When he saw the teams of horses dragging interlocking wooden barriers between the steam chariots and the open gate, Agog's gut wrenched in frustration.

Consul Magnus had baited them with the siege towers, knowing they would counterattack with the steam chariots and open up the gate. The men on the steam chariots were only just now noticing the barrier. Some tried to turn back, but it was too late.

A new drumbeat announced itself with a slow then fast repeating rhythm. The legions responded by reforming into hundreds of diamond patterns with shields interlocking for protection. Agog saw the brilliance in the formation immediately and hoped his steam chariot pilots saw it as well.

One of the Rhinos made a run for a clump of Roman soldiers, expecting to crush them. Agog watched from his tower, digging his fingers into the stone carving until his nails threatened to snap off. When the chariot reached the soldiers, instead of trying to block it, or even let it pass, half of them fell to one side keeping their shields on their backs like a turtle. Agog didn't quite understand until the Rhino hit the shields, but only on one side.

When he'd attacked the Tiberius legions, his Rhinos had run up and over the shields until the weight crushed the men beneath.

This ramp of human shields only fit under one side of the Rhino.

The vehicle flipped onto its side throwing men and crushing more, both Alexandrian and Roman, but the steam chariot was neutered. Roman soldiers rushed in to kill the survivors.

Similar scenes played out across the field, though not all performed the maneuver so adroitly. Some Roman clumps failed to move as one and were crushed by heavy wheels, while others only managed to tilt the vehicle, but enough managed to disable steam chariots that Agog knew his side would not see the end of the day alive.

While the battle raged, Roman soldiers rushed toward the open gate to secure it. Agog had kept Manticores in reserve, but so few wouldn't hold out for long.

Agog eyed the proud flags of Consul Magnus, and wondered where on the battlefield the man stood. The outcome of the battle had probably always been in the Roman's favor, but Agog admired the subtle adjustments that made victory absolute. Agog imagined the general had his men practicing these new maneuvers in the dark so they'd be a surprise. Magnus had turned Tiberius' defeat into both a military and political victory, using the legate's failure to instruct his own victory.

As the battle turned to chaos, and steam chariots were hunted down by Roman soldiers, Agog pondered his exit from the conflict. Should he join his soldiers in battle to die gloriously with warm soil between his toes, or offer surrender and be carted off to Rome in a cage, only to be hung for the amusement of the masses.

His only regret was that none of his companions were with him. Hoth was busy with Vestalis hounding the Parthians, while Jarngard was locked up in Beroea. The others were dead: Tormod had died with him outside the walls of Alexandria, Grimm during the exile's uprising, while Agnar had been captured and presumably killed trying to organize a revolt in Greece.

Agog wondered at the foolishness of sending those three wet-nosed soldiers with his steam chariot to find Vestalis. He could only assume they failed in their task, and even if they hadn't, another hundred steam chariots wasn't going to turn the tide now.

He was defeated.

The only choice he had left was the manner of his death. Seeing the results clear on the field of battle, Agog made his way down the steps of the tower.

Inside, the air was cool and refreshing as he blindly moved down the steps, keeping his hand along the wall for guidance. He knew once he gathered his weapons and made the short trip to the gate, he would find comfort no more.

Agog was near the bottom when the tower shook. He looked up and prepared to take a second step when the tower shook again. He paused, undecided. Delay would only ensure his capture. When the third rumble shook the tower, sending dust upon him, Agog raced up the stairs.

When he reached the top, he found a scene dramatically changed than what he'd just left. Agog first looked to the sky, expecting to see the gods descending on the field of battle, but then he saw the glint of racing steam chariots on the far side of the Roman line.

But what had caused the tremors?

He didn't have long to wonder when a fireball rose into the sky. Moments later, the air slammed against him, even from this considerable distance. Agog swore the destruction had come from a steam chariot speeding into a mass of Roman soldiers. Now there was nothing left but a smoking hole.

Smaller flashes of light appeared at random, throwing men like a spray of pebbles from a child's hand. Agog caught the glimmer of metal from the hills overlooking the town and his heart soared, knowing it was the steam catapults firing their loads into the Roman side. Vestalis had snuck the weapons into good position during the night.

When a fifth ball of fire and smoke and heat erupted on the field, Agog wondered again if the gods were involved, and without thinking, he knew the answer. Yes, the gods were involved, or at least one god, the one on his side, the Machine Man, the *Michanikos*.

Agog smiled grimly. This work could only be the third weapon of Archimedes. Heron had disobeyed him and went after it, and Agog would reward the man with whatever he wanted for such defiance.

As waves of smoke, black and white and gray, mixed and rolled over the field, Agog knew he had to end it. With a nod to the steam catapults on the hills, delivering death from a distance, Agog made his way down the stairs, the bright flashes from the Archimedes weapon still playing across his sight.

When he reached the gate, he would rally the men with the sole purpose of pushing through the scattered skirmishes and taking Consul Magnus before he could get away.

And with that, this war could end.

FORTY SIX

Heron listened to the gentle waves lap upon the shore, pushing foam upon the sand. Not far from her location, a row boat was anchored in the water, tilting slightly with each wave.

Seagulls clucked and screamed overhead, while she could taste rain on the wind despite the sky being perfectly clear.

She heard the light but proud steps upon the sand behind her, and knew who approached.

A hand touched her shoulder and she turned to gaze into Hoth's friendly face.

"Ave, Hoth."

"Ave, Heron," he said, crinkling his nose and glancing at the row boat before speaking again, "how do the gods treat you today?"

She tried not to scowl. He was trying to be nice. "Well enough, I suppose."

Hoth paused, the lack of ease an unfamiliar cast on his normally grinning face. "I should go. Storms are moving in and I have a ways to row to reach deep waters so the ship can pick me up."

The mention of the ship brought her gaze up. A white sail rested on the horizon.

"Then you should be going," she said.

Hoth did not move. He stood nearby, hands clasped in front, until after a while he spoke again. "Will you tell anyone else?"

She frowned. "I don't know."

"Why did you tell me?" he asked.

She couldn't help but let the hint of grin appear briefly on her lips. "You were acting the coward."

"And you're a lunatic, making a machine that flies through the sky."

She nodded. "We did almost die that day, I suppose."

He gave a belly laugh. "Almost? I still have nightmares."

"Your hair is growing out," she said.

"No thanks to you," he said. "Was it really necessary for the disguise?"

She shook her head.

"I thought so," he sighed.

Hoth glanced at the row boat. He took one step forward, cracking a seashell in the sand before pausing.

"Did you want to say goodbye?" He nodded towards the row boat.

Heron gritted her teeth. "I already did. When the men brought his body by. I'd say it again but—" She motioned toward her mechanical leg, "—you know."

"I'll miss him," said Hoth, looking stoically toward the wide sea.

"I will, too."

She looked at Hoth and almost said more, but as the words bubbled up, she shoved them back down. It was better that way.

Hoth pulled something out of his knapsack and handed it to Heron. "Sepharia saved them."

The charred bone dice felt weightless in her palm. Heron squeezed her fist around them, letting the sharp corner dig into the soft flesh.

"Why did he roll them?" she asked, though she knew the answer he would give.

"Answers?" Hoth shrugged, and that was that.

Heron released her grip and stared at the blackened cubes.

"What will you do now?" he asked.

"Though I'd prefer to return to my workshop, Agog has asked me to go with him to Rome so I can figure out the best way to use the spark powder," she replied. "He wants to get there before Magnus rallies the other legions and he has to fight for the city."

"It's a shame Magnus got away," said Hoth.

"No one's to blame. The confusion of the battle was immense." She shook her head. "But at least we captured the other commander, the legate Tiberius."

"Tiberius," Hoth said skeptically. "It would have been better had it been the other way around."

"Tiberius has promised himself to Agog."

Hoth narrowed his eyes. "Quick to change allegiance."

"Like Vestalis?" she questioned.

Hoth shook his head. "No. I don't question that one's loyalty any longer. Count me a believer. He outmaneuvered a force ten times his own and created a masterful ambush that allowed us to come to Agog's rescue. That, and he was the one to figure out the best way to use the Archimedes gifts."

"Gift? Maybe a curse," she replied with a heavy heart.

"Regrets for finding the weapons?"

"We had to keep them from Rome." She paused. "But I understand his reluctance to publicize them. I feel we've unleashed a terrible weapon on the world."

"We?" Hoth chuckled. "I'm just a sea captain."

"Back to Alexandria?" she asked.

He nodded. "Nektam promised me a new ship, the largest iron boat yet. I mean to make sure he fulfills that promise."

"And then we'll never see you on shore again," she said, smiling.

"Probably," he said. "You could come with me."

She thought about it, but shook her head. She couldn't go back with Jarngard's body, no matter how much she missed her workshop.

"I almost forgot." She handed him the scroll case under her arm. "It's the instructions for his burial. Give them to Plutarch, he'll know what to do."

They stood quietly for a while longer, and Heron sensed he had more to say, but he gave her a friendly bow and marched into the sea, climbing carefully into the boat.

Heron found a chuckle trickle up as she thought about what would have happened if Hoth would have tipped the boat over and thrown Jarngard's body into the sea. She would have laughed, if only because Jarngard would have.

Hoth took the center plank and grabbed both oars confidently and after a nod, stroked backwards, propelling the boat out to deep waters.

Heron watched for a spell, enough to remember that her knees ached and Sepharia had promised to work on fixing her arm in Antioch before they left for Rome. Agog planned on taking the city by early spring.

She raised her hand to wave, but felt foolish for doing so, so instead ran the hand through her short hair, feeling the grit of the road and promised herself a bath. When she could no longer hear the slap of the hull on the waves, Heron turned and headed back to her waiting steam chariot.

FORTY SEVEN

From the far hills, outside the city proper of Rome, Agog witnessed the shade of dusk pass across the glittering domes, silencing their dominance on the horizon.

He'd camped east of the city, tents and banners of the Alexandrian empire fluttering in the evening breeze, bringing hearth fires and wood smoke. Envoys had been sent to the Senate and he would receive them on the next day.

The winter journey through the mountains had proved harder than he expected. The steam chariots didn't travel well in the snow and ice, even with the *Michanikos'* adjustments.

He never encountered Magnus' small force either, even when they broke Rome's last defenses. His banners had never been amongst the defenders. Spies claimed he'd gone west to Gaul to take command of the legions there. Other rumors had him north, but west of the Black Sea. A problem for another time.

Agog tugged at his bushy beard. He'd let it grow out during the cold months. Vestalis had been urging him to shave it, better to present the façade of the well-mannered conqueror than the ill-made barbarian, and he would heed that advice. The old soldier had served him well.

"Ave, King Wodanaz."

Heron came limping up, the mechanical knee grinding and wheezing at each step. Agog wondered if the envoys from Rome weren't more interested to see the *Michanikos* than their new ruler. The messages practically begged for Heron to be at the negotiations.

"Can't you make that thing quieter? I can hear you over the hill," said Agog smiling.

"So now he complains after dragging this mechanical through water and air and earth and then a winter frozen up? If I were back in my workshop, I might have remade it, better to withstand such hardships, but I foolishly agreed to come to Rome."

Agog tried to pat his belly, but it was mostly gone, replaced with hard muscle earned from pushing steam chariots through the snow. "And for that, I thank you. I would have never thought to use Archimedes' spark powder for removing avalanches in the mountains. You saved us weeks of time and countless deaths."

Heron shrugged and took position next to him. "I guess the advantage of these mechanical limbs in winter is there's less of me to be frozen."

"It's good to see you in a better mood," said Agog.

"I'd be in a better mood if I were in my workshop," replied Heron.

Agog extended his arm toward the city. "You'll have all the workshops of Rome at your disposal."

"And no Plutarch or Punt to run them," replied Heron. "Are you trying to put me in a worse mood? I *was* feeling better, if only to be warm again."

"Apologies," chuckled Agog. "I'll end my teasing and tell you why I asked for you."

Heron gave him a hard glance. "You want me as a show, nothing more than a mechanical miracle, just like the temples."

"Yes, that's true, but I need you there for your eyes and ears, too," he told him.

"I thought this meeting was a formality, to negotiate the details of the surrender," said Heron.

"It is, but conquering Rome and ruling Rome are two entirely different things," he said. "Tiberius has been quite informative to the various power struggles within the city."

"I don't trust that man," said Heron grimly.

"I don't either, but he's all I've got for now. Spies or not, Vestalis has been away from the city too long to know the true score," said Agog.

Heron nodded thoughtfully. "Is it true they killed Claudius?"

"Stoned him in the Circus Maximus after they caught him trying to sneak out of Rome with a chest full of gold," said Agog. "That was proof enough for me that they were serious about surrendering."

"What choice did they have, you'd beaten their last legions and we carry enough sparkpowder to turn the city to dust," said Heron.

"Do you regret finding it?" asked Agog.

"Men will always have to make choices. We could burn the city to ashes if we so chose. A newer, easier way doesn't absolve us from using our intellect."

A long pause gathered momentum until Heron broke it.

"I'll be there, of course."

The land had turned blacker and lights in the city flickered to life. As far as the eye could see, there was Rome.

"I never realized how big it would be," said Heron.

"Five times the city of Alexandria, my scholars tell me."

Heron scowled. "And how do you propose to rule it? Even with the reinforcements arriving by ship, we barely have ten thousand."

"I'm not," he told Heron, watching for his reaction, "you're going to rule it."

Heron turned on him, red-faced. "Are you mad?"

"Not the whole empire," he smirked. "Just the city of Rome and the Senate. Until I find a suitable replacement."

"Why?" Heron stuttered. "Give it to Vestalis? Or keep it yourself?"

Agog shook his head, enjoying the moment. "I've got to chase down Magnus and quell the rebellious countryside. Even though we've beaten them again and again, parts of the Empire will grow wild or resist, if only for the comfort of their former masters. As for Vestalis, as much as I trust him, I cannot put a Roman in charge. They need an Alexandrian."

"I wasn't born there," replied Heron.

"But you *are* the city. More than anyone else. Alexandria adores you."

"Which is why I should be back there, instead of this poisonous, back-stabbing, power-mad city," cursed Heron.

He nodded. "And you will, eventually. The citizens love you already, you're the best person for the job."

"I can't," said Heron, shaking his head. "My workshop needs me. There are so many inventions to create."

"You can do that, too. Just send your drawings back to Alexandria. When have you ever needed to be present?" he asked.

Heron scowled again.

"You must accept. I've got no one else," he said honestly.

Heron put a slender hand to his chin and wrestled with internal thoughts.

"For how long?" asked Heron.

"Six months at most. With your steam chariots and the spark powder, I should be able to track down Magnus by fall and return to Rome to rule."

Heron gave a heavy sigh. "Six months, no longer."

"Deal."

Agog offered his hand and they shook.

They watched the lights of the city come alive as dusk passed them into night. Agog placed his hand on Heron's shoulder and chuckled lightly.

"Don't worry, my friend. Six months will pass quickly, and the Senate can do the heavy lifting for you. The only thing you'll have to do is send your drawings to Alexandria, let Vestalis advise you, and occasionally make a decision. Nothing can go wrong."

"Nothing?" asked Heron skeptically.

"Nothing," said Agog. "Nothing, at all."

§ § §

Continue Heron's adventure in Book Five of The Alexandrian Saga

EMPIRE
OF
ALEXANDRIA

OTHER BOOKS BY THOMAS K. CARPENTER

The Hundred Halls Universe

SEASON ONE
THE HUNDRED HALLS
Trials of Magic
Web of Lies
Alchemy of Souls
Gathering of Shadows
City of Sorcery

THE RELUCTANT ASSASSIN
The Reluctant Assassin
The Sorcerous Spy
The Veiled Diplomat
Agent Unraveled
The Webs That Bind

GAMEMAKERS ONLINE
The Warped Forest
Gladiators of Warsong
Citadel of Broken Dreams
Enter the Daemonpits
Plane of Twilight

WANIMALIANS HALL
Wild Magic
Bane of the Hunter
Mark of the Phoenix
Arcane Mutations
Untamed Destiny

STONE SINGERS HALL
Song of Siren and Blood
House of Snake and Tome
Storm of Dragon and Stone
Sonata of Shadow and Thorn
Well of Demon and Bone

THE ORDER OF MERLIN
The Order of Merlin
Infernal Alliances
Tower of Horn and Blood

ABOUT THE AUTHOR

Thomas K. Carpenter resides in Colorado with his wife Rachel. When he's not busy writing his next book, he's hiking, skiing, and getting beat by his wife at cards. He keeps a regular blog at www.thomaskcarpenter.com and you can follow him on twitter @thomaskcarpente. If you want to learn when his next novel will be hitting the shelves and get free stories and occasional other goodies, please sign up for his mailing list by going to: http://tinyurl.com/thomaskcarpenter. Your email address will never be shared and you can unsubscribe at any time.